Stephen Hunter is the author of thirteen novels. Chief film critic at the *Washington Post*, where he won the 2003 Pulitzer Prize, he has also published two collections of film criticism and a nonfiction work. He lives in Baltimore, Maryland.

THE 47th SAMURAI

Bob Lee Swagger's past was bloody, as a
Marine Corps sniper and later a self-
appointed avenger. But it seems he's not
finished with combat, when he receives a visit
from Colonel Philip Yano, who has come to
America to find a samurai sword that Bob's
father took from Yano's dying father in the
battle for Iwo Jima in 1945. Yano believes
the sword to be of political significance
to whomever can get hold of it. Bob agrees to
help and delivers the sword to Yano in Tokyo,
but then the Yano family are murdered, and
the sword stolen. Dark forces are at work.
Bob enters Tokyo's criminal underbelly
— and the violent world of the samurai. Once
more he is on a mission of vengeance . . .

Books by Stephen Hunter
Published by The House of Ulverscroft:

HAVANA

STEPHEN HUNTER

THE 47th SAMURAI

Complete and Unabridged

CHARNWOOD
Leicester

First published in Great Britain in 2008 by
Arrow Books
The Random House Group Limited
London

First Charnwood Edition
published 2009
by arrangement with
The Random House Group Limited
London

British Library CIP Data

Hunter, Stephen, *1946 –*
  The 47th Samurai
  1. Swagger, Bob Lee (Fictitious character)- -Fiction.
  2. Samurai- -Fiction. 3. Swords- -Japan- -History- -
  Fiction. 4. Tokyo (Japan)- -Social conditions- -Fiction.
  5. Suspense fiction. 6. Large type books.
  I. Title II. Forty-seventh samurai
  813.5′4–dc22

  ISBN 978–1–84782–652–7

Published by
F. A. Thorpe (Publishing)
Anstey, Leicestershire

Set by Words & Graphics Ltd.
Anstey, Leicestershire
Printed and bound in Great Britain by
T. J. International Ltd., Padstow, Cornwall

With thanks, respect, and appreciation to the samurai of the Japanese cinema:

Masaki Kobayashi, Hideo Gosha, Akira Kurosawa, Hiroshi Inagaki, Kenji Misumi, Tokuzo Tanaka, Kimiyoshi Yasuda, Kihachi Okamoto, Tadashi Sawashima, Toshiya Fujita, Haruki Kadokawa, Yoji Yamada, Kazuo Kuroki, Yojiro Takita, Ryuhei Kitamura, Satsuo Yamamoto

and

Takashi Shimura, Isao Kimura, Toshiro Mifune, Yoshio Inaba, Daisuke Kato, Mioru Chiaki, Seiji Miyaguchi, Tatsuya Nakadai, Shintaro Katsu, Raizo Ichikawa, Tomisaburo Wakayama, Tetsura Tambo, Sonny Chiba, Meiko Kaji, Michyio Aratama, Yunosuke Ito, Datsuke Kato, Yuzo Kayama, Machiko Kyo, Kashiro Matsumoto, Akihiro Tomikawa, Kiichi Nakai, Koichi Sata, Aya Ueto, Masatoshi Nagase, Mieko Harada, Hiroyuki Sandada

and

the great Shinobu Hashimoto

Turn, hell-hound, turn!
— MACDUFF IN *MACBETH*

1

ISLAND

SHOWA YEAR 20, SECOND MONTH, 21ST DAY
21 FEBRUARY 1945

A quiet fell across the bunker. Dust drifted from the ceiling. The burnt-egg stench of sulfur lingered everywhere.

'Captain?'

It was a private. Takahashi, Sugita, Kanzaki, Asano, Togawa, Fukuyama, Abe — who knew the names anymore? There had been so many names.

'Sir, the shelling has stopped. Does this mean they're coming?'

'Yes,' he said. 'It means they're coming.'

The officer's name was Hideki Yano and he was a captain, 145th Infantry Regiment, 2nd Battalion, under Yasutake and Ikeda, attached to Kuribayashi's 109th Division.

The blockhouse was low and smelled of sulfur and shit because the men all had dysentery from the tainted water. It was typical Imperial Army fortification, a low bunker of concrete, reinforced over many long months, with oak tree trunks from what had been but was no longer the island's only oak forest, the sand heaped over it. It had three firing slits and behind each slit sat a

1

Type 96 gun on a tripod, a gunner, and a couple of loaders. Each field of fire fanned away for hundreds of yards across an almost featureless landscape of black sand ridges and marginal vegetation. The blockhouse was divided into three chambers, like a nautilus shell, so that even if one or two were wiped out, the last gun could continue to fire until the very end. It was festooned everywhere with the latest imperative from General Kuribayashi's headquarters, a document called 'Courageous Battle Vows,' which summed up everyone's responsibilities to the Sphere.

Above all else, we shall dedicate ourselves to the defense of this island.
We shall grasp bombs, charge the enemy tanks and destroy them.
We shall infiltrate into the midst of the enemy and annihilate them.
With every salvo we will, without fail, kill the enemy.
Each man will make it his duty to kill ten of the enemy before dying.

'I am scared, sir,' said the private.
'I am too,' said Yano.
Outside, the captain's small empire continued. Six pits with Nambu guns in each, each gun supported by gunner, loader, and two or three riflemen flanked the empire to left and right. In further spider holes were martyrs with rifles. No escape for them; they knew they were dead already. They lived only to kill those ten

Americans before they gave their lives up in sacrifice. Those men had it the worst. In here, no shell could penetrate. The concrete was four feet thick, riven with steel rods. Out there a naval shell from the offshore fleet could tear a man to shreds in a second. If the shell landed precisely, no one would have time for a death poem.

Now that the attack was upon them, the captain became energized. He shook off the months of torpor, the despair, the terrible food, the endless shitting, the worries. Now, at last, glory approached.

Except of course he no longer believed in glory. That was for fools. He believed only in duty.

He was not a speech maker. But now he ran from position to position, making sure each gun was properly cocked and aimed, the loaders stood ready with fresh ammunition strips, the riflemen crouched to pick off the errant demon American.

'Captain?'

A boy pulled him aside.

'Yes?' What was the boy's name? He could not remember this one either. But these were all good boys, Kagoshima boys, as the 145th was drawn from Kyushu, the home of Japan's best soldiers.

'I am not afraid to die. I am eager to die for the emperor,' said the boy, a superior private.

'That is our duty. You and I, we are nothing. Our duty is all.'

But the boy was agitated.

'I am afraid of flames. I am so afraid of the

flames. Will you shoot me if I am engulfed in fire?'

They all feared the flamethrowers. The hairy beasts were dishonorable. They chopped gold teeth from dead Japanese, they bleached Japanese skulls and turned them into ashtrays and sent them home, they killed the Japanese not decently, with gun and sword — they hated the blade! — but so often from miles out with the big naval shells, with the airplanes, and then when they got in close, they used the horrible hoses that squirted flaming gasoline and roasted the flesh from a man's bones, killing him slowly. How could a warrior die honorably in flames?

'Or the sword, Captain. I beg you. If I burn, behead me.'

'What is your name?'

'Sudo. Sudo from Kyushu.'

'Sudo from Kyushu. You will not die in flames. That I promise you. We are *samurai*!'

That word *samurai* still stiffened the spine of every man. It was pride, it was honor, it was sacrifice. It was worth more than life. It was what a man needed to be and would die to be. He had known it his whole life; he had yearned for it, as he yearned for a son who would live up to it.

'*Samurai!*' said the boy fervently, now reassured, for he believed it.

★ ★ ★

Able Company caught primary assault. It was simply Able's turn, and Charlie and Item and Hotel would offer suppressive fire and flanking

4

maneuvers and handle artillery coordination, but it was Able's turn to go first. Lead the way. Semper fi, all that fine bullshit.

There was a problem, however. There was always a problem, this was today's: Able's CO was shaky. He was new to the 28th and rumors had it that a connected father had gotten his son the command. His name was Culpepper and he was a college boy from some fancy place who talked a little like a woman. It wasn't anything anybody could put a finger on, not homo or anything, he just wasn't somehow like the other officers. He was fancy, somehow, from fancy places, fancy houses, fancy parents. Was Culpepper up to it? Nobody knew, but the blockhouse had to go or Battalion would be hung up all day here and the big guns on Suribachi would continue to shatter the beachhead. So Colonel Hobbs assigned his battalion's first sergeant, Earl Swagger, to go along with Captain Culpepper that morning.

'Culpepper, you listen up to the first sergeant. He's old breed. He's been around. He's hit a lot of beaches. He's the best combat leader I have, you understand.'

'Yes sir,' said Culpepper.

The colonel drew Earl aside.

'Earl, you help Culpepper. Don't let him freeze, keep his boys moving. I hate to do this to you, but someone's got to get them boys up the hill and you're the best I've got.'

'I'll get 'em up, sir,' said Swagger, who looked like he was about 140 percent United States Marine Corps, chapter and verse, a sinewy string

5

bean of a man, ageless in the sergeant way, a vet of the 'Canal, Tarawa, and Saipan and, someone said, Troy, Thermopylae, Agincourt, and the Somme. They said nobody could shoot a Thompson gun like the first sergeant. He'd fought the Japs in China before the war, it was said.

Swagger was from nowhere. He had no hometown, no memories he shared, no stories of the good old days, as if he had no good old days. It was said he'd married a gal last time home, on some kind of bond tour for the citizens back there, and everybody said she's a looker, but he never pulled pictures or talked much about it. He was all guile, energy, and focus, seemingly indestructible but one of those professionals with what some would call a gleam in his eye who could talk any boy or green lieutenant through anything. He was a prince of war, and if he was doomed, he didn't know it, or much care about it.

Culpepper had a plan.

Swagger didn't like it.

'Begging the captain's pardon, it's too complicated. You'll end up with your people all running around not sure of what to do while the Japs sit there and shoot. I wouldn't break Able down by squads but by platoons, I'd keep a good base of fire going, and I'd get my flamethrowers off on the right, try and work 'em in close that way. The flamethrowers, sir, those are the key.'

'I see,' said the young man, pale and thin and grave and trying so hard. 'I think the men are capable — '

'Sir, once the Japs see us coming, it's going to

be a shit storm out there. They are tough little bastards, and believe you me, they know what they are doing. If you expect men to remember maneuver patterns keyed to landmarks, you will be disappointed. It has to be simple, hard, basic, and not much to remember, or the Japs will shoot your boys down like toads on a flat rock. The important goddamn thing is to get them flamethrowers in close. If it was me, I'd send the best blowtorch team up this draw to the right' — they looked at a smudged map at the command post a few hundred yards back — 'with a BAR and a tommy-gunner as cover, your best NCO running the show. I'd hold your other team back. Meanwhile, you pound away from your base of fire. Get the bazookas involved. Them gun slits is tiny but a bazooka rocket through one is something the Japs will notice. Sir, maybe you ought to let me run the flamethrower team.'

But the colonel said, 'Earl will want to lead. Just let him advise, Captain. I need him back this afternoon.'

'But — ' the young captain protested.

'Sergeant Tarsky is a fine man and a fine NCO. You let him move some people off on the left when we go. He's got to get a lot of fire going, and the people here in front, they've got to be working their weapons too. I need a lot of covering fire. I'll take the blowtorch team up the right. The Japs will be hidden in monkey holes, but I can spot 'em. I know where to look. So the BAR man can hose 'em down from outside their range. We'll get in close and burn 'em out, then

7

get up there and fry that pillbox.'

Culpepper hesitated a second, realized this smart, tough, duty-crazed hillbilly from some dead-end flyspeck south of perdition nobody had ever heard of was dead right, and saw that his own prissy ego meant nothing out there.

'Let's do it, First Sergeant.'

★　★　★

The Type 92s fired 7.7 mm tracer. White-hot bolts of illumination cut through the mist and the dust. Through the gun slit, you could not see men, not really — but you could *sense* them, maneuvering a foot at a time through the same chaos. Where the bullets struck, they lifted clouds of black sand.

'There,' said the captain, pointing, and the gunner cranked his windage to the right, the finned barrel revolved on its mesh of gears, and the gun rocked, spent cartridges spilled, the tracer lashed, and in the vapors shapes stumbled and went down amid the stench of sulfur.

'Sir,' someone yelled from the leftmost gun chamber.

Holding his sword so it would not clatter, the captain ran through the connecting tunnel.

'Yes?'

'Sir, Yamaki says he saw men moving off on the left. Just a flash of them moving directly away from our position.' Gun smoke filled the room, thin and acrid, eating at nasal tissues, tearing up eyes.

'Flamethrowers?'

'I couldn't see, sir.'

Well, it had to be. The American commander wouldn't move his people directly at the guns. The hairy beasts never did that; they didn't have the stomach and they weren't eager to die. They would die if necessary, but they weren't hungry for it. Glorious death meant nothing to them.

The captain tried to think it out.

He'd either go to his left or right, and you'd think he'd go to his left. There was more cover, the vegetation was thicker, and it was hard to bring direct fire because the ridge was steeper. You were mostly in danger from grenades, but the Americans didn't fear the Japanese grenades, because they were so underpowered and erratic.

The captain tried to feel his opponent. His imagination of a white man was someone impossibly big and hairy and pink. He conceived of a cowboy or a ghost, but he knew there'd be intelligence guiding it. The Japanese had learned the hard way over the years that the Americans may not have had honor but they had intelligence. They weren't stupid, they weren't cowards, and there was an endless supply of them.

It came down to left or right? He knew the answer: the right. He'd go to his right. He'd send the flamethrowers up that way because it was less obvious: there wasn't much cover, he'd run into spider holes, but he had the skill to overcome the spider holes. It seemed more dangerous, but a smart hand would have the advantage if he knew how to use terrain and was aggressive.

'I'll take care of it. You men, keep firing. You

won't see whole targets, you'll see shapes. Fire on shapes. Be *samurai!*'

'*Samurai!*'

The captain ran back to the central chamber. 'The little gun,' he ordered. 'Quickly.'

A sergeant brought him the submachine gun called the Type 100, an 8 mm weapon whose central design had been stolen from the Germans. It had a wooden stock, a ventilated barrel, and a magazine fitted horizontally to the left from the breech. They were prizes; there were never enough of them to go around. What we could have done with a million of them! We'd be in New York today! The captain had to lobby General Kuribayashi personally to get one assigned to his position.

He threw on a bandolier hung with pouches full of grenades and spare magazines, buckling it tight to his body. Carefully, he disconnected his sword from his belt, laying it aside.

'I want to ambush the flamethrower attack. I'll intercept them well beyond our lines. Give me covering fire.'

He turned, nodded to a private, who unlatched the heavy steel door at the rear of the blockhouse, and scrambled out.

★   ★   ★

'What's your name son?'

'MacReedy, First Sergeant.'

'Can you shoot that thing?' Earl said, indicating the sixteen pounds of automatic rifle the boy held.

10

'Yes, First Sergeant.'

'How 'bout you, son? Can you keep him loaded and hot?'

'Yes, First Sergeant,' said MacReedy's ammo bearer, laden with bandoliers of BAR mags.

'Okay, here's what we're going to do. I'm squirming up the ridge. I'm going to check out the draw. When I see a monkey hole, I'm going to put tracer on it. You're with me in a good prone. Where I put tracer, you put five rounds of ball thirty. Hold tight, stay on my forty-five tracer. Tracer won't go through them logs the Japs use as revetment, but the thirty will, 'cause it's moving three times as fast. Your buddy there's going to feed you mags as you run dry. He'll switch them on you. You got that, son?'

'Got it, First Sergeant,' said the assistant gunner.

'Now you blowtorch guys, you hang back. We got to clear this out before I can get you up on the ridge and you can get to work. Okay?'

There was a mumble of reluctant assent from his loose confederation of troops clustered just below the ridge, a couple of low, 'Yes, First Sergeant.'

'And another thing. Out here, where there's Japs, I'm Earl. Forget all the First Sergeant bullshit. Got it?'

With that Earl began his long squirm. He crawled through volcanic ash and black sand. He crawled in a fog of sulfur-stinking dust that floated up to his nose and tongue, layering him with grit. He held his Thompson tight like a woman, felt the two BAR gunners with him

11

close, and watched as Jap tracer flicked insolently above. Now and then a mortar round landed, but mostly it was dust in the air, cut with flecks of light, so brief, so fast you weren't sure you really saw it.

He was happy.

In war, Earl put everything behind him. His dead, raging father no longer screamed at him, his sullen mother no longer drifted away, he was no longer the sheriff's boy, hated by so many others because they so feared his father; he was nobody but First Sergeant and he was happy. He had the United States Marine Corps as a father and a mother now, and the Corps had embraced him and loved him and nurtured him and made him a man. He would not let it down and he would fight to the death for its honor.

Earl got to the crest of the little ridge and poked his head up. Before him he saw a fold in the sandy soil that led up to the blankness of a higher ridgeline, a rill that was a foothill to Suribachi, which rose behind them, blocking all view of the sea. It was 2/28's job to circle around the volcano, cut the mountain off from resupply, then inch up it and take out the mortars, the artillery emplacements, the artillery spotters, and the spider holes and pillboxes that dotted its scabrous surface. It had to be done one firefight at a time, over a long day's dying.

The landscape of the draw seemed empty, a random groove cut in the black sand, clotted with clump grass and bean vines. The odd eucalyptus bush stood out amid the desolation.

Once he would have led men up and all would

have died. But like his peers, he had learned the craft of war.

He looked now for gnarled root groupings in the clump grass and eucalypti, for patches of lemongrass, for small, stunted oak trees, for the Japanese had a genius for digging into them, for building small, one-man forts, impregnable to artillery but at the same time inescapable. There was no such thing as a back door. Thus they would die to kill. *Retreat* and *surrender* were terms they did not comprehend.

'You set up, MacReedy?'

'Yes, Earl.'

'On my fire.'

Earl marked the target, thirty yards out, a tuft of vegetation in a crest of black sand that had a too-studied look to it, and he knew a man lurked in a chamber behind the screen of fronds, and he put four rounds of tracer onto it, watching as the neon flickered across the distance and whacked into the green, throwing up clouds of black dust. He was so strong and so salty he could hold the gun with no rise; it never sent .45s careening wildly into space. He could shoot skeet with it and had famously put on an exhibition on shipboard for all the squad officers.

Next to him, MacReedy jacked a heavier .30 caliber burst into the position; these bullets exploded in geysers of angry power when they struck.

'Good work. That boy's gone to his ancestors.'

Earl worked the slope. His eyes picked out things few others would have noticed; he put the tracer on them, the BAR kids followed with the heavier .30 caliber ball, and in minutes, the draw seemed clear.

'Now's the hard part. See, the Japs have guys on this side. I mean, facing toward their lines, guys we can't see. That's how their minds work, the smart little monkeys. They been at this a while; they know a goddamn thing or two.'

'What's our play, Sergeant Earl?'

'We're going to roll grenades down this slope. I'm going to take the BAR. After the grenades pop, I'm jumping down there. I can pick out the monkey holes and lay fire on them. You move over the ridge and cover me with the tommy. Got it?'

'Earl, you're sure to get yourself killed.'

'Nah. No Nip's quick enough to hit old man Earl. Okay, I want the gun loaded and cocked. MacReedy, take the bipod off too. You, get your grenades out. Ready?'

'Yes, Mr Earl.'

'Okay, on my count, pull, pop the lever, then just dump the grenades over the crest. Got it?'

★   ★   ★

Battle was weather. He ran through clouds of vapor, dust in the air, through layers of sulfur. There was no sun. His boots fought for leverage in the black sand. The thunder pounded, except that it was gunfire. The slope was alive with rounds striking, and it looked like small animals peeping about. Below he could see nothing but dust and shapes scurrying through it, hairy beasts trying to squirm ahead, get within

14

grenade range, always hunted by the whiter tracers his own men fired.

He ran from gun pit to gun pit.

'Keep firing. We'll drive them back. You have ammunition, water? Any wounded?'

The men were wonderful. All believed in the hundred million, all believed in duty to the emperor, all had already made peace with death and sacrifice, saw and believed in its necessity, and would not bolt or flee; they were the best men on earth. *Samurai!*

'There, to the left!'

He pointed and the Nambu cranked around, sent a burst skittering through some vegetation, and all were rewarded with a rare sight of an enemy rolling out of the brush limply.

'Search for targets, keep shooting, they will tire of dying and fall back soon.'

Now Captain Yano reached a last shelf. By geographical oddity, a few feet of ridge lay where the far slope was too severe to negotiate and no trenches had been dug. It was wide open. It had to be crossed.

'Captain, be careful!'

'Long live the emperor,' he cried, as if to invoke a higher purpose.

Did he believe it? A part of him did. You gave yourself to it, you accepted your death, even in pain or fire, you embraced the suffering, you longed for the void. You raced through fire, in search of your duty and your destiny.

But another part said, Why?

What waste!

These fine men, they could contribute so

much, they die on a crest of black sand on an island of sulfur that held no meaning at all that could be divined. For the emperor? How many of his men knew that the godlike, all-knowing, all-demanding emperor was a recent invention and that for three hundred years had been the puppet-joke of Edo, while in Kyoto stronger, subtler men ruled and only tolerated an emperor as a useful fiction, a figure around which to build distracting (and therefore helpful) ceremonies?

He knew too: the war is lost. All our armies have been crushed. No island has been successfully defended. We die here for nothing. It would be comic if it weren't so stupid. It's a racket, a jest, for the seven men who run Japan to chortle at over sake.

But still he ran.

He was visible for no more than seven seconds. The Americans fired quickly, and he felt the hot whisper of bullets pushing the air to the left and right as they plunged past. The earth erupted around him and filled the air with grit that assailed his nose and throat.

The bullet that would kill him did not find him.

He slid to earth behind a hummock, gulped for air, then heard a series of blasts from the draw below.

He slid to the crest of the hummock and watched from a hundred yards out as an American raced down the hill with a big automatic rifle — they had so many different kinds of weapons! — sweeping quickly, sending cascades of bullets into counterlaid spider holes whose existence only the captain himself knew, as he had designed them.

It was over in seconds.

The big hairy beast yelled and gestured and two men came down the hill and another few around it, as they joined in the middle of the draw, and the American ordered them into a hasty line and led them forward.

The captain saw it then: a flamethrower.

The last two Americans in line had the flamethrower. One of them wore it on a harness, a cluster of tanks centered on his back, so heavy with jellied fuel that he bent under it and held a tubular nozzle with a pistol grip, which concealed a pyrotechnic igniter, literally a match that when struck would unleash the spurting fuel. They would come up the draw, pivot left, and under covering fire burn out the gun pits. Then the Americans would blow the steel door into the bunker and burn that out too.

The captain reached for grenades. They were absurd things, called Type 97s, unreliable and untrustworthy. Cylindrical and grooved for fragmentation, they were designed with four-and-a-half-second fuses, which meant they either had one-second fuses or six-second fuses, if they detonated at all. You primed them — this was beyond comedy! — by first pulling a pin, then smashing their fuse housing hard against your helmet and driving a striker through a primer to light a powder train.

He almost laughed.

We are the Yamato race and we cannot build a

hand grenade to save our lives. The men joked, We can survive the Americans, but . . . our own grenades?

But the Buddha smiled. He pulled the pin on the first cylinder, smashed its fuse housing against a stone, the striker flew and lit the fuse, and it sizzled to life. He held it one second (so dangerous!) then threw it over the crest. He repeated the process, and heard the first detonate. Possibly a cry was lost in the explosion. The second grenade he didn't hold, on the sound principle that no two in a row would work properly, but just hurled it, and it was the right decision, for just an instant later it went.

The captain pulled himself over the crest of the draw.

All the Americans were down. One of the boys with the automatic rifle was shrieking hysterically, his left arm bloody. Two were still. The flamethrower operator was trying to regain his feet.

The captain shot him first. He put a stream of five 8 mm Nambu slugs into him, and another burst into the assistant, even though that man was down. He shifted to the automatic rifleman, who labored with the bloody arm to raise his weapon, while behind them his loader tried to grope for a dropped carbine. The captain finished them in one long burst. Then he rotated to the downed leader and put a burst into him. He raced down the draw, went to the flamethrower operator, who, unbelievably, still breathed. He fired into his head and tried not to notice and, when that proved impossible, not to feel shame at the impact of the bullets on the young face. Then he pulled his bayonet and sawed the hose through and tossed the pistol-like igniter housing away.

No blowtorches for his men today.

He spun and began to race back to the blockhouse.

★ ★ ★

Earl somehow regained consciousness. He was not dead. He tried to reassemble what had happened, and finally identified it as either an errant mortar shell or grenades. He shook his head, trying to drive the jangles of pain out, but they remained. His hip throbbed. He looked down and saw blood. His canteen was punctured twice, there was a groove cut in the brass keeper of his web belt where a bullet had spanged off, and a bullet had grooved his side, a slow leakage of blood accumulating on his heavy USMC twill shirt. He looked around.

Gone, all gone.

Fuck, he thought.

Finally met a Jap smart as me. Smarter even, goddamn his little monkey soul to hell.

The draw was quiet, though the noise of the firing was close at hand. The Japanese still held the blockhouse; his flanking thrust had been defeated. He'd gotten four men of Able Company wiped out and himself damn near killed, and only because, now that he thought of it, he must have heard the *chink!* of a Jap arming his grenade that got him to the ground before the first blast, and he now realized there were two blasts.

He looked about; his Thompson was a few feet away. He picked it up, blew sand out of the trigger assembly, and rotated down the safety. No need to check the chamber for he carried it in combat with a round sitting there, the bolt held back. He started up the draw.

He climbed the crest, pivoted, and could see nothing. Ahead lay a crest line, where a hummock of black sand was anchored by a netting of scraggly vegetation.

He lurched ahead, slipped once, then got around the hummock to find himself a hundred yards or so from the blockhouse. Three gun pits, sandbagged revetments reinforced with palm, held gun crews with riflemen, all working frantically to keep their fire up. The guns hammered away like industrial implements.

Earl didn't pause a second. It wasn't in his nature. He had the advantage of surprise, and he was on the first pit before the men realized. He fired a long burst, the gun steamy and jumpy in his hands, and just cut them down.

A man in the second pit, thirty yards farther out, rose to his racket, fired at Earl, and the bullet banged off his helmet, the helmet itself flipping away. Earl fired from the hip, catching him, then raced to the pit, firing, and as he reached it ran dry of ammo and so leaped in, using his gun butt. He drove the heavy thing forward, smashing a Jap in the face, spun sideways, and smashed another. He returned to the first with several savage butt strokes, his heart empty of mercy.

Around him, the world lit up. Nambu fire from the third pit. Earl went down, reached for his own grenade, pulled the pin, and threw it. As he waited for the detonation, he hastened through a magazine change. When the grenade fired off, he rose to see three men with a light Nambu racing his way and he took them down with a raking burst. He rose, ran through fire to the third pit — why he wasn't killed was a mystery he'd ponder for the rest of his life — and finished the clip on the wounded men who struggled within it. When the gun ran dry, he killed two wounded men with his gun butt, not a thing you'd tell a child about, but a necessary part of the job.

He sat back, exhausted, sucked in air that was heavy with the chemical stench of this goddamned place. He saw the blockhouse lay a few yards away and knew he'd have to blow it. Yeah, with what? No grenades left, no satchel charge, no bangalore torpedo, no flamethrower. Then he flipped a Jap over — the body was so light! — and found a pouch of grenades. He knew the Jap grenades were no good, but maybe a bagful would do the trick. He reached for his Thompson and saw why it had quit. A wedge of sand had jimmied the bolt halfway back. You'd have to scrape for a month to get it cleared.

Okay.

He took a breath and ran to the blockhouse, squirmed along the back of it, his shirt scraping the concrete. He could hear its guns working the slope. He found a chamber, and peeking in, he saw a black steel door.

Earl pressed himself against the wall, took out one of the Jap grenades. With his teeth, he got the pin out. Then he slammed the end of the thing against the wall, felt it fizzle, and watched the dry thin smoke of burning powder pour out of it.

Oh, shit, these things scared him.

He dumped it in the bag, tossed the bag flush against the steel door, and headed back across the sand to the gun pit.

He needed a weapon.

★ ★ ★

The captain made it back inside. In the dankness, in the darkness, there was a moment's respite from the storm of the battle. The noise went way down, the glare ceased, the stench of sulfur was supplanted by other stenches.

Someone clapped him on the shoulder, someone hugged him, someone cried with joy.

'I stopped their flame team. Now we've got them. They won't be getting up here this morning. *Samurai!*'

He handed the Type 100 to his sergeant and went back to his little corner. He picked up his sword, a prosaic blade probably ground out by a machine in the Naval Sword Company, polished on a machine, assembled by a worker. Yet it was strangely sharp and twice men had tried to buy it from him. There was something about it that he couldn't quite define.

Now he fastened it to his belt by its clip, drew

the blade out, and set it before him.

He felt he had done his duty. No one would perish in flames. They would achieve death with dignity.

He picked up a calligraphy brush and dipped it in ink. He thought of Lord Asano in 1702, seconds from his own death by his own hand, bowing to pressures so great as to be incomprehensible.

Asano had written

I wish I had seen
the end of spring
but I do not miss
the falling of the cherry blossoms.

Asano knew what was important: the end of spring, his duty; the falling of the cherry blossoms, the emptiness of ceremony. Then Asano had plunged his blade into his stomach and drawn it cleanly across the midline of his body, cutting entrails and organs, spraying blood everywhere until the mercy of the sword had sundered his neck, ending all.

Now it was clear before Yano. He had to record what happened here, what this place was, how hard these men had fought, how hard they had died. Inspiration suddenly arrived, along with enlightenment, and in a few deft strokes, he sent kanji characters spilling vertically across the rice paper. They seemed to tumble from his brush, feathery, almost delicate, a testament to the artist's genius amid the slaughter. It was so human.

It was his death poem.

He removed his sword and laid it before him on the small writing table. With the nub of his brush, he pushed out the bamboo peg that secured the grip to the tang. Smoothly the grip slid upward, but instead of taking it off, he wrapped his death poem around the tang and remounted the grip. Then he thrust the peg back through the hole. But he thought, Too loose. With the still-wet calligraphy brush, he quickly applied a dollop of ink to the peg. It would slide into the hole, thicken like lacquer, then eventually harden into a cement bond that would keep the sword tightly assembled forever.

For some reason this small task — in the face of death — gave him immense satisfaction. It meant that his last conscious act had been the act of poetry.

Then the world exploded.

2

THE SCYTHE

CRAZY HORSE, IDAHO, TODAY

There was no why to it, not really.

You couldn't put it into words. His daughter had said, You have too much time on your hands. His wife had said, You cannot tell that man a thing. Who knew what the people in town said or what the Mexicans or the Peruvians who herded the sheep and mended the fences said, but of the last category, the words *muy loco* were certainly uttered.

Bob Lee Swagger, nearing sixty, stood alone on a slope in the American West. The property was his own. He had bought it upon discovering, in this new stage of life, an unexpected prosperity. Two layout barns he owned in Arizona, in Pima County, were doing well, managed astutely by a high school friend of his daughter's, a young woman who loved horses and had a practical streak. So a check arrived from Arizona every month. There were two more layout barns here in Idaho, east and west of Boise, which Bob more or less managed, except that they managed themselves and Julie did all the book-keeping. So there was money from that too. Then the United States Marine Corps sent him a check every month as well, for all the bleeding he'd done in far-off places nobody remembered. There was a VA disability check for the bad business about the hip, that steel joint that was always ten degrees colder inside his body than the weather outside it.

So he'd bought this nice piece of land on the Piebald River, still a ways out from Crazy Horse, itself still a longer way out from Boise. You could see the Sawtooths, a blue scar across the sea of green that was a valley. The land was serene: no human structure could be discerned. If you looked at the land, under the big Idaho sky piled with cumulus, hawks rotating in the thermals, and you saw the smeary white of the antelope herds, you might feel a little peace. A man who'd done some hard things and had finally come to a land where he could live untroubled with a wife and a daughter would love such a place, even if the daughter was off in graduate school in New York City and he and the wife didn't speak as much to each other as they once had. But the idea was splendid: he would build a fine house, looking across to the Sawtooths, with a porch on it. All summer long it would be green, in the fall red and gold, and in the winter white.

You earned it the hard way, Bob, Julie had said.

Well, maybe I did. Anyhow, I'm just going to enjoy sitting under a blanket in the mornings and watching.

I wouldn't bet on that, but if that's what you say.

But there was one thing. Before a house could

26

be built, the land had to be cleared and irrigated and Bob just didn't want another man to do that job with a machine and a crew. He wanted to do it himself.

It was called a scythe, an ancient, curved blade, rusted and nicked but still sharp as hell, affixed to the end of a grip with enough bend in it and enough knobs on it so a fellow could get behind it with his weight and strength and swing. What he swung at, he cut. You found the rhythm, the blade did the work, your muscles stretched, your stamina built. There was something nineteenth century about it that he liked, or maybe even eighteenth or seventeenth or sixteenth century.

It takes some time to work a good-size piece of land, and the more he got into it, the more it got into him. It was an hour from his home in Boise, mostly on dirt roads; to save a little time, he'd bought and taught himself to run a Kawasaki 450 off-road bike, and tore across the desert in a more direct route than via the crazy-quilt switchbacks his truck would have required. Then, in jeans and boots and an old undershirt, he'd begin. He'd been at it a month, 197 paces one way, then 197 paces the other, six, seven, sometimes eight or even ten hours a day. He no longer ached, his back no longer throbbed. His body had finally gotten used to, even come to need, the labor. Back and forth, his calluses protecting him, the blade biting the scrawny vegetation, and with each swing, a spray of stalks and leaves flew away, cutting a swath maybe two feet wide. He was halfway done now. Half the field was cut to nubbiness and had died; it could be plowed under and planted. The steeper half still beckoned, a stretch of prairie grass and tumbleweed and cacti and other tough, scrawny, high-desert growers. Yet somehow it pleased him. It meant nothing to nobody, but it meant a little this day to him.

This particular day was no different than any other. Why should it be: sun, sky, brambles to cut, scythe to swing, progress to be made. Up one track, back another, the steady swish of the blade, that swath two feet wide, the feel of the sweat building, the sense of giving himself up against and —

Then he saw the car.

Who the hell could this be?

He didn't think anyone knew he was here alone in the wild, or knew the strange linkage of dirt roads that got you here. Only Julie did: he figured then that she'd told whoever this was, and so it was all right.

It was a Mercedes-Benz S-Class in black, a very nice car, pulling up a rooster tail of dust.

He watched as it slewed ever so gently to a stop. One by one two men got out.

He recognized one right away: it was Thomas M. Jenks, a retired marine colonel and sometime friend of Bob's, a biggish wheel in Boise who owned a Buick dealership, a radio station, and a mall or two, very nice fellow, active in the Marine Corps League, a man Bob trusted. The second was Asian. There was something about him that radiated Japanese, Bob thought, but he didn't know quite what. He recalled a letter that had come a week or so ago, full of puzzling possibilities.

Gny. Sgt. (Ret.) Bob Lee Swagger
RR 504
Crazy Horse, ID

Dear Sergeant Swagger:

I hope this letter finds you happy in a well-earned retirement and I hope you pardon the intrusion, as I know you to be a man who treasures his privacy.

I am a retired full colonel USMC and currently head of the Marine Historical Section at Henderson Hall, Arlington, VA — Marine Headquarters.

For some months I have been working with Philip Yano, of Tokyo, Japan. I have found Mr Yano to be an excellent man. He is retired from the Japanese Ground Self-Defense Forces, where he was a colonel and a battalion commander, with special duty attachments to a variety of American and British Military Training Schools, including Ranger, Airborne, SpecOps, British SAS, and the Command and Staff College at Ft. Leavenworth, Kansas. As well, he has a master's degree in business administration from Stanford University.

Mr Yano has spent the summer researching Marine records as part of a research project regarding the campaign on Iwo Jima February-March 1945. As your father figured significantly in that battle and was one of twenty-three Marines to win the Medal of Honor for actions there, he hopes to discuss this with you. I gather he's doing a book on Iwo from a Japanese point of view. He is a polite, respectful, and even an endearing man and a military professional of the highest order. I hope you can be of assistance to Mr Yano.

I am requesting your full cooperation with him. Possibly you would not be averse to sharing your father's memories with him. He is, as I say, an admirable man deserving of respect and cooperation.

I will put him in contact with you and sometime in the next few weeks he will be in touch. Again, my thanks and best,

Sincerely,

Robert Bridges
Historical Section Superintendent
Marine Headquarters
Henderson Hall, VA

Bob hadn't felt up to this. When he'd read the letter, he'd thought, Well, now, what the hell? What do I know about it? The old man never talked, just as he himself, years later with tales of this and that when the lead was buzzing through the air, never talked either. That was somehow part of it: you didn't talk about it.

But he also knew that in a strange way, his father, who fought, hated, killed, blew up, and burned the Japanese for three years in the most

30

horrific way possible, also respected them in the way that only enemies unto death can respect each other. To call it love was to say too much; to call it forgiveness and redemption, maybe too much as well. But call it healing and you'd have it just about right. He had an image of the old man at a drugstore, must have been '52 or '53, couple of years before he died, someone said to him, 'Say, Earl, them Japs, they'se little monkey devils, huh? You fry them Japs by the bucketful, right?' and his father turned instantly grave as if insulted and said, 'You can say anything you want about 'em, Charlie, but I'll tell you this: they were damn fine soldiers and they stood their ground till the last drop of blood. They stood and fought even when they's burning alive. No one ever accused a Japanese infantryman of not doing his duty.' Then he felt his father, so voluble and commanding, turn the conversation skillfully to other subjects. There were certain things he wouldn't share, particularly with folks who hadn't been out there, on the beaches and the tiny little islands.

He turned to face the gentleman.

He saw a man his own age, square-headed with a neat crop of short gray hair, steady-eyed, stocky where Bob was lanky. Even in the heat and the rugged terrain, the man wore a dark suit and tie and radiated military dignity from every pore.

'Bob,' said Tom Jenks, 'this is — '

'Oh, I know. Mr Yano, retired recently from . . . ,' and then he paused involuntarily, noticing that Mr Yano's left eye, though almost the same

31

color as the right, wasn't focusing even as it moved in coordination with its brother, signifying that it was glass, and Bob then noticed a line running above and beneath it that, though neatly mended with the best skill that modern surgery could manage, was evidence of an ugly, violent trauma. 'From his country's service. Sir, pleasure to meet you. I am Bob Lee Swagger.'

Mr Yano smiled, showing white, even teeth, and bowed in a way that Bob had never seen except in movies: the bow was deep and deeply felt at once, as if the man were taking pleasure in it.

'I did not wish to intrude, Sergeant Swagger.'

Bob recalled something somewhere he'd heard about the Japanese and their humility and fear of acquiring obligation and causing difficulty and saw how from that point of view it made more sense to drive an hour through back roads than to come up to the house.

'So what can I do for you, sir?' asked Bob. 'Some research project about Iwo, is that it?'

'First, Sergeant Swagger, if I may.'

With that he pulled from his pocket a small gift box, bowed, and presented it to Swagger.

'As an expression of thanks for your time and knowledge.'

Bob was a little stunned. He wasn't much on gifts or bows or the kind of formality that seemed pointless in ninety-degree sunlight in the high desert of a western state, on his own land, when he was damp in sweat.

'Well, I can't say how nice this is, sir. I certainly appreciate it.'

'The Japanese always give gifts,' said Tom Jenks.

'It's their way of saying howdy and thanks.'

'Please,' said the Japanese fellow.

Bob saw that the box was so precisely wrapped that opening it seemed slightly sacrilegious. But he felt also an obligation and tore into it, marveling at the intricate folded structure of the paper, until finally he got it open, discovered a tiny jewel box, and opened that.

'Well, that is really swell,' he said.

It was a miniature sword assembled with high artistry. The tiny blade gleamed and the miniaturist had even wrapped the grip in individual thread strands.

'The sword is the soul of the samurai, Sergeant Swagger. You are a great samurai, as I know, so I bring this in salute.'

In a funny way, the gift touched Bob. It was so unexpected and, he guessed, quite expensive, for the craftsmanship was exquisite.

'You shouldn't have. It's so impressive. Believe me, all that samuraiing is way behind me. I just run some barns. But you put me in a helpful mood, so whatever it is you're interested in, fire away and I'll see if I can't pitch in. My old man never talked much about the war.'

'I understand. Few do. In any event, as possibly Colonel Bridges's letter noted, I've spent the last few months at Henderson Hall, examining the original documents pertaining to Iwo Jima. Before that I spent almost a year in Japanese defense archives, examining the same thing, though as you might imagine, Japanese records are rather incoherent.'

'Yes sir.'

'I have ended up concentrating on an action that took place February twenty-first, at a place on Japanese maps called Point I-five. It was a blockhouse on the northwest slope of Mount Suribachi.'

'I am familiar with Mount Suribachi and what happened on its northwest slope February twenty-first. Sir, may I say something. Sometimes you don't want to look too carefully or learn too much about what happens in battle. People do things in battle they wouldn't dream of doing no other way, time, or place. I speak from experience, sir.'

'I know you do.'

'You might learn something about us or about your own people that would prove upsetting.'

'I understand that too. This isn't about atrocity, however, or national policies or even about the movement of troops across the landscape, say the Twenty-eighth Marines circling the southern tip of the island to cut off, then assault Suribachi. It's about something far more intimate. Your father destroyed the blockhouse at Point I-five and killed most of the soldiers. That was a remarkable, courageous act of heroism. I have nothing but respect for it. The battle is interesting to me because my father, Captain Hideki Yano, was an infantry officer in the Japanese Imperial Army, Second Battalion, One Hundred Forty-fifth Infantry Regiment. He was in command of Point I-five, or the blockhouse on Suribachi's northwest slope. In other words, I believe as the battle progressed, your father killed mine.'

34

3

THE BLOCKHOUSE

Earl was trying to dig out and master a Nambu Type 96 light machine gun in the nearest gun pit when the grenades detonated. Though he was forty feet from them and they'd been wedged deep in a trench against the steel door of the blockhouse, the concussion still swept across him, punching him to the earth. He fell on a dead soldier, the man's face beaten in by the butt of Earl's Thompson. Earl saw the hideous rearrangement of features, the swelling, the shattered delicacies of the face and teeth, the bloated lips — then looked away. You train yourself not to see that stuff. He knew he had to focus. The gun, the gun!

The 96 was no BAR, but enough of them had shot enough lead at him for him to respect it. He looked at it, understanding its principles immediately; machine guns were pretty much alike in most respects. He rummaged around for a pouch of mags, found one, shifted to a new, fresh tin of ammo, locked it in, looked for, found, and locked back a bolt. Now he lifted it, feeling the ungainly slippy rotation of the loose bipod on the end of the finned barrel, and raced back to the rear of the house. If men shot at him, he wasn't aware of it.

He slipped down. The door was blown

asunder and black smoke boiled out of the entrance. It was like the doorway to hell. This is where you needed a flamethrower, for one cleansing stream from outside would search out nooks and crannies, crevices and corners, and take care of business and you didn't have to crawl in and go from room to room, killing.

He took a breath and entered a subterranean world, fighting the acrid drift of smoke, the stench of latrine and blood and food, the sudden clammy coolness of the underground chamber. It was like entering an insect nest.

He heard the heavy rhythm of a woodpecker from the left and turned, stepping over a body. *Bap bap bap bap bap*, the pound of the slow-firing heavy machine gun. An entrance yielded a chamber, and indeed three men serviced one of the big Nambu 7.7 92s, concentrating on downhill targets, one locating them, one firing, one feeding ammo strips into the big gun, fighting hard to the end. They hadn't even noticed the blown doorway.

It was pure murder. Usually you didn't see it; shapes moved and stopped moving or disappeared. Now he pressed the trigger, felt the hot sputter of the gun, the tracers just swept them away in less than a second, so goddamned easy. It shouldn't be as easy as with a hose against flowers. The gun in his hand emptied in a spasm and the soldiers never had any idea what happened, they just went down, flipping this way and that, this one fighting it, that one going down hard and fast, this one just slumping, caught and lit in a neon net, the Jap tracers white-blue and hot. It was over in a second.

Earl rotated to his left, stumbled a bit, burned some skin off his forehead on a low ceiling, and moved to the next chamber.

★ ★ ★

The captain shook spiderwebs, broken glass, fly wings, and dust from his brain. He was in pain everywhere, and when he breathed, only hot stench poured into his lungs and rasped at his throat. He thought he was drowning in an underwater of smoke and fumes. He gripped his skull to squeeze the pain out, but it didn't help. Where was he, what was this, what was happening?

It was his chamber that had caught most of the blast when the steel door was blown. The big Nambu wasn't firing; it was tilted askew to the right and the loader was either dead or dying; at any rate he lay on his back, his face and chest bloody, his eyes unseeing. He was gone, some piece of shrapnel to brain or spine, turning off his light in a microsecond of mercy.

It was Sudo of Kyushu.

Your sacrifice wasn't by fire, he thought. I kept my word.

One of the privates, though, had gone to the gun and was fighting to get it righted and the third man joined him, albeit feebly as he too was seriously hit.

Then the captain heard the sound of fire from close at hand and knew one of the hairy ones had penetrated. He reached swiftly for his pistol but found the blast had torn his belt off. He was defenseless. He looked about. The sword lay to his right.

He bent, picked it up. It was, of course, ridiculous. In this modern age, Japanese NCOs and officers went into battle with these frog-stickers, helpful in executing Chinese partisans and waving in staff photographs and patriotic rallies and little else. Yet throughout the army they were beloved, because they connected to a thousand years of the bushido way of the warrior and conjured up men in elaborate armor or brilliant robes meeting and destroying each other in battles or back alleys for the sake — this was the lie, at any rate — of the hundred million. In the sword was freedom from the *gaijin*, dignity, spirituality, *samurai*. The captain drew the sword from its metal scabbard, feeling the friction of metal on metal, and then it sprang free and described a fine, glorious arc across the smoky space as the American approached.

In truth, it seemed to be not much of a sword. It was but *shin-gunto*, short, almost stumpy, its brightness suspect upon inspection, because the skin was a mass of scratches and hazing, and a bit of edge here and there had chipped off, in some forgotten adventure. The captain had drawn it from resupply as part of his kit when he'd left Tokyo for the Volcanics, and it was one of thousands in a room of reconditioned swords recovered from returning soldiers back from the Sphere's expansions all over the southern half of the globe in the last decade. Possibly it had been carried by a now-dead man in China or Burma or Malaysia, who knew, who could possibly know?

But it was always weirdly sharp. This one, despite its mundane, even shabby appearance, had a will or destiny toward cutting. You could shave with it, or cut paper with it, and it had a lively quality unlike the heavier, duller sword that had been his first issue in China. It seemed to want flesh; it sought battle, destiny, fate. In some odd respect, he felt unworthy of it, though it was but military issue, presumably manufactured in a plant with thousands like it.

Yet it reassured him, and he drew it back in both hands, above his head, slightly separated for leverage, assuming position *jodan no kamai*, or 'high-level stance,' or even 'fire stance,' because his spirit was so strong it meant to burn the opponent, oppressing his resolve. He saw the next second perfectly: the downward diagonal between neck and shoulder (perfect *kiroshi*, cutting technique), the sword traveling straight without wobble, cutting cloth, skin, muscle, bone, the newly approved seventh kata of 1944, *kesagiri*, the preferred killing stroke of the diagonal cut, the clavicle stroke. Then the quick withdrawal, followed by *chiburi*, or that flick of blood removal before resheathing. The ritual was pleasing; it gave him comfort and brought calm to his tumultuous mind. He became one with the sword; he waited.

★　★　★

Earl killed the six men in the central chamber in a single second. It was just like the last: the

39

tracers ate them up, tossed them up and down, and they fell, some mute, some twitchy. This was war: all the bullshit about doing your bit, about the team, about gung ho, semper fi, was forgotten: in the end, it was killing and nothing but.

He withdrew, aware that the gun was either empty or near to it. He diddled, unlocked the empty magazine, and it fell away. He inserted a new one, locked it in, drew the bolt back, slid down the weird hallway, low, burning yet more skin off his bare head, and came to the last chamber.

He knew they were waiting for him.

God help me, he thought, this one last time.

Then he plunged in.

4

A REQUEST

'I don't know about that exact thing, Mr Yano,' said Bob. 'I do know that in fights things get all mixed up. You can never tell who's done what. Official reports don't usually come no place near the truth.'

'I understand that. It could have easily been a shell, a ricochet, a sniper, any of a dozen things, and it doesn't even matter. I also understand that if he did, it was because it was his duty, because he had no choice, because it was war. But I do know for certain that he was there, that he actually penetrated the bunker. The medal attests to that, as do the witness reports.'

'That much is known, sir,' Bob said. 'Battle is a terrible thing, as is killing.' Something drove him to rare confession. 'I have been cursed to have seen and done a lot of it. For the Marine Corps, I hunted and killed other men in Vietnam. I've thought a lot about it. I can only say, it was war.'

'I understand. I've seen some battle too. That's the way we chose, the path we followed.'

The sun was bright.

'But I am hoping so much that you will understand where my destination lies. I must ask one more question,' said Mr Yano. 'It's only out

41

of a love for my father as intense as the one you still feel for yours.'

'Go ahead,' said Bob. 'I see that's why you came.'

'There was a sword,' the Japanese said.

Bob blinked, not sure what he meant. Did he mean the miniature sword that he, Yano, had given Swagger just a few minutes ago? That sword? Then he saw: no, no, his father's sword. His father had a sword that day, of course. The Japs called them 'banzai swords' or something like that: he remembered them not from anything his father ever said but from the war comic books he had read religiously in the '50s. He saw in his mind a wicked, curved thing, with a long, tape-wrapped grip with a snakehead at the end of it. 'Banzai! Banzai!' some bearded, cavemanlike Jap sergeant in gogglelike glasses shouted in the comic books, waving it around, stirring his men to a human wave attack. Bob realized his idea of such a thing was probably crap.

'I know young soldiers in battle,' said Mr Yano. 'In the aftermath of survival, they want something to commemorate their triumph, something tangible, that speaks of victory. Who can blame them?'

'I've seen it myself,' said Bob. More memories stirred, forty years old, memories he had no interest in sifting through. But the man was right. It happened.

'I know,' said Mr Yano, 'that hundreds, thousands, possibly tens of thousands of swords were taken in the Pacific. Along with Nambu

42

pistols, flags, especially flags, Arisaka rifles, helmets, souvenirs of a fight so hard.'

'Mostly it was guys in the rear who ate that shit up,' said Bob.

'My father had a sword. His death was part of your father's greatest triumph. I've read the medal citation and the after-action reports in the Marine Historical Section and I know how brave he was.'

'My father was an extraordinary man,' said Bob. 'I've tried my whole life and I ain't yet come up to his waist. I imagine yours was as well.'

'It is true. But I must ask, is there a possibility that this sword was part of your inheritance? That you now have it? It was the sort of thing a father passes on to a son. There are far finer swords. But that sword: it would have enormous meaning to me and to my family. I really came to America in search of that sword.'

Bob wished he had good news for the man. He understood that it was more than right that such an event might transpire all these years later, the sword returned to its place of honor with the family of the man who had carried it and died with it. The symmetry of the idea pleased him; it seemed to signify a final closing up of old, raw wounds.

But he had no good news.

'Mr Yano, I would in a second, believe me. It would please me. For some damned reason, I have this feeling that it would please my father, and that would do me proud.'

'I feel the same.'

43

'But my father wasn't a man for trophies. He had no trophies except a forty-five he brought back from the Pacific, and that was a tool, not a trophy. But no flags, no trumpets, no swords, no helmets, not even much chatter. He just put the war behind him and got on to the next thing. He never talked about it. He never wore the uniform again, until the day he died, not even on parade days when some of the other boys did. He wasn't the sort of man who talked himself up, or tried to remind others of what he'd done. You don't see that much no more.'

If the Japanese felt disappointment, he didn't show it, and Bob realized it was not their way to show such things.

'I didn't think I'd ever heard you say anything about a sword,' said Jenks, who'd been standing idly by while the two conducted business. 'Bob's not a showy kind, and I don't believe his father would have been either.'

'No, I understand,' said Mr Yano. 'Well, so be it. That is what the gods have decreed. The sword is where it is and that is where it will remain.'

'You sure tried,' said Bob. Then he added, 'Possibly there are still some men left in that platoon? They'd be in their eighties now. But couldn't Marine Historical put you in contact?'

'There are two and I've actually talked to both. One in Florida, one in Kansas. But I came up empty.'

'That's too bad. I'd really like to help. And — hmmm,' he said.

'Yes.'

'Oh, I don't know. All this talk about so long

44

ago. I am hearing something,' said Bob.

'Hearing something?'

'I'm getting a buzz on something. 'Sword.' You say that word, meaning World War Two Japanese sword, I get a little kind of image.'

'A memory, like?' said Jenks.

'Not even that. I don't know why it would be or what it would be. Somewhere deep down, I have this little bug. Maybe it's a mistake.'

'Still, it's something.'

'Mr Yano, because we're connected in such a hard way, let me make you a promise. It ain't much. It's all I got.'

'I'm moved.'

'There's stuff in my attic. It was in the house in Arizona; I moved it when I sold that place. I looked through it a couple or so years ago when some business about my father came up and I had to go on a little trip back home. But I didn't look *thoroughly*. Obviously, I wasn't looking for anything having to do with a sword. So, I'll go back through that stuff over the next few weeks. Maybe get a sense of what's there. Who knows, maybe there's a lead of some sort. You came all the way out here to No Place, Idaho, I feel I owe you, soldier to soldier. Also, son of hero to son of hero.'

'You're very kind. I know you'll examine until there's nothing left to examine. Here's my card. Please accept it, and if there's any news, you'll be able to reach me.'

5

THE OLD BREED

The young faces stared out at him. They were so thin, so unmarked, in many cases so unformed, with eager eyes and knobby cheekbones, tan in the tropic sun. Each man clutched a vicious KA-BAR knife, or a Garand or a carbine or a BAR. They were revving themselves up for war, this young marine platoon somewhere in the Pacific, somewhere in World War II. Finally one face in the back row materialized and Bob knew it to be his father's. It was thin too, but if you looked hard, you saw the pure animal confidence. His father wore the NCO's weird combination of foreman's savvy, father's sternness, mother's forgiveness, teacher's wisdom, and coach's toughness beautifully, and the picture somehow captured a professional at the apex of his game, with a crushed boonie cap pushed back on his head, his teeth white and strong as he smiled, his utility sleeves rolled up, showing strong forearms that seemed to be curled on what Bob thought was maybe (most of it was hidden behind a man in the row in front of him) a tommy gun.

He had no idea when the picture was taken. Maybe before Guadalcanal — no, not with M-1s and carbines — maybe before Tarawa, maybe before Saipan, maybe before Iwo. There was one other too, Bob couldn't remember, but he knew his dad was one of the few marines who had hit five separate islands and lived to tell about it, though the wound on Tarawa from the Jap sniper would have killed a lesser man.

The photo, old and curled, was one of a few that remained testifying to the war adventures of Earl L. Swagger of Blue Eye, Arkansas, who entered the war a corporal and got out a first sergeant even if wounded seven times. It was a real hell-and-back story. Audie Ryan didn't have anything on Earl. He fought hard, he almost died; somehow, like little Audie, he came back. He never became a movie star, but instead became a police officer and he got ten more years of life out of the deal.

But that was all. Bob was alone in the attic and it hadn't been easy digging through this stuff, which had been hastily moved from a house in Ajo, Arizona, never categorized, never examined, just lumped together as junk from the past and shoved up here. The cardboard box — 'Buster Brown. Size C7, Dark Brown Oxfords,' inscribed in his mother's script 'Daddy's Things' — contained little else. The medals, even the big one, were nested together, the ribbons faded, the metal tarnished. Bob thought maybe he should have them polished and mounted, a display to the man's courage. But his father would have been embarrassed at such show. There were police marksmanship medals, and yellowing newspaper clippings from the month of his death in 1955.

Well, I tried, Bob thought.

He thought of Mr Yano's card in his wallet.

Dear Mr Yano, he imagined the note he'd write, I went through what remained of my father's effects and found nothing that would help you in your quest. Maybe if —

And then yet another possibility occurred to him.

This here was the stuff his mother had gathered, after the funeral, before she launched into the land of drunkenness. But there was another three years when her sister, Agnes Bowman, a schoolteacher and spinster who had not yet found a man good enough, had come and stayed with them, and Aunt Agnes had raised him, sternly, not with love or tenderness, but out of a grim sense of family duty while Erla June drank herself to death and died before reaching the age of forty. Aunt Agnes was not a giving woman, which was all right. Aunt Agnes did the things that had to be done and didn't have a lot of time for nursing boys like Bob, who in any case retreated into someplace dark for a few years after his father's death, and so never made contact with her. Perhaps she was in her own dark place. That was okay; Aunt Agnes provided and guided and paid the bills and fed him; compared to that a squeeze or a hug wasn't much of anything.

But then Bob gravitated toward Sam Vincent and his big, rambling, loud, smart, funny, competitive, welcoming family and eventually, through high school, lived with Sam, almost as a Vincent. Aunt Agnes saw no purpose therefore and moved away, sending a Christmas card every year.

Bob had visited her after his first tour in Vietnam in 1966 and as an adult discovered a decent, quiet woman, finally married to a widowed schoolteacher, living in Oranda, Virginia, in the Shenandoah Valley. It had been a nice visit, though not much had been said and damned if he could remember —

Goodwin!

Agnes Goodwin, her married name.

He didn't know why, he hadn't thought of it in years, but somehow it flew at him out of some lost file in his brain.

On Anywho.com he couldn't even find an Oranda, nor on any map; he found an old map with the town located next to Strasburg, and identifying the town as Strasburg finally turned up a Goodwin. He made the blind call and located a cousin who knew other branches of the Goodwin family and guided him toward a Betty Frawley, of Roanoke, whose maiden name had been Goodwin and was that person's uncle Mike Goodwin's daughter.

'Ms Frawley?'

'We don't want none, if that's what this is all about.'

'No, ma'am, it's not. I am Bob Lee Swagger, a retired marine, calling from Crazy Horse, Idaho, on some family business. I am trying to locate my aunt, whose name was Agnes Bowman and who late in life married a Virginia man named Goodwin — '

'Aunt Agnes!'

'Yes, ma'am.'

'Well, she was a good soul, bless her heart. She

married Daddy after Mother died and although I would never be one to criticize Mother, I will tell you those may have been the best years of his life. And she nursed him through to the end.'

'She was good at that.'

'Her end followed shortly after, I'm sorry to say. You were a marine?'

'Yes, ma'am.'

'In nineteen sixty-six, did you come and visit Agnes? I was eleven at the time and I have a very distinct memory of a tall, handsome young man who set all the hearts aflutter. He was just back from Vietnam, where he'd won some medals. He was Agnes's nephew, I believe. Would that be you?'

'Yes, ma'am, though I'm far from handsome these days, if I ever was. I remember that day in Oranda well. It was the last time I saw her. She helped raise me after my father died and my mother — her sister — had some problems.'

'Families in those days pitched in. That's the way it was. It's not much like that anymore, but in those days, families helped out.'

'Ma'am, I'm just playing out a long shot here. My father died in nineteen fifty-five, and that's when Aunt Agnes came and stayed with us, through 'fifty-eight or 'fifty-nine. As I say, it was then my mother's decline began. Agnes ran the house for a time. I'm trying to gather up any mementos that might remain of my father. He was a marine too, and a law officer who died young. I thought that she might have had some effects, that you might have them, that something there might somehow relate to my father, something I missed or never knew about.'

'Sounds like a man trying to recover his father's memory.'

'It may be that, ma'am.'

'Well, I think there's a box somewhere. I'm not sure it made the move with me. It was all such old stuff, but I hated to just throw it out. It was somebody's life, you just can't throw it out.'

'Do you have it?'

'If I do, it's in the basement and I'd have to look for it.'

'Ma'am, I'd be happy to come on out there and help you.'

'Well, I don't have much to do these days, so I may as well go look for you. You leave me your address and we'll see what we can find.'

And so, three weeks later, three weeks he'd spent alone on his property swinging that scythe every day, cutting down the brambles and thorns, a big envelope arrived from Roanoke, Virginia.

He opened it that night.

Oh, Christ.

First thing out was a picture of himself, his mother on a rare sober day, and stern Aunt Agnes, at a picnic table somewhere, '57, '58. He wore a Cardinals baseball cap, a T-shirt and jeans, and had scrawny arms and legs. 'Bob Lee, Erla June, and Agnes, Little Rock, June 5, 1958,' the inscription read, in fading purple ink.

It brought back nothing, nothing at all.

Then came his mother's death certificate, some yellowed insurance forms, her driver's license, a bank book with NULL AND VOID stamped across it, a few Christmas cards from

51

neighbors whose names meant nothing, Erla June's obituary from the paper up in Fort Smith, a small gold crucifix with a pin that his mother had evidently worn, a few more photographs, mostly of strangers, a few more official forms and a few letters, most of them unopened.

There were eight in all. Evidently they'd arrived over the three years Agnes had lived with Bob and Erla June, some addressed to Mrs Swagger, some to the Widow of Sgt. Swagger, some to Erla June by name.

He opened them, one by one. A former platoon member wanted to express his sadness and talk about the time Earl had saved his life on Guadalcanal. Then there was a schoolmate of Erla June's, inquiring as to her health and welfare and expressing gratitude. There was a tax bill from Garland County and Bob realized he had finally paid it in 1984. The daughter of Col. William O. Darby, another Arkansas war hero, famous for having led 'Darby's Rangers' in Italy before he died in France, wrote to express her sorrow and offer moral and even financial support in case of family emergencies. Boy, Bob thought, talk about class.

Then, finally, an unopened letter, postmarked Kenilworth, Illinois, October 4, 1959, on creamy stationery with expensive lettering proclaiming the sender's name and return address, John H. Culpepper, of 156 Sheridan Road.

Gently, he opened the heavy envelope, pulled out an equally heavy, creamy piece of stationery with Culpepper's name and address tastefully emblazoned across the top.

Dear Mrs Swagger:

I'm very sorry this letter is so late. I only learned by chance yesterday about your husband's tragic death four years ago. I haven't kept up with marines from the war. But I felt I had to express my sorrow at learning of the event. Earl Swagger was a very great man and helped me on my greatest day of need.

I was a young marine captain, and by default became commanding officer of Able Company, 2nd Battalion, 28th Marines during the battle of Iwo Jima. To say I was overmatched is to understate the situation considerably.

Things came to a head on D plus 2, as we called it, when it was my company's turn to lead an assault on a particularly well-designed and well-defended Japanese emplacement. Left to my own devices, I would have gotten myself and more importantly my men slaughtered, because, quite frankly, I didn't know what the hell I was doing. (I had used family connections to get myself a combat command, because I just had to fight.)

In any event, Earl, who was the battalion first sergeant, was sent down from headquarters to assist me. He certainly assisted me!

I'm sure you've read the citation. I'm proud to say I wrote it and worked hard to get it approved. I think it was my finest accomplishment in an otherwise — between you and me — completely mediocre military career. What he did that day was beyond question one of the great feats of arms in military history. From my vantage point on the slope beneath, he was literally Superman. How many Japanese shot at him we'll never know, but he never showed a single moment's hesitation and managed to single-handedly destroy the emplacement. He saved the lives of a hundred men that day!

Anyway, a few days later I was hit, thus ending my adventure in combat. Because I had not been a dynamic leader, I was not the focus of a lot of attention and I was feeling pretty blue on my cot in the hospital tent awaiting evacuation. Who should walk in but the legendary first sergeant himself. I'll never forget that day! He was a god in that battalion, and here he was coming to visit me.

He said, 'Well, Captain, I see you managed to get yourself banged up a bit.'

'Yes, First Sergeant,' I said, 'I jumped this way and the Jap knew exactly which way that would be. I was lucky he was in a hurry.' (It was a leg wound.)

'Sir, I wanted you to have this. You were in command that day, you headed up the assault, I was just the fellow who was left standing. So it's yours. Maybe it'll cheer you up.'

He handed me something wrapped in cloth, about two feet long. I quickly opened it to discover a Japanese sword, what's called a 'banzai sword,' of the sort the Jap officers carried and all too often used in combat.

He said, 'Your boys gave me that when I was heading back to Battalion after the fight. It

54

came out of the blockhouse. Someone took it off the dead Jap officer just before they burned the place out with flamethrowers. That fellow tried to comb my hair with it. I thought you might want to have it.'

I should tell you that Japanese swords were prized war trophies, especially when taken in combat. I could have sold it, and indeed, over the next few weeks many officers tried to buy it off me, one offering $500. But it was one of my treasures.

The truth, however, is that it's not mine. I didn't earn it. Earl did, and it was given to me only out of his compassion for young men who'd done their best, even if the best wasn't all that great, as in my case.

Now I think, What right do I have to have this sword? Please let me send it back to you. I understand Earl had a son. He should have it — though I should tell you, it's very sharp and one of my own children has already cut himself with it. But it demonstrates what Earl did that day. Please let me know if you'd like me to send it on.

John H. Culpepper
Kenilworth, Ill.

Julie dropped him at the Boise airport, named for a hero of World War II, an aviator. He had a flight to Denver, then a longer one to Chicago, where he would arrive at another airport named for a World War II hero, also an aviator. He had reserved a car.

'I'll be back tomorrow night,' he said. 'Ten fifteen. Do you want me to take a cab home? I know you've got a rough day.'

'No, no, I'll pick you up.' She was still the most beautiful woman he'd ever seen, still straw-blond with some gray in her hair and possibly in her eyes. She was a nurse and now administered a clinic in East Boise, a job she loved and gave herself to. The mother of his only child, she'd taken him in years ago and given him a chance at life when the whole world had seemed set on destroying him. But it was an old marriage by now, somewhat burnished, edging more to friendship and partnership than passion.

'Okay, I'll — '

'Bob, this isn't turning into one of your things?' She knew him so well it was a little frightening.

'Well, I don't think so.'

'I know you. You're really happiest out in the bush with Donnie Fenn, hunting other men and being hunted by other men.'

She knew Donnie Fenn well; she'd been married to him when he was KIA Vietnam while going to rescue his sniper team leader, who lay with a shattered hip. That team leader was Bob.

'I'm just trying to find a sword for this Japanese gentleman. He seemed like a very decent guy, I'd like to help him. That is all.'

'Yes, but I know your obsessions. You get something in your mind and it gets bigger and bigger and pretty soon you've talked yourself into Vietnam again.' It had happened a few times. 'Sometimes you can't help it. Someone

56

comes for you and you must respond. No man on earth responds better or truer.'

'Sometimes I do okay.'

'But nobody is coming for you now. This is what I don't understand. What you're doing for this man, it's very decent. But it's so much. What's going on? Why do you feel this obligation so intensely? Why is it so big to you? This isn't some dry drunk thing, some excuse to go off on a crusade and get crazy?'

'No. It's something I feel I owe my father. And the Japanese father.'

'Your father's been dead since nineteen fifty-five. And his since nineteen forty-five. It's all so long ago. How can an obligation remain to men dead half a century ago?'

'It don't even make sense to me, honey. I have to do this one. I just do.'

'Just don't find a way to go to war, all right? The good life is here. You've earned it. Enjoy it.'

'I'm too old for war,' he said. 'I just want to drink and sleep and you won't let me drink, so I guess I just want to sleep.'

'That'll be the day,' she said.

6

THE BIG WHITE HOUSE

He missed it on the first run through Kenilworth, which seemed to be but a mile or so long on the edge of Lake Michigan about fifteen miles north of Chicago. The houses were big, mansions really, and clearly this Kenilworth was a spot where the rich lived, and if they lived overlooking the lake, they must be even richer.

But then he found it: the reason he had missed it was that there was no house at all, only a gateway, sheathed in vines and buried in the shadows of elms. You had to look hard for the numbers 1 5 6 on the pillar. He turned in, guided the rented Prizm a few hundred feet down what seemed a tunnel in the trees, and then at last burst into light at a circular driveway and a big, fine white house, one of those legendary places with about a hundred rooms and tile floors and a six-car garage. It was the sort of place where great families lived, back in the time when there were great families.

Bob parked and knocked, and after a time was greeted by a heavy, bearded man his own age in black, mainly. He was also a drinking man. He had a glass of something brown in his hand.

'Mr Culpepper?'

'Mr Bob Lee Swagger, I'm guessing.'

'Yes, sir, that's me.'

'Cool name. So southern. 'Bob Lee.' Come on in. You're right on time. You said two and two it is.'

'Thank you, sir.'

He stepped into a house that was magnificent, though in a museum kind of way. It seemed to be not lived in but preserved.

'Nice place,' Bob said.

'It sure is, but try unloading it in a market like this. You don't have six million bucks in your pocket, do you?'

'No, sir.'

'Just a thought. Anyhow, care for a drink? I'm betting you're a drinking man.'

'I was, but good. Thanks, no, sir. One drink and I wake up three days down the pike in Shanghai with a new wife.'

'That actually happened to me! Well, almost. Anyway, I sympathize. Been divorced?'

'Once. The drinking was part of it.'

'No fun, huh? I try to stay pleasantly lubed all day, at least until all this bullshit is over. I'll refill if you don't mind.'

He stopped at a bar, added a slug of Maker's Mark to his glass and another cube, then turned.

'As I said in my letter, I remember the sword. I cut myself on it pretty badly in the fifties. It was *sharp*. You looked at it and something started to bleed.'

'As I understand it, the war swords were just meant to kill. Otherwise they were junk. They weren't like the fancy ones the older Japanese in the flashy bathrobes carried.'

'My arm remembers how sharp it was.'

He pushed up his left sleeve. The scar was long and cruel.

'That there's a forty-stitch scar, pard,' he said. 'My one claim to macho. People look at that and think I've been in a knife fight. Have you ever been in a knife fight?'

'I had to kill a man with a knife once, sorry to say.'

'I thought so. I'm not impressing you any, I see. Anyhow, as I said, Dad died some years ago. As the only kid, I inherited the house. He went into advertising after the war, and he did very well. But we were from different planets. He went his way, I went mine. Advertising wasn't for me. I never wanted to say the word *client* in my life, so I went into TV. I never had to say *client*. Instead, I had to say *sponsor*. Anyhow, I've got to sell this place to pay for my third divorce and this one's a mess. Why are the beautiful young ones so hard to get rid of?'

'I couldn't tell you that, sir,' Bob said with a smile.

'It's because they've never heard the word *good-bye*. So when you say it to them, they take it *personally*.' He laughed. 'This one wants my spleen for lunch as well as my dad's fortune. Amazing.'

'Sounds rough, Mr Culpepper.'

'Listen, even a genuine tough guy like you would get a cold sweat on this mission. Anyway, if you don't mind, I'm going to take you to the storeroom in the attic and let you be. Maybe it's there, maybe it's not. I honestly don't know what happened to it. I just don't have it in me to go through all that stuff. You understand?'

'Sure. My attic's a mess too.'

'Now — how can I say this? If you find something, you know, *private*. Uh, *intimate*. Maybe my dad had a stash of porn or letters from some girlfriend or even a boyfriend or something like that. Something *indiscreet*? Just leave it where you find it, all right? I'm not too interested in what is called *the truth*. I'd like to remember him as the distant, frozen, grim cadaver he was in life, all right? I'd hate to find out he was actually human.'

'I got you.'

They reached the third floor, the end of a hall, and entered a room. 'Anyhow, I'll leave you two old marines alone. If he didn't get rid of it, it's probably still here. Really, help yourself, take your time. The bathroom's down the hall. If you want a drink, want to break for dinner, anything; I'm here alone with my legal problems and trying to get in contact with a daughter who seems to have run off with somebody calling himself a documentary filmmaker. Have you noticed? They're *all* documentary filmmakers these days. If you need me, just holler. It's your sword, really, more than it's mine and it would make the old bastard happy to know it finally went to you and then back to Japan.'

'Thank you, sir.'

'Please don't call me sir. I'm just Tom. John's boy, Tom, son of *the* Mr Culpepper of Culpepper, Townsend & Mathers.'

'Loud and clear, Tom.'

'Can I call you Sarge? I always wanted to call

61

someone 'Sarge,' just like in the movies.'

'Sure, but the name I answer to mostly is 'Gunny.' It's from gunnery sergeant, a rank only the Marine Corps has.'

' 'Gunny.' Oh, that is cool. Gunny, go to town!'

So Bob turned and faced what remained of the life of a man who once had commanded, however briefly, Able Company, 2/28, on a far-off place called Iwo Jima, a hell that neither his only son nor even Gunny Swagger, three-tour survivor of Vietnam, could imagine.

Back and back, the boxes took Bob through Culpepper's life, and a biography somehow formed. Two wives, one much prettier than the other, and younger too, picked up sometime in the mid-'60s, by which time the only child, Tommy — he was evident too, a towheaded fatty, somewhat overwhelmed by his glamorous and successful dad — was in his sullen, shaggy teens.

Finally, an hour in and thirty-five boxes deep, having passed through adventures in advertising, he came to World War II. Presumably there was a box for Yale or Harvard too, wherever the guy went, but the war box held the usual junk, good conduct ribbons, battle stars, the Purple Heart, a few other trinkets, but the treasure was a marine seabook, chronicling assignments and a surpassing adequacy of performance. Bob went through it quickly and saw that yes, originally John Culpepper had been assigned to command a thirty-man marine detachment on the battleship *Iowa* in 1944. That was really a ticket to survival. That was saying, Rich boy, we're looking out for you. You get to go home when it's all over with a couple of Pacific battle stars, a captaincy, some nice stories to tell, and a leg-up on all the O'Tooles and Zukowskis who were bobbing facedown in the red surf.

John had wanted to fight. He could have sat it out, but the records showed that late in January, he transferred, at sea, from the *Iowa*, to the troopship *LCI-552*, where elements of the 28th Regiment droned toward a date with death in the center of the largest Marine Corps invasion force ever assembled. It certainly was unusual. Possibly there'd been an injury aboard the LCI and a 28th officer injured himself and couldn't continue duty, so John was shunted in fast. Or possibly John fucked up in some big, hideous way on the *Iowa* and was sent to the line company punitively. But more than anything, the move had the marks of pull all over it. Happened all the time. In 'Nam, boys would suddenly disappear a month into their thirteen-month tour, called stateside to work in the Pentagon. Somebody had complained to Mommy who complained to Daddy who'd done a congressman a million-dollar favor and so Junior caught the freedom bird home.

But not John Culpepper. He used his pull to get into battle, not out of it.

It couldn't have been easy. A year on a battlewagon isn't the best training for something like Iwo and when he got to the 28th the CO wouldn't know him, the other officers wouldn't know him, and the men wouldn't know him. He'd go into the fight without much psychological support, not easy and made harder by far by the peculiar savagery of Iwo.

So John fought on Iwo for a week. On the third day, Earl Swagger came down from headquarters and got his men through the successful assault against the blockhouse on the northwestern flank of Suribachi as the 28th circled and cut off the five-hundred-foot tall volcano. Then, a few days later, a shell landed close at hand; the young officer's legs were shattered. He spent three nights in an aid station and was evacuated by hospital ship. He recuperated in Hawaii, where he married his fiancée, Tommy's mother, Mildred, a plain girl also from the Boston area. By the time he was duty-ready, the A-bombs had been dropped, the war was over. He got to go home a hero, even if he'd probably never fired his carbine once.

It didn't matter. He did what he was supposed to, even if he was scared shitless the whole time. That's what won wars, the thousands of reluctant John Culpeppers, not the two or three Earl Swaggers.

But there was no sword.

Where could it be?

Maybe it got thrown out and off it went to the Kenilworth dump, to rust away to oblivion or be crushed to junk by a bulldozer.

Bob tried to think hard on the issue.

What is the quality of a sword?

Well, its sharpness, but that's the sword as weapon. Think of the sword as object: the answer is, its awkwardness.

It's long and thin and curved. You might display it, but it wouldn't fit neatly into one of those standard cardboard boxes; no, you'd have to wedge it in.

Who's packing these boxes? Probably some workingmen hired by the surviving son who has suddenly acquired a house he doesn't particularly want and never remembers fondly, but he's got to get it into shape, sell it before his wife files for divorce. So someone packs all this stuff, thinking not a bit about it, not engaged in the family's life, having no special sense of the meaning of a sword taken in battle and —

Bob went to the first closet. No. But in the second one, he found three golf bags, and there, in the third one, amid the sixes and sevens and the drivers and the wedges and the putter was Captain Hideki Yano's *shin-gunto*.

★   ★   ★

'Tom?'

'Oh, yeah, you found it,' said Tom Culpepper, rising from a desk in what had been his father's study. He had his ever-present glass of Maker's with him, apparently just recently freshened.

'I did, yes. It was in a golf bag. I thought you might want to have a look.'

'Yeah, I suppose I do. Yeah, that's it,' he said, taking it, holding it to the light. 'Here, let me point out something. See this peg or whatever it is?'

He pointed to a stub a few inches above the circular hilt of the old thing. It seemed clotted with some kind of black tar or something, smeary and gummy. But it also, in the right angle of light, threw up tiny puncture wounds.

'I remember the day I got cut. I'd snuck it out of Dad's study and we were waving it around, playing pirate or something. 'Fifty-seven, 'fifty-eight, sometime around there. Then we got the bright idea to take it apart. Don't ask me why. We examined it and it seemed to be held together by this little wooden pin through this hole. See, it runs from one side to the other. That secures the handle to the blade, I'm guessing.'

'I see,' said Bob, who already knew the correct terms from the Internet: the bamboo peg was *mekugi*, the hole into which it fit *mekugiana*.

'But it was stuck. We tried to drive it out with a hammer and nail and all we did was dent it. God, when I think of it now, I'm a little ashamed. We had no idea. It was just a big sword thing for killing pirates.'

'You were just kids. How could you know?'

'We never got it out. I hate to remember this thing on the floor and I'm whacking on it, the blade is getting all crudded up on the floor. It's got some kind of gunk on it. Real thick black stuff. I don't know if the Japanese officer put it there, or your father, or mine, or someone at the factory, or what. But it's not coming out easily.'

'No, it's not. Someone wanted to hold it together. Go on, pull it.'

John Culpepper's son Tom drew the sword out. It buzzed against the tightness of the metal scabbard, then described an arc across the room as he brandished it.

'Wow,' he said. 'This baby still wants to cut something. Here, it scares me a little.'

He handed it over to Bob, who in taking it felt some kind of charge — what? a thrill, a buzz, a vibration — as indeed the baby still wanted to cut something.

You could tell in a flash it was superbly designed for its purpose, a thin ridge running each side of the gently curving blade, reaching the tip — *kissaki*, he knew it to be called. He felt the blasphemous power of the thing. It had exquisite balance, but the blade seemed something even more, somehow weirdly alive. He waved it just a little and could have sworn that it contained some soft core that pitched forward in the momentum, speeding toward its destination.

He held it up to the light. Indeed, the blade had seen hard use. The steel was dull upon close inspection, a haze of cross-hatched nicks and cuts. Small black flecks attacked it randomly. On the edge — *yakiba*, he knew — almost microscopic chips were missing, whether from small boys whacking it against a tree or a Japanese officer drawing it against a marine's neck. The handguard — *tsuba* — was a heavy circle of iron, like an ornate coaster almost. The grip was tacky: the sword was covered in gritty fish skin, then wrapped elaborately in a kind of flat cotton cording that was darkened with sweat or grime, worn in places and frayed.

If you waved it, the sword rattled ever so gently, because, he now saw, the guard wasn't secured tightly by spacers.

'I remember as a kid you could slice paper with it, that's how sharp it was,' said Tom

67

Culpepper. 'Here, let's try it.'

He grabbed a heavy piece of stationery and Bob touched edge to paper and felt the sword pause, then slide through neatly. Tom dropped two pieces of paper to the ground.

'I can't believe it's that sharp,' he said. '*Nothing* should be that sharp!'

7

NARITA

You can't get mad.

You can't get mad.

Yet it was all he could do to sit there.

It's a test, he told himself. They're testing the *gaijin*. They want to see if I have the maturity, the patience, the commitment to politeness and ceremony to be worth talking to in Japan.

Or maybe, he thought, they're like cops everywhere: they just don't give a fuck.

Whichever, the result was the same. He sat in the Narita International Airport police station, forty miles outside Tokyo. It was a stark, functional space with nothing like the swanky, shopping-mall flash of the public hallways on higher levels.

The process had all been set up. Having discovered the sword, he had called the retired Colonel Bridges of the Marine Historical Section, explained all, and Bridges had volunteered to run the paperwork, which was considerable. He had the D.C. contacts and knew someone who knew someone at the Japan External Trade Organization, or JETRO, on the West Coast, which had some mysterious, influential connection with the Ministry of Economy, Trade, and Industry, known as METI, one of those large governmental entities with fingers in many pies. Arrangements were made with customs to let the sword into the country. It would be removed from quarantine immediately to the Narita Airport police department, where a license would be duly issued. Thus with the customs certificate and the license, it was all supposed to be legal.

But something was wrong. Now he waited in the central room, near the desk, with beaten Korean workers, with angry salarymen who'd gotten drunk and acted out and had to be put down with a thump on the head, with grifters and cheats, maybe with the odd minor gangster or two, as gangsters were said to be spread widely throughout Japanese society. They were called *yakuza*, he knew, yaks for short.

But, Wait, wait, wait.

Finally, Ah, yes, you have sword.

His interrogator wore a pale blue uniform with a small handgun — a Smith & Wesson possibly? — in a flapped black holster. He was an unprepossessing man, not one of your beefier cop types.

Yes, sir. The documents are there. I just need the license, and that was supposed to be arranged.

Arranged?

Yes, sir, here's the letter.

He handed it over.

It's a relic. It's from the war. Mr Yano's father died in battle and lost his sword. I believe this was it, that it was taken in battle by my father. Mr Yano came to America looking for the sword. I didn't have it then and it took me a couple of

70

months, but I think I have it now.

The uniformed officer took the document.

The sword is supposed to be delivered here from the customs office upstairs. It's all arranged.

Swords are very dangerous. You must wait. I will go check and call your name. Please return to your seat.

And so Bob sat. He thought it would take a few minutes, but the minutes dragged on until sixty of them mounted up, then sixty more. Maybe he could go out, get a book, a newspaper, a cup of coffee, something.

Everyone else in the waiting room had more patience. They could sit without making a sound, without fuss; the passage of time meant nothing to them.

A name would be called out, off they'd go, to be interviewed, deposed, to give a statement, make an identification.

Finally in the third hour a name was called and after a second he realized that it was some sort of approximation of Swagger. It came out 'Su waggaa.'

'Yes, here.'

'Ah. Yes. You come, please.'

He went with the officer — a different one, slighter, younger, though in uniform with a little gun in a holster as well — and back through squad and staff rooms, more insurance agency really than cop shop, because there wasn't the sense of bully-macho, of men who used their weight to require obedience, that you felt in an American variation.

Finally, he was led into a room; a uniformed senior police officer gestured for him to sit down.

'Sorry, we had to do some checking. It's fine for METI to have plans, but no one here knew a thing. Bureaucracy.'

'I understand. Sorry for the trouble.'

'Called your embassy, had to check with METI, the man there was out to lunch. This is unusual.'

'People don't usually bring them *into* Japan. Sure, the swords are so beautiful it's usually the other way around. Sorry for the problem.'

'Tell me please again.'

Bob went through it, trying to keep his sentences short and clear. His father, Captain Yano, Iwo. The surprise visit, the request. His discovery, his decision to honor his father. Mr Yano's father, Mr Yano and his family. JETRO and METI, his talks with the METI rep in L.A., the letter, the sense that arrangements had been made. He concluded with, 'Is there a problem?'

'A small one. You see, this is *shin-gunto*. You know *shin-gunto*?'

'Sure. Army sword. I know it ain't nothing fancy, not like the beautiful swords that are so much a part of the Japanese heritage.'

'Yes. You see it's not much. Not a beautiful piece by any means, like some. Old, rather hard used. What you don't see is that we have a regulation forbidding this kind of sword, the army sword, from coming in.'

'That kind of sword?'

'Yes. You see it's *gendaito* — '

'Modern.'

'Yes, and so officially it's not an antique that

72

tells us of our heritage and reflects the skill of our artisans. It's merely a weapon. We would regard it as we would regard a gun. You know there are no guns in Japan.'

'That's why I left my bazooka at home.'

'Excellent decision. Anyhow, the *gendaito* sword, the gun, in Japanese eyes, legally, they would be the same thing.'

'Okay.'

'But I understand and I appreciate. The man who visited you probably wasn't thinking precisely about this issue. METI wasn't thinking about this issue, only about necessary import forms, difficulties with customs, that sort of thing.'

'Sorry for the trouble. See, I wanted it to be a surprise. The man I mean to present it to, he doesn't know I'm here. I only wired him, told him I thought I'd have some good news for him. The reason I did it that way was that when he visited me, he preferred to do it without making an appointment. He didn't want me going out of my way to arrange hospitality. He was trying to be as helpful as possible. I felt I owed him the same. I knew if I told him I was coming, he'd make a big to-do, he'd meet me, he'd have the house cleaned, all his kids would be dressed up, it would be a major event. I didn't care to do that. I was trying to act appropriately.'

'I see. I believe you. What I'm going to do is bend the rules a little. I have prepared a sword license for you.'

He produced the document, which looked a little like the Treaty of Ghent, with all its formal kanji characters in perfect vertical columns, utterly meaningless to Bob. It had been stamped dramatically with some kind of red image, and it also had an impressive official serial number.

'See here, where it says 'year of fabrication.' By our standards anything that is *showa* is *gendaito*, *showa* meaning from the age of the Emperor Hirohito onward, that is, from nineteen twenty-six onward. So in 'year of fabrication' I have written eighteen twenty-five, which puts it in the legally acceptable antique category of *shin-shinto*, meaning anything from eighteen hundred up to the first year of Emperor Hirohito's reign, nineteen twenty-six. Given the deep curve of the blade, I am told by our sword expert, that is at least arguable. Therefore neither you nor the man who receives the gift should be in any legal jeopardy. That is what has taken so long.'

'I'm very appreciative.'

'No, it is we who should be appreciative. As I say, I have an officer here who knows a good deal about these things. He understood what a warm gesture of friendship and reconciliation it was for you to return the blade to the family of the original officer. It was his idea how to proceed. He examined the sword very closely. That gesture should not be hindered by stupid regulations.'

'Again, I say thank you very much, sir.'

'All right now. You must keep this license with the blade at all times and I would keep the sword bagged until you make the presentation.'

'I will of course do so.'

'Mr Swagger, I hope you enjoy your visit to Japan.'

'It is my pleasure, sir. I know I will.'

74

8

THE YANOS

After a night in a hotel in a part of town called Shinjuku, which he picked at random for economy, after a shower, a western dinner, a walk, a western breakfast, he walked to the train station, through mobs that astonished him.

The city was like being inside a television set. It seemed to be comprised mostly of vertical circuitry, very complex, very miniaturized. He was suddenly transported to somebody else's future. The reigning design principle seemed to be no wastage. Things were crammed in, built within bigger things, wedged this way and that. Even the alleyways were jammed with restaurants, stalls, and retail shops, each with a worm of neon above it and, of course, a sign. It was a literate society: writing was everywhere, in big signs that counseled certain consumer choices, in the endless series of official designations, of regulations and rulings and serial numbers, or directional indicators.

The Japanese hurtled by him; all were on schedules, no one lagged, all had destinations. The intensity of the crowds was somewhat shocking. At least in this Shinjuku place it was like New Year's Eve in Times Square 24/7. The crowds seemed organisms of their own. A red light stilled them all, but no other force on earth could, and when the green came on, baby, it was D-day, everybody hitting the beach at once. It was all go, go, go, now, now, now. Most of the men wore suits, most of the women wore suits. He knew they were called salarymen; they worked like slaves, they made the country go, they conformed, they never let loose, they always stayed on track.

You know where that leads you. All that repression, all that discipline, all that pressure to conform, all that rigidity. It builds, it builds, it builds, and so when they blow, they blow. Examples of the blow are rife in history: thus a Nanking, a Pearl Harbor, a kamikaze. No prisoners. Australian pilots beheaded for the cameras. Killing ten enemy soldiers before you go, thus choosing death over life every damn time.

And when the wiring blew sexually, it really blew.

On the JR train to the suburbs, which arrived on the minute, probably the second, he sat next to a fellow who could have been an accountant, a salesman, a teacher, a computer designer — neat suit, horn-rimmed glasses, hair slicked down, unselfconscious, focused, driven. But Bob saw what had the fellow's interest; it wasn't the *Wall Street Journal* but some comic book about bound teen girls being violated by other teen girls with tools that were exactly what they seemed, only bigger, the drawings voluptuous and specific and amplified. It could get you arrested in some places in America; here, a fellow who looked like he understood mortgages read it casually, apparently following the story with some kind of rapture. Bob looked up and down the crowded car and saw at least two other men reading books with brightly colored, almost gaily cartoonized rape scenes on the covers. No one noticed, no one cared.

Last night he'd wandered into a sex zone, a place called Kabukicho, where all this stuff was ramped up ever higher in blue neon, on billboards and videos in store windows, in the dives where the barkers tried to entice visitors into entering. Yet no one talked to him or beckoned him; he got the sense that the Japanese may have a sexual imagination next to no one's on earth and elaborate means of satisfying it, but it was a Yamato-only thing. No *gaijin* need apply. The alleyways and unknown byways and unnamed streets of the strange little empire of Kabukicho, lit by an infinite replication of vertically arrayed signs with names like Prin-Prin and Golden Gals and Club Marvel, were coagulated with flesh hunters: they wanted to see it, smell it, stroke it, lick it, suck it, fuck it, or maybe even eat it. It was a carnivore's glee, a raptor's urgent need, and its passion amazed him, and maybe frightened him a little.

Now he rode the train with a million or so other souls and got off at a far station, carrying his bag. He checked the instructions written out for him in painful English by the hotel's concierge, a gentleman of much dignity and precision who had made the necessary phone calls.

He knew: leave the station, find a cab. There

wasn't going to be any driving in Tokyo's mad traffic, even in the suburbs, made more lethal for Americans by the fact that it required driving on the left, not the right. Why didn't MacArthur fix *that?*

The cab was driven by a man in white gloves and was spotless. Even the seats were lined in white doily. Commercial buildings and elaborate buses floated by, and uniformed attendants were everywhere, queuing lines, directing traffic, pointing to parking spaces; again the sense of all the room being neatly organized and partitioned, controlled by some central committee some-where, so that no odd-shaped parcel went underutilized.

Finally, they found it. It was a big house, set back from other big houses — Yano was clearly well-off — and not nearly so jammed in as were most of the other houses in Tokyo. It was surrounded by an elaborate garden in which someone took a lot of pride.

He checked his watch: 7 p.m. Tokyo time, that seemed about right.

He paid, went to the trunk, took out the canvas travel bag, opened it, and out came the sword wrapped in a red scarf.

He headed up the walk; the big low house with all its wooden cross-hatching and the precision of the garden absorbed him. He knocked on the door.

There were sounds from inside, and in a few seconds, the door slid open and there, in a kimono, absolutely astonished, was Philip Yano.

The retired officer looked the same out of a

suit as in one: every hair in place, face extremely clean shaven, muscular under the blue-white pattern of his kimono. He wore white ankle socks. His right eye opened in stupefaction while the damaged one stayed flat.

'Mr Yano, sir, remember me? Bob Lee Swagger. Sorry for barging in like this.'

'Oh, Mr Swagger!' Yano's mouth fell open, but he regained control in an instant. 'I am honored to have you here. My goodness, why didn't you tell me you were coming? I was expecting some kind of letter. I am astonished.'

'Well, sir, the more I thought about it, the more it seemed to me that the occasion demanded a personal visit. Both our fathers would have preferred that. It's my pleasure.'

'Please, please, come in.'

Bob stepped into a ground-level vestibule, removed his shoes, then turned as Mr Yano quickly summoned the family.

The first thing Bob noticed was a pair of eyes peeping out at him mischievously. A girl of about four peered around a corner. His eyes met hers, and her face dissolved into delighted laughter as she ducked back, giggling. Then she peered around again.

'Hi there, sweetie,' Bob said to the child.

Meanwhile, two strapping teenage boys in jeans and sweat-shirts came in, barefoot.

'Mr Swagger, may I present my sons, John and Raymond.'

'Hi guys,' he said, bowing.

A young woman arrived.

'My first daughter, Tomoe.'

'Ma'am.'

'And the little devil down there is named Miko.'

Again Miko giggled, then buried her face in her mother's dress.

Bob had an immediate response to her. She was one of those dynamos. She hadn't mastered her culture's reticence yet and might never do so. She was, he could tell, a bold, brave child, full of beans, as the old saying went.

'Howdy, little girl,' he called, and she found that very amusing.

'And my wife, Suzanne.'

'Mr Swagger, sir, we are so honored and pleased — '

'As I was telling your husband, the honor and the pleasure are mine. I hope I haven't come at the wrong time.'

'No, no, no, please, do come in, it's so nice to see you.'

There was a lot of bowing and smiling, a lot of awkward but well-meant politeness, but he felt overwhelming warmth.

Yano spoke quickly to his wife in Japanese, then turned to Bob.

'I remind her what an extraordinary man you are, how honored we are to have a marine of such accomplishments visit our humble house.'

'You're so kind, but all that's way past. Anyhow, I found *this*. I wanted it returned to your family.'

With that, he turned the bundle over to Mr Yano.

'I think that has to be your father's. It was in

the possession of the son of the commanding officer of the unit my father was with that day. I have a later letter from him stating that my father gave him the sword on Iwo Jima, probably February twenty-seventh, nineteen forty-five, in an aid station where he was awaiting evacuation. I found that letter in some effects of an aunt and from that I traced it back to the commander's family and located his son and heir; I traveled out there and found the sword.'

'I don't know what to say. It was such a generous thing to do.'

'Well, as I told you, I don't think I could ever be the man my father was, but I wanted to do something that would honor his memory and your father's memory. Both were brave men. I hope I have.'

Yano held the thing, feeling its weight, its balance, but still hadn't unwrapped it. It was as if he was forestalling the moment.

'I do want to warn you,' Bob said, 'there's not much to see. As you said, it's a military relic, much abused, pretty grimy. The scabbard needs paint, the grip is all loose, the hilt rattles a little bit, the wrapping around the grip is pretty shabby, and it's missing that little metal loop through the end of the handle where I believe a tassel or something went. The blade has seen hard usage too; it's all scratched, nicked up, has a few bits missing at the edge. It's a sword that's been to war, not one for a parade or a court ceremony.'

'I will put it aside for now. Please, come in and rest, tell us of your journey. Sit, relax, have tea or

81

some kind of juice. I remember that you do not drink, or I would offer you sake. Please, come in and make yourself comfortable.'

He gave his guest a pair of slippers. Bob put them on and followed his host up a set of stairs, down a hall, and into the living room, which was full of western furniture though on a smaller scale.

Yano spoke quickly to his wife, who answered, bowed slightly before Bob — Bob bowed back awkwardly — and asked him if he preferred bottled water, tea, coffee, or juice.

'Ma'am, the bottled water would be fine.'

She spoke quickly to the daughter Tomoe, who hustled out and returned in what seemed like seconds with a tray and various beverages.

Yano maneuvered Bob into what had to be a preferred seat and Bob knew enough to refuse twice — 'No, no, really' — before acceding to the request. He was immediately to the left of an alcove in which family mementos were displayed: certificates of accomplishment, photographs of Yano in uniform at various military installations, pictures of the boys in baseball uniforms, and of the older girl at graduation — as one would find in any American officer's home. Down in the corner, Bob saw a sepia photo of a man in a tight tunic with a military cap rigidly in place over a clean-shaven head; that had to be Mr Yano's father.

Bob was asked about his trip and he had one story to tell, only one, but it got a laugh.

'The worst part of the flight was getting through security.'

'Yes, it's very bad now.'

'Well, for me it's always an adventure. I light up a metal detector like you wouldn't believe. Sirens go off, bells ring, guys drop down on ropes. No, I'm exaggerating, but I have a metal hip and so I always make the detectors crazy. So I'm always hauled aside and gone up one side, down the other. It makes everybody nervous. I'm sure if he knew how much trouble it was going to cause, the guy who shot me would have picked another target.'

Yano laughed, spoke quickly in Japanese to his obedient sons. Bob thought he picked out a word that had to be 'Vietnam' in a Japanese accent.

Then each of the boys identified himself: Raymond, seventeen, played baseball, was going off to Chuo University next year to study electrical engineering. John, fourteen, also played baseball, was in his second year of junior high school, wasn't sure what he'd study in college.

Tomoe, nineteen, was at Keio University, in premed. She was a grave, beautiful girl who didn't talk at all and seemed to have been unofficially designated the hostess. It was as if the family was well drilled on jobs and responsibilities: the two boys were audience; Tomoe was staff and logistics; Suzanne, the wife and mother, was benevolent godmother; and Philip was master of ceremonies, host, and interpreter. He alone spoke English with precision, Suzanne was second, and for the older boys and Tomoe English was largely theoretical. Meanwhile, the adorable little Miko was as unselfconscious as a wood sprite, giggling and mischievous. She seemed to have conceived some unique attraction to Bob, and he noted that she sometimes stared at him. When he winked at her, she dissolved in laughter.

She whispered something to her mother.

'Swagger-san,' said Suzanne, 'my daughter thinks you are the Tin Man from *Wizard of Oz.*'

Everybody laughed.

Swagger remembered the character from the movie he'd watched with his daughter many years ago. He saw the tall, glowing, strange-looking fellow with a gigantic tin chest and a funnel on his head. He must look like that to the child.

'Some mornings I feel like I could use some oil to get my joints working,' Bob said, 'so maybe she's onto something. Sweetie, I ain't made of metal, just skin, like everyone else.'

But Miko had decided. Swagger was the Tin Man.

The family sat completely intent on Bob. The Japanese were well schooled in hospitality, and as they took the *gaijin* in, the language barrier quickly seemed to melt away.

Soon enough Miko decided she wasn't getting enough attention. At a certain moment she assaulted her father like a linebacker seeking a quarterback and scrambled up to his lap.

Everybody laughed.

'She is a little cannonball,' said Philip Yano. 'A late arrival to our family. Most unexpected. Now much loved.'

She looked over at Swagger and stuck out her tongue, then, laughing merrily, buried her face in her father's chest, squirming mightily to find comfort until she grew bored, at which time she'd assault another family member.

Through all this, the red bundle sat on the sofa, next to Mr Yano. Never once did he address it, glance at it, seem to relate to it at all. For all intents and purposes, it did not exist.

But at last it was time.

'Mr Swagger, may I take you to my shop and we will examine the sword there?'

'Yes, absolutely.'

Mr Yano spoke quickly to his daughter in Japanese.

'I ask Tomoe to accompany us and take notes,' he said. 'That way I have a record of my first impressions that I may later consult.'

'Of course.'

Bob followed Mr Yano downstairs. The tiny room they entered was scrupulously neat and on one side were seven Japanese swords of various lengths and curvatures, in brightly lacquered scabbards, or *saya*, as the Japanese called them. On another wall were shelves with a variety of texts on swords. On the bench were stones, a small hammer, a few bottles of oil, what looked to be some sort of powder puff, various tools, and rags, all neatly folded.

'I see you're serious about the swords.'

'I'm trying to learn the art of polishing. It's very difficult, and I haven't really the patience for it. But I labor on, thinking, If I know this, then I really know *something*.'

'I get you. Sometimes it's best to lose yourself in the tiny. It keeps the world out; at the same time, it is the world.'

The father translated for the daughter, who replied swiftly enough.

'She says you must have been Japanese in an earlier life. It would explain much.'

'I'll take that as a compliment.'

'And so you should, and now to the sword.' He confronted the red bundle before him on the desk.

'These things have been an obsession in our country for more than a thousand years, literally,' said Philip Yano. 'A westerner might say it's just a piece of steel. But you see in it all our pathologies: our love of courage but also our love of violence. Our sense of justice but also our willingness to kill. The rigor of our society, the corruption of that rigor. Discipline, skill, but also tyranny, even dictatorship. I have been studying them hard for a year now, ever since — well, ever since retirement. Yet still I know almost nothing. There are men here who have given their lives over to the study of such things.

'Now you have given me the ultimate moment in my life. The studying I've done the past year now has formal application not merely to the nation and the culture but to the family. Really, my friend, I can't thank you enough or honor your generosity more highly. I am eternally obligated.'

'It's one soldier reaching out to another soldier to honor two other soldiers, who happen to be their fathers. We put in enough time in shit-holes to have earned this little moment. Let's enjoy it.'

'And we shall.'

He opened the bundle and the object lay before him, battered, worn thin in places, drawn through history.

He spoke to his daughter, who recorded assiduously; then Yano translated for Bob.

'I see *shin-gunto* furniture of the 'thirty-four issue, absent tassel, but the scabbard is metal, meaning the 'thirty-nine variant, and so not original to the furnishings. Hmmm, wear on the wrappings, some grime, possibly my father's sweat and a bit of his blood. Or someone else's blood. Looking carefully at the peg, I see traces of some black, gummy substance, tar perhaps, perhaps ink. I see marks of recent pressure, and the seal of the gummy material has been broken. The gum or ink just under the rupture of the broken seal is of a darker texture, suggesting that it was shielded from the light until quite recently.'

'What's that mean?' Bob asked.

'I don't know. I have no idea. I suppose someone tried to hammer out the pin.'

'Tommy Culpepper told me that when he was a kid, he and his buddies did try to get that out; they wanted to take it apart. But they didn't have any luck.'

Mr Yano said nothing.

Finally, he said, 'All right. The blade.'

Almost gingerly, he reached down and removed the sword from its scabbard and laid the weapon on the bench.

'*Koto?*' his daughter said.

'Possibly a *shinto* imitation of *koto*,' he said.

'It looks *koto* to me,' she said in English.

'Yes. Yes, it does. Maybe — ' and he paused.

In the little room the silence grew as the man studied the sword, clearly perplexed, perhaps even disturbed. His face became mute to expression, his eyelids seemed suddenly to acquire weight and density, and his breathing became almost imperceptible.

Finally, he said, 'Most provocative. Unlikely, but most provocative.'

Then he turned to Bob.

'What is it you say: the plot thickens?'

'Yes, sir. Meaning things just got more complicated.'

'Indeed. In the war, Japan needed blades. Two companies were set up to manufacture blades, in the hundreds of thousands. Those would be the blades called *shin-gunto*, judged today to be of no consequence except as souvenirs. I had always assumed that my father would have had such a weapon. Most did, or at least many did. He probably himself believed that.

'But at the same time, other likelihoods existed. Many older blades were turned into the military out of patriotic commitment by enthusiastic families, and they were rather cavalierly desecrated by the sword manufacturers, who after all were not artists but humble factory workers. Their exquisite *koshirae* — that is, their fittings, the handle, the hilt, the *tsuba*, and on and on — were simply dumped. It would make certain men weep to think of all that artwork, that craft and skill consigned to the dump pile. The swords were shortened from the rear to bring them to the prescribed length — that is, the tang was cut off and with it was lost much of the inscribed information from the original smith, information as to the date of smelting, the lord for whom the work was done, how the blade cut, perhaps even giving the sword a name or offering a prayer to a god of war. Part of the original lower blade was ground off to lengthen the tang, a new hole was drilled in the grip, and the military mounts were put on. The whole thing was shoved into a metal scabbard and sent to — well, wherever the Sphere was operating, be it China or Burma or the Philippines. And thus a masterpiece was effectively hidden in a wartime disguise.'

'Is that what happened here?'

'I don't know. It's not impossible. Clearly this is an ancestral blade, shortened for wartime use. By shape and grace, as my daughter has noted, it appears to be *koto* — old. *Koto* blades were generally thinner and more graceful and sharper, meaning livelier in the hand than *shinto* blades. *Koto* means 'old' as in — well, it differs, but roughly 'old' as in before sixteen hundred. Of course there are complexities. Possibly a *shinto* smith — that is, someone after sixteen hundred — merely duplicated the shape of the *koto* blade. It happened frequently; the swordsmiths, after all, were merchants, they did custom orders, they responded to market forces, they tried different things.'

'So you're telling me this sword might be some kind of antique, a historical artifact. Would it be valuable?'

'Very possibly, not that we could ever sell such a piece. It is ours, it is of our blood. It is my father's. What I'm telling you is that it might be, ah, *interesting*. Meaning of interest to more than just our humble Yano clan. Interesting to scholars, interesting to historians, interesting to the nation and the culture. What is far more provocative is the sword's heritage, what we can learn of it from what's left of its tang. If that looks promising, we might have the sword polished. I'm not good enough to attempt it. It's a time-consuming discipline only practiced by a few at the highest level, but if the sword has secrets, a polishing will liberate them. We'll see its soul if we polish it.'

9

NII OF SHINSENGUMI

Nii of Shinsengumi was an obedient samurai. He obeyed his great lord Kondo-san in all things. He would die for Kondo-san. Kondo-san, after all, had seen talent in the wild street-boy, aggression, perhaps even a future. Many hoped for such a thing, but it had actually happened to Nii. Nii was taken from nothingness into Shinsengumi. He finally belonged to somebody, to something; he was no longer an orphan, dirty, laughed at by other children. His fluffy body hardened under discipline. He learned things that astonished him, and his faith in himself grew appropriately to his love for his great lord.

He was still young, but in Shinsengumi, all things were possible. The group was comprised of the best men, and though its discipline was severe, the pleasure and the privileges attendant upon joining such chosen ones were omnipotent.

He learned the *katana*, the long cutting sword, its intricate economy of force and power, its strength and its grace. Applied correctly, with judgment and experience, *katana* could cut through anything including bodies, fully, one side to the other. He imagined unleashing it: the swing, the thunder of the cut, the spewing, jetting blood, the scream of the stricken, his stillness.

He learned *wakizashi*, the shorter, personal defense sword. It was an indoor sword. It would not catch on ceilings or doorjambs, and yet it too had almost the same power as *katana*. No one could stop it if a determined Shinsengumi applied it; he saw short, harder cuts, the slack stunned look of the cut, dissolving into pain, a cough that issued blood, the collapse to the floor like a sack of grain.

He learned *tanto*. *Tanto* was short, and without nearly the curve of *katana* and *wakizashi*, for it was not made for cutting but for thrusting. If he put his strength behind it, Nii could shove it deeper into a body than anyone in Shinsengumi. He could easily reach the blood-bearing organ and he knew exactly where to pierce: down, through the shoulder on a slight angle, into the pumping heart. Or up from the back, next to the spine, seven vertebrae from the neck up, again piercing the heart. Pierced, the heart would yield its treasure in seconds; the body it sustained would go instantly soft as if its knees had melted, its eyes would roll up into its skull and it would fall without discipline to the floor, frequently shattering teeth when it landed. The blood would pool like an ocean.

But *tanto* held another possibility. Disgraced or surrounded, in *tanto* lay a hope for dignity. Nii of Shinsengumi knew what he must do to spare himself the shame and sustain Kondosan's affection forever. He knew he could do it too; he didn't need a second.

He'd ram the blade fiercely into the left side of the pit of his own stomach, a minimum of three inches, more likely four to five. Better yet, six, though not many could force themselves to push for that long. Then one would smartly draw it across his belly, just under the navel. *Tanto* was always kept sharp for that purpose. His guts would slip out wetly amid a flood of blood, shit, urine, and other substances. It was said that one had eight seconds of consciousness after the blade reached its point of arrival. They would be an interesting eight seconds. Would one scream? Would one beg for the pain to stop? Would one be unmanned?

Not Nii of Shinsengumi. He could not disgrace himself before his lord. He would be silent, for in his pain would be the sheer rapture of a warrior's pure death. That was the way of the warrior. Death was the way —

The music on his iPod stopped.

Damn, the battery was running down. Again! He had the worst iPod! It always let him down.

He'd been listening to Arctic Monkeys live in concert at the Brixton United football stadium, the great song 'Whatever People Say I Am, That's What I'm Not.' The beat had him really pumped up. He'd felt it to his bones.

Aghhhh. It would be a long night without Arctic Monkeys. He reached for and lit a Marlboro. He sat in a sleek Nissan Maxima, jet black, five on the floor, half a block down from the Yanos' house.

His job was the American; he would stay with the American, and he would call in and report to Kondo-san any movement or change in plans. He'd stay the night if he had to.

He had a Chinese-made *wakizashi* in *saya* wedged into his belt diagonally up his back; he had a Smith & Wesson Model 10.38 Special. He wore a black Italian shirt, a black Italian suit, a black Italian hat, and a pair of extremely expensive Michael Jordan Nikes. He wore Louis Vuitton sunglasses, which had cost him more than 40,000 yen. They were really cool. He wore his hair in a glistening crew, held taut and bristly by Yamada Wax. It was perfectly trimmed. He was twenty-three, strong as a bull, and ready for anything. He had chosen death.

Nii of Shinsengumi was a very good samurai.

10

BLACK RUST

'The rust,' said Tomoe Yano in English. 'Look at the rust, Father.'

'Oh, what beautiful rust,' said Philip Yano.

Bob thought, Are they nuts?

'That's *koto* rust. No rust is so black as *koto* rust.'

'Beautiful, beautiful black rust,' said Philip. 'Oh, so beautiful.'

Wearing rubber surgeon's gloves, the father disassembled the sword. He used a small hammer and a pin, perfectly sized, to drive the bamboo peg out of the grip. It popped out effortlessly. He tracked the little nub of bamboo down as it rolled on his bench, then stared at it.

'*Shinto*, at least. Maybe original, maybe *koto*.'

'Then why so easy? It just fell out.'

Bob remembered: the peg had been stuck. But he didn't say anything; what did he know?

'I don't know. Maybe it was disassembled recently. I can't say. One of many questions. This is *very* interesting.'

Philip Yano slid the grip off, then carefully disassembled the guard — *tsuba*, Bob knew — and several spacers, *seppa*, and finally the collar, *habaki*, and laid out the parts symmetrically on the bench, blade at the bottom of the formation, grip above, hilt laid flat, and four spacers.

Then they saw a piece of paper folded tightly

about the metal of the tang.

'The paper,' the young woman said gravely.

'Yes, I see it.'

'Father, pick it up. See what it is.'

'No, no, not yet. Pen ready?'

'Yes.'

He spoke in a swift blizzard of Japanese. Then he translated.

'The *tsuba* — that is, guard — is government issue, the model of 'thirty-nine also. So when it found its new scabbard, it was rehilted, this is what I tell Tomoe. Spacers — *seppa* — also military issue, as is *habaki*, nothing special. Two holes, indicating it has been cut down, but we already knew that.'

'The rust,' Tomoe said.

'What is it with the rust?' asked Bob. The tang itself was swallowed in black erosion, so much so a fine black dust had fallen on the bench beneath it.

'The blacker the rust,' said Philip Yano, 'the older the blade. What it means, Swagger-san, is that this sword is at least four hundred years old. Somehow it ended up in the military furniture of nineteen thirty-four.'

'Is that uncommon?'

'It happened.'

'So it's not a blade manufactured by machine in some factory in the forties. It's much older. It's a real *samurai* thing. That is why it's so sharp?'

'Exactly. Think of some genius in a small shop in near-feudal times — before the year sixteen hundred — working at a forge, turning the orange metal in upon itself time after time, taking two or three different orange pieces and hammering them together after each had been folded over twenty times, beating them into a shape, then quenching them in cooling clay. Then he began filing, shaping, sharpening. It's three kinds of steel, soft for the spine, which gives it weight and flexibility, a liquid feel; softer still in the core, more pure iron, more flexibility; and a sandwich of harder, tempered steel — *yakiba* — for the edge, sharp, to cut through armor, flesh, and bone and get deep into the body. Oh, it's a war sword all right, and if my father carried it on Iwo Jima, he wasn't the first soldier to sling this beauty about, not at all. It's old, it's venerable, it's been to the dance many a time. Born in fire, cooled in earth, destined for blood. Maybe the inscriptions will tell the story.'

He indicated the line of Japanese characters deeply chiseled in the tang, as the maker of the blade those centuries ago accounted for himself and his creation, and explained for whom he had toiled.

'Can you read the inscriptions?' asked Bob.

'That'll be the fun part. There were thousands of *koto* smiths, and we will have to track through the records and find who made this sword. We will be able to learn the smith, maybe even the lord. Then we'll look at history and begin to assemble a biography of this blade. Where it went, what it did before it somehow came to my father, and then yours, and then their sons.'

'It all has meaning,' said the girl. 'Father, read the *nakago* for Swagger-san.'

'Nakago is the rusted tang under the hilt. Even it is full of tantalizing communications from the past. It's *suriage nakago*, or possibly an *o-suriage nakago*. That is, it's right on the edge between 'shortened' and 'greatly shortened,' the determining factor being how much of the signature is left. Usually, the butt end, even when shortened, retains the shape of the original. It was as if the desecrator were paying homage to his superior. This style is called *Iriyama-gata*, which places it sometime in the sixteenth or seventeenth century. The cutting-edge side of the tang is at an acute angle to the bottom end of the *shinogi* line; the other side runs either straight or at a slight upward angle to *mune*.'

Lost me, Bob thought.

But he guessed Philip Yano was telling him the very shape of the end of the tang held clues to its origin.

'You sure know this stuff.'

'I know nothing,' said Yano. 'There are many to whom this language is as supple and expressive as poetry. I struggle, doubt my knowledge, wish I knew more, curse myself for not knowing yet.'

'But do I get the bottom line? That this is a very old blade, and it could have some meaning beyond your family? Experts should examine it.'

'That's right. It may be nothing. Not every old blade was used by Musashi Miyamoto, just as not every old Colt was carried by Wyatt Earp. So the odds are very small. But still . . . they exist. Remember, *someone* always wins a lottery. I will

98

learn what I can before I make any consultations. It'll take me longer than it should, and it is foolish, as many could know in a flash. That's all right, though. It's time spent with my father.'

'The paper,' said the girl.

'Yes, finally.'

'It looks like some kind of note,' Bob said.

'This is why I fear it. It is possibly a death poem. We do that, we Japanese. It is because death is so welcome to us, that we reach to embrace it and celebrate it with poetry.'

'Yet you hesitate, Father,' his daughter said.

'Suppose it says 'Dear god, save me, I cannot stand this anymore.''

'Then it proves your father was human,' said Bob. 'I've been shot at a lot, and my thoughts have been 'Dear god, save me, I cannot stand this anymore.''

'Swagger-san speaks a truth, Father. You must face it. You must reach out to your father.'

'Do you want to be alone?'

'No, no,' said Yano. 'Much better to be with one I love and one I respect.'

He took the paper off the *nakago*, shaking it so that an ancient fine powder of black oxidized steel fell away.

He read it, and began to weep.

His daughter read it, and began to weep.

Bob thought it best to say nothing, but the girl looked over at him, the tears running down her face.

'I think it's for all the boys of Iwo Jima,' said Philip Yano, 'no matter the color of their skin.'

He read:

Above the volcano
a moon over hell
lights the faces
of the doomed and dying.
Soldiers buried in black sand
on the black island
await their destiny.
We are the broken jade
of Sulfur Island.

11

STEEL

On Tuesday night, the boy Raymond had a baseball game and got a single and a double. He played left field, appeared to have a sound arm and an instinct for the ball. On Wednesday, the daughter Tomoe had a recital; she played the cello, and to Bob at least, she was superb.

It wasn't that the kids were so well behaved and such high performers that so thoroughly attracted him, or even that the darling little Miko reminded him of his own daughter, Nikki —Y2K4 she had christened herself when young. It was that in some way the family unit was like an idealized Marine Corps. Everyone knew his duties and did them; there were no rogue neuroses, no raw egos, no angry resentments; if there were, they were held so far inside that they were never seen and never blew. But the Yanos laughed a lot and seemed genuinely to enjoy each other's presence, to the exclusion of the world. He really felt happy among them.

'No, I've enjoyed it so much, and you've been so hospitable. But I have to go; I have a life back in the States.'

'I had hoped to have news for you on the sword before you left,' said Mr Yano. 'I have exhausted all my books and have begun to make inquiries. There are many antique volumes from the nineteenth century, with much information. *The Book of the Sword* was published in many editions in the last one hundred years. The best collection is in Osaka at the university there. I had planned a trip; you would enjoy that part of Japan.'

'I'm sure I would; I have a wife and daughter, however, several businesses to look after, and remember that field I was cutting? I still want to finish that damned thing. Remember, I'm the Tin Man. Chop chop chop.'

'I understand.'

On the last night, he and Philip Yano sat up after the family had gone to bed. Yano drank sake from a ceramic bottle, in a little flat cup. Bob had tea. It was time to talk of that which united them and made them trust: war and wounds.

'How is the hip? Is it painful?'

'You get used to it. It's always ten degrees colder than everything else, and as I said, getting through airport security is a mess. It's not so funny now.'

'You have other wounds?'

'I seem not to be able to get out of the way of little pieces of flying steel. I have been shot and wounded a variety of times. That one was the worst. It took a friend from me, I am sorry to say, and he was a boy who would have given the world many gifts, so I mourn for him still. The other wounds sting sometimes, but it ain't nothing I can't live with.'

'My daughter says you sleep poorly.'

'Sorry, hope I didn't scare nobody. My dreams aren't the softest. I took many lives. I thought I

102

was a big samurai. And for what? Nothing I can lay a hand on. Well, something called 'duty.' I ain't smart enough to define it, but I felt it then, and goddammit, no matter what, I still feel it. They ain't takin' it away.'

'That is the burden of the samurai, that commitment to duty. That is why we are only happy among other samurai, who have taken lives, seen blood and ruin, tasted defeat and bitterness. No one else can truly know. They can guess; they cannot truly know.'

'I'd drink to that if I was still a drinking man. I have to ask you, Philip. Your eye. You don't talk of it. But I recognize scar tissue when I see it.'

'Oh, that. Really nothing. Iraq.'

Bob thought he misheard. Had he been drinking? Did the guy say *Iraq*, where the marines were still fighting?

'I thought that was our little pile of bad news.'

'Japan, in a spirit of support, sent small numbers of noncombat support troops, nominally guarded by Dutch combat troops, assigned engineering duties in a town in the south called Samawah. But you know the thorough, boring Japanese. We didn't quite trust the Dutch, and so secretly a small unit of paratroopers was sent as actual security. It was my honor to be selected as commanding officer. They even postponed my retirement. Normally, you must leave at fifty-five, but because they trusted me, they asked me to stay in uniform through the assignment.'

'You must have been a superb officer. That's

not a job they give to second-raters. But I already knew that.'

'I worked hard but of course have no genius for it as do you. You were a hero, I was an officer who tried his best. On the third of February, two thousand four, an IED went off next to a Japanese troop carrier, which was pitched over and started to burn. Some men had difficulty getting out. As commanding officer, it fell to me to make the effort. We did in fact get them all out, but not before one of those RPGs detonated nearby and my face was sliced open, my eye destroyed. That was it. Thirty-three years of service, ten seconds' worth of action, and a career-ending wound. So it goes. I did what I could, I got my people out, and I trust that the men remember me with respect.'

'Getting blown up in somebody else's war ain't no picnic.'

'The funny thing was that since we didn't officially have combat troops in the engagement, my eye wasn't officially damaged. However, my eye disagrees with that assessment. In any event, it was enough to serve.'

'Well, your father would be proud of you. He would salute you, if nobody else did. And so would mine. They knew.'

'You are very kind. Now I have a gift for you.'

'Oh, really?'

'Yes, very Japanese. Perhaps it will mean nothing. But it's a credo to live by, as in our ways we both have, after the ways of our fathers, who were the better men.'

'Yes, by far.'

Yano left and came back with a carefully wrapped package, which looked like a book or something book-size.

'Should I open it now?' Bob asked.

'Yes, as I must explain.'

The paper had been so perfectly folded that Bob again felt like a desecrator. Inside the ruptured nest of paper was an oblong frame in some ancient wood. Turning it over, he came across a series of Japanese characters in beautiful calligraphy, running down the center of a piece of yellowed rice paper. Looking at it, he felt something in the brush-strokes: lightness, deftness, precision, artistry, like falling water or the color of leaves.

'It's beautiful,' he said.

'The calligraphy belongs to the man called Miyamoto Musashi. He is regarded as Japan's greatest swordsman. He fought over sixty duels and won them all. He is revered though for his wisdom; he retreated from the world and wrote *The Book of Five Rings*, his guide to the sword and to life. To him, the sword was life.'

'I see,' said Bob. 'A professional.'

'Yes. Samurai. Warrior. My father, your father, the same. So I give this to you. No, it's not original, for that would be priceless, but the calligraphy was done by hand by a superb local after Musashi.'

'Please tell me what it says.'

'He wrote this in sixteen forty-five. The old one knew. He says, 'Steel cuts flesh / steel cuts bone / steel does not cut steel.' Do you see?'

Bob saw.

'The rest of them: they are flesh and bone. They will be cut. The regular people. The sleepers, the dreamers. The soft. We are the hard. We are the warriors. We cannot be cut. That's our job. And that's why they need us in ways they can't even imagine,' said Philip Yano.

12

SAKE

Nii of Shinsengumi stayed with the American all the way out. The man took a taxi from the Yanos' after a bright morning's formal good-bye in the front yard, but not to the station, as you might expect, but to Yasukuni, the shrine dedicated to the fallen of Japan's wars.

It wasn't a place most westerners went to. While the taxicab with his luggage sat racking up the yen in the parking lot, the American went into the shrine and stood humbly before the altar for some time. Nii wondered, What the fuck is this all about? It made no sense to him whatsoever.

Then the man walked the grounds. He was a *gaijin* and others avoided him, but he didn't seem to notice or care. He walked about slowly, with that odd trace of a limp, again as if trying to make communion with something immaterial. He stayed longer than the young *yakuza* could imagine anybody staying. He stood under the soaring steel torii gate that seemed to reflect the spirit of the samurai who died in battle. That it was steel, and not wood like the many conventional Japanese gates, seemed to mean something to him; he touched it several times and looked at it as though it communicated a certain meaning. Then he walked the broad concrete promenade all the way to the white and timbered shrine 250 yards from the gate. He examined the screen of serene trees that cut this place off from the craziness of Tokyo. He went to the shrine, looked in, possibly meditated — who could tell with *gaijin?*

But finally he returned to his cab and the driver fought through traffic to a JR station. Nii simply abandoned his car on a wayside street — it would be towed, of course, but was easily retrievable — bought a ticket from the machine on the JR Narita express, took up a position down the aisle, and watched the American go all the way to Terminal 2, forty miles outside Tokyo.

The *gaijin* was in the JAL line, with his two light bags, casually dressed in jeans and a tan jacket over a polo shirt. His body betrayed no impatience; he waited his turn in line, presented his documents, turned over his luggage. Nii watched from afar, as the American went through security, and watched a little drama transpire as the American was pulled out of line, examined closely by inspectors, had a sensing wand waved over his body time after time, had his papers examined by three different levels of bureaucrat, and finally was waved clear. That was the last he saw of him, a tall stranger with a bland, blank face, not one of those mobile, yappy monster faces the hairy beasts were so known for. The man's eyes were strangely powerful — that meant bad luck for enemies, the suspicion went — as if the man held a fund of secret knowledge.

But for now Nii of Shinsengumi was done.

The perfect samurai, he took out his cell and called headquarters to report in. They told him to get back fast. Tonight was the night.

★ ★ ★

Now it was over. He had his boarding pass, his bags were checked, he'd board the plane in an hour, happy he had an aisle seat. He was headed to the departure gate. The flight would last fifteen hours, but he'd be fine through dinner, then he'd take a pill, and when he awoke they'd be landing in LAX. Then it was an hour or so and off to Boise.

He felt good. He'd gotten some satisfaction at last. He felt the old man would be pleased. He'd repaid the debt, the obligation, as best he could.

Hey, old man, I'm still trying to do what you'd want me to do. Sorry you ain't here to see it.

Too bad he wasn't a drinking man anymore. He had an ache in his gut for it. He felt so good he wanted to commemorate duty and closure and pay homage.

The more he thought about it, the better an idea the drink seemed. Just this once.

No sirree. So sorry, Charlie. Nada.

You take one of those and you float away on the tide and god only knows where you come down. It had happened before.

He had spent most of the seventies drunk, going through jobs, pain, a wife, a couple of houses, the patience of his friends, the respect of his peers, almost pulling the trigger on his sorry self a dozen times. Then, somehow, he beat it, by

109

giving everything up. He couldn't take the world. He couldn't take the memories. He had to leave both. So he lived like a monk, among rifles, a dog, hills, and trees, an exile, speaking to no one, reading, shooting, walking, caring for the dog, making do on a tiny retirement, trying somehow to recover what he had lost.

He could have lived that way forever. But things began to happen. It was a busy time for a while as he was forced to recover skills he thought long gone. They weren't gone. He still had a little something that could get him through, and the terrible thing was, that was really his best self. The Swaggers were men of war. They were warriors. Nothing else. Could add and read and make polite for a time, but that wasn't them. That sure wasn't Earl with his duty-craziness, whether he was walking in through the high tide and blue-white Jap tracers off Tarawa or stalking the cornfields of Arkansas for armed robbers. And that wasn't Bob, three tours in 'Nam, America's second- or third- or fourth-leading sniper depending on who was telling the truth.

So why would you want to drink?

You do not want to drink.

It is unnecessary.

I have a beautiful wife, I have a beautiful kid, I'm building a house where I can look across the meadows of the valley to a purple range of mountains, and whoever thought I'd have that? What old snipers get that? You hunt men and watch them flop and go quiet through the scope close on a hundred times, maybe you get so far out you don't ever come back.

I am back, he thought. I don't need no help.

But then he thought, Goddammit, I did something for my father today. That pleased him immensely. He remembered the old man from so long ago: the father who didn't hit him. All the other kids, damn, they'd say, Lord almighty, my father tanned my hide yesterday but good. Wooiee, hurt so bad, I ain't never missing on sloppin' them hogs again. But Earl Swagger never hit him, not once. Years later he asked his mother on a rare sober day why.

''Cause his daddy whipped both his boys so hard he left scars. Your daddy thought that was the coward's way, man beating on boys, and he stuck to that rule. That's the kind of man your daddy was, and Lord I miss him so.'

Bob missed him too: he remembered the old man in the black-and-white state police cruiser in June of 1955 pulling out of the farm. He didn't look back, but he caught his son in the rearview mirror and raised a hand, and Bob waved back. 'Bye, Daddy, bye.' The old man was dead two hours later. Bob was nine.

So he thought, I have done something my father would have liked. If he's up there he's smiling. I paid off an Earl Swagger obligation, the last one in the world, and I have served the old man. If anything calls for a drink, that does.

And so he wandered out of security and went up into Narita's flashy mall of restaurants and souvenir shops and duty-free jewelry places and found a little bar, almost French-looking, not Japanese at all, all brown wood and brown

111

bottles, the whole place with the comforting feel that only a bar can give a thirsty man. He slid to a stool and caught the eye of the young man behind it in a white coat, and said, 'Could I have a sake, please?'

The kid smiled. He looked like so many young men Bob once knew, even if this one was Japanese.

'Sure,' the youngster said, speaking his English well, almost without accent. 'You want it heated?'

'How do y'all drink it? I saw a fellow who drank it out of a little ceramic pan, like. A tiny, flat little glass thing.'

'Oh, we drink it that way. But we also drink it in a square wooden box called a *masu*. Want to try that? We even heat it! Yep, I can fire it up in the microwave if you want, sir. That'd make you a Japanese through and through.'

'Son, I don't think your beautiful country is ready for the likes of me. Nah, I'll have it like my friend Philip Yano, straight, but in one of those little flat deals.'

'Coming up.'

The boy pulled a large bottle off the shelf, unlimbered a kind of flattened dish about half an inch high, and poured just a small jolt of the clear fluid into it.

Bob held the odd cup up, sniffed it. It had a medicinal quality. He thought of all the time he'd spent in hospitals, too much time, and fluids that had come out or gone into him, or that burned when some orderly put them on his ruptured flesh.

'Semper fi,' said Bob, 'catch me if I fall now.'

112

'What do you think?'

'Hmmm. I see how you could grow to like it. It's all right.'

It had a biting odor to it, then in the throat a kind of subtle sweetness, not overpowering, with a hint of fruit, but it left an afterburn as it went down, suggesting the presence of fire under the sweetness.

'Another?'

'Hell, why not. I've still got an hour before my plane and I'm not going to do anything on the plane but sleep the Pacific away.'

He semper-fied the second one down, then had one for the road, one more for the Corps, one for the dead of Vietnam, one for the dead of the Pacific, one for the living, one for the thought-they-were-living-but-were-dead, and one for the hell of it. Somewhere in there he wondered whose feet were on the ends of his legs, and meantime the boy responded to him, as boys did to men who clearly knew their way about the world, as many young marines had, and bought him another. He then had to buy the boy one, it made perfect sense. Then of course he had to go to the bathroom and he got directions, found the room, and went in to discover what he already knew, the Japanese bathrooms were like science fiction, and somehow on their own they stayed perfectly clean. He negotiated that transaction, then checked his watch, realizing it must be time to board. He headed to the departure gate.

Then he made a disturbing discovery. They'd come and changed the airport while he'd been sitting at the bar. It was now a different airport, and the more he tried to find his gate, the stranger it got. He noticed he'd tired considerably, probably from carrying someone else's feet around, and decided to take a rest.

He awoke as a janitor shook him, but quickly went back to sleep, and awoke a second time to find a policeman shaking him, looking stern.

Lord, what a headache! It felt as if someone had put his head in a vise and a couple of sumo wrestlers had put their full weight against the tightener.

Then he thought, Hell, I am not on an airplane.

He looked at his watch.

It was 6:47 a.m. Tokyo time.

The plane was long gone.

He sat there for a second, aware that his life had just gotten extremely complicated.

Oh, you stupid fool. You *moron*. You cannot ever touch even the first drop or this is what happens.

He looked up and down the airport, saw that somehow he'd taken a wrong turn out of the bathroom and compounded that error with other errors and ended up in a wrong corridor. He tried to map out what he had to do: return to the main terminal, get in line, turn in his unused boarding pass and ticket, get himself rebooked on the next available LAX-bound flight — how much would that cost? — call Julie and let her know, then get something to eat and hunker down. He'd have to catch up with his luggage at LAX and the anger he now felt was because of the possible loss of the calligraphy Philip Yano had given him: Steel cuts flesh / steel cuts bone /

114

steel doesn't cut steel.

You idiot.

Next thought (his mind was moving so slowly!): maybe there was a way to rebook without leaving the departure terminal, which would spare him the nonsense with security.

So finally he got up and decided on a first course of action: coffee. Then food. Then he'd be ready to face the ordeal his own stupidity had created.

So he walked the terminal and, in ten minutes or so, indeed found a JAL office and counter. Unfortunately it wasn't open yet. It opened at eight, still an hour and a half off. Down the way, he found the flashy international departure mall, and soon enough a Starbucks, and managed to talk the young men behind the counter into firing up a coffee for him, though they weren't technically open. The new *USA Today International* was out, so he read it, then an *International Herald Tribune* and an Asian edition of *Newsweek*.

Eight o'clock rolled around; he went back to the JAL counter, was first in line, turned in the boarding pass and ticket, gave a somewhat vague description of his adventure with the sake and the bathroom, and without difficulty was rebooked on a 1 p.m. flight to LAX; he even got another aisle seat. There was no problem with his luggage; it would be held at U.S. Customs at LAX. She even smiled at him.

Then he found an international phone, called his wife, who was out, thankfully. He left a message and decided it was best to tell the truth;

115

she'd be unpleasant for a week, but in the end it was better than a pointless fib.

Now, by nine, he was done and caught up and only had to wait another few hours.

I won't be sad to leave this damn airport.

He sat down, took his load off, and decided on another course of action. He found that Starbucks, waited in a long line, got another cup. The place was crowded so he wandered into the terminal and found a seat.

That was when — it was 10:30 a.m. — he noted an image on one of the television monitors. It took a while to organize in his slow-moving mind: it ran from something vaguely familiar to something sharper until finally it became knowable.

It was Philip Yano.

Then came a family portrait of the Yanos, one that he'd seen in their home. Philip, Suzanne, the grave doctor-to-be Tomoe, the sons Raymond and John, and finally the little sweetie, Miko.

Then the house in which he'd spent such pleasant hours — in flames.

Bob simply sat there, trying to make sense of it, trying to get it organized in a way he could deal with.

He turned to the person next to him, a Japanese man in a suit.

'Sorry, sir, the TV. What does it say?' he blundered, not even remembering to ask the man if he spoke English.

But he did.

'It's very sad,' the man said. 'He was a hero. A fire. He, his family. Wiped out.'

13

KONDO ISAMI

He was in his shop. His family slept above him, but late in the night Philip Yano was alone with his father's blade before him.

It lay, with its broad curvature, its obscured *hamon* where hard cutting metal met soft supporting metal, its mesh of scratches, burrs, blurs, spots of rusts, chips, and *ware*, on the bench before him. The light gleamed dully on its surface, showing its imperfections, with stains of toxins running riot, radiating stench and miasma.

What secrets do you hold? he wondered.

Should I invest six months and 15,000 yen per inch to have you polished? And suppose that reveals . . . nothing. Suppose you're a tired old hag of a blade, polished so many times that now you're brittle and will shatter at the merest breath. You yearn for oblivion, and another polish — the tenth, the fiftieth, the five hundredth? — would just take away more of you, make you weaker and yet more nondescript.

I would waste my money, my time, and my spirit on you.

He tried to accept what lay before him: an unremarkable ancestral blade created sometime in a forgotten past by a smith of no particular talent. You were all right. You served: a war here,

117

an execution there, maybe a duel, an ambush, a plot, maybe politics and ambition and strategic planning, an Edo or Kyoto ceremony or two, and finally, hundreds of years after your birth in fire and clay, you were clapped in military furniture and went off to war and ended up briefly in the possession of a forgotten officer named Hideki Yano, who died on Sulfur Island in service to — well, to what? His forgotten ancestors. Of what significance could that be? Almost none: it's the story of a million other blades and a million other men.

You have your father's blade. It's enough.

And yet . . . and yet . . .

It's so old. It's *koto* at least, made sometime in the 1500s. It's unusually, even mythologically, sharp. Even now, centuries later, when Swagger-san and I throw paper against it, it cuts deep, fast, and straight.

He thought of a story:

A disciple of Japan's greatest swordsmith, Masamune, believes he has finally made a better blade than his teacher. Being vain and ambitious, he demands a competition.

The old man resists but ultimately relents.

The young man's blade is placed in a stream. Things drift down: it cuts . . . everything, twigs and leaves and fish. It cuts garbage and paper and bubbles. Everything that floats it sunders.

Then the old man's blade is placed in the water. It cuts . . . nothing.

Whatever floats to it is magically diverted.

After a time, the young man exults.

I have won! My blade is better! My blade cuts

everything, his nothing!

Old Masamune pulls his blade from the water with a smile.

Admit it, Master, says the young man. Mine is better. It cuts everything.

Old Masamune walks away, satisfied.

The young man sees a priest, who has watched the action.

Priest, tell him how much better my blade is. Make him see.

No, says the priest. His blade knew the way. It saw nothing that had to be cut. It brought no harm into the world. It has come to help the world; it is a blade of justice. Your blade, on the other hand, cut *everything* without discrimination. It is an evil blade. It has no morality. It should be destroyed.

Yano looked at the dull thing. He had a premonition, like a chill, as if an *oni*, a demon, had passed through him. It is an evil thing, he thought.

The young swordsmith's name was Muramasa, and his blades acquired a reputation; there was something evil about them, they yearned for blood, whoever wielded them became a great killer but died by the blade as well. The blades had a particular hunger for the shogunate's blood; over the centuries Muramasa blades accounted for several deaths in the Tokugawa family and were finally banned. Those that could be found were gathered up and destroyed; only a few remained. Could this be a Muramasa blade?

He had never seen a blade cut so straight, so clean, so quick.

The American didn't understand it, the child Tomoe didn't understand it. But he did.

It cut like a legend. It cut everything. It wasn't Masamune's blade, it was the young man's.

He looked now at the tang.

The kanji lettering, each unit a visual poem in itself, climbed the shaft of the metal, blurred by age, subtlety lost in rust, its history written in the holes — three of them — that were drilled each time the blade acquired a new owner-warrior, until finally some dreary mechanic in the Naval Edge Company in Tokyo in 1941 or so clamped it in a set of fixtures, lowered the grinder, and punched a final hole through it, before burying its secrets in the cheap metallic furniture of the *shin-gunto*-issue 1939 trappings. If it had ever been sublime, it was now banal.

He examined the inscripted lettering and for hours looked in the volumes he had on hand.

There was *Zusetsu Toso Kinko Meishuroku*, of the limited edition of 1,200. There was Sasano Masa's *Tosogu No Kanshu*, Kajima's *Tsuba No Bi*, and Ikeda Suematsu's *Kano Natsuo Meihin Shu*, not that this smith was a *gendaito* like Natsuo, but possibly Natsuo had gotten an idea from him, and Yano might have recognized it in the steel. *Kanzan Shinto* was also there, for the same reason, as Nagayama's *The Connoisseur's Book of Japanese Swords:*

At the university, he would have access to *Koson Oshigata*, *Umetada Meikan*, and the first half of *Shinto Meijiro*, and possibly there was something there. However, almost entirely lacking would be references to the run-of-the-mill

120

koto smiths whose swords form the bulk of most collections, and possibly the answer lay there.

There was one possibility: a book called *Koto Bengi*, which included a lot of lesser smiths, with surprisingly accurate reproductions and details of chisel strokes that enabled checking for forgeries. The years from 1345 until 1590 were represented; rubbings that had been taken from almost-new, unrusted tangs yielded clear reproductions.

But who had it? That would take some digging. It had never been reproduced, but if any book held the key, it would be that one.

Then a thought occurred to him.

He went to his computer terminal, swiftly logged on. He checked e-mail and saw nothing, not that there was ever anything, and he went to Google in English. He typed in 'Koto Bengi' and the system searched the computer universe and churned out ten possibilities.

Hmmm, one was an online encyclopedia, another few conventional sword-for-sale sites where blades were traded to wealthy Americans at only a 700 percent markup; a few others were indexes or rings that connected to still other sword sites; and a few led to shops offering books or sword memorabilia or small sword accessories like *meuki*, the metal inlays for the grip, or *seppa*, spacers, or *kozuka*, the small sub-sword blades that were sometimes inserted into the *saya*.

An hour into his search he came upon a small store in Tulsa, Oklahoma (!), calling itself the Samurai Shop. He looked briefly at the overpriced but clearly genuine swords (many were papered, meaning they'd been examined and certified by the Japan Sword Association), then finally clicked on 'Books' and called up a list of volumes. Halfway down the list he found it: *Koto Bengi*, 1823 edition, very rare, good condition, spine weak, spots on cover, $1,750.

For $1,750!

Certainly there was a *Koto Bengi* in Japan that could be examined; a library would have one in its collection, or a shrine.

Samurai had become international and you were just as likely to find rare artifacts in the American Midwest or the Scottish highlands or the Italian peninsula as anywhere in Japan. The collectors were like swarming insects: they came, they bought crazily, they resold, and many of them learned. That was the oddest thing: many of the most knowledgeable men in the world on blades were not Japanese at all. Here, a sword scholar in Japan in 1823 had examined blades of the late 1400s through the year 1600, had meticulously redrawn or taken rubbings of *nakago* for a volume that survived a tumultuous 184 years of war, strife, revolution, and extreme violence and had ended up in a store in Tulsa, Oklahoma, where a clever merchandiser displayed it on something called the Internet. Now it flashed back across time and centuries to a retired soldier in the suburbs of Tokyo!

The website for the Samurai Shop displayed the cover of the treasured old volume and its title page, and there were further icons for 'Random Pages' and a lengthy description.

All right, he thought. I'll play your little game, Mr Oklahoma Samurai.

He clicked on 'Random Pages,' and one by one, a set of pages flashed before his eyes.

And then he stopped. He realized as he looked at the tang of a long-lost blade that it was his sword. That was the Yano blade.

Yes, that was it.

It had to be.

The tang on the computer screen was longer, of course, because the barbarians of the Naval Edge Company preparing for the Sphere's mad war had not yet sheared off half the kanji lettering.

But Yano looked closely at the very end of his tang, and there indeed he saw the nub of three letters that had been rudely cut by the band saw or the file. They matched perfectly.

The computer screen showed the complete and undistorted tang of the very blade he held before him in his rubber gloves; he had its pedigree, its smith, the lord or house for whom it had been prepared, the results of its cutting test, the —

He saw with a quick pang of disappointment that it was not a Muramasa blade. No, how could it be? That's a one-in-a-million shot, like a lottery ticket paying off big. He wasn't familiar with the smith's name, which he read in its two kanji, one for *nori* and the second for *naga*, thereby a yeoman called Norinaga, possibly of the Yamato school (the blade looked Yamato). But Norinaga-san, you're one of thousands. This happens to be your sharpest blade; you should be proud.

123

But then he noticed another thing, a small indentation on the hilt, almost too small to see against the dapples of the black rust and the rise and fall of the rough unpolished old steel.

He got out a jeweler's loupe and studied the mark carefully, turning it in the light.

It was a symbol, not a kanji, what is called a family crest, in Japanese a *mon*.

Taking up a pencil and a sheet of paper, he drew what he saw, and when he looked at it, it astounded him. It looked like a naval propeller, three-bladed, mounted on a hanging medal of some sort. It puzzled him, the contemporariness of it. It was some device an Imperial Navy torpedoman would have worn. It seemed to have nothing to do with the seventeenth century.

He went from there to his *Mon: The Japanese Family Crest*, assembled by one of the western pioneers in Asian arts, a strange California man named Willis M. Hawley, who dedicated his life to all things samurai. Hawley was one of the few westerners admired by the polishers and sword makers of the '50s and '60s and his specialty was the encyclopedic. He alone in the West would have the patience to collect and classify thousands of Japanese *mon*.

Yano sighed. It would take him hours to track through the pages and pages of symbols. He looked at his watch. It was so late. He should be in bed.

And then he thought: Well, start. Just start. Then tomorrow, do some more.

But it turned out the book was organized not alphabetically but by pattern. He slid through

124

the pages, looking at the eighteen or so renditions of patterns in stark black-and-white, seeing such images as the ever-popular chrysanthemum, the persimmon, the melon, the arrow-root, the Chinese bell-flower — but of course no torpedo propeller. But there was a maple, a chestnut, the hawk feathers, the roll of silk, the rabbit, the bat, the dragonfly, the arrow notch. Then — the torpedo propeller! No, no, it was the military fan. It was a fan!

He quickly turned to page fifty-nine, found eighteen variations on the fan, none of which matched, went back a little and found dozens of other fan shapes — the cypress fan, the feather fan, the folding fan, the hemp fan. He applied his tired eyes to each three-bladed symbol, until there it was. He compared the three images over and over again. The slightly fuzzy image in the loupe, brought out by the correct angle into the light, built of tiny chisel marks four hundred-odd years old; his own much larger but necessarily cruder rendition of it in pencil on the white sheet; and Hawley's bold black-and-white variation, barely an inch by an inch, but nevertheless bone clear: three blades, mounted atop some kind of V device that he now saw represented the fan. Who knew what the three propeller blades meant? It didn't really matter, now that he had found it. He tracked over to the kanji name of the family, then the romanized version . . .

It was the House of Asano in Ako.

He sat back, astonished. His heart began to pound.

It was from the house of the most famous samurai in history.

Yet elation was not what he felt.

A ghost returned. If the blade could be rooted in the Asano house and its bloody history, and if the name Norinaga could be likewise linked to Asano, then suddenly the blade was of inestimable worth, but to Yano what mattered was the glory: this would be the rare 'cultural treasure,' worthy of careful restoration and display in the great museums of Japan. Its provenance associated it with a plot, a raid, a fight, a death, then the mass *seppuku*, belly splitting, that perfectly summed up the samurai ethos and represented at its purest and highest what the samurai meant to Japan and to the world.

He thought, How could — ?

But it was more than possible. His mind ran through possibilities. The blade is stolen or lost somehow after it is confiscated from whichever of the ronin carried it on that bloodiest of all samurai nights, and no one, for a hundred years, realizes its meaning, as the story is devoured by other stories, just as violent, just as bloody. But then in 1748 comes the puppet play *Kanadehon Chushingura, Treasury of Loyal Retainers*, which popularizes the story and becomes the basis for many kabuki plays. But it is the woodblock artists who make the story immortal, among them Utamaro, Toyokuni, Hokusai, Kunisada, and Hiroshige. However, the most famous are those by Kuniyoshi, who produces eleven separate series on the subject, as well as twenty triptychs.

By that time the sword is lost: it floats from family to family, from sword shop to sword shop and somehow is turned in to the government in a spasm of great patriotic fever, along with a hundred thousand other blades, and it is hacked and shortened and ground and machine-polished — buffed, buffed! — and sent off to war, where it has its further adventures, ending up finally in his father's hands and then in an American's hands. And now it's back.

Yano felt fear.

It wasn't a fortune he had discovered but an immense responsibility. The sword wasn't just worth millions but was an artifact of the nation. That made it worth killing for. It was leverage, it was status, it was fame, it was . . .

If anyone knew.

That was the key question: Did anyone know? Who would know?

Then he heard the glass break.

He waited, breathless. His heart began to pound again.

He heard a cry: '*Hai!*'

It was a war cry.

He reached for the only intact weapon close at hand: a *shin-shinto katana* from 1861.

★   ★   ★

Nii listened.

'Young men of Shinsengumi, this is your blooding. Is this for you? Have you the steel, the strength, the determination? Or are you one of them, one of the dissolute?'

Kondo-san spoke quickly and fiercely.

'Do you hang out in the malls and paint your hair blue and your nails black? Do you dance to barbarian rapture, and pierce yourself with gewgaws? Do you have sexual congress like a rabbit, without meaning, rutting in alleyways and gymnasiums? Do you fill your system with drugs and live your life in a blur of pleasure? Or are you hard and resolute, men of bushido, men of courage and commitment? Are you samurai?'

'We are samurai!' came the cry.

The four of them were in the back of a truck. It was 4 a.m., in the quiet suburbs of Tokyo. They were parked in front of the Yano house. They wore black *hakama* kendo trousers and jackets and black *tabi* over black *tabi* socks, which isolated the big toe so they could wear the zori sandals. Each carried sharp Chinese-made *wakizashi* and *katana*, the two swords, and each carried a silenced Glock 9 mm.

'Then, my children of the spirit, you must *go!*' said Kondo, and the four felt the excitement rise and crest.

Noguma was first, Muyamato second, he, Nii, third, and Natume fourth. They leapt from the truck and advanced in low, stealthy strides to the house.

The door was locked.

Noguma kicked it in, and as he kicked it, performed *nukit-suke*, the drawing cut, except there was no one to cut. Meanwhile, the others unlimbered their swords, possibly without the grace and beauty of Noguma, who had practiced this move a hundred thousand times. It was truly unfortunate that nobody was there to absorb his elegant energy.

He ran into the house, shouting, '*Hai!*' and looked for something to cut. There was nothing.

But downstairs he spied light.

'*Hai!*' he shouted again, and raced down the steps to the corridor, followed by Nii, while the other two went upstairs.

As Noguma ran along the corridor, he saw a man step out of a door with a sword and he raced toward him, full of lust for blood, full of energy, and executed a perfect *kirioroshi*, that is, downward cut, fully expecting to sunder the man from tip of crown to navel.

Alas, the man adroitly sidestepped and slipped with oily speed into *ukenagashi*, or 'flowing block,' which enabled him to slide off into a horizontal attack and lay his blade's edge at full force into Noguma's guts through the navel, the side, almost to spine, cutting through to the core, slicing entrails and organs and everything else in the way, then withdrawing on the same plane so as not to ensnare the blade, and poor Noguma fell spurting, for the body is really nothing more than a thin bag of blood, and when it is ruptured, it empties rather quickly.

Brave and determined, Nii meant to unleash *kirioroshi* on his target and raised his own sword but the man was too fast and drove forward with the hilt of his already-raised weapon and hit Nii under the eye with a thunderous blow, pounding illumination and incoherence into his skull, and he slipped in pain, then lost all traction in the lakes of Noguma's spewing blood, and went with a crack to the floor.

★ ★ ★

Yano cut down the first man in an elementary college kendo move he hadn't realized he still knew, and the blade bit deep but with stupefying ease, and he didn't even have time to mark it as his first kill, for now the only thing in his mind was his family.

He continued through on the same line, minimizing motion, and drove the hilt of his grip hard into the face of the squat second man, sending a vibration through his weapon. He drove a huge gash into the muscleman's face, and watched him spill out of the way as well, with a possible skull fracture.

A third was before him, and he coiled around into the power-stance position, elbows back and cocked, and deployed *kirioroshi*, but this fellow was far trickier, parried the blow, and slipped off and by Yano.

The father turned as the man flashed out of the way. Yano lifted again, then realized he'd been cut bad. His legs went, his knees went, he slid down, down, down until he lay flat on the floor, staring up.

Above him, he saw his antagonist perform *chiburi*, the ritual flicking of the blood off his blade, then *noto*, the ceremonial resheathing in *saya*, a smooth ballet of practiced moves, then lean forward. He had a square, fierce face, eyes bright with exultation, a mouth so short and flat

130

it expressed nothing at all. Yet it was familiar. Who was he?

'Why?' Yano asked. 'God, why?'

'Certain necessities,' said the man.

'Who are you?' Yano said.

'I am Kondo Isami,' said his victor.

'Kondo Isami has been dead a hundred years. He was a murderer too.'

'Where is the blade?'

'Don't hurt my family. Please, I beg you — '

'Life, death, it's all the same. Where's the blade?'

'You piece of shit. Go to hell. You are no samurai, you are — ' and then he coughed blood.

'Die well, soldier, for you have nothing else left. I'll find the blade. It belongs to me, because I was the strongest.'

With that he turned, leaving Philip Yano in a pool of his own blood in the darkness.

14

RUINS

By the time he arrived by taxi, it was all over. The last of the TV trucks was pulling out. There was a crowd but by now it had thinned. People stood about listlessly, aware that the show was almost over.

The house smoldered. In a few spots, raw flames still licked timbers, but mostly it had fallen in on itself, a black nest of charred spars, halfburned boards, broken porcelain fittings, blackened flagstones. The odor of burning hung thick in the air.

The garden was a riot of smashed plants, footprints, the treads of tires where the fire engines had pulled up. A few shingles lay around, a few pieces of broken, scorched furniture.

He ran to the yellow public-safety tape. A few cops stood by, not particularly interested in the situation, in their navy-blue uniforms with the tiny pistols in the black holsters. Beyond, Bob could see some sort of conclave of investigators, men in suits or light jackets who had gathered at the sidewalk that once led into the Yanos' vestibule. The whole scene felt moist, somehow, from all the water spent to fight the blaze; the ground was soft, in places muddy, the water pooled into puddles.

Bob pushed through the crowd, no longer really interested in the rules of politeness that defined the culture of Japan. He didn't care about the polite mob of witnesses.

He ducked under the yellow tape that cut off civilian world from public-safety world and immediately attracted the attention of first one, then a second cop, and finally a third.

'I have to see the investigators,' he said.

'*Hai!* No, no, must wait, must — '

'Come on, no, who's in charge? I have to see the — '

Somehow weight was applied to him. The Japanese uniformed officers were amazingly strong given their height, and with three of them gathered and more assembling, and the investigators looking his way, he felt the urgency of the collective will: go back, do not make a disturbance, you have no place here, you are not a citizen, do not interrupt, these are our ways.

'*I have to see the man in charge!*' he yelled. '*No, no, let me through,*' and he squirmed away and quite logically, it seemed to him, made to approach the investigators or executives or whatever they were. '*I have to explain. See, I knew these people, I had business with them, you will want my testimony.*'

It seemed so logical to him. All he had to do was make it clear.

'*Does anybody here speak English, please?*'

But for all his good intentions, he seemed to excite nothing but animosity on the part of the Japanese, who appeared not at all interested in his contributions.

'You don't understand, I have information,' he explained to two or three of the men who were forcing him back. 'I need to tell people something, please, don't push me, I have to talk to the man in charge. *Don't touch me, don't shove me,* please, no, I don't want any trouble, but don't *touch me!*'

The Japanese barking at him seemed to be spewing gibberish, and their faces gathered into ugly, monkeylike caricatures, and he experienced the overwhelming melancholy that *they really didn't care* and it infuriated him, and just at this moment, someone pushing on him slipped, a hand broke free and accidentally smashed hard into his chest, and the next thing he knew, he shoved back.

★　★　★

He swam to consciousness. He was in some kind of ward, his head felt like a linebacker had crushed it against a curb, and he was sore everywhere.

He tried to sit up, but handcuffs on one wrist had him pinioned to the bed frame.

The room was pure white, brightly illuminated. How had he been unconscious in such a place?

A slim Japanese woman in glasses and a business suit stared at him. She looked about thirty, which meant she was probably closer to forty, and sat across the room in a shabby, plain chair. She was reading *Time* magazine. She had beautiful legs.

134

He put his free hand on his forehead, felt its heat, then ran it down to his chin, which was sheathed in whiskers, two or three days' worth. Yet he was clean. The Japanese had beat him unconscious, then in their thorough way cleaned him, sedated him, stitched him, and committed him.

'Oh, hell, where am I?' he said to no one, blinking at the brightness of the light, feeling deep pain behind his eyes.

He tried not to think of the loss, but the more he denied it, the more it hurt. An image of the perfect family came before his eyes, the little Yano unit, each committed totally to the other, the love that was duty that held them together.

It was all terrible, but the worst was Miko, the child.

Who could kill a child? he thought, and he felt killing anger rise and knew it would kill him before it would kill anyone else. The grief was like a weight on his chest, trying to squash all the oxygen from his lungs. He thought he might have a heart attack.

'Is there a nurse?' he said.

The woman looked at him.

'Sorry, do you speak English?'

'I was born in Kansas City,' she said. 'I'm as American as you. My dad is an oncologist and a Republican and a two-handicap.'

'Oh, sorry, look, please get me a nurse or something. I need another shot. I can't, it's — it's just, I don't know.'

'Just relax, Mr Swagger. You've been heavily medicated for three days now, I don't think you need more medication. Let me call a doctor.'

She punched a button on a science-fiction control panel next to his bed, and indeed in a few seconds a staff doctor in a white coat with grave Asian seriousness came in. Pulse taken, eyes checked, head wound examined, Bob passed muster.

'I think you'll be okay,' the doctor said to him in English. 'You're a pretty tough old bird. You have enough scars.'

'Really, doctor, I'm fine, it's my — I need a sedative or something. I'm feeling very bad. I just can't lie here. Can you get someone to release me?'

'The cops don't want you free,' said the young woman. 'The Japanese have very strict rules about certain things and you broke all of them and even invented some new ones.'

'I was a little out of my head. Come on, doctor, please?'

'Sorry, Mr Swagger. You're going to have to come to terms with it sooner or later. What you need is relaxation, peace and quiet, a good therapist, and your own country, your family, people you love and who love you.'

'I'd settle for an aspirin. Some kind of sleeping pill would be better.'

The doctor spoke in Japanese, then said, 'I'll give you aspirin for the pain.'

A nurse brought a tray with three white pills and a glass of water; Bob gulped them all.

Suddenly he was alone with the woman.

'You're from Kansas City?'

'Yeah. I'm with the American embassy here in

Tokyo. My name is Susan Okada. I'm head of the Bob Lee Swagger department. We specialize in deranged war heroes.'

'How's business?'

'It was crappy for the longest time. Now it's finally heated up.'

'Where am I?'

'The Tokyo Prison Hospital.'

'Jesus Christ.'

'Yeah, it sounds so nineteenth century. You've been here for three days. Your wife has been notified.'

'She's not coming, is she?'

'No, we didn't see the need.'

'I just don't — Ah, Christ, I don't know what to say.'

'Well, we need a statement from you. Then we'll get you to Narita and off you go. The Japanese won't press charges.'

'I didn't do anything.'

'That's not how they see it. They have you for assault, disrespect for a police officer, public drunkenness, disturbing the peace, and worst of all, for not being Japanese. They'll put you away and forget about it. They're not that interested in your version of things.'

'Oh, Christ. My head hurts. God, I feel so awful.'

'Have a drink of water. I could come back tomorrow, but I think you'd be better off to get this over with. The sooner you do, the sooner we get you out of here.'

'All right.'

She opened her briefcase, got out a digitized tape recorder, and moved close.

137

'All right, the whole story. Your involvement with the Yanos, start to finish. How you ended up punching cops at the scene of a fire.'

'At the scene of a murder. Okay . . . '

He told it, not enthusiastically or well, but doggedly, the whole thing, the visit, the sword, his drunkenness at the airport, his discovery the next morning, his arrival at the site, his recollections of the troubles there.

'I don't recall hitting anybody. If I did, he hit me first.'

She put the tape recorder away.

'That doesn't matter,' she said. 'Anyway, I'll have this typed up. Tomorrow, you sign it. I'll have you on the one p.m. JAL to LAX and booked through to Boise. All right?'

'No, not all right.'

'Work with me on this, okay, Mr Swagger?'

'You have to tell me. What is going on? What is happening?'

'The Tokyo police and the arson squad are investigating. We don't know much, we don't have good sources with the cops. And it's not what is diplomatically classified Official American Interest, so they're under no obligation to answer our queries.'

'Ms Okada, six people, a family of decent, normal, distinguished, happy people, were wiped out. Were murdered. There's such a thing as justice.'

'The Japanese haven't confirmed anything about murders. The official line has to do with an unfortunate fire, a tragedy, a terrible, terrible — '

'Philip Yano was an extremely capable

138

professional soldier. He was a paratrooper, for god's sake, the elite. He'd been under fire. He'd commanded men under fire. He was one of the best in his country. He was trained to handle emergency situations. If his house caught fire, he would have gotten his family out. If he didn't, something is very, very wrong. That, coupled with my presentation of a sword that he believed might have been of some value, adds up to a very complex situation, requiring the best of law enforcement efforts and — '

'Mr Swagger, I am aware you are a man of some experience in the world and that you have been around the block more than once. But I have to say that in Japan we are not going to instruct Japanese official entities how to do their job and what conclusions to reach. They will do what they will do and that is it.'

'I cannot leave six people dead in — '

'Well, there is one thing you don't know. There is some very good news. The child, Miko Yano. She is still alive, Mr Swagger. She was at a neighbor child's that night. Praise be to Buddha or Jesus H. Christ for small miracles, but Miko made it through the night.'

★ ★ ★

Narita Terminal 2 again.

The embassy van, driven by a uniformed marine lance corporal, scooted through the traffic, carefully found the lane to international departure, turned into a gate where a magnetized card reader permitted swift VIP access.

A police car, with two grumpy Japanese detectives, followed but did not interfere.

'They really want you gone,' said Susan Okada, sitting in the back with Bob, who was now rested, shaved and showered, and dressed in clean clothes.

'That's fine,' said Bob. 'I'm going.'

The van pulled up, and Bob and his new pal Susan got out, took an escalator up, and went through the vast gray room where the ticketing desks were. All the paperwork had been taken care of; he was waved through security, so there was no comic scene about the steel hip. And soon enough he was in the departure lounge at the gate. Through the window, he could see the vast, blunt nose of the 747. The plane would board in a few minutes.

'You don't have to sit here with me,' he said. 'You must have better things to do.'

'I have lots better things to do. But for now, this is my job.'

'Okay.'

'I'm on the drunken idiot patrol. I have to make sure a certain guy doesn't tie one on and end up in the hoosegow again. You get that.'

'I get that. No drinks ever. I get that. I only fell off the wagon once in years and years. I am a good boy. I thought I had the drinking beat.'

'How do you feel?'

'All right.'

'All kinds of people wanted to be here. The commanding general USMC Western Pacific wanted to be here. Evidently you know him.'

She gave a name.

'He was a battalion executive officer my first tour in Vietnam. 'Sixty-six. Good officer. I'm happy he did so well.'

'Well, he wanted to make sure you were well treated by everyone, that this went smoothly. I saw your records. I see why they think so highly of you.'

'All that was a long time ago.'

'We have a minute. Let me speak with you frankly.'

'Please do, Ms Okada.'

'I am so frightened you will try to make something of this tragedy. Yeats said, 'Men of action, when they lose all belief, believe only in action.' Do you see what he was getting at?'

'I sound like a country-western hick, ma'am, and now and then I break a sentence like an egg, but it may surprise you that I am familiar with that quote, and I've read them other guys too, Sassoon, Owens, Graves, Manning, a whole mess of writers who thought they had something to say about war and warriors. I know who I am and where I fit in: I am the sort of man people like to have around when there's shooting, but otherwise I make them very nervous. I am like a gun in the house.'

'Well, I don't know about that. But you know where I'm going. You can't let this become some kind of crusade. You can't come back. You don't know the rules here. The rules are very, very strange, and you could get yourself into a lot of trouble and make a lot of trouble for a lot of other people. You must make peace with what happened: it's a domestic matter, the Japanese

141

will handle it. There have been allegations of criminal behavior but no findings yet. You have to play by their rules. Do you see what I am saying? The Japanese have kicked you out and never want to see you again. If you come back, there won't be a second chance. You could do hard time.'

'I hear you.'

'It may seem unjust to you, or unbearably slow, or corrupt, even. But that is the way they do things, and when you try to change their system, they get very, very angry. They *are* their system, do you see? And you can live here for years and not understand it. I don't fully understand it.'

'Will you keep me informed?'

'No,' she said, looking him in the eye. 'It's not a good idea. Put it behind you, live your life, enjoy your retirement. You don't need to know a thing about it.'

'Well, you tell the truth.'

'I'm not a bullshitter. I will not 'keep an eye' out on things. I want you to let it go. Let it go.'

'What about the girl?'

'She will be taken care of.'

'I have to — '

'She will be taken care of. That's all you need to know.'

The flight was called.

'Okay,' he said. 'It's against my nature, but I will try. But since you don't bullshit, I won't bullshit. I feel *obligated* here.'

'What do you mean? You couldn't have known — '

'It's a war thing. I'm a war guy, he's a war guy. His dad, my dad, war guys. Us war guys, we're all connected. So I picked up an obligation. It's something ancient and forgotten and not in existence no more. Lost and gone, a joke, something from those silly sword-fight movies. Something *samurai*.'

She looked at him hard.

'Swagger, what men in armor believed five hundred years ago is of no help or meaning anywhere in an American life. Forget *samurai*. They're movie heroes, like James Bond, a fantasy of what never was. Don't go *samurai*. The way of the warrior is death.'

15

TOSHIRO

What was *samurai*?

It wasn't *bushido*, the way of the sword; he read books on that and found nothing that really helped. It wasn't any of the other things — calligraphy, computers, automobiles, screen paintings, woodcuts, karate, Kabuki, sushi, tempura, and so forth, at which the Japanese had such eerie talents. And it didn't just mean 'warrior.' Or 'soldier.' Or 'fighter.' There was some additional layer of meaning in it, something to do with faith and will and destiny. No western word equivalent seemed to quite get it or express it.

Part of it was that kind of man, fascinating in himself, *samurai*. He wore a kimono. He wore wooden clogs. He had a ponytail. He carried a batch of blades. He would fight or die on a bet or a dime or a joke.

He was lithe and quick and dangerous. He was pure battle. He was USMC NCO material to the max, hard, practical, dedicated, if not exactly fearless then at least in control of his fear and able to make it work for him. If *samurai* was to be understood, it would be understood through him.

Bob watched movies over and over. He had a hundred of them, not just the ones the smart boys said were great like *The Seven Samurai* and *Yojimbo* and *Throne of Blood* and *Ran*, but

144

movies nobody ever heard of in the West, like *Sword Devil* and *The Sword That Saved Edo* and *Hanzo the Razor* and *The 47 Ronin* and *Samurai Assassin* and *Harakiri* and *Goyokin* and *Tale of a Female Yakuza* and *Lady Snowblood* and *Ganjiro Island.*

He watched them on a DVD player in an apartment in Oakland, California, with bare wood floors, a thin mattress for a bed, and nothing else. Each morning he rose at five, ate a breakfast of tea and fish, then went for a six-mile run. He came back, watched a movie; then he read for an hour, on swords, on history, on culture, books he understood, books that seemed bullshit, books even on calligraphy. Then he ate lunch in one of a dozen Japanese restaurants nearby, because he wanted to be used to them, to their smell, their language, their movements, their faces; then he returned home at two, rested, watched another movie; then he went out to dinner, sushi usually, sometimes noodles, occasionally Kobe beef; after nightfall, another two hours of reading, then another movie.

There had to be answers in there somewhere.

Bob had never seen such grace. Their bodies were liquid, so malleable, so changeable, so flexible in subtle, athletic ways that defied belief. They could run and dodge and dip, pivot, feint, stop, change direction fast, all in wooden clogs. They carried the swords edge up in scabbards that weren't even secured to the belt; in fact, indoors they took the long sword off and carried it around like an umbrella. Yet he noticed: no matter the movie, when they sat on the hard

145

floor, they put the sword in the same place, to the left of the knee, blade outward, hilt just at the knee, grip angled at 45 degrees before them. They never deviated. That was the thing, the core of it: no deviation.

And they were fast. He'd never seen such speed. It was like they were oiled, and when they moved, they passed through air and time at a rate other mortals could barely comprehend. It began with some kind of draw, an uncoiling with blade, so that the sword came out and began to cut in an economy of movement. Sometimes you couldn't even see the cut it was so fluid; sometimes it was a thrust, but more usually it was a cut, conceived from a dozen different angles, the cut hidden in a turn or a pivot, dancelike but never effeminate, always athletic. And always the conventions: the samurai usually fought against three or four at a time, and often when he would cut, the cut man, feeling himself mortally wounded, would simply freeze, as if to deny the end of life and stretch the final second out over minutes. The samurai would resheathe with some kind of graceful mojo, the sword disappearing with a piston's certainty into the scabbard, then he'd turn and strut away, leaving behind a collection of statuary. Then they'd topple, one after another.

Was that, somehow, *samurai*?

In one movie, a guy fought three hundred men and beat them all. It was funny and yet somehow just barely believable. Was that *samurai*?

In another, seven men stood against a hundred. It was like a Green Beret A-team in

Indian country in a war he knew too much about, and these guys were as good as special forces. They stood, they died, they never cried. Was that *samurai*?

In another, an evil swordsman became possessed of the sword; he couldn't stop killing, until finally he perished in a blazing brothel as his enemies closed in, but not before he cut down fifty of them. Was that *samurai*?

In still another, a father avenged himself upon a noble house that had urged his son-in-law to commit suicide with a bamboo sword. The father was swift and sure and without fear; he welcomed death and greeted it like an old friend. Was that *samurai*?

In still another, a brother, mired in guilt, returned home to face his sister's husband, who had advised him in aiding the clan and ultimately massacring a peasant village. The hero paid out in justice, finally. Was that *samurai*?

In another, a man said, 'Sire, I beg you. Execute us at once!'

Was that *samurai*?

In still another, a man said, 'I am so lucky it was you that killed me!' and died with a smile on his face.

Was that *samurai*?

In most of them, the brave young men were drawn to death; they would die for anything, at the drop of a hat.

How the Japanese loved death! They feared shame, they loved death. They yearned to die; they dreamed of dying, possibly they masturbated to the idea of their own death. What a race of men they were, so different, so opaque, so unknowable . . . yet so human. *Samurai?*

Sometimes the westerner in him got it. At the end of *The Seven Samurai*, the three survivors head out of town, the battle over; they turn and look back to a hill and on the hill are four swords, points down, thrust in the ground, next to four rough burial mounds. A wind whistles and blows the dust across the hill.

He got that one: he'd seen enough M-16s bayonet down in the dirt, as the squad moved on, and the weight of melancholy of young men lost forever, of heroes unremembered, of comrades who died for the whole, was an ache that never went away.

But some of the stuff was so strange.

In one, the hero, a dour samurai who wanders the landscape with his kid in a baby carriage, kills a guy and the dying man says happily, 'At last I got to see the Soruya Horse-Slaying Technique.'

He had really wanted to see the hero's sword-fighting skill; it was worth his life to see it, and he felt privileged even as he bled out!

★ ★ ★

One day there was a knock on the door. He answered it and discovered a beautiful young woman, serene, poised, possibly a little annoyed. It was his daughter.

'Hi, sweetie. What are you doing here?'

'The question is, what are *you* doing here?' Nikki said.

148

'I guess Mommy gave you the address. How is she?'

'She's fine, she contends. That's her talent.'

'Right.'

Nikki walked in as if she owned the place. She was wearing jeans and a ponytail and cowboy boots. She was twenty-three and in graduate school in New York to be a writer.

'You were going to come visit, remember?'

'Yeah, well, you know Pop, sometimes the old goat forgets.'

'You never forgot a thing in your life. Daddy, what on earth? I mean, really? This Japanese thing? What on earth?'

She looked around: the kanji composition that he had received from Philip Yano hung on one wall and on the other was a brush painting of a bird called a shrike sitting on a twisted piece of limb. There were piles of books, a huge TV and DVD player, and a hundred-odd DVDs, most with kanji lettering and pictures of lurid men in ponytails on them.

'Do you want a Coke or anything?'

'How about some sake? Wouldn't that be the beverage of choice?'

'I'm not drinking again.'

'Well then, you've apparently managed to go insane without the booze.'

'Opinions vary on that issue.'

She sat down next to the wall.

He sat down across from her.

'What's with the bird?'

'It was painted in the year sixteen forty by a man named Miyamoto Musashi.'

149

'And who was he?'

'A samurai. The greatest, many say. He fought sixty times and won them all. I like to look at it and think about it. I like to try to understand the flow of the strokes. He also wrote the kanji over there. Do you see it?'

'What does it mean?'

'It means 'Steel cuts flesh / steel cuts bone / steel does not cut steel.' It was given to me by Mr Yano the night he and his family died.'

'God. Do you understand how nuts you sound? Do you understand how upset Mommy is?'

'There's plenty of money for her. She shouldn't have any problems.'

'She has one huge problem. A husband who's gone crazy.'

'I'm not crazy.'

'Tell me. Tell me as if it makes any sense at all. What is going on here?'

'Sure, okay. You'll see, it's not so nuts. It's all about swords.'

'Swords.'

'Japanese swords. 'The soul of the samurai,' or so they say.'

'It sounds like you've started to believe all those screwball movies you have lying around.'

'Just listen, all right? Hear me out.'

He narrated, as plainly as possible, the events of the last few months, beginning with the arrival of the letter from the superintendent of the Marine Historical Division and ending, essentially, the minute before she knocked on the door.

'And so you never returned to Idaho? You came here instead, and took up this life.'

'I have principles for a hard job. One, start now. Two, work every day. Three, finish. That's the only way you get it done and any other way is a lie. So when I got off that plane, I thought, Start now. *Now*. So I started.'

'What on earth are you planning next?'

'Well, there'll come a time when I feel I'm ready. When I've learned enough to go back. Then, somehow, I've got to look into things, I have to make sure that some kind of justice is done.'

'But — correct me if I'm wrong — you have no evidence whatsoever there was some foul play in the case of these poor people. I mean, fires do happen, families do die in them. It happens every week.'

'I understand that. However, Philip Yano had an idea that the blade I brought him had some historical significance. Now, reading about this stuff, seeing how important swords still are to the Japanese, how they still dream about the damned things, how they study and practice with them, it gets damned interesting.'

'How much are they worth? Top end?'

'It's not money. There would be a lot of money, yes. But to the Japanese the sword ain't about money.'

'Don't say *ain't*.'

'I'm trying. It keeps creeping in. Okay, the sword *isn't* about money. It's more important than money. They have some peculiar beliefs that you would find very strange. I found them

151

strange too. But as I learn about them, they begin to make a kind of sense. You can't think about this as an American would. It's a *Japanese* thing. It has to do with the meaning and the value of the sword, and the prestige a certain sword would have.'

'Now here's what someone else would say. A clinical psychologist, for example. He'd say, There was a man who was vigorous, heroic, and extraordinary, but also stubborn, obsessive, and somewhat self-indulgent. Even narcissistic. He loved the warrior reflection he saw in the mirror. He never talked about it, but he loved it. He loved the silent respect he got everywhere in life, and the way his presence could quiet the crowd with a single harsh glance. But then he got old, like all men. Suddenly, he's facing retirement. He secretly doesn't want to sit on that porch. And watch the seasons change and count his money. He wants a mission. He wants something to define his warrior life. He's not the sort to go fishing. So something comes along, and using his considerable cunning and intelligence, he insists on seeing reasons, patterns, clues, hints, all kinds of things that he fancies only he, in all the world, not the professional investigators, not the fire department arson squad, none of them, can see. And it adds up to conspiracy, plots, murder, exactly the sort of thing that demands forceful action from a forceful man, a warrior. And he happens to be that forceful man. He happens to be that warrior. Do you see where this is going?'

'I'm sorry you see it that way.'

'There's no other way to see it. Oh, Daddy.

You're too old. You're slow, you're old, it's over. You were a great man; you can be a great old man. But don't be the man about whom they say, No fool like an old fool.'

'Sweetie . . . let's go get some dinner or something, okay?'

'Yes, in Idaho.'

'No, here. We'll get sushi.'

'Ugh. Raw fish. Please, anything but that.'

'I have to tell you this. There are obligations here you don't know anything about. Deep, family obligations. Long story, no one would care, except me. But . . . *obligations*. This goes a long way back, and my father in the war, and the Japanese he fought.'

'I wish your father had never won that medal. It has haunted you your whole life. You don't owe the Japanese he killed a thing. It wasn't your war.'

'Honey, it was.'

'You've seen too many of these silly movies where guys in bathrobes, flip-flops, and ponytails cut each other's heads off.'

'Maybe so. But to me, it feels like I'm going home.'

'Just promise me one thing: you won't grow a ponytail.'

After that, it was pleasant, but Nikki felt her father's need to return to his obsessive course, and so after dinner — she got through the sushi, somehow — she left, leaving him to his self-decreed mission.

★　★　★

153

His days were the same. The next development was the arrival of a package with a blue label, marked SAL, from Japan, wrapped in that perfect Japanese way.

Had he ordered something? Some book, some pamphlet? He'd bought a lot of weird stuff off the Internet, out-of-print books, Japanese sword exhibition catalogues, guides to sword fighting. But no: it was a thin package of copied documents, official in nature, no source given; they were typed in kanji with utmost precision, and included hand-drawn diagrams, badly Xeroxed and difficult to read. The whole thing had a spy quality to it; it seemed somehow illicit, the product of a penetration.

He'd have to have someone read it to him but he knew well enough what his anonymous donor from a Tokyo post office had sent him: it was the Yanos' autopsy report.

16

KIRISUTE GOMEN

Nii handled the negotiations because, even among the most trusted, most senior of the 8–9–3 Brotherhood, Kondo Isami would not show his face.

Nii met with Boss Otani in the latter's office suite, a corner of a tall building in West Shinjuku, the fifty-fifth floor. The office was luxuriously appointed as befitted a man of Boss Otani's accomplishment: he controlled much of the action in Kabukicho, more than a hundred clubs. He employed in his main group and in several subgroups one hundred of the fiercest yaks in all of Tokyo, men who would die for him instantly. He owned a controlling interest in three gambling syndicates, the north and west sides of the Tokyo amphetamine franchise, and more than a thousand prostitutes. He himself had killed many times on the way to his current lofty position.

It helped, of course, that at one time his ascent had been blocked by a certain ambitious boss in another organization, who could not be reached and who waged a terrifying war on Boss Otani. This man's gang of killers had left Boss with the hundred-stitch scar that ran from his nipple to his hip. It was then that the boss made the acquaintance, anonymously, of Kondo Isami of

Shinsengumi. In a week, the boss's rival dropped by for a tête-à-tête. Boss Otani did most of the talking, for of the two têtes, his was the one still attached to a neck.

In black suit and somber mien, young Nii tried not to pay attention to the Tokyo skyline, which stretched to the horizon outside the fifty-fifth-floor window. It was, nevertheless, truly magnificent, the double towers of the Tokyo municipal government buildings, the fabled Hyatt hotel made famous in a movie, the cheesy Washington Hotel, which Boss Otani partially owned.

'Man or woman?' said the boss.

'It doesn't matter, *Oyabun*,' said Nii, careful to use the term of respect.

'What does matter?'

'Corpulence. He wants a tubby one. He likes a certain density of flesh.'

'What happened to your head, young man?'

Nii's left eye was still swollen shut. It looked like someone had puttied a large grapefruit to the left side of his face and the grapefruit had begun to rot and turn weird tones of purple that were shot with veins of red and smears of green-blue.

'It was unfortunate,' said Nii. 'I forgot to duck.'

'I hope whoever had the temerity to strike such an important man paid for it.'

'He did. Most quickly, *Oyabun*.'

'Were you the author of this justice?'

'No sir. Kondo-san himself was. It was magnificent. I have never seen such speed.'

'Did you learn from Kondo-san?'

'I believe so.'

'You are quite lucky to have encountered such a *waka-gashira*, a young boss, so early in your life. Study hard, *kobun*. Acquire knowledge and experience and give yourself over. You will prosper, or die gloriously.'

'Thank you, sir.'

'Anyway, a fat one?'

'A jelly-belly. You can see why.'

'Yes, of course.'

The older man, whose face looked like a Kabuki mask shaped to express decadent rage, punched an intercom button, and another man in an exquisitely tailored black silk suit, came in. He wore horn-rims and had neat hair. He bowed deeply before his employer and spiritual leader.

'Yes, Otani-san?'

'I require a woman.'

'Certainly, Otani-san.'

'She needn't be a beauty. She needn't be a top producer. In fact, it's probably best if she's not. She should, of course, be a guest worker. She should have no family in this country. She should have no reputation, no charisma, so that when her circumstances alter, her absence does not cause comment. She must live alone, she must work a very late shift. She must have no bad habits or infections of any kind.'

'There are dozens of such candidates. Alas, none of them live alone. At the rate they are paid, none can afford to live alone. Plus, one of every group, sometimes two, must report secretly to their bosses.'

'I understand. So be it,' said Nii. 'He would consider it an acceptable risk.'

'Yes, and if there's fuss, the remaining hens can be plucked too.'

'At the Club Marvelous, the guest workers are Korean ladies. They tend to corpulence and keep to themselves when not in the club. One of them should suffice. What is the timing to be, sir?'

'Nii?'

'Oh, sooner rather than later. He wants this cutting test done, and then the restoration must begin and that will take some time. We must be ready by December.'

'Did you hear?'

'I did,' said the factotum. 'I will supply name, time, route home. I assume Kondo-san prefers his pleasure at night? Things are much easier to arrange at night. We own the night.'

'He would prefer daylight, of course,' said Nii, 'for more exact details are revealed. But he understands the impossible cannot be done. Night is acceptable.'

'Who disposes?' said Boss Otani.

'It's certain to be unpleasant. Perhaps the testers should provide disposal,' said the factotum.

'Nii?'

'Yes. We'll dispose.'

'Good. Then it is settled.' He addressed Nii. 'Tomorrow you call the Club Marvelous and the manager will supply you with the details.'

'Kondo-san thanks his friend and mentor,' said Nii.

'I would do any favor for Kondo Isami,' said Boss Otani.

***

The Korean woman left much later than her sisters. They got off at five and walked, en masse, to the subway station at Shinjuku. It wasn't the danger, for Kabukicho was patrolled by police and yaks, both intent on crushing disturbances, who kept the crime rate to almost nil. However, unpleasantness could occur if a single woman met a group of men. Westerners were the worst, especially the Canadians and the Texans, though Germans occasionally acted out as well, and some nasty Iranians might be encountered. If the men were drunk and horny and angry, and had received the age-old message 'For Japanese men only' in many bars, it could be awkward for everybody and end with teeth knocked out, eyes blackened, feelings ruffled.

But on this night the woman, a corpulent enough country girl from outside Pusan, had been stopped unaccountably by her boss. She had been quizzed about another girl, who was suspected of sleeping with westerners on her own (rare) spare time. All proceeds must be generously shared with management and a strict no-freelancing rule was enforced.

But this woman did not room with the suspect, so what was the point? It made no sense to her and cut into the five hours she had off, and she had now missed the 5:40 a.m. train and another wouldn't depart until 6:10 a.m.

She hurried alone across the splotches of illumination, the dark shadows of Kabukicho, as dawn approached and another night of expensively purchased sin put itself to sleep. She headed east down Hanazono Dori, heading toward Shinjuku station. Her cheap wood-soled sandals clattered on the empty street as she rushed, the clubs now mostly deserted, the barkers gone, the sailors headed back to the harbor, the airmen to the air bases, the tourists to their giant hotels. It was the hour of the hare.

The street, which drew its name from a shrine a few blocks behind her, was featureless in the low light. She didn't like this part of the walk; she focused on the brighter lights of a major cross street ahead.

And then she saw — *hmmm*, a blur, a move, some kind of disturbance — and, with it, heard a rustle, a shift, a clunk, some weird night noise that had but one characteristic, that it didn't belong.

She turned, looked back into the blur of countless vertical signs, brightly lit from within, blazing into infinity. The rain spattered on her glasses. She drew her cheap raincoat more tightly against her, annoyed that it was useless against the sudden chill. It was probably nothing, but she felt that someone was waiting for her just ahead. You could never be sure, and she had so much responsibility, she could not afford to be robbed or injured. She hurried back along Hanazono Dori, hoping to get to a large avenue that would still be populated, like Yasukuni Dori.

And where were the cops? Normally, she hated the police cars, particularly the sullen young officers who looked at her as if she were a

160

member of the herbivore kingdom, but now she wished she saw the red light of official presence. Nope, nothing. Not far off she saw the jagged skyline of East Shinjuku, lit with spangles of illumination, promising a new world order or something.

Her life was crap and would never be anything but crap. She worked for next to no money under tight supervision, giving hand jobs and blow jobs and greek the night long. She had absorbed enough Japanese sperm to float a battleship. On a good month, she scraped together a few thousand yen to send back to Korea, where her mother, her father, and her nine brothers and sisters depended upon her. She suspected that it was her father who had secretly sold her to the Japanese man, but family loyalty was nevertheless something she felt powerfully, a Confucian conceit that gave everything she did the faintest buzz of virtue. It meant that in the next life she would be something higher, better, easier.

She turned back, to check again. It was then that she saw the two men. They were in the shadows, moving stealthily, matching her movements, but when her eyes fastened on them, they froze, almost melting into nothingness like skilled Red guerrillas. She stared and in seconds lost their outline. Were they really there? Was she dreaming this?

'Hey,' she called in her heavily accented, grammatically fractured Japanese. 'Who you? What want? You go away, you no hurt me.'

In the beautiful Korean of her consciousness,

she was far more articulate: are you demons come to take me? Or drunken, fattened American fools who want a free greek fuck to brag about on the flight home? Or young, angry yaks, annoyed that the boss thinks so little of you and therefore look for someone upon which to express your rage?

But they were so still they seemed not to be there. In a second she had convinced herself that it was her imagination. It was punishment for thinking unkind thoughts about her father.

She turned and headed again down Hanaz —

She heard a sound. There were two men behind her. But she was not stupid or panic-prone. She did not scream and run hopelessly into the middle of the street. Instead she accelerated her pace just enough, tried hard to give no sign that she knew she was being stalked. She tried to think. The streets were dark and it was still half a mile to the bright lights of Shinjuku Dori. They could overtake her at any point.

She looked for a sudden detour. She could head for either the Lawson's convenience store or the Aya Café, both of which were open twenty-four hours a day. She could maybe find an alleyway. The prospect of getting home had become meaningless. She cared only to survive the night and if she had to lie in garbage behind some horrid club, she would do that. A better plan was to find one of the all-night joints, where she could nurse a few cigarettes until seven. It would then be pointless to return home. She could spend a couple of hours in the club, then go back on. It would be hard, but she would get through it.

She came upon an unlit little promenade ahead, not far from a section of fifties bars called the Golden-gai. There was no overhead and she thought if she darted down it, the two men following wouldn't see. By the time they'd gone beyond it and returned, she'd be out at the other end, on Yasukuni Dori.

It was called Shinjuku Yuhodo Koen, an anomaly in Kabukicho, a curved, flagstone walk set almost in a glade, two hundred yards behind Hanazono Shrine, lined with trees on either side, almost unknown to the general public and certain to be deserted at this hour. It was dark enough to hide or to not be seen. It was ideal. She darted into it, opened up her gait, and prayed that she had dumped her stalkers.

★ ★ ★

Since the promenade was narrow and the trees close, he would use *kesagiri,* a cut that began at the left shoulder and drove downward on the diagonal, splitting collarbone, the tip of the left ventricle, left lung, spine, lungs, right lung, liver. Well delivered, it sometimes flew through the curls of the intestine to exit at the right hip just above the pelvis. It was a good test for the blade, which in casual experimentation had proven astonishingly sharp. Old Norinaga knew his business, back there in his darkened hovel in 1550 or whatever, working in the light of the bright fire, as in an anteroom of hell, folding and

163

refolding as his crew of young hammerers laid their strength and will into the glowing chunk of steel and iron.

It was an unusually heavy blade, signifying that it had not been polished often, which meant it had a certain structural integrity. Not much of it had been stoned off in the 450 years since its forging. No hairline vertical cracks, invisible to the eye, ran through the *hamon*. No *niogiri* and no breaks in the *nioguchi*. No *ware*, no bubbles, no acid damage. It was merely scratched dull by a half century in a scabbard and before that however many years of mundane military duty and before that, who knew? All that was known was what it had accomplished in 1702. He had remounted it, hating the esthetics of the junky army furniture of 1939. Now it wore a simple, pure *shirasawa*, a wooden sheathing and a wooden handle that assembled neatly into one curved airtight wooden object, almost like a piece of avant-garde sculpture. The *shirasawa* was called a blade's pajamas. It was a storage mechanism, not a fighting or a ceremonial one and it meant no *tsuba* had been affixed, for the *tsuba*, the handguard that kept the fingers off the sharpness of the blade and caught opposing blades as they slid down toward the hands, was a fighting accouterment or — many were extraordinary works of art in their own right — an esthetic device. But he expected no fight tonight.

They could see her. She diverted down their little lane, a stout woman still fifty yards off, slightly spooked, moving too quickly, aware that she was being followed, unaware that she was

164

being driven. She wore a cheap cloth raincoat, a scarf, and glasses. Even from this distance, her wooden-soled sandals made a distinct click on the pavement.

'Now, Nii,' he said. 'What did Noguma do wrong?'

'He was too big in his cut,' said young Nii, crouched beside him. Nii had the plastic garbage bags with him. His was the most unpleasant task of the night.

'Yes, he thought he was in a movie. When he stepped forth, he was consumed in drama. I believe also he stopped to think. At that point it is too late to think. You must be an emptiness.'

'Yes, *Oyabun.*'

'There is no thinking, no willing. Both take time. Time means death, not for your opponent, for you. Do you read western literature?'

'I listen to western music.'

'Not quite the same. I think of Conrad. He said something so brilliant it is almost Japanese. Musashi could have said it. Or Mishima. 'Thinking,' he said, 'is the enemy of perfection.''

'I understand,' said Nii, who really did not. It was still memorization for him. You did this, then you did that, then you did another thing, all in sequence, and if you did one out of sequence, you got yelled at. But of course all the time you were thinking, your opponent was cutting.

'Be empty, Nii. Can you be empty?'

'Yes, *Oyabun.*'

★ ★ ★

The woman felt confident now. Another ordeal had passed. She was down the dark promenade and had stopped twice. The two followers had missed her detour. She was alone. It was all right. She would survive another night in Kabukicho. She would get another glorious day in that adventure known as her life. She would send another 15,000 yen back to —

He moved so silently, so speedily, he could have been a ghost.

'*Hai!*' she said.

He materialized out of the trees to the right of the promenade like a giant bat, smooth and dark, in flowing garments, his face almost Kabuki white, like a demon's, yet at the same time so graceful were his movements she could not tear her eyes from him. She knew she was dead. He was a dancer, a magician of the body, a hypnotizer in the fluid, swooping flow of his body as his arms came up. She stared at him, somehow calmed, and there was a frozen moment when she looked into his eyes and felt the compassionate touch of another human mind and then he —

★ ★ ★

Arctic Monkeys screamed. Nii simply watched in the dim light and could not look away.

He saw the *oyabun* appear in front of the woman so smoothly and so evenly there was no aggression in the move and in some way the woman was not frightened. There was no terror. So charismatic was he that he somehow blinded

166

her and took her into death as if it were a deliverance. She seemed to welcome it as a purification.

His arms went up into *kasumi gamae*, the high-right stance, the elbows near, the arms almost parallel, the sword cocked and coiled behind his head, the hands apart on the grip, one up close to the collar, one down low on the very end. He paused, musically almost, as if to obey the ritualistic demands of the drama. Then the strike and its parts: elbows apart came together as he unleashed downward, the blade flashing high over his head, then plunging downward, as the palms rotated inward. The left hand provided the power, the right the guidance as force was applied along the full edge.

Nii watched: the blade drove on an angle through her with almost utter nonchalance, as if she were liquid, driving across the chest on an angle toward the hip, speeding up as the force continued, but it was so sudden and surgical that she couldn't scream or jerk or even begin to comprehend what was happening to her.

Just as easily, just as quickly, he got through her, driving the sword edge through the inner landscape of her body, feeling the different textures and elasticities of the blood-bearing organs, the crispiness of the spine as it split, the tightening of the gristle of her intestines, the final spurt through the epidermis from the inside out. Astonishingly, almost illogically, her left quarter, the whole thing, arm, shoulder, neck, and head, slid wetly off the cut and fell to earth, little filaments and gossamer connections breaking as it went, her face with still a look of astonishment, leaving her other three-quarters erect for just a second. A jet of black spurted from the hideous opening of the cut that had become the leading edge of what remained, and when the knees went, clumsily, the whole awkward thing fell to earth, and instantly the blood began to pool blackly in the dim light.

'Yes,' said Kondo Isami. 'It's very sharp still.'

Nii said nothing.

'Now, little Nii. Get this mess cleaned up and disposed. And say a word over her when you bury her. She was good cutting.'

It was called *kirisute gomen*, meaning 'to cut down and leave.' It was the right of every samurai, according to article seventy-one of the *Code of 100 Articles* of 1742.

17

INO

'He says,' said Big Al, 'that it's not an official form, it's a draft. It was just typed from notes.'

'So there's no way of telling if it's authentic. It could be a forgery.'

They sat in an office behind Sushi Good Friends, a profitable restaurant owned by Al Ino. Al also owned three other sushi restaurants, two strip malls, a couple of pizza joints, two Hair Cutteries, three gas stations, and two McDonald's around Oakland, a few more in San Francisco, and one or two way out in Carmel County. He was a retired master sergeant, USMC, whom Bob had found through a contact in Marine HQ, under the category Japanese language specialists, as Ino had spent twenty-four years in Marine Intelligence, most of it in Japan.

'He doesn't think so.'

'Why not?'

'Because he says that although it's not an official form it is organized like an official form. He's seen a lot of coroner's reports. He was a homicide detective in Osaka for eleven years, Gunny.'

The 'he' was the father-in-law of one of Al Ino's sons, who had retired to America to be close to his daughter. Al said he was a top guy who knew Japanese crime up one side, down the other.

'That's Osaka. Maybe they do it different in Tokyo.'

'Trust me on this one, Gunny. They *don't* do it different in Tokyo.'

'Gotcha.'

They were discussing the document Bob had received a few days earlier, shipped by SAL, the big Japanese shipping company. It had turned out quickly enough that the return address was phony, as was the name of the shipper, one John Yamamoto.

'It seems like — '

'They're Japanese, Gunny. They're very careful. Every *i* is dotted, every *t* crossed at every step. They're thorough, methodical, and they have infinite patience. They work like dogs. That's how I ended up owning half of Oakland.'

Bob looked at the document. It was thirty pages long, column after column of kanji characters arranged vertically on the pages, with never a strikeover or erasure, now and then a crude stick-figure drawing with arrows or dotted lines signifying this or that mysterious pathology.

'No names?'

'No names. Just scientific fact on the burned remains of five humans found in the Prefecture of Tokyo at such and such a time at such and such a place. Five dead human beings, and some remarks, some oddities, some things he couldn't figure out.'

'I'm not sure I can get through this. I once had my own father autopsied, if you can believe it, and I got through that. I'm not sure — '

He trailed off. He needed a drink. A splash of

sake would taste so good. It would calm him just enough. Al Ino was a drinking man and Bob could see a whole rack of bottles on a cabinet on the other side of the office. In any one of them, paradise hid.

'Well, it's pretty hard stuff,' said Al. 'Maybe I could submit a report to you, Gunny. You could look at it at a better time.'

'No, I've got to do this. Just tell me. Is it bad?'

'Well, here's one thing I'll bet you didn't know. Whoever the oldest male victim is, he got one of them.'

'Huh?'

'Yeah, there was a lot of blood soaked into his trousers, and they didn't burn because they were so wet. The blood typology and DNA matched nobody in the family. Does that make you feel any better?'

Bob was surprised: it did.

Here's to you, Philip Yano. You were tough at the end. You defended your family. You went down hard. You cut.

'Is it a surprise?'

'Nah. He was pure samurai. That's how he'd go.'

'Good news, bad news,' Al went on. 'Good news. I suppose, some mercy on a cruel night. The family members were shot. Nine-millimeters, head shots, once, twice. Someone went upstairs silently, from room to room with a pistol, and put them down. So there was no pain, there was no torture, there was no rape.'

'Only murder,' said Bob glumly.

'The 'young female' was shot twice, once in

the jaw, once in the head. She must have risen, he got her as she was getting up, then he stood over her as she was still breathing and fired again. The others, the boys and the mother, it was clean.'

Bob put his head in his hands. God, he needed a drink so bad! He thought of grave Tomoe and what she would have brought into the world as a doctor, with her care, her precision, her commitment to obligation, her love of her father and mother. Shot in the face, then in the head. Lying there as he came over, she probably understood what was happening, what had happened to her family.

'Is there more?'

'Unfortunately. Gunny, are you all right?'

'Let's just get this over with.'

'The bad stuff.'

'If being shot in your bed is good, then . . . go on.'

'They were cut.'

Bob blinked.

'I'm sorry.'

'Not 'hurt yourself shaving' cut. Not 'hell, I cut my finger' cut. No. They were cut. *Cut*.'

'Christ.'

'I translate, roughly.'

Al picked up a sheet of paper out of the document that he had highlighted with a yellow Magic Marker.

''All limbs and necks were severed. Torsos were sundered diagonally and horizontally. In two cases, pelvic bones had been cut through, seemingly with one clean stroke. In another case, rib bones were sheared in two at roughly a forty-five-degree angle to the spine. All spines were severed. The instrumentation in dismemberment appeared to be a number of heavy, extremely sharp sword blades. The cleanness with which the bones were separated at the site of each incision suggests a weapon traveling at considerable velocity, as if at the end of a stroke of an extremely powerful right-handed man. Several less forceful cuts were also noted; in some cases, bones were merely broken and not fully separated, suggesting men of less intense musculature.''

'His students.'

'Yeah. Hmmm, let me see.' Al rose, walked to a bookshelf, and pulled out a volume. It was called *The Japanese Sword: The Soul of the Samurai*, by Gregory Irvine.

He flipped through it.

'Yeah, there's nothing arbitrary about the cutting that went on that night. It followed prescribed methodology of seventeen ninety-two. Here, look at it. That's any one of the Yanos.'

Bob looked at the page, trying to keep his rage buried. Rage was not helpful. Rage got you nothing but dead in a hurry.

'It's a cutting scheme according to the Yamada family,' said Al. 'It illustrated the various prescribed cuts that could be carried out when testing a sword on a corpse.'

The line figure depicted a body wrapped in a jocklike towel, with the various dotted lines signifying cuts through center mass. It was headless, and helpful lines pointed out the

173

proper angle through the shoulder on each side of the shorn neck, through the elbow and the wrist and latitudinally across the body from under the arms all the way down to beneath the navel.

'Okay,' said Bob, 'that's enough.'

He needed a drink.

18

THE SHOGUN

The Shogun liked to meet at the Yasukuni Shrine. He felt at home there, where the spirits of Japan's many millions of war dead lay consecrated, amid the woodlands and the forests where only rarely could a *gaijin* be seen, and then never one mad with cameras, hungry for Japanese pussy.

He was surrounded by bodyguards, for, of course, he had many enemies.

But it was generally a quiet place, away from the hum and throb of his many organizations, his obligations, his many lords and lieges, all of whom waited for order and direction, his responsibilities, his pleasures, his orchestrations, his plotting, his aspirations. So he could walk and enjoy, from under the steel torii gate that towered over the promenade, which ran two hundred or so yards to the shrine itself, the classical structure of timber and whitewashed stone, ornate and serene at once.

Kondo joined him precisely at 3 p.m.

'Kondo-san,' the Shogun said.

'Lord,' said Kondo, who in street clothes and unarmed appeared to be nothing extraordinary. He was a square, blocky man in his mid-forties whose awesome muscularity was hidden beneath his black salaryman suit, his white shirt, his black

175

tie and shoes. To look at his masculine face was to suspect nothing; no one could know what lay behind his opaque dark eyes. He was neither handsome nor not so handsome; he was in all ways anonymous and therefore unnoticeable. If with sword in hand he was a beacon of charisma, without one he could have been an actuary.

Kondo bowed from the neck and head, keeping the body taut, the feet close, the hands straight against the seam of the trousers. (Musashi's rule no. 8: Pay attention to trifles. Thus everything, even the bow, had to be perfect.)

'Come walk with me. Let's talk,' said the Shogun.

'Of course, Lord.'

'I suppose I should ask for a report.'

'Yes, Lord. The blade is as reported. It is absolutely authentic. It is the real thing, that I know. I have felt its power.'

'You used it, then?'

'I knew my lord would understand. I had to know the blade, and to know a blade one must kill with it. And now I know the blade.'

'Was it risky?'

'No, Lord. It was well planned. The woman was alone; she had no relatives. She was a Korean prostitute working in one of Otani's clubs. It worked out very well.'

'You say it cut well.'

' "The moon in a cold stream like a mirror." '

'That well, eh?'

'Musashi himself would have been well pleased.'

'I hope we haven't lost too much time.'

'Lord, I have made arrangements. Even now the blade will go to old Omote, the best polisher in Japan; then it will go to Hanzaemon, who makes *koshirae* like no other man alive; then finally, to Saito, the *saya* maker, again the best. Normally these men take forever, if at all. They will work quickly, however, for the Shogun.'

'Excellent. I trust you in these matters.'

'When it is done, it will be magnificent. When you make the presentation — '

'You must understand how important this is,' said the Shogun. 'What is at stake. I stand for a certain Japan. That Japan must be protected. I am that Japan even as I protect it. I cannot lose my power, and the presentation of the blade will guarantee my position for years and years to come, plus win me the adoration of the masses.'

Kondo had heard this speech many times, but he pretended, for the sake of everybody, that he had not. 'If you play your cards right,' he said, 'it might even win you the Supreme Order of the Chrysanthemum from the emperor.'

'Hmmm,' said the Shogun. 'I think the Supreme is a little much to hope for. But one of the lesser badges. That would be very nice.'

'Lord, I promise you. I am your samurai, to you I am pledged, and I will make this thing happen. I will not fail you.'

'You too stand for the old ways, Kondo-san, and I will never forget it. With you at my side, I can do anything. You give me strength. You, too, are Japan, the old Japan.'

'My reward is your happiness.'

'Is that so?'

'Well, your happiness and the four million dollars you're paying me.'

'Four million buys a lot of loyalty.'

'It bought mine, I'll say.'

'All right, then. The blade is secure. No suspicion attaches to you or to me. The blade will be restored and I will make the presentation and the people shall love me and my position and my clan's importance will be guaranteed. Imperial will go away and die. The Americans behind it will go away and die. We will have won a great culture victory. Our Japanese art will stay forever Japanese.'

'I pledge myself.'

'Excellent.' The Shogun checked his watch. 'Now I must hasten. I have a crisis to attend to. You know, Kondo-san, all this rough business, all this maneuvering and plotting and violence, I hope it never affects the artist in me.'

★ ★ ★

It wasn't the boy, it was the teacher.

It wasn't her clothes: her clothes were perfect. She had on low heels, a pair of panty hose from Tashiroya, a severe skirt cut just to her knees, a white silk blouse, some very nice pearls, and a conservative jacket. She wore glasses — the glasses were so important! — and her hair was up, pinned securely. Her makeup was exquisite.

It wasn't the set. It looked exactly like any other classroom: the phalanx of desks, the chalk-frosted blackboards, the maps, the flag on

178

a pole in the corner. It had the dusty, shabby look of thousands and thousands of classrooms and any Japanese male would grasp its essential reality in seconds.

It wasn't the lighting. Technically, his people were very good. Here, for example, at the casual pinnacle of their professionalism, they had duplicated exactly the pale wash of the ubiquitous high school fluorescents, though with enough soft underlighting to give everything within it a kind of white, dull gleam. For some reason, some magical reason, in this bath of lucidity, flesh itself took on an almost alchemical palpability. Even as each detail was revealed, each flaw, each hair follicle, the end product never looked raw or sordid. It had a kind of majesty to it, classically Japanese (as were all the other motifs) as if delicately painted on a silk scroll by a master in a satin kimono sometime in the *koto* age.

It wasn't the director, an old pro, it wasn't the camera, the stage-hands, the experience level, it wasn't any of these things, but it took the Shogun's expert eye to see in a second what the problem was. It was the actress.

'Sakura-chan,' he spoke gently to her, 'I know this is difficult. But the transition is so important. You have ripened into womanhood. Your flesh has acquired gravity, density, solidity, and amplitude. You have a woman's body. Your eyes have wisdom, your beautiful face has knowledge, your hair a silky glisten. Our makeup people have transferred your already shocking beauty into something beyond shock; you are

179

truly mythological. Do you hear, my dear?'

'Yes, *Oyabun*,' said the beautiful young woman chastely.

'But I see from the rushes that something is lacking.'

'I understand.'

'You are holding back.'

'It is difficult.'

It was difficult. Sakura had been in the business three years and was a star. She had a following, was a celebrity, had several magazines and photobooks devoted to her, could get a good table in any restaurant in any city in Japan. The Shogun had invested a great deal of money in her, had her dentition fixed (she'd had a gap between her two front teeth), sent her to the best dermatologists, the most sophisticated manicurists and pedicurists, hired a trainer to develop the muscles of her already willowy, utterly desirable body.

'I understand how difficult it is,' said the Shogun 'Shirley Temple couldn't do it. Sandra Dee couldn't do it. Some even believe that the great Jodie Foster hasn't done it. It is the hardest thing there is. Only Judy Garland was able to do it cleanly and completely.'

'I am trying so hard.'

Her problem: Sakura, in *Schoolgirl Sluts* nos. 3, 9, 17, and 26 (26 had been a huge hit!), had always played a victim. She had come up the hard way, through entry-level *bukkake* roles, moving on to her specialty, the schoolgirl rape victim, moving boldly to the geisha motif and quite successfully into a series called *Cutie*

Rangers, where in polyester sci-fi outfits with holes cut so that her perky breasts showed constantly, she moved product in the millions. But her breasts had simply gotten too big and beautiful to continue to play in kilts and ponytails. She had to become an adult woman or she was through.

It was the third day of filming *Woman Teacher in Black Sakura* and it wasn't going well.

'Possibly you try *too* hard, my dear,' he said tenderly.

'I miss the pixels.'

It was like working without a net. In all her other films, Sakura had been pixellated: that is, in postproduction, a computerized mosaic had been appliqued over her most private parts and the most private parts of her male costars. Of course it was psychological, for on the set, all things were displayed routinely, but somehow knowing that at a certain point the delicate obscurity of the pixellated smear would be applied and that one's most intimate areas were to be protected had helped liberate her to the incredible frenzy that her directors and her millions of fans so admired.

But at a certain point in an actress's career, she had to move beyond the pixels and enter the world of 100 percent nudity. Such product was of course technically illegal in Japan, by mandate of the Commission of Motion Picture Codes and Ethics, but since the commission was under the control of the All Japan Video Society (AJVS) and since the Shogun was president of the AJVS, in fact its dictator, he could sell such product without fear. He was both the criminal and the police in the issue. It was good work if you could get it, and he had gotten it.

'My darling. You know that the essence of *chijo* is honesty. You have to move into *chijo*, you have to put pixels behind you and share the beauty of your womanhood with all Japan.'

And *chijo* was the essence of his empire. *Chijo*: 'lewd woman' or 'slut woman.' It was based on a counterintuitive fantasy, that behind those demure Japanese women, soft-spoken and polite, hardworking and demure, all delicate beauty and exquisite wardrobe, there lay a demon of sexual flame.

The Shogun had been the first to see this. The teacher, revered and feared, so central to the Japanese culture and the Japanese tradition: yet behind her classical looks and reserved dignity lay a wanton, a debauchee, who would assault her students, demand sexual surrender from them, force them into girls' clothes, literally rape them in all possible positions.

It started with teachers, moved quickly to the other figures of authority: airline hostesses, office ladies, nurses, campaign girls, even finally, as they grew older, the surprising 'mature housewife' category.

He had tapped a vein. The money just poured in. The hunger out there was amazing.

'Think of it this way,' he said to the troubled young beauty. 'We have our Japanese ways. The world, particularly the Americans, hunger to dominate us. They would change what we do, and destroy us. Not with atom bombs and firestorms, but with their culture, their crude, aggressive, unknowing ways. You, you little Sakura, you must stand against that. You are not merely an actress, you are a frontline soldier, a samurai, in the battle against America. Do you see, my dear, why it is so incumbent upon you to find within yourself that samurai spirit, to display it before the cameras, to let us distribute it, to become full *chijo*. Really, *chijo* is the samurai of the flesh.

The girl Sakura delivered a boffo performance.

19

DR OTOWA

It was through the good auspices of the retired Lieutenant Yoshida of the Osaka Homicide Squad that the distinguished Dr Otowa agreed to see Bob Lee Swagger. Dr Otowa, with graying temples, was well tailored, articulate, and multilingual. He did not know Lieutenant Yoshida, but upon receipt of a letter, a quick call to people who would know (and Dr Otowa was very well connected) proved Yoshida's bona fides as a first-rate man, almost a legend, who had retired to Oakland, California, to be near his daughter, who had married an American of Japanese ancestry.

The two men met in Dr Otowa's office in the Tokyo Historical Museum, a shrine of antiquities that looked like a cathedral, grand and somber, enshrouded in its own parklands near Ueno, where the doctor was curator of swords, with a specialty (and worldwide reputation) for the Bizen smiths of the fifteenth century. His office, appropriately, was a room of blades: they glinted brightly from their glass cases, wickedly curved constructions that represented to many the highest and most articulated accomplishments of the Japanese imagination for more than a thousand years. The museum had one of the best collections in the country, only a small portion of which was on display to the public.

'Mr Swagger, would you care for some sake?'

'Thank you, sir, but no. I'm a drunk. One sip and off I go.'

'I understand. I approve of self-control. Now, Lieutenant Yoshida's letter said there had been some sword thefts in the United States, blades worth many thousands of dollars. A killing as well. As a westerner, you wonder, How could a piece of steel made five hundred years ago for slicing up brigands and executing conspirators and splitting one's own bowels be worth killing for all these years later?'

'I know the swords are works of art. They can be incredibly valuable. That would be worth killing for just on the profit motive.'

'So you are here to find out about the market. But surely you have seen men kill for insignificant sums.'

'For quarters. For pennies. For harsh words, bad jokes, and cheap gals. Men will kill for anything and nothing.'

'You know a thing or two, I see.'

'But I do believe there was some craft here. The killer had to know about swords. Possibly he represented or was himself a high-level collector. Possibly he meant to hold the blade ransom as you would a child. Perhaps . . . well, I don't know. But I've checked and the very best sword might go for two hundred thousand dollars. Would that justify such a crime?'

'Possibly it was a historical blade. It had validated provenance and was associated with something extraordinary. That would accelerate its value exponentially. That would be something on the order of Wyatt Earp's Colt.'

'Wyatt Earp's Colt sold for three hundred fifty grand. That's a lot of money.'

'Swords mean more to the Japanese than guns to Americans. Such a sword might go for ten times as much here. Say, three point five million. That's worth killing for easily.'

'Yes, but the more famous the blade is, the harder it would be to sell for a profit. You could steal Wyatt Earp's Colt or even the *Mona Lisa*, I suppose, but who would you sell it to? That's why the idea of a crime for profit seems not to fit here. Maybe just having it would be enough, but still . . . it doesn't make sense.'

'Possibly not to an American. Possibly to a Japanese,' said Dr Otowa.

'I have to hope I can make sense of it. If not, I'm pure out of luck. I have to presume some sanity and logic behind it, sir.'

'Fair enough.'

'So let me ask this. Is there *one* sword? By one, I mean something like a grail. Maybe its beauty, maybe its history, maybe both. It exists only in rumors. It's never been verified. But if it came to light, it would shake up everybody. I mean a sword so special that . . . well, I don't know Japan well enough to say. But it would translate into instant power, prestige, attention, something more valuable than money. Something really worth killing for?'

'Killing not merely a man, though. Killing a family? A wife, a husband . . . '

Swagger sat back and squinted at the doctor.

'Hmmm. You saw clean through my little game.'

'Mr Swagger,' said Dr Otowa, 'I am in regular e-mail contact with blade societies, collectors, and curators all over the world. If a man was killed in America and a rare blade stolen, I would know. On the other hand, several months ago, a man named Philip Yano and his family were destroyed not twenty miles from where we now sit. It was very puzzling, very sad. The next morning an American made a scene at the site of the crime, claiming before witnesses that he had given Yano a rare sword that had been stolen. For his efforts, he was rather unceremoniously asked to leave the country. The investigation concerning Philip Yano has stalled and it seems that nothing is being done, as if certain police officials believe some crimes are best ignored. Now there is an American in my office seeking to discover something about what blades would be worth murdering for. It wasn't a hard connection to make. I don't see how you got back in the country, though.'

'I have a very good fake passport in another name.'

'You realize what will happen to you if you are caught illegally on Japanese soil.'

'I know it will go hard.'

'Yet you risk that?'

'I do.'

'The way of the warrior is death. It is not fifteen years of masturbation in a Japanese prison.'

'I will do what I must do.'

'Mr Swagger, I suspect you are a capable man. You had the sponsorship of Yoshida, who would

187

not lend use of his name to a criminal. So the misrepresentation itself speaks of your righteousness.'

'I only mean to see this thing out, sir.'

'I'm going to tell you a story. I'm going to tell you the story of a sword. Of a sword worth killing for, a sword worth dying for, a sword that would make its possessor the most important and revered man in Japan. Are you ready?'

'I am, sir.'

'All right, Mr Swagger,' he said, 'let's begin. Now, so that you understand, let me give you something to hold on to.'

He went to his wall display case, unlocked it, and took out a weapon.

'*Katana*. Sixteen fifty-one, used by a man called Nogami.'

Swagger took the thing.

'Go ahead, take it out of the *saya*. Don't worry about etiquette now. Just pull it out and don't cut a finger or a leg off.'

Swagger pulled it out. It was heavier than it looked. It had a strange electricity to it.

The blade wore a slight curve, was dappled along its edge, where the harder steel that cut met the softer steel that supported; a groove ran up one side, and the tip was a unique orchestration of ridges upturned to a chisel point. Why was it like that? Why wasn't it just a point? There had to be a reason. These people studied cutting and stabbing, made art and science out of them; they knew the sword and no implement in history had been so engineered as a Japanese sword.

The handle was long enough for two hands and then some, but the whole thing could be used one-handed if necessary.

It wasn't beautiful. No, it looked like a weapon, like, say, an M-14 rifle, perfectly, exactly functional, meant to do one thing very well and built by people who cared about nothing but that one thing.

In his hands, it seemed to come to life. What had Tommy Culpepper said? Oh, yeah: it *wants* to cut something. It did. It yearned for flesh. A gun was different; you grew used to it, and it became a tool. But the sword thrilled you each time you picked it up.

He stood and waved the blade artlessly through the air, feeling the slight thrum as it gathered speed and momentum. The grooves made it sing a bit as it sliced left and right.

'Let's begin with snow, Mr Swagger. Snow enters the Japanese imagination by chance on a cold night in what the old calendars call December seventeen-oh-two, but which is by ours January thirty-first, seventeen-oh-three. Think of a column of men, forty-seven of them, trudging through the dark city then called Edo, through the whirling blizzard. They are hunched against the cold, but the weather is not on their minds. Vengeance is.'

Bob saw snow. He saw men jogging through it, swords such as this one slung, heads down, breaths blowing steam into the dark night air. It could have been Russia, it could have been the Chosin Reservoir, or it could have been Valley Forge. It could have been anywhere men fought for what they believed.

'They look like Green Berets or Russian Spetsnaz or Brit SAS. They wear camouflage, jagged patterns on their kimonos. Each carries two murderously sharp swords, as well as, somewhere, a shorter *tanto*, just in case. Most carry *yari*, our word for spear. Each of them has been training his whole life for this. No commando team in history has had more talent, skill, will, and violence at its disposal.

'Who have they come to fight? The story goes back two years. The shogun — military dictator, the true power in Japan — required that his lords spend every other year in Edo servicing his court in elaborate ceremonial duties that were the court's entire purpose. I know how foolish it sounds: think how brilliant it is. He wants them consumed with worry over the ceremony, far from advisors and sycophants, so that they won't plot against him. It's the time of *seppuku*. If a lord makes a mistake, if he violates a law, if he crosses his legs wrong or wears the wrong hat — '

He made a gesture, drawing his firm hand in a fist across his belly.

'In seventeen hundred a young lord from the House of Asano, in Ako, was called to Edo for his turn in the court. He was — well, opinions differ. A man of probity and strength, a great man who wouldn't kowtow, who hated corruption, effeminacy, bureaucratic infighting, all the propensities of headquarters. Or was he a silly fool overmatched, outwitted, and ultimately destroyed? He may have been a mediocrity, a retardate, a crusader. Opinions vary. What's important is that for some reason he will not play the court game, which is bribery. The most important figure at the court is the master of tea ceremonies — essentially the shogun's social secretary, secretly controlling everything. His name is Kira. He has seven other names, but we call him Kira. He's easy to get along with. Just give him a lot of money.'

'Asano won't.' The circumstances were familiar. Bob had seen movies more or less covering them.

'No, possibly out of idealism, possibly out of stupidity, possibly out of naïveté. Kira is furious. Kira, by the way, is ambiguous. Some see him as a decadent libertine, a partaker in the pleasures of the Floating World, a seducer of young maids. Others see him simply as a man guarding the traditions he had inherited, under no obligation to reform. He did as he was taught. In his way, he was obedient to the dictates of his lord too. Thus, angered and insulted by Asano's refusal to bribe him, he declares war on Asano, but not with blades. He shames the younger man, he gossips about him to destroy his reputation, and remember, to the Japanese, reputation is everything. The pressure on Asano is incredible. If he makes a mistake — ' He made a sound like a belly slitting. 'And Asano one day breaks down. In a fit of rage at some insult or other, he pulls his *wakizashi* — short sword — and lurches after the much older man in a part of the shogun's castle called the Pine Corridor. He manages to cut Kira twice, once on the forehead, once on the shoulder.'

191

Bob looked at the weapon.

'Asano has violated court etiquette; he has pulled his blade in the shogun's palace. It's an instant death sentence. Say what you will for Asano, he died with far more dignity than he lived. He wrote a poem in the seconds before: 'I wish I had seen / the end of spring / but I do not miss / the falling of the cherry blossoms.' Then he cut his own guts out.

'The shogunate confiscates his property, his mansion, and it drives all his retainers out. Now they are shamed, they are unemployed, they have nothing.'

'You know, I think I saw some movies about this. I never quite understood them, I now realize, but I know what happens. The Forty-seven Ronin. They visit Kira two years later. The government has abolished the clan, confiscated its property, and driven them out to the countryside, but they weren't quite done. One night, they came to call.'

'When it was snowing. Correct. Come look at this and bring the sword. I want the sword in your hand when you see this.'

The two men rose, and Dr Otowa took Bob over to a woodcut on the wall.

'The greatest Japanese warrior artist was Utagawa Kuniyoshi. He portrayed that night and the men who took part dozens of times, and from him come all our images of the event, even if he was working in the nineteenth century, one hundred sixty years after the fight. This is his triptych entitled 'Attack of the forty-seven Ronin on Kira's Mansion.''

Bob looked. He saw war, familiar enough. A melee, a whirl, a crazed mess, no rules, no coherence, men in desperate postures, faces grim, driving forward with the long spears and swords, just like the one he held.

'See that one there,' said Dr Otowa, pointing to a dominant armored figure in the center of the battle, with the longest spear, urging his men on with some sort of horsetail switch. 'That's Oishi, the senior retainer of the House of Asano. He is the hero of the story. He is the man who planned and led the attack, who held the Ronin together, who coordinated intelligence reports, who laid out the final strategy. He knew he was being watched by the shogun's secret informers so he went so far as to leave his wife and go live in a brothel, pretending dissolution to mislead the spies. Or that is what is said. Maybe he just needed an excuse to leave the woman and live it up with the geishas until the day came.'

'Wouldn't be the first time,' said Bob.

'Not at all. Oishi divides his men into two groups, assaults through the snow. One man is assigned to cut the bowstrings of Kira's bodyguards, so there's no way they can get their big weapons into play. Then it's man on man, sword on sword. A fellow named Horibe Yosube was the best swordsman; he was accompanied by his father-in-law, Horibe Yahei, who was seventy-seven. Many of the men were old. The youngest was Oishi's son, who was seventeen. But it is Oishi we are interested in.'

'He killed Kira.'

'Yes. After all the killing was over, they found

the vile Kira hiding in the charcoal shed. Oishi knew him because of his age and the scar on his forehead. He ripped the old man's jacket off and found the second scar on the shoulder. Oishi offered him the *tanto*. Kira was no samurai. He declined. Oishi beheaded him with a single stroke from his *wakizashi*, which was the blade that Asano had used to disembowel himself. Now *that* sword, Seppuku of Asano, then Beheader of Kira, that is a sword Japan would love to have. What happened to it? We don't know. We only know that it was made a hundred years or so earlier by a smith named Norinaga in Yamato.'

'I see.'

'No, no, you don't, because I haven't finished the story. The world would understand the story I've told you. Loyalty, courage, violence, justice. What a primal narrative. How satisfying. Now, however, comes the Japanese part. The Forty-seven Ronin? Did they run and hide? Did they sail to China and Korea and change their names? No. They marched in formation to Sengakuji Temple, where their lord was buried, washed the head of Kira, and turned the head over to the priests. Then they turned themselves in to the shogun and awaited judgment.

'There was much debate, but in the end, all of them, *all of them*, were ordered to commit *seppuku*, and all of them did. Here's the truly Japanese part: they were happy to do so. The story isn't a tragedy, it's got a happy ending. The Forty-seven, within a year, had been ordered by the shogunate to split their bellies, and on a single day, an orgy of belly splitting took place. That is why we remember them. That is why hundreds of people go to Sengakuji Temple here in Tokyo every day to visit the graves and burn incense to their spirits. That is why there is a big festival on the fourteenth of December — to commemorate the night Oishi cut the old man's head off. That's the sword. That's the *one*. It's just like the one you hold in your hand now.

Bob looked again at the weapon.

'Could it somehow have ended up shortened, remounted in 'thirty-nine *shin-gunto* furniture, and carried in World War Two?'

'There's no reason at all why it couldn't have. It was lost. It could be anywhere, it could be nowhere.'

'What would verify it?'

'The shape of the blade and the structure of the ridges and the nature of the *hamon* would place it in the right time frame; then if enough was left on the tang, the presence of Norinaga's name and the Asano crest would complete the triangulation. None of the other Ronin had swords by Norinaga. Oishi had Asano's *wakizashi* and *katana*, with a white cord around the *koshirae*. Only Oishi carried Norinaga.'

'And if you had that sword — what would you do with it?'

'Possession of Beheader of Kira would be a totem of samurai purity that would propel its owner to instant fame. Its recovery would electrify Japan. I'd donate it to my own museum and display it to the people of Japan. It would be a gift to the nation. The nation would rejoice. Or

195

most of it, anyhow.'

'What would the man who wiped out the Yanos do with it?'

'I don't know, Mr Swagger. I don't know. But he certainly wouldn't give it up easily. Mr Swagger, do you understand what you're getting yourself into?'

'I suppose I do.'

'Do you have a plan?'

'I have a lead. A policeman, said to be an expert, examined the sword I brought into the country at the airport. He was the only one who saw it. He had enough time to make an impression of the tang. When I examined the sword in America the *mekugi* was cemented in place. Yet when I watched Yano examine the sword, that pin popped right out. So someone had disassembled the sword; it could only have been that policeman, who had it in his custody for three hours. That was the only time it was out of my sight. He won't want to talk with me, but that's too bad. I will learn of a next step from him. I will pursue that next step. In the end, I will find who stole the blade and I will retrieve it, no matter what.'

'These people will come for you.'

'I have been at risk before.'

'Yes, I realize. In the military.'

'Yes, sir.'

'This is different. It's not war, it's more intimate. Are you armed?'

'No. I'm sure I could get a gun.'

'Yes, but if you were caught here without a passport and with an illegal gun . . . I hate to think of the consequences. Possibly you should hire a bodyguard.'

'He'd just get in the way.'

'Do you have any martial arts skills?'

'I know a trick or two. I was in the Marine Corps for fifteen years and took a few unarmed combat courses there. I'm not afraid of violence.'

'Fear has nothing to do with it. The bravest untrained man facing the most cowardly trained swordsman would die in a tenth of a second. Do you know the sword?'

'No.'

'If a skilled man came at you with a sword, what would you do?'

'Well, I suppose I'd go into the OODA loop: observe, orient, decide, and act. That's the core of — '

'You would die, Mr Swagger. That's all you would do. Look, I'm sure you're a very brave man. But get some instruction. Learn some fundamentals, at least, if you're determined to explore these dark Japanese alleys. They are unkind places for the uninitiated.'

'I hear you.'

'There's no way you could pick up what some have studied for a lifetime. But at least you'd have some sort of a chance if assaulted.'

'I'll consider it.'

'Here,' he said. 'Here's the number of a fellow in Kyoto. I will call him and tell him of the *gaijin* who thinks he's Toshiro Mifune. He and I will have a good laugh. We were kendo competitors many, many years ago. We pelted each other bloody over the decades. He trained my son.

He'll see you, as a favor to me, even if only to be amused. You should spend a week with him and listen to what he has to say. Or you should go home. Those are your only choices. 'Steel cuts flesh / steel cuts bone / steel does not cut steel,' as Musashi said. Become steel or get cut, that's the world you're entering.'

20

THE YOUNG MEN

Bob left the august building and headed through the parklands where dozens of brightly colored stalls, selling books and DVDs and yakitori, had been set up. He saw a cop car and thought, Do they know who I am? Am I being watched?

The trip in had been easy enough. Al Ino, through his intelligence contacts, was able to come up with a passport for Bob; soon enough, that led to a whole new identity, complete with driver's license, Social Security number, and fake pictures in his wallet; he sold some bonds and put $100,000 in a fund in the name of a Mr Thomas Lee, of Oakland, California, traveling money accessible anywhere in the world with credit card and PIN number. It went without a hitch; Bob Lee Swagger didn't exist anymore.

Now that he'd done the first thing, he had to figure out how to locate the cop at the airport, how to approach him, how to secure his cooperation.

Yet already he was exhausted. Where had his energy gone? Was he too old for this? And a week of sword lessons: what could be learned in a week? What was the point?

He looked about for a western-style restaurant. He walked for a bit, leaving the somber, grand building and its parklands, and entered the crazed utopia of modern Tokyo. In time he found a Starbucks and went in and bought a seven-dollar cup of black joe.

Gradually, the Starbucks began to fill up. The coffee was hot and strong, and he began to —

And that's when he noticed. The restaurant had filled up quickly enough, but with the same man. He was about twenty-five, all twenty-five of him. He wore his hair in a crew cut with a butch wax front fence; he was muscular, alert, oblivious, and yet at the same time aware. He wore square black-framed sunglasses, chinos, and a white polo shirt. They didn't pay any attention to the lanky, older *gaijin* sitting there, but very quietly and skillfully surrounded him. Then Bob noticed they'd each ordered a single cup of coffee.

Oh, shit, thought Bob. I don't like this at all.

One of them seemed to amble by, then, with a certain nonchalance, slid across from Bob. Not a word was said, not for a while. Finally the young man looked over and smiled and said, 'Hi.'

'Hi,' said Bob. 'Do I know you?'

'No, but I know you. Thomas Lee, isn't it?'

'What is this?'

The young man took a sip of his coffee.

'This Starbucks, really good, huh?'

'It's okay. What is this? Who are you?'

'A friend, I guess.'

'I don't have any friends. I'm a mean old bastard.'

'Not that kind of friend. The other kind. As in, we have the same enemies, so we should be friends.'

'Are you a cop? You look like a college tennis player.'

'Relax, Mr Lee. Enjoy your coffee. I just think that when you finish, you should come with us.'

'Why would I want to do such a thing?'

'Because, as I say, we're friends.'

'You say. I get in a car with you and the nine-millimeters come out and it's all over for me.'

'Guns are illegal in Japan. Let's put it this way: we can help you. We have the same goal.'

'Prove it.'

'All right. Your name isn't Lee. It's Swagger. You're an ex-marine, a war hero, known in some circles as quite capable, something of an operator. If you get caught here on that bad passport, you are in deep trouble. We know all that. If we wanted to take you down, we could do it with a single call. Yet we do not. We are nice to you. We like you. Look, let's do it this way. I'll leave, all the men here will leave. You come out when you're ready. Satisfy yourself that no one's around, no one's coercing you, that it's entirely up to you. Then cross the street and you'll see a tan van. I'll be sitting next to the driver. Come over, get in. We'll drive you to an interesting place and you'll meet some interesting friends.'

★　★　★

He rode in utter silence for about an hour. Then the doors opened but didn't reveal the bright light of outdoors. His 'friend' leaned in.

'This way, Mr Swagger.'

201

Then he heard a strange sound. It was a hollow, vibrating thunk or clank. It was a wood sound and he figured after a bit that people were banging sticks together, sometimes quite rapidly, in dizzying patterns.

He was in a vast interior space under a vaulted, curving roof, and saw that it was a hangar of some sort. As his eyes adjusted, he quickly made out that it had been converted into a gigantic dojo. Everywhere, young men whacked at each other with *katana*, wooden of course, exhibiting a great deal of elegance and power. Most wore the *hakama* pants and *shin-shaga* jacket of kendo, and the armor and masks of that game, but a few, either brave or fools, either too nimble to be held back by the armor padding or in punishment for an infraction, went at it with unprotected faces and bodies. They were really good.

He turned and saw his 'friend' had joined two men wearing uniforms that had to belong to Japan's Self-Defense Force.

'What is this, gym class?' he asked.

'Not exactly, Mr Swagger,' said the leader of the group.

'Don't know where you get your information. My name is Lee,' he said. 'Thomas Lee. I have papers to prove it.'

'That's not what Lieutenant Yoshida said.'

Oh, great, thought Bob.

He walked over, joined the officer, and the four of them walked between mats until they reached a conference room. They all took seats around a large table.

'Yoshida didn't betray you,' the officer in charge said. 'He was helping you. Yoshida informed us because he knew that you and I shared the same objective. I knew about your impending arrival before you even got the tickets.'

'All right. Who are you?'

'I, Major Albert Fujikawa, Commanding Officer, Third Battalion, First Airborne Brigade, Eastern Army, Japanese Self-Defense Forces, ground division, welcome you to Japan. The young man in civilian clothes is my executive officer, Captain Tanada, commanding officer of my Recon Company. As you might imagine, the bigger fellow is a sergeant, Master Sergeant Kanda. We welcome a retired gunnery sergeant, United States Marine Corps.'

'Well, aren't you well informed? You even know my old rank. Al Ino tells Yoshida, who tells you; you make inquiries and get all my bona fides.'

'Something like that.'

'But now I get it,' said Bob. 'You're Philip Yano's guys.'

'We were with Colonel Yano for many years. In Samawah, I was the one the colonel pulled from a burning Bradley vehicle. I'd be dead if it weren't for him.'

'He was a very fine man.'

'He was indeed.'

'He and the kids and his wife deserved better than they got,' said Bob.

'Nobody deserved what the Yanos got. And that is why you're here.'

'No one seems to be doing a goddamned thing about it!' Bob said in frustration. 'That don't sit right with me.'

'Mr Swagger, your anger, your loyalty, your fury, your drive, all that is indeed commendable. However, it is time to face some realities. You have almost no knowledge of Japan. You don't speak Japanese, you don't understand our values, our traditions, the way our society is put together.'

'I've seen a lot of samurai movies,' said Bob.

'Oh, excellent,' said the major. 'Did you see the one where the fellow outran the horse?'

'As a matter of fact, I did.'

'Or the one where the samurai defeated three hundred men in a village?'

'Yeah, I saw that one too. I also saw the one where the gal cuts the guy's head off, but he don't notice until he turns around and his head stays in place. But I also saw a lot of stories about lone men doing what they had to do and getting the job done, even if it cost them their lives. That was the lesson I took.'

'You know nothing of our politics, our corporations, our sexual tendencies, our strange relationship with the samurai past. Can you name a single city in Japan besides Tokyo, Hiroshima, and Nagasaki?'

'I think there's one called Kyoto. Oh, also the one where they held the Winter Olympics that time.'

'Do you know if you are allowed to have sexual relations with a geisha?'

'I have always wondered about that one.'

'Do you know how to tie an obi?'

'No.'

'What is the Diet? What is the name of the emperor? What is the name of the majority party? Do you know what a prefecture is? What is the difference between a shogun and an emperor? What is the family name of the great shogunate clan? Can you name a famous film director who did not make a single samurai movie? Do you know how many people we lost in World War Two? Do you know how many people were burned to death in a single night in Tokyo?'

'No. I don't know any of that.'

'Do you know our justice system? Do you understand the structure of the *yakuza*, their traditions, identification marks, tendencies, and traditions? Do you understand the difference between our National Police and the Prefectural police and how they interrelate?'

'No. I take the point. I am ill equipped for this job. I will get in the way. I will fuck things up. Is that what you brought me here to tell me?'

'Actually . . . no. All those reasons are, in fact, why you are the one man in Japan who might succeed at this job.'

Bob's mouth fell open. Had he heard right?

'I don't — '

'You see, we have a tight little island here. Rules, boundaries, traditions everywhere. Do you want to understand the Japanese, Mr Swagger? Look at a kimono or a *hakama* and see how it is a galaxy of knots, all different, all perfect, all strategically placed. That is why the

205

swords never fall out of the sashes in the movies. No westerner could tie any of those knots; every Japanese could tie all of them blindfolded. So we are caught up in our own knots, Mr Swagger. We need a westerner who can cut through knots. Fuck the kimono, fuck the obi, fuck the way *saya* fits in the obi, fuck all that shit. Cut through it. Find out who killed Philip Yano and why.'

'So you want to . . . help me?'

'By law, those of us in what passes for a military are forbidden from taking part in domestic affairs. The penalties are extreme; we are watched constantly. We represent a Japanese tradition that many Japanese have been taught to be ashamed of and cannot face. So they hammer us into insignificance. But you, Mr Swagger, are uninformed, undisciplined, unaware. You can go anywhere and ask anything. You are true *ronin*. Masterless samurai, owing nothing to nobody. You really *are* Toshiro Mifune.'

'Don't know about that, but I will try my damndest.'

'I believe you. All right then, you'll have a number. We will staff that phone twenty-four hours a day. If you get in trouble, if you need help, if you need logistics support, intelligence, we will provide it for you. In the meantime, we'll go our separate ways, seem to lose ourselves in the minutiae of meaningless existence as we have since Philip Yano and his clan were slain. I'll even divorce my wife and move into a brothel. Well, no, I won't.'

'Believe it or not, I catch the meaning. Otowa mentioned that story.'

'He would have, yes. Our retainer has been murdered, our clan destroyed. We will settle that account, Mr Swagger.'

'But there's a bargain that must be made. I will be part of that fight. That's the bargain I'm making with honorable men, right?'

'All right, Mr Swagger,' said Major Fujikawa, 'you have your bargain.'

'Now,' said Bob, 'let's see if you're as good as you say you are.'

'Go ahead,' said the major.

'At Narita, there's a cop who's the station's sword expert. Someone they call to deal with sword matters, importation, exportation, ignorant *gaijin* who bring stuff in or out without doing the necessary paperwork, that sort of thing.'

'Yes. It is logical.'

'He's the guy. He's what this thing pivots on. He's dirty. He has to be. He understood in a second the potential value of the sword I carried, he made the phone call, he's the one who made the whole thing happen. I have to have his name and address. I start with him.'

21

THE COP

Someone in the unit had a brother who was a cop at Narita, and in a few days, Major Fujikawa called with a name — Kenji Kishida — and an address. Bob intercepted him at Narita. He was the one on the brand-new Kawasaki 400, a gleamy red dream machine, bigger than all the other bikes. Obviously, he'd bought it with his *yakuza* windfall for finding the sword.

When he arrived at and departed from the station lot, parking and locking his bike in the gated compound, Bob watched from the coffee shop, where he could sit unobserved reading a newspaper. Kishida moved with an awkward limp. He didn't have the agility, the rangy grace of a young man, nor was he muscle-bound like others who spent lots of time in the gym bulking up.

This fellow wore a suit, suggesting he was a detective or an administrator, and in his bright red-and-black helmet with its darkened full-face shield he looked almost ridiculous, like a hybrid beast, part salaryman, part knight in armor.

Bob monitored the man's apartment house for a few days, until he was satisfied Kishida had no wife and kids at home.

The next week Bob noted that his candidate was working the midnight shift. One morning at

4 a.m., Bob pulled into Kishida's apartment building's parking lot, riding an identical Kawasaki 400, Metalle Majestic Red, that he'd bought in the name of Thomas Lee. He'd spent afternoons coming to terms with the left-hand driving. He was swaddled head to foot in racing leathers, and wore the exact red-and-black helmet with darkened visor that Officer Kishida wore. He pulled into the stall that Kishida always took and even aped the candidate's slight limp, his old guy's demeanor.

He entered the building, nodding at a sleepy night watchman at the desk who thought Bob was the officer, took the elevator up to the right floor, walked to the apartment, bent over, and attacked the lock with a credit card. There was no heavy security system, no deadbolts or electronic monitoring. The lock yielded in a split second. Then he was in.

The apartment, of course, was trim and neat. Three pairs of black shoes and two pairs of sneakers, with shoe trees in them were lined up in the foyer. Bob went to the bookcase and saw many English books; Kishida spoke English. The books were all about swords. Most were in Japanese, several in German, and several in French. All were arranged by nationality, then alphabetically. He pulled one out at random and found it copiously underlined and with margin notes. On the inside cover were precise notes taken in a fine kanji hand, running up and down the page, indexed to page numbers. He pulled two other books out and found them equally dissected.

No dirty dishes were in the sink in the small kitchen, and the refrigerator yielded no germy sushi, no moldy noodles. There was a six-bottle carton of Sapporo, and three cans of that famous Japanese drink, Diet Coke. Next to the refrigerator was a half-open bottle of Ozeki sake.

Bob moved to the bedroom. It was nondescript, with Musashi's famous shrike hanging on a scroll over the futon, which was flat and neatly made up. Against the opposite wall was a large TV and DVD player. In the closet were uniforms, shirts and ties, and two civilian black ties and black suits. Then polo shirts, a few pairs of jeans and chinos, all neatly pressed. Each hanger was exactly one-third of an inch from the next.

Closing the door, he went to the low stand next to the futon and opened it. There he found on one shelf, again alphabetically arranged, the crème de la crème of samurai DVDs, mostly Kurosawa but also several other top-line films he had seen, including *Samurai Rebellion, Harakiri, Band of Assassins*, and *When the Last Sword Is Drawn*. Beneath, neatly stacked and alphabetized, were porno DVDs, from a company called Shogunate AV. Shogunate AV seemed to specialize, as near as Bob could figure out, in something that might be called 'teacher films,' for each of the covers showed an attractive young woman in her mid-twenties in a business suit and glasses lecturing a batch of boys. In subsequent shots she was stripping for them, they were touching her, she was servicing them, all in the classroom, where higher mathematics had been chalked on the blackboard.

Jesus, he thought, who came up with *that*?

He left the porn stash and went to the desk. Indeed, the still shiny owner's manual to the top-of-the-line Kawasaki 22R400 bike lay on the desk, and it too had been scrupulously studied, underlined, and annotated, all in a precise kanji hand.

Where were the swords? This guy would surely have swords.

He never found them, but he found a vault in a living room closet. That's where they'd be, this fellow's small, proud collection.

Bob went back to the desk and found a photo album: our hero in kendo outfit through the stages of his life, young and proud, a winner of some local tourneys, a man in his twenties lean and dangerous. A woman appeared in some of them, but then she disappeared. Divorce, death? In the more recent photos, the swordsman had become a coach and posed with a group of younger kendo warriors.

Then, in a drawer, Bob found what appeared to be a pile of bills. They were all addressed to Kenji Kishida, of 1–23–43 Shintoyo, Apartment 633, Chiba. Many were in kanji, a few, from Citibank, were in English and Japanese, and many said the same thing: they appreciated his recent settling of debts and they thanked him very much.

There it was. The guy was bankrupting himself buying swords he couldn't afford. Then the dream sword is presented to him in the middle of a business day. He recognizes the Asano crest and the sword-smith's signature, he reads the shape of the blade, puts two and two together, and recalls that somebody in the last few weeks wants an astonishing sword. He knows the number. He takes the sword apart. He makes his tang imprint, makes the call, faxes the imprint, and connects them to Bob. It takes a couple of hours to set up a tail. Bob's sitting there like a fool; when he leaves, he has no idea he's leading the killers to the Yanos.

A week later Detective Kenji Kishida receives an envelope full of cash. He can settle his bills; maybe he buys a sword he's longed for and it reposes right now in the vault. He's got a little extra. He always wanted a bike. Why not? Who will notice? He probably never connected it with the Yanos. It was just a little favor of the sort a mildly dishonest cop might do for someone in power.

★　★　★

The officer did not go to work Saturday. He arose late and finally went to his bike about eleven in the morning. He had full racing leathers on and looked like a 'cycle knight. He examined his bike with a great deal of pleasure, checking connections, lubricants, this or that tube or pipe or cable. Then he put on his helmet, climbed aboard, keyed the engine, kicked up the stand, backed out. With a lurch — he had clearly not yet mastered the subtleties of the handle-grip clutch and the foot shifter — he shunted into motion.

Bob caught the tail end of this drama, as he'd been circling the blocks in a figure-eight pattern to keep the parking lot observed, figuring it would only be out of sight for seventy seconds out of every two minutes, and when he came by, the man had mounted up. Bob slowed, tracked him as he moved through the lot, let him join traffic, and followed a good three hundred yards behind.

Kishida threaded his way through the traffic, still clumsy and jumpy on the gears, edged his way through the suburbs of the small city of Narita to the Kanto Expressway, where, ever so tentatively, he finally got up into the higher gears and was soon humming along at 100 kmh. It never occurred to him that he was being followed, and even if it did, he probably wouldn't have had the confidence to take his eyes off the road before him. So Bob slipstreamed along without much difficulty.

Then Kenji Kishida either tired of the strain of moving at high speed or decided he wanted to see something prettier than Nissans and Mazdas playing tag at 120 kmh and the revetments of the superhighway, so he took an exit ramp. Bob easily followed him. Soon enough the houses fell away. Ahead, some mountains dominated the landscape, and rows of carefully cultivated fields lay on either side. The traffic thinned, and finally Kishida turned up a smaller road and seemed to be heading into the mountains. He still had not noticed Bob, now two hundred yards behind.

The road was empty, climbing slightly through rich pine forests. Bob had never seen a more beautiful and serene range of hills. He knew he'd never have a better chance. The guy might join a heavier-traveled road in seconds.

He gunned up into fifth gear, goosed the bike, and flew beyond a hundred miles an hour. The wind beat against him and he closed the distance like a shot, zooming by Kishida, feeling the man's sudden start of panic. Then, cruelly, he cut Kishida off, eating up his space, driving him onto the shoulder. The dust spun up in clouds as Kishida struggled with the treacherous loss of traction, got tangled up in gears and throttle and brake sequence, almost lost control, almost in fact died, but somehow managed to brake hard and bring the bike down in the dust.

Bob fishtailed to a halt, punched down his kickstand, and ran to the man lying next to the fallen, still chugging bike. He shut down the engine and saw through Kishida's shaded visor the man's fear, panic, confusion, and hesitation. Kishida tried to rise. Bob put a left-footed dragon's kick into the side of the helmet — hadn't done that in years! — and clocked him hard. Kishida fell down, slipped trying to get up, ripped at his helmet, then grabbed at his zippered jacket, perhaps to reach a gun or a *tanto*, but Bob kicked him in the helmet with another wheelhouse dragon's sweep. That put him down solidly, and he lay, shaking stars and spiderwebs out of his head, trying to figure what the hell was —

Bob jumped him, pressing his knee against the squirming man's chest. He pulled the zipper down, saw the shaft of a Glock, pulled it,

214

dropped the mag, racked the slide to toss the chambered round but there wasn't one, then tossed it twenty feet away. Kishida recoiled in horror. Bob yanked the man's helmet off.

'You stay put if you know what's good for you. I'll smack you around even more if I have to!'

'I am a police officer. You are in big — '

'Shut up. I ask the questions, you answer 'em. That's how this game is going to be played. The sword.'

'I don't — '

'*The sword, goddammit.*'

'What sword?'

'The sword that bought you this bike. The sword that paid all your debts. The sword that bought you some new toy in your vault. The sword that's going to buy you teacher porno for the next ten years.'

Kishida said nothing. His eyes suddenly went distant and he looked off, thinking. Then, finally, he looked back.

'I know who you are. I knew you'd come.'

'It don't matter a lick who or what I am or who or what you know. What matters is the sword. You were the one who spotted it. Who'd you tell? How did it happen, how was it set up, what was the deal, the connection? Don't give me any bullshit. I know more than you could guess.'

'Please, I had no idea those people would be killed. You have to believe that. I never realized . . . I just had no idea.'

'So you knew it was going to the Yanos.'

'No, but the collectors were talking afterward

215

how some American at the site of the fire was screaming about a stolen sword. That's when I saw how it could have been. I am ashamed. I should have committed *seppuku*, but I lack the courage.'

'You and me both, pal. Just tell me: who reached you? How did it happen? Who was on the receiving end of the information? How was it set up?'

'I can't tell you. Go ahead, kill me. If I tell you, I'm dead. It's the same thing.'

'You don't want to die. Not with that pretty bike lying there and brand-new swords in your vault. It ain't worth dying for, believe me. And I don't want to kill you. Too much paperwork. Tell me. Talk to me, Kenji, goddammit.'

The man took a deep breath.

'I was approached by a low-ranking *yakuza* some six months ago. He gave me a hundred thousand yen. 'For what?' I said. He said, 'Just for keeping your eye out.' He knew that I was a collector, an ex-kendo champion, something of a scholar of the sword, and at Narita I was always the one called to inspect and judge blades that unsuspecting tourists brought in or took out without proper documentation, and that I was also asked to consult on sword thefts, insurance values, that sort of thing. So he knew that I was at a kind of crossroads of sword information.'

'He had a specific sword in mind?'

'No. He couldn't have known what would or wouldn't come in, if anything. But they were looking for something big, something that would make a splash. They turn up now and then as

216

more and more swords are returned, as people look at the things they have in their trunks, as collectors and foreign buyers become more aggressive and pay more and more. *Samurai* is bigger than Japan. *Samurai* is international now.'

'So you saw the sword?'

'It was lying on a desk, just in from Customs. A fellow was typing up the license. I knew in a second it had historicity to it. I made a fuss and demanded to take charge. I told them it resembled a certain stolen sword and I had to make some phone calls. Once I had it in my office, I had some trouble getting the hilt off. Someone seemed to have poured some black tar or something into the *mekugiana* and I couldn't budge it. Fortunately, I had my kit. I was able to knock the pin out with the brass hammer. There was even a poem written by someone, I don't know who. 'Moon of hell,' that I remember. But I was too excited about the sword. I didn't recognize the smith's name, Norinaga. But I picked up the crest, looked at it through my loupe, and realized at once it was the Asano *mon*. I recognized the *koto* shape, which put it in the proper time period. It was a thrill. It was all I could do to keep from jumping up and down. It was only later when I researched the smith's name that I realized what it had to be. If I had known that — well, I don't know.'

'So you called?'

'Well, first I had to make the imprint of the tang. I did that quickly. Then I made the call. It was a young man's voice, husky, strong, not the *yakuza* I'd first talked to. He heard me describe

217

it and left the line for a second or so. He called someone. Another voice came on the line. He asked me to describe it. He was very knowledgeable. He even knew that the Asano family crest had changed over the years and had me recheck it to make certain that the one I had was right for the time. I told him the smith's name. He got very quiet. I said, 'What do you want me to do? Confiscate it?' 'No, no,' he said, 'fax me the *oshigata* and stall. Take an hour or two. Let the *gaijin* wait. Walk by him several times and note his height, his weight, his demeanor. Do you understand? We need to know what he looks like.' So that's what I did. I actually walked by you two or three times, and once sat near you. You didn't notice me. I could tell you were angry. Then I went and called them and gave a detailed description. He had me wait another few minutes and then finally okayed the next move. I reassembled the sword and went to my supervisor and told him I had been mistaken and that the license was fine and to tell you how moved we were that you were returning it.'

'And that's the time they set up to tail me to the Yanos.'

'I don't know. I never heard from them again. Two weeks later a package arrived. I opened it and found three million yen. Not a fortune but enough to pay my debts, buy a *shinshinto* that had caught my eye. I still had half of it left, so I bought the bike.'

'I don't suppose you kept the package?'

'No, of course not, I destroyed it. I had to spend all the cash. I couldn't put it in a bank because then I'd have to pay taxes on it and explain where I got it.'

'Do you still have the fax number or the original number?'

'No. I destroyed them too, after the murders.'

'Any names, any vocal characteristics, any — '

'I do recall one thing. When the young man went to call his master, he left the phone. But I heard the name. He called 'Isami-sama.''

'Isami-sama?'

'Isami, the name would be; *sama* is honorific.'

'Did you recognize it?'

'Any swordsman would recognize it. Kondo Isami, a great killer from the bloody past. Many duels and murders, many bodies. A pseudonym of a fellow with a high opinion of himself. Also bespeaking a high opinion: *sama*. It's an inflated honorific, higher than *san*. It connotes high rank or special talent, as viewed from below. The man doing the talking considers this Kondo Isami highly accomplished and is trying to ingratiate himself.'

Bob walked over and fetched the Glock. He picked it up, punched the cartridges out of the magazine, then slammed the magazine home and handed the gun back to Kishida.

'If I need more information, I may visit you again.'

Kishida said, 'If Kondo Isami catches you, he will make you tell where you got your information. You may be brave and resolute, but you will tell him. Then I am a dead man.'

'No, what's going to kill you is that damn bike you don't run worth a damn. You better get some

219

practice on a closed course.'
'I get mixed up in the gears.'
'Good way to die young and beautiful.'
'It doesn't matter. I am already dead.'
'Nah.'
'You can guarantee that?'
'Yes.'
'How?'
'Because I'm going to find him first. I'm going to cut him down and leave him for the birds.'

22

YAKIBA

She wasn't the best. But she was fast. And she had guts. He watched her from the second row. Here in the far western suburbs, he wasn't in an English-friendly tourist zone. There wasn't a lot of translation around to help the rich *gaijin*; people lived and worked and died without much thought of Americans. So the banner above the brightly illuminated mat was untranslated, but he figured the swoop of red kanji had to say something like 'Tenth Annual Women's Kendo Semifinal Match, Kanagawa Prefecture' or some such. It was in a high school gym, like the one he'd played basketball in a thousand or so years ago, and the baskets were folded back on rollers, up near the ceiling. The light was harsh and the competitors dashed through it, blades blurred in stress and skill.

Most were younger. Some were older. The fans were just as intense as stateside b-ball parents. She won her first bout easily, had some trouble in the second, and finally, in the semifinals, went down hard to some seventeen-year-old genius who moved so fast she made a blur seem lazy. But Susan Okada had poise and dignity. She countered the cuts and tried to get her own in, she gave ground, then advanced, she ducked, she thrust, she did everything but win.

She also took two or three hard claps on the side of the mask; the sword, called a *shinai*, was only sliced bamboo staves held together by twine for presence but not strength, but at that speed when it hit, it had to feel like someone had pronged a huge rubber band against her head.

When it was over, she bowed to her opponent, bowed to the referee, bowed to some kind of altar or something of kendo godhood off to one side beneath a dramatic kanji and a couple of framed photos of old Japanese guys, and finally found her way to a front-row seat, where she crashed. He watched: Boyfriend? No. Husband? No. Gals from the office? No. Nothing. She was by herself.

She sat somewhat dully during a break in the ceremony, a towel around her neck. Her feet were still bare. She didn't look particularly feminine; she looked like any jock in defeat, tired but secretly pleased she had done as well as she had, not really ready to leave the world of athletics and go back to a real one where victory and loss weren't so clearly defined.

He squirmed down and sat one seat away from her. She didn't notice.

'You swing a mean stick, Ms Okada.'

'Swagger. I thought that was you.'

'In the flesh, big as life, twice as mean.'

'Jesus Christ, how did you get in? You're on the Japanese watch list and they don't make mistakes like that.'

'I have some friends in the business. They got me some real good papers.'

'Do you have *any* idea what can happen to you?'

'People keep telling me I'm in for a big fall.'

'You are going to make *such* an unhappy inmate.'

'Well, they gotta catch me first.'

'If they do, I can't do a thing for you. If you break their law, it's tough shit, buddy. You're in their system. Off you go. The embassy will just walk away. That's our duty. It's their law, we have to respect it.'

'Just don't call the cops, that's all I ask. Anyhow, you seem to have picked up kendo fast. You looked good out there. I wasn't joking. I'd hate to have you mad at me with a live blade. You'd cut me to spinach.'

'Swagger, this is so dangerous.'

'Let me buy you a beer. You look as if you could use one, just having been clocked by a seventeen-year-old. Damn, I hate it when that happens. There's got to be a place around here.'

'I'll go shower. Tell me how it turns out.'

'The good guys win, just like in the samurai movies.'

'No, *here*. I want to see how far that little bitch who whacked me gets.'

The match had started anew and as Bob watched, the little bitch kicked ass big-time.

$\star$ $\star$ $\star$

It was a working-class bar a few blocks away, and so dark and quiet no one seemed to notice the tall white guy. Most everyone sat stupefied in front of a TV showing sumo while downing mighty tin kegs of Sapporo. They found a table

223

in the rear, thanked god there was no karaoke tonight. Finally a waiter came by and they ordered a Sapporo for the little lady and a Coke for the tall white guy.

'Why'd you take up kendo?'

'My father was a kendo champ many years ago here, before he went to the U.S. for medical school. So it runs in the family, I guess. Plus, I'm supposed to meet these people, understand them, provide little insights to the more important analysts when I'm not getting drunken Americans out of the Kabukicho tank. This is a good way.'

'It's none of my business, but no boyfriend, no husband, no — '

'It is none of your business. I have a career. It's enough for now. Swagger, what are you up to?'

'I have two items of business and I need your help.'

'You are putting me at a terrible disadvantage. My official responsibility is to turn you in, cut a deal with the Japanese, get you out of here before you do some real harm or get yourself in real trouble. I *have* to do that. It's nothing personal. You seem like a decent enough guy. But there is such a thing as duty.'

'I know about duty.'

'I know you do. I looked carefully at your record. You left everything in Vietnam. I get it, I respect it, it moves me. But I cannot let you get in trouble and I cannot let you screw things up for our country over here. You understand that?'

'Sure. I understand. But let me just tell you a thing or two. Then you decide what to do.'

'Oh, this should be rich.'

He told her the story, his assumptions and where they'd led him, leaving out only his quiet alliance with the Japanese Self-Defense Force airborne boys. He ended with the motorcycle adventure and the admission of the police officer.

She was silent for a while.

'I don't know,' she finally said. 'Maybe he just said that to please you. You'd damned near killed him, you were sitting on his chest like a baboon, you'd technically assaulted him so you'd committed about your twenty-third felony, and since he was Japanese he was used to indirection, politeness, lowered voices, discretion. You probably scared him so much he would have said anything to get you out of his face.'

'Maybe so. But how did he know about the two sword identifiers before I told him? He knew. If nothing else, that proves the sword was valuable and not some piece of war junk. If it was valuable, the whole thing swings into line. You know how nuts these people are about swords. In Dr Otowa's office I felt like I was visiting the pope. It's a religion.'

Again she looked off.

'Look, give me a few more days,' he said. 'And just a little help, okay? I won't break any more laws or beat anybody up or chase them with a motorcycle.'

'What is it?'

'The officer. He said he heard the kid on the other end of the phone call somebody 'Isami-sama.' Kondo Isami. He said that was the

225

name of a great swordsman and killer. Anyhow, I need to talk to somebody who knows *yakuza*. I have to find out who this guy who calls himself 'Kondo Isami' is. I can't just walk into a cop station and ask to see the file on Kondo Isami. You must have a contact somewhere, a cop, someone in the media, some spook or something, someone who knows someone who would know this stuff. If this Kondo is a real guy, if he has a past, if he fits, then we've got something, at least a next step. If he's nobody, if it's nothing, I'm on the first plane home. I tried, I failed.'

'No more felonies. No bull-nose macho Marine Corps bullshit. Don't call in any napalm strikes.'

'No napalm.'

'Call me at my office tomorrow afternoon. I may have something for you. You can stay out of trouble till then?'

'Sure.'

'Take a steam bath or something?'

'Sure.'

'And you said you had other business. Two pieces. That was one.'

'The child.'

'Miko?'

'Yeah. I have to know. What's happening with her?'

'She's in a hospital. There are few orphanages in Japan. Orphaned children go to relatives. But there are no relatives left. So the social services people put her in a Catholic children's hospital. She's not doing well. There's no one for her. She lost everything one night, and now she sleeps on a cot. She thinks the Tin Man is going to come and rescue her, poor thing. I haven't figured out who the Tin Man is.'

'That's so sad.'

'So it goes on the wicked planet Earth.'

'Nobody visits her?'

'Not anymore.'

'Can I visit her?'

'Not a good idea.'

'She needs someone.'

'It's not possible.'

'Miss Okada, don't you *want* these people? They killed a family and orphaned a four-year-old child. They have to be punished. Don't you see that? Didn't you send me an autopsy report? I have an idea in my head this professional objectivity is a game; you want these guys as bad as I do.'

'I didn't send you anything. That's a delusion on your part. But it's not the serious delusion. The serious delusion is that you want to believe that you and I are buddies, in this together, in a quest for justice. No way. I work for the United States government, which is where my loyalties begin and end. Don't romanticize me, because I'll disappoint you. Here's the reality: you have one inch of leash. You pursue this investigation for a little while longer. If you develop some evidence, you make sure it comes to me first, last, and only. If it's of value, I will see that it gets to the proper Japanese authorities, and at that point our interest ends. The Japanese system will deal with it, or maybe it won't, because that's the reality. If you break my rules, I'll report you in a flash and you're on your way to a Japanese prison.'

'I would say you drive a hard bargain, except you don't bargain at all.'

'No, I don't. You can't go samurai on me, do you understand? If you samurai up, I will have to take you down hard. I do not bullshit, Swagger, and I tell you loud and clear: if I have to, pardner, I will bust you up so bad you'll wish you'd never entered this rodeo.'

23

THE TOKYO FLASH

Of course she drove a red Mazda RX-8. Long hair flying, wearing aviator's teardrop sunglasses, she flew through the Tokyo traffic like a ninja, cursing at the slower, veering in and out, braking hard, gunning too fast, rushing through the gears, utterly confident in the left-handed driving. It was late afternoon of the following day, and when he called her, she told him she'd pick him up.

But they didn't go to any reporter. Instead, they pulled into a large building of gray brick, clearly Catholic, from the religious statue in the front yard. She drove around the side to the parking lot that faced a playground behind a cyclone fence.

'You stay here,' she said. 'I don't want her seeing you. We don't know what she remembers, what her associations are. Believe me, this child doesn't need any more trauma. It's hard enough.'

He sat in the car as Okada disappeared into the building and, ten minutes later, emerged with the child.

Bob watched. Immediately he saw the difference. Where Miko had been a force of nature, a naturally gregarious, adventurous child, now she held tightly to Susan's hand and didn't seem to want to go out on her own. Susan took her to a swing, sat her on it, and pushed, but in a few seconds the child began to holler.

They were too far away for Bob to hear, but he saw Susan take the child off the swing and hold her. Then they walked to a slide and, tentatively, Miko climbed and desultorily descended the gleaming surface. But there was no liberation, no surrender to the giddy power of gravity; it was a glum trip.

The visit lasted a few minutes. Miko seemed fearful, constricted, clinging neurotically to Susan, who was talking gently to her but without much effect.

It was almost more than Bob could take. He found his muscles tensing, his jaw clenching, and his anger rising.

I don't care what I said to Susan, he thought. The man who did this to her will feel fear too. Then I will cut him.

The woman and the child went inside and Bob tried to relax, but his mind was too buzzed. He wished he had a drink, but that would not solve anything. Instead, he climbed out, took a few drafts of fresh air, and tried to calm down. Pretty soon Susan arrived, and they drove off.

'Let me ask you something,' he said as she gunned through the busy avenues. 'When this is over and let's assume I'm still standing, I ain't in no jail, and I'm headed back to the States — '

'No.'

'You don't know where I'm going.'

'Sure I do. I know exactly where you're going. You want to adopt her.'

'I am already a father. Some say I'm a good one.'

'I'm sure you're a great one. Moreover, you could make her a wonderful home in the West, and sooner rather than later she'd heal, though never completely, and she'd come back to us and she'd become happy and productive and have a wonderful life. That doesn't matter.'

'What matters?'

'Connections, which you don't have.'

'What do you mean?'

'It's very hard for foreigners to adopt a child in Japan. First, few of them are available. I'm not sure if she qualifies. Then there's the shape of your eyes. They're round. The Japanese are disinclined to let a westerner adopt a Japanese child, unless there's some prior connection. It's not like China or Korea where cute girl babies are a cash crop for American yuppies.'

'There's no hope?'

'Not a whisper. Not an eyelash.'

'Suppose your boss, Mr Ambassador, used his influence.'

'He wouldn't do it for me, why would he do it for you? I don't have the juice, you don't have the juice.'

'That sucks.'

'It does indeed. But the world is full of terrible injustices. Ninety-eight percent of them can't be helped or fixed. This is one of them. Concentrate on the two percent that can. Ah, here we are.'

Nick Yamamoto lived in a quiet Tokyo residential neighborhood a few kilometers geographically and several universes culturally

231

from Kabukicho. His was one of those nondescript wooden homes behind a fence that was attached to other homes on either side, all of them squashed together like french fries in a greasy bag. They had no trouble parking in the quiet neighborhood, slipped through the gate, and knocked.

Like many Japanese males he was slender, small, wore glasses, moved fluidly. Unlike most Japanese men, he had blond hair. It was thatchy, moussed in odd directions, and suggested some kind of rock star. If you only counted the hair, he looked eighteen; the rest of him was a man of forty-odd years.

'Do you like it?' he asked Susan.

'No. It's stupid.'

He looked up at Bob.

'Is she a bitch or what?'

'She can be pretty tough,' Bob said. 'You should get her started on me if you want to hear some ugliness. Anyhow, my name is Bob Lee Swagger. I like your hair.'

'See, he likes my hair.'

'What does he know? He's a *gaijin*.'

Bob and Nick shook hands, bonding immediately on their mutual fear of the great and wonderful wizard Susan Okada. Nick took them into the place, all wood floors and luxurious western furniture. A seventy-two-inch TV hung on one wall broadcasting baseball, but everywhere else books were jammed into shelves and framed front pages hung on walls. The smell of grilled meat hung in the air; Nick had just finished dinner.

'A drink?' Nick asked.

'Can't touch the stuff,' said Swagger. 'If I do, I'm gone for a month. Please go ahead.'

'Okada-san?'

'No, I'm working. This isn't social.'

'Tea, coffee, Coke, anything?'

'No thanks.'

'Well, I think I will, if you don't mind.'

Nick went and got himself a jug and a cup and proceeded to lubricate himself with small sips of sake. He ushered them to the leather sofa and he slipped into a nice Barcelona chair.

'Nick used to be the *Tokyo Times*' Washington bureau chief, which is where I met him. But then he was recalled and in a few months got himself fired. What was it, Nick? I don't remember. Plagiarism or bribery?'

'Actually, it was both.'

'The cocaine made him do it. It wasn't his fault.'

'The cocaine made me do it. It was my fault.'

'Anyhow, he says he's clean now, and he's still a one-man show. He publishes, writes and reports, and lays out the *Tokyo Flash*, a weekly of a disreputable sort. Tokyo has hundreds of them. His is one of the best. If you want to know about Brad and Angelina, or what porn star has just left which studio to go hard-core for two billion yen, Nick would know.'

'But I know some other stuff too.'

'He's published seven books on the *yakuza*. And he knows a lot more than he's published.'

'I'd be dead if I published what I know.'

'You sound like just the man I need,' said Bob.

233

'Well, I'll try. I owe Susan for something in D.C. So try me.'

'Kondo Isami.'

'Ohhhh, I'm impressed. Which one? Kondo the original, or Kondo Two, the Sequel?'

'I guess the first to start.'

'You probably couldn't understand the second without the first.'

'I'm all ears.'

Nick poured himself a little more sake. He turned off the TV, fished among his CDs and found one, and popped it into a player.

'Soundtracks from several samurai movies.'

'Swagger's seen a lot of samurai movies. Too many. He has the Toshiro Mifune disease.'

'Well, Swagger-san, I'm a writer, so I believe in mood. This is the right music for this story.'

He took another swig on the sake.

'Westerners can't really appreciate the dynamic between shogun and emperor that played off and on in Japan for three hundred years. I won't bore you with it in detail, but we had this weird system of a showy but powerless emperor-god on a throne in Kyoto and a guy in armor who'd fought in a hundred battles and outthought everybody else running the show in Edo. They never got along.

'It came to a head in the middle of the nineteenth century, when aggressive outsiders began pressuring Japan to open up and trade with the West. The shogun opposed the move, the emperor embraced it, more or less, and that set the clans a-warring. The emperor, as I say, lived in Kyoto, the shogun in Tokyo. I'll call it

Tokyo instead of Edo just to keep it simple.'

'I'm very simple,' said Bob, 'but so far I'm with you.'

'A lot of pro-emperor *ronin* — masterless samurai, who despised the shogun — came to Kyoto and essentially turned it into Dodge City. It was violent, terrible, a city of anarchy. The year is roughly eighteen hundred sixty-two. In Tokyo, the shogun was embarrassed that he couldn't keep control of the city where the emperor resided; it made him look foolish.

'So a lord sympathetic to him, and certainly with his permission, hired a militia. Or maybe you'd call them vigilantes, or regulators, something cowboy. A gang, a posse, an outfit, whatever. They called themselves the Specially Chosen Ones, which in Japanese is *Shinsengumi*. They were led — well, there was a lot of turmoil in their own leadership, as there always is in Japan, but eventually, with the help of a really good, bloody assassination — by a guy named Kondo Isami. Big guy, tough guy, ran a dojo out west, very ambitious. So Kondo and his Shinsengumi set out to tame Dodge. They did it by killing. It's been in a thousand movies, but you probably remember either *Band of Assassins* or *When the Last Sword Is Drawn*.'

'Saw 'em both. Poor Toshiro gets beheaded in *Band*. I guess he was Kondo.'

'That's right. Kondo Isami is definitely the Mifune part. That's what happened to Kondo when the emperor's clans won and the shogun was replaced. But for a long time, in Kyoto, Kondo was the law, and he and his boys were the bloodiest mob old Japan ever saw. They killed and killed and killed. Kondo himself probably killed a hundred men in sword fights. He was your true-grit samurai, love him or hate him. So any man today calling himself Kondo means to scare you and frighten you and communicate to you that he is willing to kill. That he even likes to kill.'

'And Kondo Isami Two?' Bob asked.

'I've never seen his name in print. Supposedly it appeared only once and a few weeks later, the reporter's head was found mounted on a tripod of golf clubs outside his paper, a tabloid called *Weekly Jitsuwa*. It caused quite a stir. The three clubs were the eight and nine irons and the number three wood. *Ya-ku-za*, of course, is slang derived from a card game's losing hand, which is eight-nine-three.

'Nobody knows who he is, only what he does. He's an elite *yakuza* assassin, with a very small team of highly trained men who favor the old traditions. They still kill the old way, with the sword.'

'You'll have to explain that to me,' Bob said.

'For a westerner it seems bizarre, I suppose. But in certain applications, the sword is actually far more efficient than the gun, if you don't mind a lot of sloppy blood around. These guys spend their lives working on it and get very, very good. They can take you down as fast as a gun. It's an extremely lethal weapon and they have a butcher's knowledge of anatomy. They know exactly where to cut you or, if they have to, pierce you, to empty you of blood in a split second. They cut your lungs and take out your air supply, they cut your pelvis and shatter your support system, they cleave your brain and it all goes dark. You don't even feel the pain, you just go down in a heap. And best of all: no noise. You can have a nice little battle, a good triple assassination, a one-on-one to the death, assured that no cops are going to show up. Nobody knows until the next morning when they notice all those pools of sticky red stuff in the gutter. Here, look at these.'

He went to a cabinet, pulled out a file, and handed it to Bob.

They were autopsy and crime scene photos of men dead by sword. On the slab, the nude bodies had oval openings the size of footballs, sometimes hard to see because the skin sundered wasn't white but usually mottled red, black, and green, not from disease, as Bob initially thought, but from the dense, almost obsessive tattooing that marked the bodies. But the cuts were visible once you focused on them amid the dragon's heads and wolves' yaps and kanji characters: they exposed a butcher's festival of sliced meat inside, visible now only because the blood had drained. The cuts were gigantic, and deep, and permanent; they'd empty the sack of fluid that is a human body in a second. In the on-site photos of the rubbed-out of the underworld, the distinguishing feature was not the black suits and shoes, not the sunglasses, not the twisted postures of the fallen or the occasional lopped limb or split head, but the blood, the lakes and lakes of it. Each body sat like an island in the middle of a red sea; it lapped everywhere, spreading in satiny luster, as if by some mad king's imperial mandate.

'This Kondo Isami came on the scene about five years ago. An underboss named Otani was having trouble with a Chinese-sponsored hotshot in Kabukicho and was bedeviled by one individual in particular. 'Bedeviled' as in 'cut really bad.' Kondo Isami introduced himself to Otani by sending a business card and a head. It was very effective. As Otani rose, so did Kondo, specializing in the impossible, the discreet, the hard to do. Evidently, unlike most of the yaks, he is not tattooed. He has to be brilliant, socially adept, and completely presentable. But even so, there are weirdnesses. Many who've met him have not seen his face; he goes to great lengths, including masks or theatrical lighting arrangements, to prevent certain people from getting a look at it. But he'll meet others very casually, it is said. He goes dancing or clubbing. Suddenly, for no reason, he doesn't care if anybody sees him. Now what the hell could that be about?'

'Sometimes he's shy, sometimes he's not. Maybe that's all there is to it.'

'No, there's more. Nothing's simple about this guy. He has brilliant sword skills. He's at the level of almost transcendent technique that some of the legendary sams achieved, like Musashi or Yagyu. His boys may not be quite so advanced, but their internal discipline is tremendous. Only once has a Shinsengumi guy been taken by the cops, and he committed hara-kiri in the station

238

with a fork before he talked. He turned out to be a street gang kid who'd evidently been talent-spotted by Kondo, brought into the unit, trained, and disciplined. They found him soaked in his own blood with a smile on his face.

'Otherwise, they specialize in the hard to do. Enormously violent. There was a rumor some Chinese gangsters were going to mount a move against Boss Otani, and the Shinsengumi took them out in about thirty seconds in a Kyoto inn, where the group had gathered for recreational indulgence. They caught them in the lounge. The swords came out much faster than the Berettas, and they danced from man to man in seconds, cutting. Kondo himself split a Chinaman from crown to dick. Cut him in two, top to bottom. Amazing strength, but more. You have to know the art of cutting. He does. Then they left no witnesses.'

'Look, Nick,' said Bob, 'I think Kondo has a new client. I think he took out Philip Yano's family, stole a sword of some rare value that had come Yano's way, and now he's got some plan for the sword that I can't figure out. So can you ask around, see if you can find out who Kondo's working for and what he'd need a special sword for? And why would he have to wipe out the Yanos? Why couldn't he just send a burglary team in, crack the vault, and walk out clean? Or even buy the damned thing, not that, come to think of it, Yano would have sold.'

'Sure, I can ask. But I'm getting something out of this. I'm getting a scoop that'll make me the man in the tabloid game, and even get me back in the respectable rags.'

'Absolutely.'

'Nick, be careful,' Okada said.

'I'll be careful. Meanwhile, Swagger-san, learn to fight.'

24

THE EIGHT CUTS

The compass no longer held four directions. There was no longer a left or a right. That up/down stuff? Gone totally. As for colors, numbers, signposts, any markers of a universe to be navigated rationally: vanished.

Instead, all reality consisted of the eight cuts. There were only eight cuts.

Never more, never fewer.

Tsuki.

Migi yokogiri.

Hidari yokogiri.

Migi kesagiri.

Hidari kesagiri.

Migi kiriage.

Hidari kiriage.

Shinchokugiri.

Or thrust, side cut left to right, side cut right to left, diagonal cut right to left, diagonal cut left to right, rising diagonal cut from right to left, rising diagonal cut from left to right, and vertical downward, the head-splitter.

He stood, sweating, the very sharp blade in his hand so that his concentration wouldn't wander. A mistake with a thing so sharp could cut him badly and he already bled in small quantities from a dozen brushes with the *yakiba*, the tempered edge, of the wicked thing. Doshu paid the blood no mind: the message was, if you work with live blades, you get cut. That's all. No big thing. Get used to blood. It goes away or it needs stitches and there's nothing in between.

'*Migi yokogiri!*' the bastard commanded, and Bob obligingly performed the downward right to left cut, not a slash, not a lunge, not a thrust: a cut.

'*Kire! KIRE!*' the man yelled at him.

Cut.

Bob realized there was magic to the Japanese in the word. It wasn't like 'cutting classes' or 'cutting the rug' or 'damn, I cut myself' or 'don't cut corners,' all those little metaphorical indulgences on the principle of the sharp thing encountering the soft thing, the sort of expressions a society might create that had never taken blades too seriously.

To the Japanese the word *cut* had special significance. You didn't toss it about lightly; it was almost a religious term. With a sword, you *cut*. To cut was to kill, or to try to kill. The weapons were meant for that purpose only; they were dead-zero serious, no jokes, no jive, no sport, no fun. In their way, they were as meaningful, emotionally, as loaded guns and possibly more so because a gun could be unloaded but a sword never could.

'Left diagonal cut!'

'Right sideways cut!'

'Rising left diagonal!'

There were only eight of them. But everything depended upon those eight. If you could not master those eight, you had no chance.

'No, no. Angle all wrong! Angle bullshit. Angle must be perfect. Go *slow!*'

How long had this been going on? It felt like the crazed exercise at Parris Island, back when Parris Island meant something, where you were on a seventy-two-hour field exercise and nights bled into days, which bled into nights, until you were so aching you thought it would never end and your movements had gotten stupid with fatigue. What was your name? Where were you from?

But that's what got Swagger through 'Nam three times, so as much as every second of it sucked hard and long, it was somehow worth it. You had to do it.

'Rising left diagonal! No, no, blade bent, no! Feel!'

The small man came behind the sweating *gaijin* and with vicelike fingers took his arm through the motion, controlling his elbow, controlling the angle of the blade, which had to be precisely aligned to the angle of the cut, else the whole process broke down, you got a blown cut and the sword torqued its way from your grip, or at least took you out of timing so that your opponent could get in and cut you bad.

No, not cut you bad.

The Japanese would say, *Bassari kiru.*

Cut you through.

He thought he'd pass out. But if the little man with the wispy goatee could keep going, so, somehow, could he. But it went on for hours and hours and hours until:

'Put sword away.'

Bob bowed, not knowing how or why.

He found the *saya*, remembered to extend it from him, and dropped it over the extended sword, whose edge he'd turned to self according to etiquette, and then returned it to the rack in the deity alcove.

When he turned, Doshu was tightening a *men* around his head and had already gotten on the body padding.

'Come, come. Now, you, me, fight. Fight hard. You kill me with wood. Good cuts. Make good cuts.'

Bob must have groaned; all he wanted was a nap.

'Come on. Only do for six, maybe ten more hours. Then I give fifteen-minute break.'

Bob realized — a rarity. A joke.

★　★　★

Hmmm. He found out quickly that he could fight or he could cut. But it was damned hard to do both. He was as fast as Doshu and now and then got his licks in, though perhaps Doshu was going light on him, even if the whack of the wooden edge against his unprotected arms or torso would leave welts and bruises for days. But when he hit, he hit sloppily. When he cut well, he cut slow.

'I can't stay with you.'

'No 'stay with.' Sickness. Sickness of ego. No win, no lose. You must fight in one mind.'

One mind. Now what the fuck did that mean?

'Concentrate but no concentrate. See but no

244

see. Win but no win.'

What language was this?

'Stop,' the man said after a bit. 'You like girls?'

'Yeah, of course.'

'Remember best time with girl?'

'Well, yeah.'

'What?'

'Come on. I can't tell you that.'

'When?'

'Oh, 'ninety-three. I hadn't been no good for a long time. Hadn't been with a decent woman in a long time. Got in a bad scrape and was on the run, and I made it to the house of a woman who'd been married to my spotter in Vietnam. In some way, I'd fallen in love with her picture first. She was what I lost when I lost him. It fucked up my head. So anyway, had no place to go and I went to her and it's been okay ever since. She saved my life. And the sex part — well, hell, it don't get no better.'

'Think of sex,' said Doshu, and cut him hard in the throat.

'*Ach!* Hey,' Bob shouted.

'Think of sex,' said Doshu, and whapped him hard with the blade in the right shoulder.

'*No!*' Bob said. 'It's too goddamn private. It ain't for this. I can't think of sex. It's wrong.'

'You fool. No Japanese. Think of — think of *smooth*.'

Smooth?

What was smooth?

'I don't — '

'*No!* Think of *smooth!*'

And what came to mind when 'smooth' was

245

ordered? He thought of the scythe. He thought of his solitude on the high arroyo, the long spring and early summer months, the old blade in his hand, the suppleness through his torso, the way he could only keep it going three hours the first day and by the end, when he was damn near finished, he could go fifteen, sixteen hours at a whack, thinking nothing of it. He thought of the small, tough desert scrub, the way that old blade, nothing a samurai would look at twice, would just *smooth* through it. Sending stalks and leaves aflying in a spray, with that oddly satisfying whipping sound as it rent the air.

Somehow he found something private and his own, and using it, he blocked the next cut, stepped inside it, and cut Doshu hard across the wrists, knowing that he'd purposely missed the wrist guard by a hair so that the blow really hurt the little bastard like hell.

Think of the scythe!

★   ★   ★

He wasn't sure when it stopped, he wasn't sure when he rested, but somehow he found himself outside in the dark, rolling carpets.

'Roll tight. Not tight enough! Roll tighter.'

What the fuck did *this* have to do with anything?

'Why are — '

'No *why*, fool! No why! Do! Do well, do right, do as Doshu say, do, do, *do!*'

And so he did. He rolled the thatchy carpet squares into tight rolls, pinned them, got twine

246

around them, and tied them tight. The absurd image of tying off an elephant's penis came to him, and when he smiled, Doshu hit him hard with the switch.

'No goddamn joke, *gaijin*.'

Finally, he got them secured. It took a while to get the feel of it, but finally he could do it fast enough, and when all the carpets were rolled, he'd accumulated quite a pile, maybe seventy-five or eighty.

'Now soak!'

'What?'

'Soak, goddamn! Soak!'

What this turned out to mean was loading the carpet rolls into a trough, then going to the hose and filling the trough to the brim. It was dark. What day was it? He thought it was the third day, though maybe it was the fourth day or maybe just the second. Who knew? Who knew when this little bastard was shutting up? Who knew when it would stop —

'You sleep now. Till dawn. Two hours. Then we cut.'

'Cut?'

'Yes, no bullshit, sword is cut. No cut, no sword. We cut, cut well, cut hard, or I kick you out, you hopeless *gaijin*, goddamn you to hell.'

★ ★ ★

Three hours later, slightly refreshed but still groggy as hell, he found himself in the back courtyard. Doshu had directed him to load five of the soaked, rolled carpets on five heavy

247

wooden bases, each with a vertical rod from which sprang a spike. The carpets sank on the spike and stood upright, like little soldiers.

'*Tameshigiri.*'

'Okay,' said Bob.

'You watch, then do.'

The old fellow took the sword, bowed to it, withdrew it from its *saya*. Then he turned, faced the array of five carpet rolls on five spikes.

'*Ai!*' he shouted, and with a speed that Swagger almost could not follow he flashed through the formation, coiling and uncoiling, the blade whispering at warptime, just a sliver of light, a flash of shadow, a sense of willed disturbance in the cosmos, and in what had to be less than one second, he had precisely cut each carpet roll at about a 47.5-degree angle, talk about your 'smooth,' and stood still.

'You do. *Tameshigiri.* Test cutting. Must cut real. Pretend all bullshit. Do it. Do it now.'

Bob bowed to the little god in his sword, not because he believed there was a little god in there but because not bowing would be one thing more to be yelled at for, unsheathed, and approached the closest rolled carpet.

'*Jodan-kamae,*' yelled the man, meaning on high, and being right-handed, Bob found that position, one leg slightly ahead of the other, almost a batting stance but not quite as his hands were far apart on the hilt of the weapon and he was thinking of killing.

'*Ai!*' he shouted, and brought the sword down hard at 45 degrees against the bundled material. With a vibratory clatter, the sword twisted in his hand and seemed stuck about a half inch in the bundle.

'No, no, no,' screamed the little man. 'Angle all wrong, much stupidity. Angle of edge be same as angle of blade or you get bullshit like that. I told you. Do what I say.'

Bob readdressed his carpeted opponent, tried to shake his brain free of thought and not feel like an idiot in a bathrobe with a long knife cutting up carpets, but instead like a ferocious samurai warrior about to dispatch an enemy.

The sword seemed to move on its own; his mind was blank to results and he thought for a second he'd missed completely it was so smooth, but then with the lazy grace of the totally dead, the top half of the carpet roll fell off to hit the ground.

'Again!'

And again, and again, and again.

Somewhere in there, he progressed to two-cut sequences, cutting one way, reversing smoothly by the gyroscopic guidance in his elbows from the center of his shoulders, then coming back through it. He seemed to be getting it, feeling the power in his hands, making subtle corrections in the stroke, cutting not with arms but with the 'center of his body,' that is, with the whole weight of the body behind it; there was weird satisfaction in watching the carpeting fall helpless before his blade.

'Not good,' said Doshu. 'Is maybe okay. But no time to make good. Now you can cut a little, so tomorrow we teach you to fight.'

'Floating feeling in thumb and forefinger, with the middle finger neither tight nor slack and the last two fingers tight. When you take up sword, you must feel intent on cutting the enemy. No fixedness. Hand alive. I no like fixedness in swords and hands. Fixedness means a dead hand. Pliability is a living hand.'

Yeah, sure, easy for you to say, thought Bob, and Doshu raised his own sword smoothly and with elegant grace and rhythm, a snake coiling to strike, a swan rising, his muscles in perfect syncopation.

Bob tried to model on him, feeling his body fight him, feeling ridiculous, a barefoot Fred Astaire with a pretend sword in a gymnasium.

'No! No, again, no thought. No thought. Too much thought.'

What does *that* mean?

He tried to concentrate but thought, See, it would be easier if he broke it down, one, two, three, then four, five, six, and I could practice each one and —

He pinched off the spurt of frustration and tried to feel the move, the slow rotation of hips, the uprising of the arms, that goddamned 'floating feeling in thumb and forefinger,' and somehow it was just a little better.

'In one timing, Swagger,' said Doshu, whatever that meant.

'I — '

'No talk! One timing. *One timing!*'

What did one timing mean?

'Make shield of fists.'
'I — '
'Place body sideways.'
'Okay, but — '
'Keep shoulders level with opponent's fists.'
'I'll try if — '
'Keep rear leg open, Swagger.'
'Like this?'
'Keep stance same as opponent's.'

He tried to do it all, and of course could do none of it. There was no end, no progress, no start, no finish, no lesson plan. Doshu gave him opaque orders, shouted commands to 'Approach no-think!' as though he were ordering a trainee to drop and give him fifty. It went on, pointlessly, forever, Fourth day? Fifth? Afternoon of first? Who knew? He realized at a certain point the only way to deal with this wasn't to think about it being 'over.' Don't think about it 'ending.' It is not a thing of beginning and ending. Concentrate only on exactly what is before you. Do exactly what is stated. Do it, don't think about it, analyze it, try to 'learn' it. Just do the fucking thing, and do not place it in time or cause-effect, or this, then that. See it — this seemed to help — as shooting. You simply have to teach your body the way. The body knows the way, so that you don't have to instruct it; it is on subconscious autopilot, there's no particular sense of having 'mastered' a thing, it's just that all the work is connecting and the body is learning things without telling its owner.

Maybe he was getting it, sort of.

Swagger cleans the floor of the dojo on his hands and knees. With a soft wet cloth and a pail of warm water, he scrubs each and every square inch. He goes over the woodwork and reaches spots that have not been reached before. He gives himself to this work, taking pride in the perfection of it.

And in cleaning he came across a little corner where a few treasures of ego were on display: it was in what he knew to be the deity alcove, the spiritual heart of the dojo, where the truly supplicant went to worship.

What Swagger saw, beyond an indecipherable kanji banner and a few photos of elders who must have founded this particular style or school or way or whatever, were pictures from a past full of men and boys and, lately, girls. All were sweaty, all in triumph, all in *gi* and *hakama*, and Bob always recognized Doshu, and in some of the earlier ones he recognized his sponsor in this madness, Dr Otowa, supremely cool and intelligent. In one Otowa and Doshu stood with a boy, who by the cast of his eyes and the wit in his mouth and the sternness in his forehead had to be a little Otowa, a son, with some silly trophy or something, all of them sweaty, all of them exhilarated. It was like a Little League photo from the '70s, so far distant in time and place as to be all but unrecognizable, all of it however speaking of some unbroken line, father to son, going back through the generations.

You saw these photos all over Arkansas,

though usually a dead deer or a baseball bat or a football was part of it, instead of a kendo *shinai*; it was the same, the father passing on what he knew, the boy, though distant, hungry for it.

'Swagger! Sword, now. *Now!*'

★ ★ ★

Doshu is a drill sergeant. He's a yeller, a pressure cooker, a demander. But it's so hard because it's not progressive in a western sense; there's no feeling of going from here to there. The edges of things are blended. Somewhere — the start is indistinct — he'd moved into kata, which was a series of moves with the sword, a kind of offensive syncopation so that the blade came out, flowed around the shoulders to a certain perfect position, then was cut with, the cut riding a rhythm, never just a brute expression of force. It seemed to have something to do with wave dynamics, a sense of harnessing a blast of energy that would rise from one hip, course through the body to the opposite shoulder, flow downward into the fists, which would then surge in opposing directions, bringing the blade through with an amazement of unwilled speed and force, all without trying. Doshu would swing lazily at him with his *bokken* and Bob would block it, feel it sliding off his own wooden blade, and see how to ride it down and open up a way to the man's innards, then turn back and slip into another kata.

'Attack and abide in one,' Doshu said, '*migi yokogiri*,' and Bob delivered his side cut.

'By the false, the true is obtained,' he also said, '*hidari kesagiri*,' so that Bob tried to obtain the truth through a left-to-right diagonal.

He clarified by adding, 'Beat the grass and scare up the snake, *tsuki*,' and Bob thrust, trying to scare up snakes.

Then to make it absolutely clear: 'Use thought to approach no-thought; use attachment to be unattached.'

He then tried speed. A Swagger gift: fast, good hands.

He brought maximum speed to a horizontal stroke from the draw — *nutisuke* — and you'd have thought he'd blown his nose on a flag or something.

'*No! No!* Speed wrong. Speed bad. Speed sick, Swagger. No speed. *No speed!*'

It was not the only time the obscure little man seemed really agitated, but something about speed annoyed him deeply.

'Speed sick. Speed bad.'

He said it over and over.

Don't think of speed, Bob cautioned himself. If you connect with speed, it's all wrong. No, no, no. Slow, sure, smooth. Smooth is fast. Fast is not fast. Fast is slow. Smooth is fast. Be smooth.

'Moon in the cold stream like a mirror.' That was the strangest, yet it was what Doshu would always come back to. Opaque, cute even, some Asian cornball thing from an old TV show or other. It felt too self-consciously 'mystic.'

He remembered Yoda from some *Star Wars* thing: 'There is no *try*. Only *do*.' Something like that. Maybe he was some aged fool of a Luke

254

Skywalker on a strange planet far from home, trying to master a little wizard's poetry, which would only work if you believed it, yet he could not believe it at his heart, because he was a U.S. Marine and what he believed in was obedience to orders, obedience to traditions, never surrendering, and breaking the weapon down to clean it.

Yet he saw that was itself a form of Zen or bushido or whatever this little guy was selling. It wasn't action, it was belief. You had to give yourself to it and trust it. You had to give up on the you part of you, because the more of you there was, the less belief there was and the more vulnerable you were.

★ ★ ★

Day and night flowed together. Bob never saw the sun, not after the first morning's work outdoors. He slept in snatches, was pulled from unconsciousness, dragged to the dojo floor, and put through paces. Some children watched and laughed. They thought he was really supremely funny, big, tall, clumsy, gangly. Sometimes even Doshu smiled.

But it did seem a rhythm arrived somehow, sometime. The moves began to feel all right to him, possibly even good. The less he tried, the better he did. Maybe it was that he was so exhausted he didn't care anymore. But he was learning smoothness.

Doshu stood across from him; the *bokken* flashed toward his face, and Bob was fast enough to parry and ride the sword down. He saw three next steps: he could rise off the pinned sword and go for a horizontal cut — *migi yokogiri* — that would take Doshu across the chest; he could pivot inward, getting so close to Doshu that Doshu was helpless, and drive backward for a penetrating strike to the chest, *tsuki*; or he could float backward, find a new stance, and look for another, larger opening.

While he was thinking, Doshu was cutting. Doshu had reversed, come out of the pressure of the upper blade, and stepping away, clipped him with two inches in the larynx. If the swords had been steel instead of wood, he'd be on the floor trying to hold the last of his seven pints of blood in his body, but he wouldn't be fast enough.

This went on; the combative katas increased, and Bob got them, he saw them, he understood the principle, saw the opening, but he just never quite got there in time.

'Fuck!' he said.

'Moon in the cold stream like a mirror,' the man said.

Bob tried to crank up the concentration, but that didn't work. He was being beaten severely at every exchange, and the blows of the wooden sword were raising knots on his bones and joints. His sweat poured off him. His fingers felt numb. How much longer would this go on?

And suddenly it stopped.

Doshu drew back from him and looked at him. Then he delivered a verdict.

'First day, eight cuts. Not bad. Second day, cutting *tameshigiri*, not bad. Yesterday, fighting, good. Today, fighting, not so good. Nothing.'

'I don't have it today,' said Bob.

'Is no 'Don't have today.' No *yakuza* say, 'You got today? Okay, now we fight.' Is only *now*.'

'I'm trying,' Bob heard himself say, and waited for Yoda to answer, 'Is no *try*. Is only *do*.'

But it was Doshu who answered: 'You not know enough. Anyone beat you.'

Bob wanted to say, But you said speed is sick. Wanting to win is sick. Then he stopped. Why fight him? he thought. He knows this shit, I don't. It's not up to me to point out his contradictions. Just go with it.

He bowed, showing humility to his tormentor, and saw immediately that this pleased the man. Bob composed his face into an expression of nothingness. Is nothing. Nothing is. Only void. Enter void. Do not exist. Use thought to approach no-thought.

'You sleep now.'

'No, I'm fine. I can go on.'

'No, sleep. Tired, sore, disappointed, confused. Not concentration. You sleep now. You come when you wake. But then, you fight.'

'Fight?'

'Sure. A match. But you must win.'

'I will win.'

'You *must* win. No win, I kick you out. I cannot help you nothing. You go away. Swagger die soon anyway, no worth helping.'

'I will win,' pledged Bob, believing he would. He liked this little development; it was a return to cause-effect. It was an ending, a climax. He would fight, he would win, he would go on. The finality was pleasing.

Doshu bowed; Bob returned the bow and went off. He went to the kitchen, where a surprisingly nourishing meal had been prepared; he ate it hungrily. Then the old lady — Doshu's mother, his maid, his sister, no introductions had been made — took him to a room where he discovered a modern shower. She left, he stripped, and luxuriated in the warmth of the stinging water, feeling it soothe his bruised muscles and achy, swollen joints. Then, wrapping himself in a towel, he found his pallet behind the kitchen. Someone had covered it with a futon and a clean linen sheet and he settled into surprising comfort.

He woke sensing light.

I am ready, he thought. I will win.

He found a fresh jockstrap, pulled on *gi* trousers, covered them with *hakama* trousers, which he now knew how to tie, all the little bows and straps, all nice and neat. Attired, he stretched for twenty minutes, warming his muscles. Finally, all loosey-goosey, he put on his *gi* jacket, belting it tight, and walked to the dojo.

Doshu awaited, as did his opponent.

'You must win,' said Doshu. 'No mercy, no hesitation, no doubt. Give all. Become void.'

'I — ' said Bob, then stopped when he saw the enemy.

It wasn't merely that the enemy was about four feet tall and about ten. It was much worse. She was a girl.

25

THE FLOATING WORLD

Nick worked the clubs. Uptown, downtown, all around the town. He did the fancy glass-and-chrome joints in the Ginza, the most sophisticated of Tokyo's nighttime districts. It cost him a fortune, because the Ginza is possibly the most expensive strip of real estate in the world, but he'd just moved two pounds of pure Moroccan White Girl to a minor yak offshoot and so he had a big wad of cash in his drawers and he didn't mind spreading it around in search of a scoop that would put his rag on the map big-time.

And it would be a scoop too: Kondo Isami, the legendary yak killer, man of mystery and blood, working for a new big boss on a new big plan. That would make him in this burg. God, he loved this filthy town.

But he had no luck on the Ginza strip. He worked the gay part of the city, Shinjuku-2-Chome, on the principle that a few of the yaks were fairy or went to both coasts; they might sneak off here to relax, to get off, to forget the slicing that was so much a part of their lives, and might relax enough so that with a gallon or two of sake, they might spill something to a rent boy, he might spill something in turn. He worked Ace and Kinswomyn and Kinsmen and Advocate.

But no. The fags weren't talking, or if they

were, they weren't talking to him, a straight guy with blondish hair and too much money to burn.

He had no luck either in Akasaka, another bright grid of streets loaded with bars, clubs, joints, particularly soaplands, those slippery palaces of hygiene and blow jobs, but not quite as sophisticated as Ginza. A lot of loose lips, in more ways than one; in the soaplands. Again, nothing. Nobody was talking.

He tried bouncers, barkeeps, hostesses, jazz musicians, rockers, cops, dealers, a few low-ranking yaks, people he knew or who knew of him. He spread a fortune around doing all the places: Cavern Club, Crocodile, Fukuriki Ichiza, Gaspanic Bar, Geronimo Shot Bar, Ichimon, Hobgoblin Tokyo, Shinjuku Pit Inn, Ruby Room, Nanbantei, Milk, Maniac Love, Warrior Celt, Xanadu, and Yellow. He got names and places from guys and moved on to other guys, other places, but generally he got the same warning, high town or low.

'Baby, you don't want to ask about that guy. That guy's serious. If he finds out, he'll come to call in the night and you'll end up cut to noodles.'

'I hear you. It's just I heard a little something, I'd like to lay it out.'

'It'll lay you out, Yamamoto-san. You'll die for the glory of the *Tokyo Flash*. Is that what you want?'

'Thanks, bud.'

'Good luck, man.'

He tried Nishi Azabu, Roppongi, Harajuku, and Shibuya Center Gai, even Ebisu, popular

260

with the expatriate set, though it was almost unthinkable that a *gaijin* would know something before a Nipponese would.

No, no, no, nothing. Instead, he came upon a yak scoop, having nothing to do with anything at all. Still, it was all the buzz, and he heard it in a dozen places. The yak talk was porn talk, almost the same thing. The boys at Imperial had made some big American connection and were cooking up a deal; it looked like they'd be getting western stars, blond girls, into their product line, and that looked promising if they could only get import licenses. Anyone who got American product into Japan stood to make a fortune, as the Japanese hunger for white women was well known. And if you could get white women to do the Japanese things — *bukkake*, subway groping, pig snout rings, bondage, urination fantasy, rape, teacher, airline hostess, office lady — the profits would be huge. But until now no one had been able to break the ban on foreign product; nobody had the juice to get it through customs. One man stood against it.

Miwa, called 'the Shogun' because he was the genius at Shogunate AV, was known for his ferocious interest in keeping Japanese porn Japanese; the Shogun worked hard to keep the laws really tight so that any American outfit trying to set up business in Japan would find itself ensnared in legal troubles and police harassment. It was almost certain he was a nationalist crackpot, as were many yaks with business connections and many businessmen with yak connections.

The Shogun was head of AJVS, the All Japan Video Society, the professional group that represented Big Porn's interests and worked with the Administrative Commission of Motion Picture Codes and Ethics, which theoretically regulated the porn industry, though it was more frequently thought to be a subsidiary of AJVS by virtue of collateral interest or out-and-out bribery. The key to the Shogun's power was his presidency of AJVS, which in turn made him the most influential figure of the Administrative Commission; it made him the boss, really, of porn. If he lost that, he lost everything. And his term at AJVS was up. Word had it that for the first time in years, bribe money was being spread around to the other porn studio execs — there were hundreds of studios — to deny the Shogun reelection; if Imperial took over AJVS, they took over the Administrative Commission as well; they'd open up trade with the Americans. As rich and powerful as Miwa was, how could he stand against a huge tsunami of American capital, ravenous for the incredibly flexible gymnastics of the classic Japanese pussy? He hated the Americans. It was more than anything rational, it was cultural: their product was uninteresting, it had no ideas, it reflected a society of decadence and softness. 'Keep Japanese pornography Japanese!' the Shogun said.

That's all the boys were talking about. It was like a war was going to break out, and maybe it was, as both Imperial and Shogunate AV had their powerful sponsors in the business. Maybe the streets would run red with blood as the two porn giants tried to dominate and set the future.

'Nah. The porn people may have yak money in them, and yak influence, but they don't like to go to the blades. They'd rather sue or try to ruin each other with unsubstantiated rumors. They'd never kill. They get too much pussy. If you get a lot of pussy, you don't see the point in cutting someone's head off, especially when it might get you your head cut off.'

'Maybe Kondo is signing up with one of those outfits just as a threat, a hint of future difficulties,' Nick said to this source, a detective on the Organized Crime Squad, who knew.

'He's above that crap. His thing is the elegant, perfect hit. He's not going into alleys with hoods and start madly hacking off heads. It's too common. He picks his jobs, that's all. He'd never get involved with porn. He's old school. He's like all the stiffs who hate Miwa for making millions off pussy.'

'Sure,' said Nick. He slid over ten 10,000-yen notes.

'Wow,' said the cop, 'that's a nice tip. You won't tell anybody I talked to you?'

'You bet I won't,' said Nick, 'and you won't tell anybody I talked to *you?*'

'You think I want to spend my last eight seconds bleeding out in an alley?'

★ ★ ★

Finally, only Kabukicho was left. He was well known there, and it made him feel a little vulnerable. But he had no choice. He knew this

263

was dangerous and Kabukicho was Otani's and clearly Kondo had an Otani connection. The wires in Kabukicho would be direct; any questions he asked would get to the wrong people fast.

He knew he ought to hire somebody to do the asking for him, somebody from out of town so it wouldn't get back that it was Nick Yamamoto, the Tokyo Flash, the Clark Kent of the Tokyo tabloid scene, on the trail.

But he couldn't resist. He had that reporter gene. He wasn't an elegant writer, he wasn't ambitious for power, fame, or money, but he just had to know a little bit more, a little bit sooner. That's what drove him. It was such a high — it got you much higher than the White Girl, which is why he was able to walk away from the White Girl for personal use, though he didn't mind making a buck or two off her once in a while — to hear something first. There was that moment when you knew what nobody else knew. God, what a buzz, what a jolt.

He began casually, with people he knew were so minor they were probably unconnected to anything big.

'Anything going on? I'm thinking some kind of realignment. A certain guy who's worked with Otani on some delicate matters now working with someone else, someone big, someone from a little outside? Hear anything?'

'I think I know who you're talking about, but I don't ever discuss him. It's not healthy. He'd cut off my arm and make me eat my tattoos.'

He went everywhere, Queen Bee, the S-M

264

Club, Mysteria Purity, Le Grand Bleu, MoMo Iro, everywhere, talking to anyone, whores, image club performers, trannies, enforcers, bouncers, cutters, the odd Chinaman, the odd Korean, the odd African, impersonators, pickpockets, and everywhere it was the same.

Nothing. Nothing.

It was the nothing that had him tantalized. There was usually something, but the talk about the upcoming election for presidency of AJVS and its implications on the issue Imperial versus Shogunate AV had become so loud that nothing else was being talked about. It was as if an anvil had been laid across Kabukicho gossip lines. But then finally . . . oh, it was so small. It was so nothing. It was a wisp, a leaf in the wind.

He was in a small club closed to strangers, so late it was early. Scotch was the drink of choice, blues the music and the lighting scheme, smoke the preferred atmosphere. You could hardly see across the room. Nick threw down another Scotch and water, turned to the barkeep, and said, 'Another for me, another for Dad here.'

Dad was a bouncer at Prin Prin, an image club that catered to the fantasy life of the Japanese male, including student-teacher, airline hostess, office lady, kimono. It even had a whole set built to resemble a subway car for those who just had to grope. But even in such a kingdom of the dream cum true, trouble sometimes broke out and thus a fast big man with good hands was needed. His specialty was the 'soft punch' by which he deflated the overly amorous with a thunder blow to the midriff, yet left no scars, no bruises, nothing but a powerful sense of ill-being.

'You didn't hear this from me,' the thunder-puncher said.

'Yeah, yeah, yeah.'

'Swear to god, not from me.'

'Swear to god twice.'

'I have a bitch. She's half Korean, supervises a shift at one of the hand-job joints. Tough little gal. Pretty, but tough.'

'Yeah.'

'She says all the Korean sex workers are nervous because one of their own got disappeared a few months ago.'

'I didn't hear a thing.'

'That's just it: you weren't supposed to. Just here one day, gone the next. But here's what my girlfriend knows that nobody else knows and she didn't even figure it out till she thought about it. The next morning on the way to work, she saw a guy named Nii, some minor hood who somehow got into a good crew and is now off the street — '

'Nii.'

'Nii. She saw him stagger out of a bar where he'd clearly been for hours, go into an alley, and puke his guts out. Just puke. She swears that when he bent over, his jacket fell open and the bottom half of his white shirt was drenched in red.'

'Lord.'

'Like he'd been at some brutal hacking. So who had Nii hacked? The woman? Why would he hack some nothing Korean whore and then make it go away?'

'Maybe he's screwy that way. Jack the Ripper, that sort of thing. Or maybe it's just Kabukicho. The odd whore gets disappeared once in a while. Life goes on. Boo fucking hoo.'

'Sure. But there's something weird here. What was weird, this Korean whore thing, it was somehow set up, all the Korean girls were talking about it for weeks. Her boss kept the gal late so she didn't go to Shinjuku station with the others. She went later, by herself, and somewhere along the walk to the station, real early in the morning, she met up with somebody and just vanished. The Nii thing suggests she was cut.'

'Hmmm. Doesn't have to be Eight-Nine-Three Brotherhood.'

'Yeah, it does. Because the thing was *planned*. Somebody with juice got it set up so that this gal could be, you know, cut from the herd, held for a certain time, then released to go off and be chopped, diced, spindled, mutilated in private. No cops, no witnesses; it was all planned out. And poor Nii had the cleanup job. He wouldn't have the juice to set it up. He's nothing, a servant, a cleanup kid. But he's working for somebody with juice and somebody who likes to cut.'

Nick saw it then: sure, it fit.

Nii would have to work for Kondo. Kondo wanted to cut something. It was all arranged via Boss Otani. But why?

'Do you remember the date?'

'Only that it was just after that soldier-hero and his family got burned up. Remember that? God, that was sad.'

'It was sad,' said Nick.

But his mind was already racing. Kondo had cut the shit out of someone and Nii had helped. Nii was Kondo's boy. So if he wanted to find out what Kondo was up to, he had to find out what Nii was up to.

★ ★ ★

The police records were easy enough to obtain. Nii, Takashi 'Joe.' The photo showed a squat face under long Beatle-style hair, the eyes gleamless with a lack of intelligence or purpose. The photo was taken when he was eighteen, old enough to be arrested the first time. Rap sheet: impressive but hardly incredible. Breaking-entering, time in juvie, assault, robbery, carrying a *wakizashi*, a footloose punk hunting thrills and his own death in the alleyways of Kabukicho. He ran with a street gang called the Diamondbacks. That meant, among other things, he probably had tattoos of diamonds on his back. With his pals, he raised minor hell. Eventually, he did two years hard time for beating a shop owner half to death. He clearly was a guy trying to attract yak attention, and failing. Yet two years ago . . . he disappeared.

Has Mr Nii turned a corner and become a model citizen? Is he now selling life insurance, Popeye's chicken, Nikes, porn? It doesn't seem likely. Far more likely: he's made that dream contact, he's been taken in by somebody, cleaned up, spiffed up, given a haircut, he's put on a suit and a pair of expensive Italian

268

pointed-toe black shoes, he's learned how to tie a tie and cut his nails, and now he moves discreetly and invisibly through the world of yak crime, violent when necessary but not spastically violent, pointlessly violent, the violence of sudden rage. No, now it's controlled and deployed by a much wiser boss.

Nii? You see Nii? Any word of Nii? Where's Nii hang? Remember Nii? That kid, Nii, always gets in trouble, ran with the Diamondbacks. Funny you should mention the Diamondbacks as I think the new bouncer at the Milk was a Diamondback for a while.

Nii? Oh, yeah, Nii. Okay guy, I guess, don't know what happened to him. Not that you'd notice him. He was what you call your average-looking guy, nothing about him stood out. Oh, one thing I remember, yeah, he used to like to go to a bar called Celtic Warrior. He always had a samurai thing. He saw himself as the last of the Toshiro Mifunes. Yeah, Celtic Warrior, it's in Nishi Azabu.

Which is how come Nick found himself sitting in Celtic Warrior in Nishi Azabu on a Thursday night, alone at the bar, nursing a bourbon and water and a headache, trying to maintain his sanity as a bad multiracial goth band played heavily Japanese-influenced Celtic war melodies, an assault on the ears almost too intense to be described, much less endured. The joint was typical plastic shit, with shields and those ridiculous western knight swords like the old kings used hanging crosswise all over the place, and big mock-metallic triangles everywhere, crap

269

out of *Black Shield of Falworth*, all Hollywood phony, all plastic. Some mooseheads and deer hung on the walls too, and there was even a stained-glass window behind the bar. It was so Camelot, or a Japanese version of an American version of a story that had never been true in the first place.

And that's when he saw Nii.

It would have been so easy to miss him. It was only the sullenness in the eyes, their lack of dynamism that clued Nick in. The guy had bulked up considerably, and cleaned up; he now wore a neat crew cut moussed to an inch and a half of vertical, a white shirt, a dark suit, a tie. He could have been any salaryman unless you looked carefully at the fastidious way in which the collar of the jacket fitted the broad neck so perfectly, the way the suit hung with just the faintest dapple to it, picking up a sheen, the razor-vivid line of the trousers crease, their wondrous drape and flow that only the finest silks achieved, and the black shoes that seemed so standard but were actually extremely expensive British oxfords, worn generally by CEOs, ambassadors, and power lawyers. He was $6,000 in wardrobe trying to pass as $400 in wardrobe.

His whole manner was refined, poised, amused, confident. Say, hadn't he come up in the world? And he wore his kingliness well, as Nick observed how extravagantly he was treated by the waitstaff and how generously — but quietly — he responded. He was a happy man, Nick realized; good job, plenty of dough to spend, the future looking brighter and brighter.

Nick watched the play of the evening. Occasionally a band member would come over and pay homage to Nii, occasionally the staff. Others came and paid honor and were rewarded with a smile or a touch; girls too, he seemed to be catnip to girls, that gangster thing just drives them wild.

And after a time luxuriating in the pride of having Made Good, Nii spoke to a young woman — the most childish woman there, Nick noted — and she trotted off to get her coat and tell her friends she wouldn't be going home with them. The two walked out, holding hands, and Nick let a long minute pass before leaving a generous mound of yen on the bar and following.

He shadowed for a while from across the street, and eventually Nii took the little date into a nice apartment building and upstairs. Quickly enough Nick dashed across the street and sited himself a little to the oblique so he could see two sides of the structure. He prayed that Sir Lancelot Nii's place was on one of these two sides, and indeed, within a few minutes, a light on the fifteenth floor came on. Nick counted windows, establishing how far from the corner the apartment was, so that he could get into it tomorrow.

★ ★ ★

Nick got there early. He was wearing a wig, a dark mop, because it occurred to him that it wouldn't do to let the world on to the fact that a blond-haired man much too old for blond hair was stalking a well-known *yakuza* killer.

It didn't take long; a Mercedes pulled up, a black S-Class limo, and Nii, crisply dressed for work, and the girl, looking as if she'd had her brains fucked out and couldn't even comb her hair, stepped into it and it sped away.

Nick had a little thrill. Was Kondo in that car? It was unlikely Kondo would pick up his own crew. More likely he hired a limo service to round the boys up and bring them where they would do that day's business.

Nick crossed the road, went to the apartment's foyer, flashed a credential at the doorman. It was quite an impressive piece of paper, signifying him to be a representative of the Domestic Appropriations committee of the Diet. It was entirely authentic, in its original owner's name, and a Kabukicho forgery expert had expertly glued Nick's picture on it.

'I'm taking depositions on the land scandal,' Nick said. 'Mr Ono,' that being the first name he'd cross-referenced with a phone number listed to that address.

'I shall buzz him, sir.'

'Not if you want to keep your job, you won't.'

'Yes sir.'

'And you won't tell the houseboy either. I know how these places work. You call the houseboy, tip him, and he gets to Ono before I do, Ono has time to destroy incriminating documents, Ono gives the houseboy a huge tip, and he splits it with you. I'm not stupid.'

'Sir, Joji's on fourteen; he won't be involved.'

'You make sure Joji stays on fourteen.'

'Yes sir.'

Nick knew Ono lived on seventeen and so he took the elevator up to that floor, got out, and took the stairway down to fifteen. He quickly established the door that had to lead to Nii's and went down to fourteen. He found the houseman, a dull-looking Korean, smoking a cigarette in a closet on break.

'Oh, there you are, Joji,' he said. 'Dammit, I do this twice a week! I locked myself out of my apartment. Can you let me in?'

Joji looked at him dully, trying to place him.

'It's me, Nii, fifteen-oh-four, come on, Joji, I'm late.'

If Joji hesitated it was only to secure a bigger tip; Nick slipped him a 5,000-yen note, and they went upstairs. Joji used his house key and headed back to his cigarette.

Nick was alone in the apartment. Very nice. Had Nii gone so far as to hire a decorator? The place was very much your modern *yakuza*, without frill or kitsch. No books, but one whole wall given over to a sound system and just about every western rock or rap CD ever cut, a shelf or two of Shogun AV's teacher-blows-Koichi — and oh, say, naughty, naughty, even a few black-market items involving young girls. Nii, you've got some sick bugs in you. There was also, of course, a TV screen big enough to land a jet on.

Skipping through the apartment, Nick counted clichés: the furniture was black leather and chrome with a few modernist gewgaws here and there, crystal sculptures signifying crystal sculpture, a

273

horrible and therefore priceless piece of modern art on the big wall.

Another room was the workout palace, which explained Nii's new body. The space was half dojo; a wall rack held a batch of swords, some wood, some steel, for cutting. In the corner lay a pile of tatami mats.

The bedroom had its own special sort of cliché: the mirror on the ceiling threw back the image of the devastated bed, sodden and twisted and wrecked. Stains and the smell of sweat were everywhere. Handcuffs, lined with soothing foam, still attached to the bedpost, suggested the way the night had gone. Also a coil of rope lay on the bottom half of the bed, so Nii had probably done some tying too. He must have had that Japanese thing for a well-tied knot. As an aphrodisiac, the form of the beautiful young girl, bound and helpless before him, had done wonders for Nii: three discarded, half-full rubbers lay like squashed snakes on the hardwood floor. Nick thought, Oh, to be twenty-five again!

Next, the closet: ten black silk suits, each with a swanky Italian tailor's label, three pairs of black oxfords, twenty pairs of almost-new Nikes, and a pile of neatly ironed and folded white silk shirts.

Nick sat at the desk and began to work through it very carefully. One drawer had a collection of sports magazines, another bank statements, which showed the guy was indeed doing very well, and other bills: dry cleaning mainly, rent, and . . . well, well, well, here we have something very interesting.

It was a series of drawings: three diamonds, crude and amateurish, in the first. In the second, the diamonds had begun to be subsumed by superior imagery, as the new forms obscured the crudity of the original pattern. In the third, the imagery, drawn by a master, had triumphed, and no trace of the diamond remained. The third, a kind of design proposal, had been signed with a name from a tattoo parlor in Shinjuku, Big Ozu. Nick had once done a story for the rag on Big Ozu, favorite skin artist of the *yakuza*. He was your man for snake scales, imitation Kuniyoshi faces, lions, tigers, and bears, as well as fans, scrolls, bamboo, and kanji, all popular *yakuza* motifs. He still tattooed the traditional way: not by electric needle, but more slowly, more painfully by bamboo sliver. So now that he was in the bucks, Nii had hired Ozu to craft a design to absorb his no-class street-gang origins, as if obliterating his sordid past.

The big guy owed Nick a favor, for his piece had driven Ozu's customer list through the roof, including some movie stars and rock singers. And he also knew that men tell their tattooists what they don't tell their wives, bitches, shrinks, and buddies.

26

KATA

'I am not going to strike a child,' Bob said.

'Probably true. But she strike you, often,' said Doshu. He spoke quickly to the girl, who began to carefully assemble her kendo armor.

'This interesting,' Doshu said. 'My pupil Sueko. She will be safe from your blow and armed with a *bokken*. As she short, *bokken* long. When she strikes, much pain. You wear no armor. On the other hand, with a *shinai*, even your strongest blows will not affect her, that is, if you are even able to strike her. Also, as you long, *shinai* short. Yet you must defeat her.'

'Sir, you don't understand. I cannot strike a child.'

'Do not look and see form. Look at what is close as if distant and distant as if close.'

Bob dropped the *shinai* on the floor.

'No, sir. I come from a father whose father beat him terribly when he was a child. He never struck me and he made me understand, one does not strike a child.'

'Then you must go.' Doshu pointed to the door. 'You do not know enough yet. Your mind is soft. You will die quickly if you stay. Go back to America, drink and eat and forget. You are not swordsman. You will never be swordsman.'

Bob saw how cleverly Doshu had penetrated

him. The man had put him in a situation where his strength and speed were meaningless; he could not use them against a child, even if he had wanted to. Something deep in his fiber would prevent him. On the other hand, he had to win. If he didn't win, he'd failed. He would not be a swordsman.

So how could he win? He had to find some way to fight soft. He had to anticipate, move, parry at a level higher than he'd ever been, much higher, and when he saw his opening, he'd have to take it but willfully disconnect from those things that made him a man — his strength, his speed. He had to take command of his subconscious and will it to govern him to a smoothness he didn't have, a quickness no one had. He was trapped.

'I will fight,' he said. 'But if I hurt her, I will hurt you. Those are the stakes here, sir. You understand that. You can't put her in jeopardy without risking your own ass. And don't think you can go aikido on me. I know that stuff too. I've been in a few dustups. Here, look, goddammit.'

Bob yanked down the corner of his little stupid jacket and showed the old man a few places where hot metal had tried to interrupt his life span. They were puckers, frozen stars of raised flesh, long gashes, healed but never quite vanished, relics of a forgotten war.

'I have seen much blood, my own and others'. I can fight, don't you forget it.'

Doshu was not impressed.

'Maybe then you be good against little girl.

But I think she whip ass.'

Bob faced the child. She looked like some tiny druid priestess. Her *bokken*, stout white oak, looked like Excalibur or Beheader of Kira and when she drove it into him, it would bruise to the bone. Her head was encased in a padded helmet, her face covered by a steel cage; the helmet wore two thick pads that flared laterally to cover her neck and shoulders. Her torso was encased in padding, and both arms and wrists as well; she wore heavy gloves; she looked part goaltender, part catcher, part linebacker, and 100 percent pure samurai.

They moved to the center of the dojo floor, bare feet on bare wood, under the wooden struts that sustained the place, which felt more like temple than gym. Swords hung on the wall, ghosts flitted in the distance.

She bowed.

He bowed.

'Five strikes wins. Also, kendo much head. I have asked Sueko not to hit head unless necessary. Also, war, not kendo. So any killing strike wins, not only kendo targets. Understood?'

He waited a second, permitting no questions, and then said, 'Guard position.'

Bob stepped back, to *segan-kamae*, the standard high guard, his sword before him at 45 degrees, both elbows held but not locked, the tip pointing to her eyes. It was a solid defensive position, but you couldn't do much with it. She, meanwhile, fell to *gendan-kame*, with her sword held low, pointed down and to the left. It was an offensive position, quick to lead to stunning blows, less efficient for blocking.

Bob tried to find the rhythm that had sometimes been there for him and sometimes not. He tried not to see 'her,' that is, the child; instead he tried to see her *bokken*, for it was his real enemy.

Doshu stood between them, raised a hand, and then his hand fell.

He stepped in fluidly, she countered a little to the left, and suddenly, like quicksilver, she went low to high — 'dragon from water' — and he could not get his *shinai* into a block fast enough by a hair, and she slipped her blade under his guard, screamed '*Hai!*' with amazing force, and he felt the bitter bite of the white oak edge, classic *yokogiri*, against his ribs. God, it hurt.

He realized, I have just been killed by a child. With live blades, she would have cut his guts out.

'One for Sueko. Swagger nothing.'

Rage went through him, red and seething. He had an impulse to revert to bully's strength, flare and howl and race at her, using his bulk to intimidate, but he knew he wasn't fast enough or smooth enough and that no answers lay in the land of anger. She would coolly destroy him.

She attacked, he gave ground and parried two of her blows; then, being limber and flexible, she split almost to ground level and swept at his ankles, but somehow the solution came exactly with the attack itself, and he found himself airborne — he knew that leaving the ground was a big mistake, one of the 'three aversions,' to be avoided at all times, but in this case unavoidable

— to miss the horizontal cut and, as he came down, he tapped her on the thick pad of the shoulder, near the neck, a somewhat uninspired *kesagiri*.

'Bad cut, Swagger. But still, you get point. One to one.'

The next two flurries were in hyperspeed. He could not stay with her for more than three strikes and she seemed to gain speed as he lost it, and each time, '*Hai!*' the *bokken* struck him hard, once across the wrist, making him drop the *shinai*, once on his good hip, a phenomenon known in football as a stinger. Oh, hoochie mama, that one hurt like hell.

Sweat flooded his eyes and he blinked them free, but they filled with water and the keenness of his vision went.

He felt fear.

He had to laugh. I've been shot at ten thousand times and hurt bad six times and I am scared of a little girl.

Was it the fear or the laughter or both? Somehow something began to come through him. Maybe it was his blurred vision, maybe that thing in sports called 'second wind,' maybe a final acceptance of the idea that what came before meant nothing, there was only now, and her next kata seemed to announce itself, he took it on the lower third of the blade, ran her sword to ground, recovered a hair faster, and slashed the *shinai* across her center chest, *kesagiri*. She didn't feel it, given the heavy padding, but Doshu's educated eyes were quick to make note.

'*Hai!*' Bob proclaimed.

'Too late. Must deliver blow and shout in one timing. No point.'

Bad call. That was kendo; this was war. But you forget bad calls, as every athlete knows, and when she came, he knew it would be from the left, as all her previous attacks had been right to left; in the split second she drew back to strike, he himself unleashed a cut that seemed to come from nowhere, as he had not willed it or planned it; it was his fastest, best cut of the afternoon, maybe even the whole week, and he got his '*Hai*' out exactly as he brought the *shinai* tip as smooth and soft as possible across the left side of her head, and felt the bop as it hit her helmet.

'Kill, Swagger.'

He dropped back, going again to *segan-kamae*. He saw what she had that he didn't. It wasn't that she was stronger or faster. It was that she got to her maximum concentration so much quicker than he did, and her blows came so fast from the ready position; he could stop the first, the second, maybe the third, but by the fourth, he was behind the curve and he missed it.

Yet the answer wasn't in speed.

Not if you 'tried' speed, in the Ooof!-I-must-do-it! way. You could never order yourself to that level of performance.

What was the answer?

The little monster, however, had altered her stance. She slid into *kami-hasso*, issuing from above, the *bokken* cocked like a bat in a batter's stance, spiraling in her grip as she would not hold it still because stillness was death.

281

She stalked him, sliding toward him, and now that he was tired, he knew that he'd lost much speed and if he struck first, he'd be slow and she'd nail him for the fourth point, then finish him in seconds and it would be over.

What is the answer? he thought, backpedaling, going through his small bag of tricks, and coming up dry.

Oh, shit.

What was —

He tried to read the eyes, could not see them in the darkness of the helmet; he tried to read her sword, it was a blur; he tried to read her body, it was a mystery. She was just it: death, the enemy, all who'd sought to vanquish him and failed, coming in this time on a surge of adrenaline and serious attitude, sublimely confident, aware that he could do nothing but —

'The moon in the cold stream like a mirror.'

Musashi said it four hundred years ago, why did it suddenly appear in his mind?

Suddenly he knew the answer.

What is the difference between the moon in the sky and the moon in the water?

There is no difference.

They have become one.

You must become one with your enemy.

You must not hate him, for in anger is sloppiness. You must *become* him. And when you are him, you can control him.

Bob slid into *kami-hasso* and felt his body begin to mimic hers, to trace and somehow absorb her movement until he felt her and in some strange way knew her. He knew when she

282

would strike for he could feel the same wave building in himself, and, without willing it, struck first with his shorter sword and would have sliced both hands off had there been an edge to his weapon. The sword had done it. The sword saw the opening; the sword struck, all in microtime.

'Strike, Swagger. Three — three.'

It was like he'd found a magic portal to her brain; the next strike went quicker still, a tap through her defenses to her solar plexus, so soft he couldn't exactly recall delivering it but just felt the shiver as the split bamboo splines of the *shinai* bulged to absorb the impact.

'Hit, Swagger, four — three.'

She suddenly knew rage. Champions are not supposed to fall behind. He had broken her; she lashed out, issuing from above, yet as fast as she was, he felt tranquillity as the blade dived toward him in perfect *shinchokugiri*. He turned, again without force, and caught her under the chin, a blow that in a fight would have decapitated her.

'*Match!*' yelled Doshu.

He withdrew, assumed a formal position, and bowed deeply. Becoming her, he now loved her. Becoming her, he felt her pain at defeat. He felt no pride. It wasn't Miller Time. He felt honored to have fought one so valiant.

She took off her helmet and reverted to child: the face unlined, unformed, though dappled with adult sweat, the skin smooth, the eyes dark and piercing. She returned the bow.

She spoke.

'She say, '*Gaijin* fight well. I feel him learning.

283

I feel his strength and honor. He an honorable opponent.''

'Tell her please that I am humbled by her generosity and she has a great talent. It was a privilege to learn from her.'

They bowed again, then she turned and left and at a certain point skipped, as if she'd been let out of school early.

'Okay, it worked. I learned something. The moon thing. I got it, finally.'

'Tomorrow I will speak certain truths to you. I must speak Japanese. No English. You know fluent Japanese speaker?'

'Yes.'

'You call. I tell this person some truths, he tell you.'

'Yes.'

'I give you truth. Are you strong for truth?'

'Always.'

'I hope. Now wash floor of dojo. Scrub, water hot. Wash down all surfaces. Go to kitchen, assist my mother. Then cut wood.'

★　★　★

Okada was surprisingly agreeable. She left Tokyo early the next morning and rammed her RX-8 into Kyoto in about five hours, arriving at noon. She parked out front, and Bob, who'd been washing dishes under Doshu's mother's stern eye, saw her arrive, in her neat suit, her beautiful legs taut, her eyes wise and calm behind her glasses, her hair drawn up into a smooth complexity of pins and stays, tight like everything about her.

284

She came in, having replaced her heels with slippers, and was greeted by a child, then led into the dojo. She didn't even look at Swagger; instead, she bowed to the approaching Doshu.

'Hi,' Bob said, 'thanks for coming.'

She turned. 'Oh, this ought to be really good.'

Then she turned back to Doshu and they talked briskly. She asked questions, he answered. She asked more questions. They laughed. They talked gravely. He made policy statements, she gently disagreed, and he defended his position. Swagger could hear the rhythm of discussion, the rise of agreement, the fall of disagreement, the evenness of consensus.

Finally, she turned to Bob.

'You got it all?' he asked. 'He says I'm a moron and I ought to be kicked out. I thought I did pretty well yesterday. I beat a ten-year-old girl.'

'That ten-year-old girl is Sueko Mori, the prodigy. She's famous. She won the All Japan Kendo Association for twenty-one-unders a week ago. She's a star. If you beat her, you did okay.'

'That little kid?'

'That little kid could beat most men in this country. Are you ready?'

His annoyance tamed by this information, Bob nodded.

'Doshu says you learn fast. You are athletic. You are strong, with quite a bit of stamina. Your left side is stronger than your right side, and your rising diagonal is stronger than your falling diagonal. He does not know the explanation.'

'Tell him I spent a summer swinging a scythe, low to high, left to right. Those muscles are

285

stretched and overly developed.'

'Well, he really doesn't care. Next, he says you have good character and work habits. He worked you like a dog. If you had a weak character or bad work habits you would not have stood for the grueling ordeal and the humiliation. He was very impressed with that aspect of your behavior. He thought, after the first day, you might make a swordsman. Your mind was right. Untrained but right.'

'Well, thank him.'

'He doesn't require thanks. He's not congratulating you, he's telling you what is.'

'Sure.'

'But, he says, it is possible to be too athletic, too strong, too hardworking. The hard worker tends to oversegment, the athlete to trust reflex and muscle. So, though you picked up the moves very quickly, you had trouble integrating.'

'He said 'integrating'?'

'He said 'becoming one timing.' I said integrating.'

'Okay.'

'He says that yesterday, finally, under pressure of the match with Sueko Mori, you integrated. Your learning curve in that match was extraordinary. You went in a nobody, you came out a swordsman. You must learn to develop that feeling, that sensibility; it is your only hope.'

'So he thinks I'm okay?'

'Well, that's where he goes a little opaque on me. He stops well short of declaring you the next Musashi. He says you still have problems. But he says you have advantages too. Thus he has an idea of what you can or can't do, and how you must operate.'

'Please, go ahead.'

'He says you are not Tom Cruise. There is no Tom Cruise. No one can learn the sword in days or weeks, except in movies. He hated that movie, by the way. However, you have done a great deal more than most.'

'Okay.'

'You must know your weaknesses and strengths and maneuver accordingly. That is strategy. You have *not* become a great swordsman. You have become an almost proficient swordsman. You will lose to any proficient *yakuza* swordsman. You will only win under one circumstance: against someone younger, who hasn't been in a fight and will panic at the sight of his own blood. You're a warrior, you've seen blood, others' and your own. Blood doesn't scare you, turn you to jelly. Thus, you know that in a fight you will be cut, you will bleed. Your opponent may not. He will see blood, his own or even yours, and he will tighten, lose his rhythm, his concentration. He will die; you will survive.

'Other than that, stay away. If you fight others, you will die. You are not strong enough to cover all the sectors of defense. The longer you go, the slower you will get. A good swordsman will play you out, waiting for your sword to still or drop, for your concentration to falter, and then he will kill you. In fights, you must win quickly, one, two blows, or you will die. The longer you fight, the larger the chance that you will die. You survive not merely on your sword, but on your guile in fighting only those you can beat and never those you cannot beat. A great swordsman will kill you in a split second.'

'He knows,' Bob said. 'He sees where this is going. He's telling me I cannot fight Kondo.'

Doshu heard the name and turned to Bob.

'Swagger-san,' he said, with something almost but not quite like affection. 'Kondo: death.'

★   ★   ★

They roared through the Japanese night in her Mazda, the rush of the wind so intense it precluded conversation. Maybe there wasn't much to say, anyway. Kyoto was a blur of light behind them, Tokyo not yet a blur of light ahead of them. She kept the red sportster up well over eighty miles an hour, driving with calm deliberation, all intensity and concentration.

But after a couple of hours, it began to rain. She pulled over to the shoulder. A car, too close behind, screeched and honked.

'What's his problem?' Bob said.

'He was too close. I should have signaled. Can you latch the top?'

'Sure.'

She pressed a button and the rubberized roof came out of its compartment, unfolding on an ingenious structure until it covered the cockpit. He got it latched without trouble, though the mechanism, clever and Japanese, was new to him.

'Do you want me to drive? You must be exhausted. Now it's raining.'

'I'm fine. I'm a big girl. Anyway, you're just as tired as I am.'

'No, I didn't get much sleep there, that's for sure. That old guy worked me to the bone. 'Eight cuts! Eight cuts!' I haven't worked that hard in years.'

'You are a hardworking guy,' she said. 'Believe me, I know plenty who aren't. My supervisor likes to cultivate 'the big picture,' which means I do the work and he's out on the links chatting up businessmen. But I guess it's okay that he's lazy, because he's so stupid if he worked hard he could really screw up.'

'Amazing how full the world is of assholes,' he said. 'Anyway, have you heard from Nick yet?'

'No, nothing. I checked my phone and e-mail before we left. I'll check again.'

She flipped open the little jointed piece of plastic, worked it over, its bright glow illuminating her grave face, and then announced, 'No, nothing yet.'

'Okay.'

'What are your plans? You have to tell me, Swagger. I'm so afraid, now that you think you're Yojimbo, you'll go out on your own.'

'No, I told you I'd clear everything through you and I will. I'd hoped to hear from Nick, that's all.'

'Suppose you don't.'

'Then I'll try and find a private investigator, a guy with *yakuza* connections, maybe an ex-cop, and we'll turn him loose on the case. Maybe I should have done that already. I didn't think of it. I was just thinking of how to keep that old man from whacking me black and blue.'

'A private eye won't work. If Kondo doesn't want to be found, the PI will know it and he will just take your money and conveniently come up with nothing. Nick's got the guts to ask around; I doubt anybody else does.'

'Then I'll go to Kabukicho and start kicking in doors on *yakuza* joints and asking loud, impolite questions about Kondo. That should get me noticed.'

'That should get your head delivered to the embassy by Black Cat Courier by Monday.'

'Then I don't know. Maybe I *am* overmatched on this one.'

'On the other hand, you've learned stuff — '

Her cell phone rang. She checked the number ID and said, 'It's Nick.'

She hit talk.

'Hello, Nick, what is — '

But then she was quiet.

'Oh, hell,' she said.

'What?'

'It was Nick. But he said, 'Susan, I fed the dragon.''

''Fed the dragon'? What the hell could that mean?'

'I don't know. But it was also his voice. It was full of fear. Real, ugly fear.'

'Oh, Christ,' Bob said.

She dialed Nick's number. There was no answer.

27

THE SAMURAI

Nick had it, or most of it. He sat in his kitchen under a bright lamp, looked at his notes, an outline, a time line, charts of consequences, phone numbers, the whole thing: amazing how it came together, how quickly.

The tattoo artist, Big Ozu, had told him of Nii's bragging about easy street from now on, and how he could afford to have his back finished and the horrible, crude diamonds hidden in an abstract of classical Japanese shape and color and the kanji inscription, 'Samurai forever.'

It took some doing and a mighty investment in the world's best sake, but Nick finally got Ozu to reveal the darkest secret: the name of the man to whom Nii, through Kondo, was now pledged. It was as if Kondo's clan had found a new daimyo, its connection to the ruling powers was now so much more powerful.

It was a name he already knew: Miwa.

Miwa, the shogun of Shogunate AV and head of AJVS, at that very moment stuck in a power struggle with Imperial to maintain command of Big Porn, trying to keep it Japanese against Imperial's hunger to Americanize the industry and bring white women in.

Now, what could Kondo do for this man, and

of what meaning would a sword, a special, important, historical sword be?

Nick could have left it there: the man just wanted the sword because he was a collector, this was the mother of all swords, to add it to his collection would be —

But then why didn't he just buy it from Yano? And why were Yano and his family wiped out, why were certain suggestions given so that the unfortunate tragedy of the Yanos was not pursued with alacrity and instead allowed to drift? It hadn't even been assigned to a senior investigator.

So Nick began to look at Miwa. It turned out there was quite a lot of data: Miwa's career was storied, publicized, even self-publicized. It was the tale of a poor boy, going from nothing to something and conquering Japan in a way few men had since the shogun, an irony in itself. Miwa lived in luxury with houses everywhere in Japan, seven in Tokyo, two in Europe, one in Vail, one in Hollywood, one in New York. He traveled by private jet, he consorted with millionaires and movie stars, his amorous adventures were legendary.

How could such a man want one thing more?

And Nick realized that it wasn't 'one thing more' — it was simple survival. He saw now how a sword could help Miwa and establish his line forever.

Against that, the deaths of the Yanos was nothing. Really, what was it? A mother, a father, four children? You could cut them down and leave them. That, simply, was the eternal order of the universe. Who were they next to greatness? What were they? Compared to the fabulousness of Miwa and the scope of his ambitions, what did they weigh? Who cared for them? No samurai would rise to their defense. They must yield to the inevitability of it all, and cease to impede Miwa in his march to glory.

Nick needed a drink. He went to the refrigerator and got out a bottle of sake. He struggled with the plasticized cap and finally, in frustration, got out a small kitchen knife, sliced the plastic off, and poured himself a drink.

Ah. The taste of sake, so utterly Japanese. He set the knife down on the table and sat back. He allowed himself to take some pleasure.

Nick saw a golden life before him, where it would all go: his scoop would shock the world, an arrest would follow, Japan's foundations would be shaken, the world's journalists pouring in upon him as the scandal reached epidemic proportions, his own redemption.

He would be back after his various misadventures with Lady Kokain. It would be —

Nick heard something, a strange sound, he didn't know what it was, then realized it was some heavy object being laid against his doorjamb, and in the next second he heard the crash of wood splintering, of the door giving, and the sound of footsteps.

Nick knew immediately.

He scooped his notes up and stuffed them in a manila envelope.

He had seconds.

He fought panic.

Then he saw where he could hide them.

He raced to that spot, rolled them up, and shoved them in.

Then he picked up his cell, punched Susan Okada's number, worried about being tapped, tried to think of some unique way to reach her, a suggestion, a code even, that she and she alone would recognize.

'Susan,' he said when she answered, 'I fed the dragon.'

Then he turned and saw his old friend Nii advancing on him with a pugnacious look and a *wakizashi* in his hand; behind him came Kondo, and Nick had the biggest scoop of his life.

Now he knew who Kondo was.

Now he knew why some people got to see Kondo and others didn't.

He also realized they would torture him beyond description to learn what he knew and who he had told and who he was working with.

Nii raced to him but wasn't in time.

Nick plunged the knife into his own carotid and bled out, smiling, in eight seconds.

28

DRAGONS

They got there by midnight. The traffic in Nick's neighborhood was normally nonexistent at this hour, but tonight it was terrible. Four blocks from Nick's, the lanes froze into gridlock; nobody was going anywhere.

'There's a cop up ahead, trying to get this sorted out,' Susan said.

'I'm going to slip out and see what I can see. If I don't make it back in time, I'll meet you at Nick's.'

'That doesn't make any sense. Everybody will notice a *gaijin*. I'll go. You scoot over and stay with the car.'

She got out; he moved behind the wheel and waited.

Ten minutes later the car hadn't moved an inch, but Susan was back. As she approached, he could see, from the slowness of her movements and her downcast expression, that the news was very bad. She ducked into the seat.

'They burned it. Like the Yanos'. Burned it to a crisp. Burned the houses on both sides too.'

'Maybe he got out.'

'No,' she said from far away, 'he didn't. The cop said a man was dead. A suicide. He set his house on fire, then he cut his own throat. They carted him away to the morgue an hour ago.'

Swagger tried not to concentrate on Nick, poor Nick. He tried not to feel rage or pain or despair. He remembered Doshu: 'Only now.' Only now. Yeah, right, but get me off this goddamned frozen star, the alien place where everybody I talk to gets whacked hard and ugly by men of shadow I have never even seen and the game is nothing I understand.

Only now. Only now. Think it through.

She didn't say anything but just sat there for the longest time. Her almond eyes seemed unfocused; maybe she was seeing afar with a close-up eye and seeing close-up with a distant eye.

'Poor Nick,' she said at last. 'I think he was finally in the clear.'

'Smart guy. Brave guy. The best.'

'Poor guy — '

'Look, I'm not the boss or nothing, but we have to think this through. If Nick cut his own throat, it means Kondo Isami found him and he knew he'd be tortured. He knew these boys. So he went out samurai.'

'I hate to think of that.'

'Well, ma'am, somebody has to think of that, so I guess I'll go ahead and be the one.'

'You know, it makes me sick how good at all this you are.'

'I understand that. I make a lot of people sick. I'm a sergeant, it's my job. We are in a war, people are dying, people are in danger, so let's just figure out a next move.'

She was silent. Then she said, 'I can't think in this car. We'll go to a coffee shop. I have to get out of this stupid traffic.'

The place was half-empty. They got coffee at the counter, then found a table at the back. Starbucks. It was like being in Iowa.

'Okay,' Swagger said, 'you tell me if I'm right. You're smart. I only went to high school.'

'New rule: sarcasm not permitted. Sarcasm out of bounds. Get it?' she said angrily.

'I apologize. It was stupid. It won't happen again. Okay, here's where we are. Nick found something. We don't know what. But somehow they heard about it and came after him. He gave you a clue. So somehow he had enough time to hide what he had and to call you. 'Susan, I fed the dragon.' Then he cut his own throat, knowing that if they got to him, they'd torture him and he'd give everything up. Little skinny Nick, more samurai than any of those boys. And here's another thing I have figured out. See if you agree.'

'Okay.'

'They didn't burn the place for no reason. They figured out he'd learned something, and they were worried he'd left it. They couldn't find it. They burned the place so that whoever he was working with couldn't find it either. There's no point in burning the place otherwise. It just attracts attention and the last thing these people need is attention.'

'That makes as much sense as anything.'

'Okay, so let's think about the clue Nick gave you. Maybe I'm full of shit, but it can't be that hard. He cooked it up in two seconds. You said he sounded scared on the phone. He knew they were there. He hid whatever it was fast, he came up with a clue fast, and it was something only you knew.'

'But what does that tell us?'

'It means it plays off something you know. 'I fed the dragon.' No, no, 'Susan, I fed the dragon.' Not dragons in general, not dragons in history, not dragons in no poetry or movies or songs, but a dragon that Susan knows. So what we have to do is find a point where three things touch: Susan, Nick, and a dragon. What does Susan know about dragons?'

'Nothing.'

'Did you ever discuss dragons with him?'

'No.'

'Did he ever mention them to you?'

'No. Never. The first time I heard the word 'dragon' from his mouth was last night.'

'What was the first thing you thought when he said 'I fed the dragon.''

'Oh, this is helpful. I thought, What the fuck is he talking about?'

'Are there any dragons in your past?'

'I dated a couple, that's all. I was married briefly to one.'

'Think of what a dragon could be or relate to. A team name? Your high school football team — I'm betting you were a cheerleader — was it the Dragons?'

'I was the head cheerleader. It was the Panthers.'

'Ever study, uh, what's it, dinosaurs?'

'Paleontology, archaeology, geology. No, never.

Russian and Japanese literature.'

'Oh, *that's* helpful. You can make a lot of dough off *that*.'

'Swagger, I gave you sarcasm warning number one. One more violation and you're on your way to Arkansas.'

'Idaho. Let me say some dragon things to you. You react. Maybe it'll jog a memory.'

'Fire away.'

'Flying dragons.'

'Nothing.'

'Sleeping Beauty.'

'Nah.'

'Prince Charming?'

'No such thing.'

'Reptiles.'

'Are dragons reptiles?'

'Well, they're green and scaly. They're like dinosaurs or big alligators.'

'Do they have two-chambered hearts? Are they cold-blooded?'

'I don't know.'

'I don't know either.'

'Chinese dragons?'

'No.'

'Dragons in parades? You know, people under a long dragon thing?'

'Wouldn't that be a Chinese dragon?'

'Dragon bones? Dragon wings? Dragon tracks? Dragon breath?'

'No, no, no, no.'

'Flying Dragons.'

'You said that.'

'A gang called the Dragons?'

'No.'

'A triad called the Dragons?'

'No.'

'A flying dragon kick from karate?'

'No.'

'The sleeping dragon? That's kendo move, low to high.'

'I *know* what it is. No, not that.'

'A Chinese restaurant called the Dragon.'

'No.'

'Saint George?'

'No.'

'Saint Andrew?'

'No.'

'Prince Charming.'

'You did that one already. This isn't working.'

'Well, I'm pretty much out of dragon stuff. Could it be a picture, a movie, a book, a poem, an article, a paper, a — '

'Hmmm,' she said.

He saw something in her eyes. It was that faraway look: seeing the mountain as if it's close at hand.

'Article?'

'Paper. If dragons are reptiles, does that make them lizards?'

'There are no dragons, so can't they be anything?'

'Well, as you said, green and scaly. That makes them reptiles. So wouldn't they be lizards?'

'I suppose. Why?'

'It's just that — oh, it's nothing.'

'Try it. What the hell?'

'Lizards. I have something in my life dealing

300

with lizards. I *may* have mentioned it to Nick.'

'But you're not sure.'

'Swagger, nobody can remember everything they've said to a casual acquaintance over a five-year period.'

'Of course. Sorry. But you said a paper. School paper. Lizards.'

'Yeah, it's a story I've told a few times in embassies and at the department, at parties and dinners, that sort of thing. Did I tell it to Nick? It's possible. I met him at a party at the Japanese ambassador's residence on Nebraska in D.C. about five years ago. It was low-key professional: I was supposed to chat him up, he was supposed to chat me up. There was some drinking. I may have told him.'

'Tell me.'

'I had a petty good-girl's ambition to graduate from high school with a four-point-oh average. I had to be perfect, and for three years, I was perfect. But my senior year, I dropped a couple of points in advanced-placement biology. I had to somehow make it up, or I'd get a B, and there would go the four-oh. So I went to the teacher and I said, you know, I can't quite make it up on the remaining tests. If I ace them, I still just get an average of three-nine-nine in here. Is there any extra credit thing I could do? He was a good guy. He said, 'Well, Susan, if you wrote me a paper and it was really good on an original subject, I don't see how I could keep from giving you the A that you need so badly.' The joke is, I have no feeling for biology. I just learned it by rote. I had no gift at all and there was nothing I

301

was capable of writing an A paper on. I had no inspiration, no anything. So I went to the *National Geographic* bound volumes in the library and just paged through them. I was looking for something that might stimulate my imagination.'

'And you found something?'

'A lizard. A big, ugly lizard. God, it was ugly. It was about ten feet long, green, carnivorous, with a forked tongue. It was limited to seven islands in the West Pacific near Java. The biggest island was called Komodo, and so the lizard was called a Komodo lizard. So I became an overnight expert on the Komodo lizard — this is before the Internet, I should add — and I did a paper on its prospects in an environmentally diminishing world. I got the A, I was valedictorian, my parents weren't disappointed, and I went on with my life as planned, except of course I didn't marry Jack McBride, but that's another story. The funny thing is, that lizard really helped me by being so interesting. So the joke is, now and then if I'm happy and I've had a few drinks and people are toasting, I toast. My toast is 'Here's to the lizard.' And they all laugh, because it's so unlike little Susan Okada, the Asian grind with the four-oh average who never makes a mistake. I may have told that to Nick, after toasting the lizard. I think a bunch of us, some Japanese journalists and some State people, I think we went to a sushi place in Georgetown. That may be where I did it.'

'And that's it?'

'Yeah. But see, here's the thing. That creature

is also sometimes called a Komodo dragon. Maybe I toasted the dragon and that's what Nick was thinking of.'

'Komodo? Is that a Japanese word? It sounds Japanese.'

'No, it's Indonesian, I think.'

'It sounds Japanese. *Os*, lots of syllables. It could be Japanese.'

'It does sound Japanese. It actually sounds like a Japanese word, very common, *kamado*. *Kamado* simply means stove or oven. It's an inverted ceramic bowl or something. In the old days, most Japanese homes had one. It's a grill, I suppose. You grill fish in it. Usually small, it's — '

They both let it lie there, on the table.

A few minutes passed. Then Bob said, 'Nobody would see the correspondence between the word *Komodo*, the name of the lizard, and the word *kamado*, meaning grill, unless they spoke both English and Japanese well. That would be you. And nobody else would have a Komodo in his background except you. Now, the next question: would Nick have had a *kamado*?'

'He shouldn't have. They all have microwaves now. But he did have one. Don't you remember how his house smelled the night you were over? He had just eaten and he'd grilled some meat. He grilled his meat in a *kamado*.'

'Now, Nick's sitting there, somehow he knows he's about to get hit. It's over. But he doesn't panic, not Nick, he's a cool hand, he's samurai all the way. He knows he can't get out, but he tries to preserve what he's got, which is some documents, that's how he beats his killers. Where's he put them? He slides them into the *kamado*. Maybe there's a liner and he puts them under that, in the bowl. Then he calls you and he's afraid the phone is tapped and the only thing he can think of is that little anecdote from your first meeting and the correspondence between *kamado* and *Komodo*, that only you would see.'

'He was good at puns. He said he loved to write his headlines in his rag because he liked the puns, the more outrageous the better.'

'I think,' said Bob, 'tonight I'm going to pay a visit to the ruins of Nick's house. You tell me what I'm looking for and where it'll be. I'll find it if it's there.'

29

THE SHRINE

It was one of his favorite spots: the secluded cemetery at Sengakuji, the Shrine of the 47 Ronin behind its gate and its imposing statue of Oishi. Here lay the remains of the 47 who'd forged through the walls at Kira's, slaughtered his bodyguard in furious battle, then beheaded the old man. It was as sacred a spot to the Japanese imagination as was possible, and when the Shogun visited, he always called ahead, made certain that the place was 'closed for maintenance' so that he would have it to himself and that the usual clouds of incense smoke from the hundreds of joss sticks lit by supplicants would have cleared away.

Here was naked bushido. It expressed itself on many levels. The bodies themselves, after the mass *seppuku*, were buried at the highest level, in Buddhist fashion, a thicket of vertical grave markers and ceremonial wooden stakes weathering in the rain and snow. One could — and many did — buy a bundle of joss sticks to lay in tribute to the 47 or their lord Asano, who was here also, which was why a low, smoky vapor lingered among the headstones. Below was a museum, for tourists; a courtyard, wide and gravelly, the shrine itself, the typical Buddhist structure of timbers and white plaster of a pattern spread widely

305

across the whole of Asia, under a tile roof with tilted corners, an archetype that on a thousand Chinese restaurants had become a cliché. Here also — between the courtyard on one level and the cemetery on another — was the stream in which the men had washed the head that night so long ago. Here was the vengeance and the loyalty of the retainers. Here were men who'd die before they'd live with dishonor. Their head-stones lay alongside the paths, under the shade of trees. Here is where they presented Kira's head and got a receipt — preserved and displayed in the museum — from the priests:

Noted:
Item: One head
Item: One paper parcel
The above articles are acknowledged
to have been duly received.

Here is where they waited to be arrested; here, months later, after they'd been ordered to commit *seppuku*, here is where their bodies had been taken.

The skylines of Shinjuku or central Tokyo were far away. Fall was upon them, a chill bit the air, soon winter would arrive. The leaves, russet, red, gold-brown, orange, fell to earth in riots of color. He drew his muffler tighter against his neck, pulled his cashmere overcoat tighter, looked and saw bodyguards with receivers in their ears all around.

'You're sure?' the Shogun asked Kondo.

'Not totally, no. But I'm sure that he had

nothing set in type, as we found no page proofs. I'm sure he had made no attempts to talk to police sources because we've canvassed. As far as I can tell he spoke only to a few sources: the tattooist and several, uh, 'experts' in Eight-Nine-Three affairs. All have been spoken to, all have owned up, all have been remonstrated against. They will not betray us again. For Yamamoto, I'm sure he had nothing except the possible suspicion that you and I had made an alliance.'

'Still, it's disturbing. At this time, particularly, when things are so delicate and hanging in the balance.'

'Most likely, sheer coincidence. Someone saw something, and maybe this reporter had a hunch. He was well versed in the ways of our brotherhood, he knew who to ask, and he made some slight penetration into our business. Alas, his hair was blond like Charlize Theron's and someone noted him and sold him to us. We dealt with him. That is the order of business. As for any information he may have learned, it almost certainly died with him.'

'You're sure?'

'Well, Lord, of course there is no 'sure.' I'm as 'sure' as I can be. But I can only talk in probabilities. We never had a conversation with him. His actions precluded that. He knew the conversation would have been unpleasant. But there's no evidence at all he was working for someone and no reason to believe he was. He had as yet assembled no product: we examined his house seriously before lighting it. No notes, no story, no time line. He had nothing but suspicions and they died with him. That is the highest probability.'

'But what were the probabilities that Spruance's Dauntlesses would catch our fellows on their decks refueling? Why would they come in at just that precise moment? The probabilities were infinitely tiny, yet the Americans fell out of the sky, and in five minutes we lost three carriers, three hundred of our best pilots, and the war. I think about that moment often, Kondosan. That moment. Not one minute before, not one minute after. The carriers were turned into the wind, their decks laden with refueling planes. It was Japan's moment of maximum vulnerability during the war, and in that moment the Americans struck.'

'The Americans cheated. They had the codes.'

'I hate the Americans. They *always* cheat. They are stupid and blundering and it doesn't matter because they cheat.'

'I cannot protect you from God's apparent enthusiasm for the Americans, Lord. He makes the unexpected happen, as Midway proves for all time. I cannot protect you from it, just as no one could have protected Nagumo from Spruance's Dauntlesses. No one can protect you from Buddha's whimsy, God's will, the indifference of Shinto, or the sheer random drift of chaos in the universe. It sticks its ugly little head in at the most inopportune time. But we have done everything rational to protect you and to make this thing work and to get you what you so richly deserve. The only thing we can't protect against is bad luck.'

'The Americans always have good luck,' said the Shogun bitterly. 'Now they think they can take over my business, that I am vulnerable, that my planes are on the decks refueling. They are cheating by spreading millions around. It's so unfair.'

'Lord, it will not happen.'

'That's what Kusaka, Nagumo's chief of staff, said too,' said the Shogun glumly.

'I understand. Therefore I have sent my best men to the polisher's, and the security at that point is perfect. These are the boys who visited Yano-san and his family with me — all sworn, all bloodied, all who have cut before. There isn't a man in Japan or even the world who could force the issue at the polisher's. It would be one against six, and six of the best. Nii leads them and he will willingly give his life. He is true samurai. Your head is safe. And so is mine.'

30

SWORD OF LIFE

It was the next evening, past midnight, at the same Roppongi Starbucks.

He put it before her. It was slightly scorched, but he gently opened the manila envelope and one by one spread the documents out onto the table of the coffeehouse. He could see Nick's handwriting in kanji running up and down the pages of vertically lined *genko yoshi*.

'And no one saw you?' Susan asked.

'I done some crawling in my time. I got in close as I could, then crawled past the other houses till I reached the ruin. I didn't even have to go inside; I found the *kamado* buried under some fallen timber close to the first-floor patio in the backyard. Half the bowl remained intact and the envelope was in the lining between the charcoal chamber and the outer wall. It slid right out. I got my ass gone fast. Total time onsite, less than five minutes. Just in case anyone was watching, I doubled back three or four times. Nobody could have stayed on me, way I ride. I'm in the clear.'

Susan applied the full force of her intelligence to the pieces of paper, now and then shuffling them, now and then righting them, trying to make them assemble into coherence. Bob sat quietly, aware that he no longer existed.

Finally, fifteen minutes and another cup of coffee later, she said, 'Okay.'

'He had it?'

'Most of it.'

'Does it make any sense?'

'Yeah. In fact, it's simple. It's just business.'

'The guy we're after, he's a businessman?'

'Is he ever. His name is Yuichi Miwa, called 'the Shogun.' His fortune is based on pornography: he is the founder of Shogunate AV. Miwa got into DVD early and onto the Internet early; thus he made millions, which, reinvested in newspapers, television, software, games, and so forth, became billions. But now he may lose it.'

'Someone's coming after him.'

'Someone is. It's an up-and-coming AV company called Imperial. Imperial, evidently, has American money behind it; they want to take over the Japanese market, import American women, blondes mostly, to perform in Japanese-style porn. The government has forbidden that for many years, but if Imperial can get it done, their profits would go through the roof. Miwa happens to be president of something called AJVS, the All Japan Video Society, the industry rep group, I guess a kind of MPAA for dirty movies. AJVS works with the government and controls the regulations of the business; under the Shogun, the government has kept American product out of Japan. Miwa's term is almost up and there's an election. He's won unopposed for sixteen consecutive years, but now he's opposed. Imperial is spending a lot of money and is running a slate. There's dozens of smaller porn studios, and they're either going to follow the Shogun or the usurpers from Imperial. See, it's like a lot of industries and regulatory agencies. If you control the industry association, you really control the regulators, in this case something called the Administrative Commission of Motion Picture Codes and Ethics. Really, as it functions, AJVS controls the commission. It *is* the commission.'

'So what does the sword have to do with any of this?'

'Miwa has to win that election. If he loses it, he loses everything. So he needs to do something bold to make himself a beloved institution. He has to transcend porn and become a hero to the people. At that point, the smaller studios and Imperial cannot vote him out. He's too big. He in essence becomes president-for-life. He maintains control of AJVS and the commission and ipso facto the industry; he prevents the American product from coming into Japan. His business thrives; Imperial withers and dies.'

'Now I get it. Yuichi Miwa understands how sword-nuts the Japanese are,' Bob said. 'It will be his publicity masterstroke: he will make a big-deal announcement that he found the most revered relic in Japanese history. It's the actual blade used by the great Oishi in the attack of the Forty-seven Ronin against Lord Kira in seventeen-oh-three. It's the thing that took Kira's head. He'll get all kinds of media. He becomes a hero. That'll establish him as the Great Man of the People who cannot be replaced.'

'The little guys know if the election goes

312

against him, it will be a complete loss of face for the industry. They cannot afford the shame.'

'I see.'

'Yes,' she said, 'and now it swings into line. *That's* why the Yanos had to be wiped out. It had to be entirely a Miwa production, his campaign, his search, his recovery, his restoration, his presentation, all under his auspices. The Yanos mess up that narrative and show the random nature of the process. He's not a campaigner for the culture, he's just a rich guy who bought something off someone. So they had to be eliminated entirely, and their deaths had nothing to do with anything else in their lives. They were just the people who were in possession of the sword. They were in the way. They had to be destroyed for the welfare of the Shogun, their property confiscated.'

'So the Yanos had to die,' Bob said, 'so some creep could win an election for king of teacher-blows-Johnny.'

'Well, you could have put it more eloquently, but essentially that's right.' Suddenly a deep melancholy seemed to overtake her. 'The terrible thing is, I think he wins.'

'Why do you say that?'

'Now it's too late. He has the sword. It's protected, it's guarded, it's hidden. No one could ever get it back. There's no connection to the Yanos. He'll announce it in time for this ridiculous porn election, get all the media, get the TV and the print, and win his little contest. I don't see a legal way of reaching him. I suppose you could give a statement to the police identifying the sword as the one you brought into the country, I suppose we could find police factions that would see it our way, I suppose — '

'Yagyu Munenori, sixteen thirty, *The Life-giving Sword:* 'It is missing the point to think that the martial art is solely in cutting a man down. It is not in cutting people down. It is in killing evil.''

'Forget it, Swagger.'

'I can't. I didn't come across no ocean to give a statement.'

'It's moot. You forget, we don't even know where it is. You can't be Toshiro Mifune because there's no place to be Toshiro Mifune.'

'I'll find the goddamn thing in ten minutes.'

'Swagger, you're proposing a felony. I have a duty to report you to the authorities. I always told you this.'

'Okada-san, you know the authorities have been bought off by Miwa. There ain't no authorities in this case. It's just you and me, redneck and cheerleader. We do something or that little girl is orphaned and there's no justice in it at all. It's just a thousand years of history all over again: big guys with swords cutting people down and laughing about it.'

'That sword is locked and guarded in one of Miwa's seven estates around Tokyo.'

'I can find it in ten minutes.'

'Swagger, it is locked and guarded in — '

'It's being polished.'

'What?'

'The blade needed restoration. He would hire the best polisher in Japan to bring out every last wiggle of the *hamon* on the blade. It has to be beautiful, don't you see? He can't take the blade into his mansions, because the sword polisher's equipment is heavy stone and the art of polishing a sword is delicate, slow; it demands total concentration. Somewhere right now, within a few miles of us, there's a sword polisher working the blade to perfection under heavy guard. The polisher probably doesn't want to work on the sword, but Miwa and his pal Kondo Isami don't care what the polisher wants. They don't care what anybody wants.'

She looked at him.

'So what are you proposing?'

'I go to the shop. I get the sword.'

'That's a plan?'

'I'll knock on the door. I'll say, 'Please give me my sword back.' They will say, 'No, that is not possible.' 'Hmmm,' I will say, 'I'm afraid I must insist.' We will have a spirited discussion.'

'You are insane. You're not a samurai.'

'The samurai left town. You're stuck with the old white guy.'

'They'll kill you, Swagger.'

'Think of something better.'

She couldn't.

31

BATTLE

Susan dropped him at the museum at 6:30 p.m. and it took some yakking to get by the guards and the receptionist as the institution was about to close. But Dr Otowa himself okayed the entry, came down and met Bob at the elevator, and took him through the somber gray light, the solemn quiet, the dignity of the displays, up to the office, where they sat among swords. The swords, behind glass in a humidity-controlled environment, were everywhere, except for the large black door that signified the presence of a vault. Inside it, there had to be more swords.

'Doshu said you learned well. He was very impressed with your skill and character. He is an astute judge of men.'

'Well, sir, glad I came through and that he thought I did okay.'

'Now, you said an emergency.'

'Yes, sir. I think I know where Philip Yano's stolen sword would be. Well, it would be in the restoration process. That being the case, odds are it's at a polisher's because that's the longest, hardest part of the process. I could kick around making phone calls and visits for a week, but I know you're wired into that world. You could find out in a second.'

'You want me to make some inquiries?'

316

'Sir, the way these people operate, I don't think an inquiry digs them out. These people want this blade restored now. They want someone good working crazily to finish the project in a certain time frame. They're running low on time, they have a schedule to meet. They also have to restore the furnishings and scabbard, all at the very top of the art. What that means, I'm afraid, is that there's a polisher who has suddenly disappeared. He's no longer a part of the mix. He hasn't been heard from and his friends are getting worried. He's out of the loop, he's gone off on an unexpected 'vacation,' something like that.'

'I know a journalist who would know. Please sit down while I e-mail him.'

The doctor went to his terminal, logged on.

Bob sat and let his eyes trace the curve and shimmer of the beautiful blades that surrounded him, while hearing the *tappity-tap* of keys. You could watch the comings and goings of designs, as the curves got deeper and deeper, then began to shallow out and rise toward a straight line. Or you could watch the *tsuba* change from a single iron ring, as rugged as a Viking oar, to an elaborate, gold-etched carving, elegant, too beautiful for its ostensible purpose, which was to keep enemy blades from sliding down one's own, to cut the hand off. You could watch the points elongate or shorten, the grooves on the blades reach farther and farther, double up, shrink, then disappear altogether. You could see the play of *hamon*, sometimes feathery and insubstantial where the hard tempered steel of the edge met the softer embracing steel of the spine. All in all, it was quite a display, and even knowing as little as he did, Bob had the sense now of a secret world. *Kissaki, yokote, mitsugashira, hamon, shinogi, shinogi-ji, hira, ha, mune, munemachi, hamachi, mei, mekugiana, nakago, nakagori,* that was it, tip to butt, and he knew what each meant. It was a universe.

'Mr Swagger?'

'Yes, sir.'

'The best sword polisher in Japan is in London, restoring blades for the Victoria and Albert Museum. The second best is in San Francisco, giving a seminar for your countrymen. But the third — '

'The third.'

'The third used to be the best. Only time eroded something of his skill. He is eighty-four. His name is Tatsuya Omote. I have his address.'

'Yes, sir.'

'You're on to something. I fear that three weeks ago, he abruptly canceled an appearance at a conference in Osaka. He's missed the deadline on a commission he undertook for a shrine in Hiroshima. His shop doesn't answer and he no longer responds to e-mail. This is very troubling to his friends, but he did send one e-mail several weeks ago telling them not to worry, he was fine, he simply had an all-consuming project.'

Bob looked at his watch. It had taken seven minutes.

'What now?' the doctor asked. 'Should we call the police?'

'I think that's likely to tip people off rather than set anyone free. I think I'll drop by and see what's going on.'

'That could be dangerous. Are you armed?'

'No, sir. Of course not.'

'Come with me.'

The doctor led him to the vault and spun the dial of the combination lock. He pulled the door back, and Bob had the sense of a great weight shifting on ball bearings.

Bob didn't enter because he wasn't invited. But the doctor emerged in a few seconds with a white weapon.

'*Gendaito wakizashi*. Modern short sword. It was forged in nineteen forty-three by one of the leading *showa* smiths at the height of his powers. It was meant for the smith's son, who was then an officer on an island called Tarawa. Obviously, the son never came back. After the war, the smith remounted the blade in the civilian furniture you see now, which is why the *saya*, the *tsuba*, the *same*, the *saego* are all white. White is our black. It reflects grief.'

The doctor held the sword before him, cutting edge up, and with his left hand removed the white-lacquered *saya*. The naked blade gleamed in the light, beautiful and hungry.

'The old man told me, when the museum acquired his collection, that this was the sharpest, strongest blade he ever made. It was made with love to protect his son. But his son never got to carry it. The old man gave it to me with the idea that I would give it to my son, to protect him, but my son never got to carry it. He died early also. So I give it to you, because you are a son too. I give it to you in hopes that it can protect you with its magic ingredient of a father's love. So this is really a gift to your father, from me. I hope he was a good man.'

'He was a very good man,' said Bob.

'Good. I'm praying that you don't have to use it, but if you do, I know this: it will cut swift and fast and true.'

★ ★ ★

They drove through the suburbs, then farther into the farmlands surrounding Tokyo, the famed Kanto plain. Mountains loomed on the edge of vision, including the great one, Fuji, gigantically big, the clear fall day revealing it vividly. It looked like an advertisement for a Japan that only existed in the minds of western tourists.

'You don't have to do this,' he said. 'I have the bike. I could have found the place on my own.'

'Suppose you get cut. Suppose you're bleeding and you can't work the bike. Suppose someone calls the cops and you have to run away and have no place to run. You're just a big *gaijin* and they'd pick you up in thirty seconds. No, Swagger, I do have to do this. I can't *believe* I'm doing this.'

'It'll be fine.'

'And that's why you're carrying something under your jacket? Something about the length of a sword.'

'Otowa gave it to me, just in case.'

'Swagger, you are going to be so dead or so

locked up and my career is going to be so over.'

'I can handle this.'

'Yeah, the white guy with a week of training. Uh-huh.'

'Don't forget, I beat a little girl.'

At last they found it, on a nondescript street in a nondescript town, a nondescript commercial building with a few ground-floor shops, one of them clearly closed, its curtains drawn. The others in the line sold noodles, sushi, sex movies, liquor, and software games. But the sign over the closed shop simply read Nihonto.

'That's it. That's Tadaaki Omoto's place. God, it looks like a place where they sell cheeseburgers.'

'*Tatsuya Omote*. Can't you get the name right?'

'You're very edgy, Ms Okada. I know what you need. How about some shopping? It's time to go shopping.'

'What?'

'Sure, that always settles folks down. Let's go buy some stuff.'

He got out of the car and strode across the lot. A few steps behind, she followed. He went straight to the liquor store. By the time she'd caught up to him, he had bought a pint of Jack Daniel's.

'This is a very fine drinking whiskey,' he said. 'Would you like some?'

'Swagger, I — '

He paid, about 3,600 yen. He held the bottle out to her, but she shook her head no.

'Okay, in a few minutes. Now, what about a

nice cup of noodles?'

'Mr Swagger, have you had a breakdown? Really, I — '

'No, ma'am, I am fit as a fiddle. I do think we should have some noodles.'

'You are — '

'We should watch for a while before I go into my Toshiro imitation. Come on.'

So the samurai and his companion went into Solo's noodlerama and had a nice cup of noodles each, and a diet Coke. It was actually pretty good. They sat near the window.

'What do you see?' she asked.

'Well, I see a large Mercedes S-Class, black, very shiny, parked in the lot. Your standard yakmobile.'

'You have no idea how many of them are in there. We should call the police.'

'Yes, and what do they find? An old man polishing a sword in the presence of several thugs in suits. Where would the crime be? Would the old man say, 'These guys have terrorized me into polishing this stolen sword'? He would not, because he fears retaliation, and rightfully so. The cops would say, 'How is this sword stolen? Has it been reported stolen?' And of course we'd have to answer, 'We have no proof except for the crazy accusations of Slim Whitman here who claims it's a sword he brought into the country a few months ago.' Then the yaks would say, 'And here's the license for the sword,' which they got from Yanosan. So the sword goes back to the yaks, we're booted out of town, and Mr Tatsuya — '

'Mr Omote, dammit. Can't you get *anything* right?'

'Mr Omote gets back to polishing. Meanwhile, the cops discover my passport ain't no good and I'm arrested. That don't sound too good to me.'

'Come on.'

She led him back to the car.

'Get in.'

She opened her purse, a rather large green leather bag, and handed it to him. He looked inside and saw the grip of a small pistol.

'It's a sterile Chinese Makarov. I got it from a couple of the Agency clowns on the fourth floor. It's loaded with some magic candy called three-eighty hollowpoints, whatever that means, it had the boys all giggly. Take it.'

'No.'

'Swagger, you can't go in there with just — '

'Yes, I can. This game is called swords. It's their game. I beat them at it and that makes me the winner. And throw that thing into Tokyo Bay. It'll get you sent to Japanese women's prison for the next fourteen years and they don't have no Kate Spade bags there.'

'I hope you survive long enough to tell me how a bumpkin from Utah who sounds like Johnny Cash before the cure can identify a Kate Spade.'

'I'm from Idaho out of Arkansas. My daughter made me buy her one. I also bought one for my wife. You must do okay. They ain't cheap. Sure you won't have a drink?'

The question wasn't even sane enough for an answer. She just looked at him. He took the small, flat brown bottle out of the paper bag, cranked off the cap, smiled, toasted her, and said, 'Cheers.'

Then he poured some of it into his hair, and ruffled his hair with his other hand.

He splashed some on his neck.

He handed her the bottle.

He pulled down his tie and unbuttoned four buttons on his shirt and tugged his shirt up on the left side.

'"The foundation of the Way is always deception." Yagyu, sixteen thirty-five,' he said.

'All right, Swagger. I give up. Go to your little war.'

'See ya,' he said, stepping out.

'I'll be waiting for you to come out, that is, *if* you come out.'

★　★　★

Nii was amazed. The old man, barefoot and in black like some kind of hipster, with glasses so big they blew his eyes up like a bug's, sat on a low stool on a platform. He looked like some kind of musical performer. He was bent over the long curve of steel, his eyes fiercely concentrating, his left hand securing the blade against a block of wood, his right gripping a piece of flat stone. A water bucket sat at his right foot.

He was in the part of the process called finishing. It had been a long, slow war, starting with foundation stones and the full power of his imagination and his stamina and his know-how, all applied against the blade in an act that was part love and part hate and all art. The blade, for its part, fought him stubbornly. Its scars were proudly earned in forgotten battles, its surface was stained by the blood of many, some justly taken, some not so justly taken. It did not want to return to the ceremonial pristine.

In the war, the old man's weapons were stones. There were dozens of them, each with a specific name, a specific grain, a specific face, to be used in one place, in one direction — *arato, kongoto, binsui, kasisei, chunagura, komanagura, uchigumori hato, uchigumori-to* — and the art of the campaign was in knowing the place for each in the time-consuming ritual. The old man's face was as wrinkled as a prune's, but his hair was long and fluffy. He looked more like a saxophonist than a warrior, but a warrior he was, and the glitter of a million particles of ground steel were the evidence of his attack, even if, every hour, he vacuumed them up, for an unvanquished particle could slide between stone and blade and cause havoc.

Nii watched as something beautiful emerged with slow precision out of something mundane. What had seemed to be a common chunk of old steel, smeared, spotted with rust, nicked, and hazed, was now an elegant sweep of colors and textures. It didn't shine, not really; it glowed, as if lit from within. Somehow as the old metal was removed, the blade regained its life and power. It was alive now. The smeary, milky line (or smudge, really) of the *hamon* ran along the whole edge. The tip, *kissaki*, was cruel and perfect, a couple of inches of eloquent steel that

325

would penetrate anything. The thicker metal of the *mune* had a golden quality, substantial and embracing, solid yet giving rather than crudely strong and brittle. And the two grooves (*bo-hi*, they were called) gave the blade an aerodynamic purity and would make it sing as it cleaved the air. It looked hungry for blood. It was one of those objects that was sacred and profane at once. It wanted but one thing, to drink more blood, and yet it was also an expression of the distilled genius of the people of the little island who had created and spread its soul and spirit across half the known world. Nii knew none of this. He could express nothing of it. He felt all of it. It had gotten his mind, for once, off little girls.

The old man worked steadily, without seeing anything but the sword, six inches from his face. He was, in his way, too cool to see the gaudy, fashion-obsessed yaks of the world. He communicated to them that, though loud and forceful, they were trivial, meaningless. He lived to work. He accepted that day some weeks ago when they had simply shown up with guns and a large pile of money.

'You will do this work. This work and no other. You will keep it secret from everybody. You will be watched. You must finish by the first week in December.'

'It cannot be done in that time.'

'Yes, it can,' Kondo had said to him. 'You must know who I am, and what I am capable of. I would hate to spill your blood — '

'Life, death, it's the same.'

'To you, in your eighties, but perhaps not to

326

children, grandchildren, wife, friends, and so forth. We will leave a big hole in this small town.'

Glumly, the old man accepted the new now. He gave himself up to the blade. What choice did he have, really?

And now he was done. A final burnishing, an inspection, the full power of —

'Nii!' someone called.

Nii looked up. He saw that the old man had stopped polishing, something he'd never done before. That disturbed Nii.

Then Nii heard it: someone was banging on the door.

'Who is that fool?' he demanded.

'It's a *gaijin*. It's some stupid-looking *gaijin*.'

'Fuck. Well, I'll get rid of him,' Nii said. 'You, back to work.'

But for some reason the old man would not work. He stared at Nii with great intensity, as if seeing him for the first time or as if he knew something. Then he smiled.

He spoke for the first time in months.

'This is going to be good,' he said.

★ ★ ★

Bob knocked hard on the door. He heard stirring inside. He tried the lock, felt it rock in the jamb but not give much at all. He knocked again, harder.

'Hey!' he said. 'Hey, goddammit, open up. I got a sword needs polishing!'

Something stirred inside, and through a small crack in the curtain behind the glass, he sensed a

327

flash of movement. What he could see was otherwise unimpressive: shelves and on the shelves what looked to be shoeboxes, and in the shoeboxes what looked to be stones, some flat, some jagged, all different in shape, texture, and color.

'Hey,' he shouted again, 'goddammit, I have a sword! You want some money? I have money for you. Don't you want to work? Come on, goddammit, open the hell up.'

He did this for about three minutes, loudly, a drunken *gaijin* who would not go away, not soon, not ever.

'I hear you! Goddammit, I hear you in there, open up, goddammit!'

Then he saw movement in the dark, which soon resolved itself into two husky young men in suits. They had impassive faces and one wore sunglasses. They were about 240 each and lacked necks. They had short arms that hung at a slight bend because the muscle was so overdeveloped it kept the arms from straightening.

They came to the door, and Bob heard clacking as the lock was released. The door slid open an inch but no farther and both young men crushed against the opening with their full linebackers' weight and strength, giving no quarter.

'Hey, I — '

'You go away. Shop closed. No one here. He gone. Go away now, please.'

'Come on, fellas,' he said with a drunk's belligerent stupidity. 'I bought this thing for a thousand bucks. It needs a shine. This is the place, ain't it? Guy told me this place really shines 'em up good. Come on, lemme in, talk to the fella.' He held up the white-sheathed, white-gripped *wakizashi*.

'Go away now, please. No one here. Polisher gone. Go elsewhere. Not your business here.'

'Guys, I just want — '

'No business for you here.'

The door rocked shut and Bob heard it click.

The two men edged back, then disappeared into a rear room.

He stood there a second, then reached into his pocket and pulled out a metal pick. The clickings of the door had informed him that it was a standard throw-bolt, a universal fixture, easily overcome. He slid the pick in the keyhole, felt the delicate mesh of tumblers and levers, wiggled this way and that, and felt each tumbler eventually give up its position. He put the pick away, took out a plastic credit card, drew that up the door slot to the bolt, and began a steady upward tapping, gentle and persistent, urging the bolt off the spring-driven lever that secured it. In two seconds, with a snap, it yielded to these probings and popped open.

He stepped into darkness.

'Hey,' he said, 'anybody home? Goddamn, the door wasn't locked, you must be open.'

He heard shuffling from behind a curtain, some whispers.

He bulled his way back with a lurch, stepped through the curtain, spilling awkwardly into the larger rear room, and there beheld a strange spectacle. A small old man with hippie hair and spaceman goggles sat on a platform with the blade, which Bob recognized instantly by shape and length, though now it gleamed like some rare piece of jewelry.

Six extremely husky young men, all in black suits, three in sunglasses, all holding sheathed *wakizashi*, stood across from him. He almost laughed: they looked like the Notre Dame interior line doing an en masse imitation of the Blues Brothers.

Suddenly the Japanese began to jabber, an excited, stunned blast of men talking over other men, until finally one yelled loudly and seemed to take command. He leaned forward and sniffed.

'You drunk. You go home. Go now, go fast.'

'Just want to get this here sword shined up so it's like that thing there. Damn, that's a pretty one. Sir, can you make this one like that one?' He held the sheathed *wakizashi* and waved it about theatrically.

The leader spoke harshly and two of the linemen came at Bob, bulking up as they came, their muscles bunching as they tensed, their right hands forming fists.

'Whoa, whoa,' he said, 'no rough stuff, fellas, please, *please!*'

The bruisers halted.

Then he looked at the old man, who looked back. He winked. The old man winked.

A frozen moment transpired as everybody took stock. Eyes flashed this way and that, hands tightened on hilts, breathing became harsh. Bob was suddenly quiet, wary, eating them up. It was a moment that seemed to last an eternity. One could compose a haiku during its exquisite extenuation.

Bob looked at the fat leader.

'The one he's polishing? The one you killed the Yanos to get? I want it back. And I want you knocking at the door to hell.'

Then it was over, as if no concept of quietude or peace existed anywhere on earth. It was time to cut.

The two closest yaks went for their swords to cut down the American, but they were not fast enough. Iai-Jutsu. The art of drawing and cutting. It was called *nukitsuke*. With his off-the-charts hand speed Swagger got the blade out — it clacked dryly as the transaction between blade and *saya* occurred — and into a horizontal cut called 'crosswind' by Yagyu, one-handed, the cut landing with his front foot, the body weight behind it for power, so full of adrenaline he drove through both of them. *Hidari yokogiri*, his old friend, cutting horizontally from left to right. He thought he'd missed, for he only felt the slightest resistance, and for a nanosecond had an image of disaster. But the disaster was theirs. The blade slashed deeply in a straight line, gut to gut, through suit, shirt, undershirt, skin, fat, entrails, viscera, spleen, liver, whatever, and just kept on going in a mad driving arc, leaving in its wake nothing, and then everything. The blood pushed out with a good deal of power. It didn't explode, as in too many movies, and spritz as though a sprinkler had projected it, it just sloshed out heavily, along with two breakfasts. And it kept on coming, seemingly gallons of it, in a red dump that literally sounded tidelike as it splashed against the floor. One stricken man went down like a sack of potatoes fallen off a truck; the other just stood there, stupefied, stepped back, trying to hold his guts in, and then sat down to die.

Without thinking, Bob's blade rode the energy high and came up into issuing from above, better known in the country of its origin as *kami-hasso*, and he watched as another man, sword high in *jodan*, came galloping at him. Under such circumstances, most men would panic: a huge, angry, bulged-eye man of immense strength charging full bore, the sword raised in his hands as he gathered strength to unleash a sundering blow, he was every mad psycho in every bad horror movie ever made. He screamed dramatically. But with eyes that saw far as though it were close and close as though it were a distant mountain, Bob waited until the clumsy drive of the blade announced itself and then with a quick small movement slipped to the left and shimmied into safety exactly as, trailing blade, he cut the big one's belly open deeply, and the sword never fell. This one instead kept going by him, turned, eyes now spent of rage and filling instead with horror at the immense damage that had been done to him, went to one knee, dropped the sword, then toppled clumsily forward.

Bob saw none of this. He turned and watched as the three remaining split up, two going one way, the third the other as they came around the

332

old man on the platform, who watched the craziness largely indifferent. Bob's lizard brain understood without actual thought that fighting one was better than fighting two, so he rotated to the left, coming around to meet the lone man on the left side of the inert polisher on his platform. His enemy was a slight but older fellow, not given to panic or stupidity. His long face intent, the sword before him, he approached steadily, just watching, waiting for Bob to give him an opening, which Bob of course didn't, so he attempted to make one. His sword flashed laterally, the classic *kesagiri*, shoulder to navel, left to right, on the diagonal, but from somewhere at a speed that has no place in time, Bob read the cues — 'The eyes are the key to reading the actions of the mind: the light or gleam in an opponent's eyes is as revealing as the movements of the rest of his body' — and rose to take the cut on his own blade, rode the blade down, and then reversed. It was *uke-nagashi*, the flowing block, and he absorbed the energy from his opponent, seized it, then unleashed it, snapping through with his wrist and extending one-handed in as small a space as possible. Throat. At the end of the arc, the point was traveling at stunning speed, generating amazing foot-pounds of energy, taking all of Swagger's strength and distilling it to one small cutting edge.

Results looked unpleasant, even shocking, but worse than that was the sudden noise the man made, a hideous wailing, as air and blood were forced from his split larynx and the realization of his own inevitable doom overcame him, causing his lungs to expel their atmospheres forcefully. But he did not fall. By one of the eccentricities of a dying body's last spurts of energy, his knees locked and he stood still, arms fallen, sword lost, spewing blood from the cut throat — though in a kind of gurgly fountain style, not the patented Toho spray — as his eyes looked at nothing. Then, finally, like a tree, he fell, hitting the puddled blood so hard he kicked up splatters, some of which suddenly danced across Bob's face, the old man's face, and the ceiling.

The other two came around the old man's platform and confronted Bob, separating slightly; they dropped into classic *tachi*, relaxed standing, the sword before them, as they slid through the blood steadily on small, floating steps, eyes steady, faces intent, not angry or frightened. Bob found himself — who the hell told him this was best? — in *kamehasso*, sword higher, almost a batting stance but relaxed, trying and finding it within himself to stay calm as they rotated around the front of the platform and came at him smoothly. He looked for his opening, they looked for theirs and had the advantage because they could spread out on the sound idea that he could not — being no Musashi — fight in two hemispheres at once, and whichever he chose to defend, the fellow assaulting from the other would deliver the death cut.

He knew without thinking it, he had to be the aggressor. He didn't come to a conclusion, it was just there before him, as certain solutions to certain vexing problems had come to him in his last fight, against the little girl.

He lunged left, but it was a feint, meant to drive back the one on the left. It worked. This fat boy stepped back for just a second. But seeing that move, the fellow on the right foolishly interpreted it as commitment, his heart filled with greed and visions of victory and reward, and he drove forward with the horizontal cut, the same crosswind Bob had used earlier. Bob knew it would come and pulled a move of his own devising, which was to thrust forward low, one knee plunging, the other back-kicking, flattening and lowering him. He felt the opponent's sword roar by his hair, fluffing it, and he cut the man through the knee with a strike that felt slow and weak but that must have been strong and powerful, for it got through the one leg completely and the leg fell away to the right. The one-legged man hopped in screaming horror. Some things can't be stopped, however, and the blow was too good: it continued, though much less forcefully, and bit halfway through the other leg, trapping itself for a second as the man fell.

He was dead. A brilliant move against one opponent, it was a foolish one against two, for now the fat one, who'd done all the talking, had the advantage and surged forward, flowing smooth and soft like a beautiful river — from somewhere Bob noted that he was well schooled — to deliver the diagonally angled *kesagiri* issuing from above to split the crouching *gaijin*.

I die, thought Bob, knowing that he was so far behind the curve he'd never make it, even if he felt his blade pull free. What happened next he saw clearly. Both his opponent and he had forgotten one thing: it didn't matter to him because his center of gravity was so low and his supporting feet were so widely spaced, one before him and bent, the other stretched behind him and straight, but the venue in which they fought was slick with blood. Fat boy, on the other hand, had a high center of gravity, an unstable one in the slipperiness of the blood. He lost his footing, his sword wavered, oops, *oof!* omigosh! *ulp!* He struggled with his balance, the rhythm and timing of his cut utterly wrecked, and by the time he delivered it at about one-quarter speed, Bob got the blocking blade, even turned to take it on the *mune* of his sword, found the leverage in rising and pushed the enemy blade away and, finding himself in a nicely set-up *shimo-baso*, with the blade now back and the hilt forward, simply drove the hilt with a monstrous thud into the fat one's face just below the eye. He fell like the giant in Jack and the Beanstalk, all dead weight, *ker-splash* in the blood, throwing splatter everywhere. With one hand he waved the sword and Bob hit it hard with the lower half of his own blade just above the *tsuba* and it flew away with a clatter. He leaned close, smelled breath, saw sweat and teeth and venting nostrils and fearful eyes, and hit the guy exactly where he'd hit him before with the hilt. It was a solid drive that echoed through his bones. The fat boy groaned and lay flat.

Bob stood, breathing hard. He flicked the blood off his blade, heard it splatter against a wall. He realized he still gripped the *saya*. All his blows had been one-handed, against all doctrine.

He turned and walked just a few feet to the amazingly contained old man.

'Cut *down*,' said the old man. 'Not just cut. Cutting no good. Blood, no death soon enough. Cut *down!*'

Christ, Swagger thought, everybody's a critic.

'Better footwork. Feet all tangled,' said the hipster. 'You fight two, no good. Go to dojo. Get sensei. Must learn. You lucky. You use up all luck this life and next life. No more luck for you. You must practice with sensei. Much work to do.'

'You got that right,' said Bob. 'I definitely was lucky. Now, old fellow, give me what I came for and I will get out of your way.'

'Fat one not dead.'

'I get that. I've got some words for him.'

'Okay. Very nice sword here. Honor to work on. Highlight of life. I appreciate much. Here, let me finish sword.'

He applied himself to it for another minute, held it to the light, pronounced it done, and put it into a red silk bag. It seemed to take him hours to tie the fucking thing, and Swagger saw that he had to do it just right.

Finally, he handed it over.

'No touch blade with stinky Merikan fingers.'

'I understand that. You'll be all right?'

'Fine. I go stay with family in Sapporo.'

'Can we drop you anywhere?'

'No, I catch bus. It's fine.'

Bob turned. He walked to the supine form of the one survivor amid the carnage as the polisher Mr Omote put on some slippers, got a coat on, and made ready to leave.

Bob poked the live one, felt him stir, then groan. The eyes finally came open, blinked as he reacquainted himself with unpleasant memories of the last few minutes.

He touched the wound under his eye, from which blood flowed. It had already started to puff and would soon grow to the size of a grapefruit.

'Hey, you,' said Bob, 'listen here or I will do some more cutting on you.'

'Please don't hurt me.'

'Why not, it's fun.'

'Oh, my face,' said the guy, who, Bob now saw, was about twenty-five or so. His mug issued blood, tears, and snot from a variety of damaged sites.

'Pay attention. You have to deliver a message, all right?'

'Sure, Joe.'

'My name ain't Joe, asshole. See this?' He brandished the red silk sword bag. 'It's the sword. It's *my* sword, I have it back. Kondo Isami wants it bad. Fine, I'll barter it to him. He has something I want. When I get it, I'll give him the sword.'

'I hear you.'

'In three days, I'll take a classified in the *Japan Times* personals column. It'll be addressed to a 'Yuki.' It'll be in alphabet code from *The Nobility of Failure* in English, not the Japanese translation. Got that?'

'What's that?'

'A book, you moron. Way too hard for you.

338

He'll know what it is. Can you remember that?'

'Sure. J — sir.'

'Sir I like. The ad'll give a location, a park probably. He's to meet me at that park alone the following evening. He gives me what I want. I'll give him what he wants.'

'Sure,' said the fat yak. Then his eyes clouded over with puzzlement. 'You want money? A pile of it?'

'I don't give a shit about money, clown-san.'

'What you want, then?'

'His head,' Bob said. 'Tell him to bring it.'

32

KONDO

Kondo was fascinated.

'He said that? He actually said that?'

'Yes. He did.'

'Nii, tell me again. Tell me exactly.'

'I asked him what he wanted from you. He said 'His head. Tell him to bring it.'

'Cheeky fellow.'

'He was, *Oyabun*.'

They were in Nii's apartment. A private nurse in 8–9–3 employ had stitched and bandaged Nii up, as his own fellows cleaned the sword polisher's shop after dark, making sure the bodies and all the carnage on the floor — and the chopped leg — were neatly disposed of. Nii, stitched, swollen, returned to his own place, and a few other men of Shinsengumi lingered about, dark-eyed, dark-suited, wary. Kondo, however, was lit up by the situation. Something in it pleased him immensely. He could not keep a half smile off his face.

'Describe him again, please.'

'American. Tallish, not gigantic. When himself, composed. Not one for excitement. His eyes were very still. He knew where to look, how to move. He'd killed before. Blood, the ugliness of the cuts, none of that had any effect on him.'

'Tell me again how he fought. Details this

time, Nii. Tell me everything.'

'He was shrewd. We were stupid.'

'*You* were stupid, Nii.'

'I was stupid. He smelled of drink. He was wild and loud and out of control. His hair was a mess. He was any *gaijin* you see in Kabukicho, full of wild plans, knowing nothing. I was thinking how to get him out of there without incident, without the police becoming involved. I knew it would be difficult. I missed something.'

'What?'

'He picked the lock. I heard it lock yet in seconds he had penetrated it. He was an experienced man. I sat there, trying to remember whether or not we had locked it. Now I know we had.'

'So he deceived you.'

'With the drunk act, completely. It was brilliant. If he had announced himself at the door, he would have greeted six men, blades out, hearts strong. Instead he got close with his absurd drunken act. Then, in a flash, he was sober and deadly. He cut down the first two in one stroke, expertly delivered. His best cut of the fight, I think, though the cut he made on Kamiizumi was also excellent. Anyway, they were gone and lost in the first second, Johnny Hanzo in the next. Johnny Hanzo lost his head and charged and the *gaijin* quietly let him come, then pierced him in the second before Johnny could unleash a cut, and Johnny was gone. In less than three seconds three men were out of the fight.'

Through the narration, Kondo sat quietly, in rapt concentration, as if he were working on serious visualization skills. He was seeing all this in the dark space before him.

'So then there were three?'

'Yes. And all three could not get around the old man on his platform. So Kashima and I went one way, and Kamiizumi the other.'

'Kamiizumi was the best of you six. The oldest, the most experienced. He'd been in fights before.'

'He was magnificent. I thought for certain he would achieve victory or cut the man so bad the victory would fall to us. But the *gaijin* anticipated his cut, took it, and used it to propel himself into flowing block, threw it off, then came through with something I'd never seen before, a kind of one-handed drive, amazingly fast. He had to anticipate which way Kamiizumi, blocked, would break. Perhaps it was just luck, but he hit Kamiizumi in the throat. Unbelievable. Such blood. It was — '

'Did he watch him fall?'

'No, *Oyabun*. Instead he turned immediately to face us as we came around the old man. He went under Kashima and cut him through the leg. He sundered it. That's when I had him. His blade was momentarily trapped in Kashima's second leg, because he didn't anticipate getting through so easily and had lost a firm grip on the sword as it bit into the second leg. It was a blown cut, trapped, tying him up. But then Kashima toppled and his blade came free.'

'You had him.'

'I did. Him below, sword down, myself above, driving full strength toward my target, his neck.

If you try for speed, you do not achieve speed.'

'It must be no-try. Always, no-try.'

'It was try. Too much try, *Oyabun*, I slipped, lost my footing, and when I was back in timing, he was ready; he took it, slipped it, and drove his hilt into my face.'

'It wasn't pretty.'

'It wasn't. The last was sheer improvisation on his part. Very sloppy. I think he was running out of energy.'

'How old was he?'

'Advanced. Not ancient. Oldish. Late forties, maybe early fifties, maybe older. Very brown from a lot of sun, as if permanently tanned. Thinning hair. His face never got passionate, except the last time he hit me. I think he enjoyed that.'

'What a man. This is so wonderful. I can't begin to tell you. I have never fought six. What were his strengths?'

'Spirit. He was very hard of resolve. He was not scared, excited, scattered, angry, or anything. He was empty of everything except his professionalism.'

'I like that.'

'He was fast. He was very fast. His hands particularly. I will say, however, that he fought much better against one than against two. He easily defeated every single man he fought, he vanquished the first two with *nukitsuke*. He only faltered when the two of us moved in, where he made a mistake and I almost had him.'

'Excellent.'

'*Oyabun*, may I be permitted to commit *seppuku* now?'

'No. no. no. There's too much to do. I have nobody to spare as your second. We don't have time now.'

'I am so ashamed. I cannot face my parents' ghosts, my friends, our other Shinsengumi. I can hardly face you.'

'Don't be an idiot. It would accomplish nothing. Plus, I've seen it and it hurts. It's very messy. You may have to die, Nii, but at least let it mean something. Now look at Kamiizumi and the others. Their deaths were helpful. They exposed the strengths and the weaknesses of the man. They died well. You conveyed the information that they unearthed to me. It's valuable information. If you had cut yourself after the fight and killed yourself, that information never would have reached me. What good would have been accomplished?'

'I survive only to serve. When no longer needed, I will express my shame and try to get my honor back with the *tanto*.'

'Yes, yes, if that's what you want. You could also go off and get laid, and maybe that would be enough for you. Anyhow, Nii, listen to me. I am going to get a police artist. I want you to describe this *gaijin* to him very carefully. We will spread a net to catch this fresh fellow and get our sword back. We have to get him *before* the night of the exchange because if he controls the exchange, we're at a great disadvantage. We don't know who he represents, what his goal is. I can't believe it's simple *kataki-uchi*. Westerners don't understand the concept of vendetta. Maybe Sicilians, but no others, not really. He's

344

playing an angle, and he could have snipers on the roofs, a team of fellow professionals. It's too big a risk to run. I'd hate to go into that blindly.'

Nii nodded solemnly. He tried to remember details, to assemble them in his mind so that he could assist, but he was aware that something wasn't adding up. Then he saw what it was.

'*Oyabun?*'

'Yes, Nii,' said Kondo, who was already striding out to make his arrangements, even as he debated whether to tell the Shogun of this disturbing yet provocative development.

'I'm sorry. I regret. I did not recognize.'

'What?'

'I realize now: I know who this *gaijin* is.'

'You do?'

'Yes, *Oyabun*. I regret that I did not recognize him at the shop, but it was so out of context that I — '

'Stick to the message, Nii.'

'Yes, *Oyabun*. I once sat two seats behind him on the JR Narita express. I followed him from the Yanos' to Narita the night we — '

'*That* gaijin?'

'Yes, *Oyabun*.'

'That would be the *gaijin* who brought the sword in.'

'Yes.'

'He was with the Yanos.'

'He stayed at their house for several days.'

'He was close to them?'

'Yes, now I recall. I watched from just across the street that last night. He hugged them all. I followed him to Narita and watched him check

345

into the flight. I watched him pass security. That's when I left to join you and we went to the Yanos'. With Kamiizumi, Johnny Hanzo, Kashima, and the others.'

'He knew the Yanos,' Kondo said again, deliciously. 'Then it *is kataki-uchi!* Oh, splendid.'

'I suppose we could contact the inspector. He would know the name.'

'We don't need the name. Now I know how to catch the *gaijin*. I'll reel him in and cut him down.'

'And when it's over, I can have my *seppuku?*'

'Nii, you shouldn't be so selfish. Think of your *oyabun*, not yourself. Find dignity and worth in service. Then, if you've been good, I'll let you kill yourself. But as a treat, Nii, first I'm going to get you a nice little girl.'

33

ORDERS

With your typical order of yakitori, you got four edible, even delicious skewers of meat and one so repugnant it was almost kind of funny. The smell of chicken cooked on an open fire filled the place. No Popeye's ever smelled so good. At other tables men and women were lustily gobbling their food. Bob had eaten the hearts, he'd eaten the meat, he'd eaten the gizzards, he'd eaten the other strange things, but he was left with the knees.

Well, maybe they weren't knees. Maybe they were elbows. Whatever, they were twisted little chunks of glistening sinew. Even the flames of Mama-san's blazing fire behind the bar hadn't blackened them. In truth, in the curves and folds of each there seemed to be some gobbet of protein, and maybe a truly hungry man would scrape it out and go to town, but he just didn't have the heart. Instead, he looked across the smoky space, across the rude tables and floor, half-expecting Toshiro to come blasting in and start cutting people at any damn time, until he caught Mama-san's eye, pointed to his empty plate, and somehow communicated the idea, Bring me another order, touched his empty Coke can to request more of that too. She nodded. He could have been in the fourteenth

347

century, except for the Coke. He went back to the puzzle before him.

He almost had it. He'd been scouting Tokyo by bike for a nice private place for his meet with Kondo and finally found just what the doctor ordered: he'd have the man travel to Asakusa and walk the street outside the shrine, where all the stalls were. For some reason, that zone closed early and went largely unpatrolled. He'd meet him there, in the street, and he wouldn't jump until he was satisfied the man was alone, not trailing a crew of goons. He didn't want to fight six again, or more likely thirty, for Kondo would travel with his specially chosen group.

Now he worked on his code, primitive as it was, finding the right words in *The Nobility of Failure*, marking page number, paragraph, sentence, and word so that the message was shaping up to read 'Dear Yuki, 233–2–4–3,' denoting page 233, second paragraph, fourth sentence, third word. It went on and on, gibberish if you didn't know the key. Decoded, it would read 'Asakusa, Temple Street, midnight tonight, alone.'

He felt her before he saw her. She strode in manfully, as per her style, and sat down. He didn't look up for the longest time.

'I'm almost done with this. I think I've got it set up just right.'

It was several minutes before he finished, and when he came out of his zone of concentration there was another interruption, as Mama-san brought the plate of skewered chicken parts and another Coke, asked Susan what she wanted, and received only a drink order, then scurried away.

'You shouldn't be anywhere near us tomorrow night, in case it goes bad. But I wanted you to see what I was doing; I told you I'd keep you in the loop.'

Then, finally, he looked at her and knew instantly that something was wrong.

'All right,' he said, 'what's up? You haven't said a thing.'

'You remember I once told you I wasn't a bullshitter?'

'Yes.'

'I'm not going to start now. I'll be honest and blunt, all right. So no matter what, you can never say, She misled me.'

'Oh, Christ, Susan. I don't like where this is going.'

'I'm closing you down, Swagger. It's over. It's finished. Time to go home.'

He didn't feel anger or rage or betrayal. She had never exactly pretended to be his pal in this and had always told him she'd do what was best by the rules of her duty, not her feelings. And she'd never quite bought into it, the whole warrior thing. On the way back from the fight at the polisher's, with the blood soaking his pants and spattered on his face, she'd said nothing except:

'Did you hurt anybody?'

'No, but I killed five men.'

'Oh, god.'

'It wasn't no movie. It was like a pie fight in a sausage factory. I didn't like one goddamn thing about it, but they would have cut me deep as I cut them, so I did what I had to. The old man is fine and has left. I have the sword, so that's fine. The yaks will clean up, once they find out, because they don't want no cops nosing into their business. It'll be fine, no mess.'

She had only said, 'No mess *this* time.'

Now she said, 'This can go one of three ways. I hope you see that it is best if it goes the first way.'

'And that would be?'

'You give me your false passport. You go out with me to a government van and you are driven to a U.S. Air Force base not far from here. I have arranged, or rather with some dickering and string pulling the ambassador has arranged, for you to be flown home, gratis, by the United States Air Force, outside all channels. You will be landed in California, escorted to the gate, and permitted to exit. That's the end of your involvement. What has happened over the past few weeks here in Japan ceases to exist. There was no — I can't even remember what your passport says.'

'Thomas Lee.'

'There was no Thomas Lee. He's gone, you're gone, it's over. You go back to Arkansas.'

'Idaho.'

'Whatever. Meanwhile, the ambassador finds a way to slip a report on your findings that I have written to certain sympathetic Japanese Ministry of the Interior officials. It will give them some guidance. I hope they act on it, and I feel certain that within the Ministry of the Interior, there is a clique that will want very hard to proceed. It may take some time and there will be no illusion of progress for a long time. But eventually, as the Japanese sort this out, they will proceed and the thing will be done, and those who killed Philip Yano will be punished. In any event, since we now have the sword, the immediate plan of the man who styles himself a shogun has been disrupted. He will not win reelection to AJVS, he will be undercut and destroyed. So that's something. And in the end, we will achieve justice.'

'You know that won't happen.'

'Way number two. Exactly the same outcome, except that you make some sort of ruckus or act irresponsibly. Four large gentlemen enter the restaurant. They happen to be former South Korean Special Forces guys who handle contract work for certain embassy departments when needed. They are very tough. Something like seventeen black belts among them. Lots of combat. They subdue you. It hurts. Then you are taken to the van, only you are wearing handcuffs and are severely bruised. Et cetera, et cetera, et cetera. Swagger, don't do that. Don't put yourself and me and them and everybody through that. It would be such a waste, so foolish, so pointless. It would break my heart.'

'Okada-san, possibly at this moment I ain't too worried about your heart.'

'Way number three. You bolt. There's probably a rear entrance to this joint, and you are, as we know, an extremely capable, resilient, creative man, particularly in dark arts like escape and evasion. You break out, you get away, and try and finish on your own. Then we snitch you out to the Japanese authorities. A tall *gaijin* with no Japanese language skills, I don't like his odds. Maybe it takes two days, maybe it takes three. But they catch you, divine that your passport is fake, read our signals and see we are not interested in helping, and off you go, before the judges. No juries in Japan. Second offense, off you go to prison. Five, maybe ten years. What a waste. What a foolish, sad, absurd ending. What a way for a great hero to end his days. No wife, no daughter. I will come visit you until I get bored, and then I won't anymore.'

'What about way number four?' he said.

'There is no way number four.'

'Way number four: You send the big boys back to their cages. We proceed. I only need two days more. I meet Kondo Isami on the street at Asakusa at midnight. Your four ROK Special Forces guys handle security, so there ain't no interruption. Kondo and I fight.'

'That is one of the things I am trying to prevent. He will kill you.'

'Maybe. Or I will kill him. If the first happens, you go ahead with your plans. On the other hand, if the second happens, you go ahead with your plans. Maybe the Japanese eventually bring down Yuichi Miwa, maybe not. The point is, the man who killed Philip Yano and his family is dead. Justice has been served. Or someone has died trying to do that justice. He failed, but at least he tried. Somebody called it 'the nobility of failure.' That's the world I'd rather live or die in.'

'No. It's not going to happen. It has been decided. We cannot have a dangerous, violent American citizen in this country illegally mixing it up with Japanese criminal elements, in ways that can't be controlled and could explode into scandal, damage, death, anarchy, humiliation at any moment. We need the Japanese, we need their cooperation in a lot of bigger battles. There's a war going on, in case you haven't noticed.'

'Philip Yano noticed. He lost an eye and a career in that war.'

'What happened to Phil Yano and his family was a tragedy and an atrocity. But the wicked, wicked world is full of tragedies and atrocities, and they can't all be avenged. Other things may matter more, like national security, like smooth relations between allies, like truth in dealing with allies, like any number of things that will be decided by people who see the big picture and live with responsibilities you and I can't imagine.'

'What is Okada-san's attitude in all this? I hear the State Department. I don't hear Okada-san.'

'Okada-san is samurai. She works for a daimyo. She lives to serve him. It defines her. She obeys her daimyo. She made peace with that decision years ago. Her feelings are her business and nobody else's. Duty is the only thing that counts. Now, Swagger, please, finish your motherfucking chicken skewers and leave quietly with me. It's the best way. It's the only way.'

'You are a tough one, Okada-san. I give you that. Nothing gets in the way. Professional to the

353

core. You sure you weren't a marine?'

'If it matters, I hate to see this end. What you've done — well, I've never seen anything like it. But that's neither here nor there. I am samurai. I obey my daimyo. Now it's time to —'

A strange noise came between them.

'Shit,' she said.

She bent, picked her green Kate Spade bag off the floor, and fished out her cellular. It buzzed irritatingly.

'Your daimyo wants an update.'

'It's not my daimyo's number.'

She popped the thing open.

'Yes. I see. No, no, that was the right thing to do. And when? All right, thanks. I don't know. I — I just don't know. No, don't call them. I don't know, I have to think. If you call them, it makes even more problems.'

She closed the phone and put it back in her purse.

'So,' he said. 'Let's go to the van. Let's get this over with.'

'No,' she said. 'It's all changed.'

He saw now something in her eyes that could have been the beginning of tears. Even her tough warrior's face and its self-willed impassivity, a signal mark of her beauty, seemed slightly affected. Gravity somehow had altered it into something darker, sadder, and more tragic.

'That was Sister Caroline at the hospital. Armed men just broke in and kidnapped Miko Yano.'

354

34

THE TAKING

It still made no sense to the little girl. She had been at her friend Beanie's house and they had a party and played with Pretty Ponies and watched a movie about a funny strange green man in a forest and giggled the night away and the next day two strange men and a strange lady took her away to this place full of nuns and nurses and hurrying and scurrying. She didn't belong here, but there was no other place for her.

She understood, of course, that something had happened. A sister led her in prayer and finally told her about a fire and that Mama and Dada and Raymond and John and Tomoe were now with God. That was fine, but she had to know. 'When can I see them?'

'My dear, I'm afraid you don't understand. Let us pray again.'

The days passed, then the weeks. Every time someone came in the room, she looked up, felt a surge of joy and hope, and thought, Mama? Dada?

But it was only a nurse.

They dressed her in strange clothes. The toys were dour and limp, many broken. The other children stayed away from her as if she were infected. She was so alone.

'Mama?'

'My dear, no. You have to understand. Mama

and Dada have gone to be with God. He called them. He wants them.'

In her mind, she could see only one face that comforted her. It was from the TV, a fabulous story she loved so much about a little girl and her three friends who went off to fight a witch. One of the friends was a tall, almost silver man with a great cutting tool. He was the Tin Man. She loved the Tin Man. He was in her life somehow. She associated him with her father, for she'd first seen him with her father. The man was kind, she could tell. She remembered him in her own house, and she saw that in some way her father loved this man and the man loved her father, something she saw in their bodies, in the way they related and joked and listened to each other. If Daddy and Mommy and her sister and brothers were gone, she wondered about the Tin Man. She dreamed about him. Maybe he would save her from all this.

But the bed-wetting started and it annoyed the sisters and the nurses. They tried to hide their anger, but a child is sensitive to nuances of face and tone and body, and she realized that she was letting them down horribly. It made her sad. She could not help it. It humiliated her, because hygiene (she didn't know that word but thought only of her mother's term for it, 'being fresh') meant so much and she had been coached in it so powerfully by Mama and now she couldn't control her dirtiness. Voices weren't raised, punishments weren't threatened, blows weren't unleashed; still, she felt the nuns' disappointment like a powerful weight.

She didn't know when the screaming started. But after a while, it seemed that there had always been screaming. She had no idea where it came from, but some nights, when she was alone in the dark and sometimes asleep, and sometimes not, she began to hear the screaming.

Mama? Dada? Raymond? John? Tomoe?

It wasn't them, but it was. She missed them so. Why had they left? Why did God want them so badly? It seemed unfair.

'You must be strong,' the nuns told her.

But what was this *strong*? Her brothers, especially Raymond, the ballplayer, were strong. They lifted weights and their muscles bulged and shone in the light. They laughed and teased and needled each other about school and girls and homework and other things, and it had been so wonderful, though of course at the time she didn't know how wonderful, and that it would soon end forever.

But that seemed not to be the *strong* the nurses wanted. It wasn't muscles, but some other thing that she could not understand and could never do. It had nothing to do with each morning's wet bed and every other night's screams.

'It's you that's screaming,' one of the nurses said. 'Not anyone else. Please, darling, you have nothing to fear. You are among friends who will take care of you. You must be' — that word again — 'strong.'

And then one afternoon the screaming was so loud it woke her. But then she noticed she hadn't been sleeping. It was daylight. There were no shadows. It occurred to her that it was not, this time, her own screams or the screams of Mama and Dada and John and Raymond and Tomoe but of Sister Maria.

At that point the door to her room exploded open, and a giant monster crashed in. He was a very bad giant monster, she could tell. One side of his head was swollen and yellowish, he had a bandage over the lower half of his face, and blood spots stood out against the white. He looked her over and she was so scared she peed.

He grabbed her.

'Little girl,' he said, 'you will do exactly what I say or I will hit you hard. Do you understand?'

She felt the full force of adult will against her and if she wanted to scream, she couldn't, for she was too scared.

Holding her roughly, he proceeded to the hall. She saw Sister Maria on the ground, her face bloody, and Nurse Aoki kneeling over her trying to help, afraid to look up, shaking with fright. She thought of the Tin Man. The Tin Man could save her. But the Tin Man was not there.

As the giant monster roared along the hall, two other giant monsters joined him, in the same black suits.

In seconds they were outside. Nobody had bothered to get her a coat or anything.

A sleek black car pulled up, and the giant monster shoved Miko into it and sat next to her, his bulk dominating.

'You,' he said. 'No noise, no screaming, do

what you are told, or it will be hard on you. Squat down so nobody can see you.'

He forced the child to the floor and threw a blanket over her as the car pulled away with a screech.

35

FACE-TO-FACE

Exactly as Bob had planned, an ad keyed to *The Nobility of Failure* appeared in the *Japan Times*' Personals section. The difference was that it was not sent from him to Kondo Isami but from Kondo to him. It deciphered neatly enough to 'Yasukuni gate, 10 a.m. Tuesday.'

'They'll kill you,' said Susan Okada.

'No. Not if I don't have the sword. What he'll do is set up a second meet. That's when they'll kill me.'

'Oh. That's so much better. Look, we have to call the police.'

'No. You know that Kondo, or his boss, Miwa, have sources and influences in the police. If you tell them, in ten seconds Kondo knows. And what does that get? It gets Miko killed, it gets me killed. I will go to this meeting, I will set up the next meeting, the exchange, and we'll go from there.'

'But he's holding all the cards and he knows it. You can't negotiate with someone who has an advantage. He will get you to some deserted place, kill you, take the sword, kill Miko, and go ahead with his plan. They'll win.'

'Maybe I can — '

'*No!* You'll get her killed. You'll get yourself killed. Miwa will win. And then what?'

'Okada-san. I will go to this meeting and come back. And then we'll see.'

'If something I did gets that child killed — '

'You did *nothing* but your duty. This is not about any failing of yours. It's about guys who will do anything to get what they want. That's what it's always about. And you and I are lucky that we have the privilege to fight them. And we will fight them. And we will stop them. They think they're samurai. They're not. We'll show them what *samurai* means.'

But Susan wasn't convinced; Bob left her in a state of despair.

★   ★   ★

It had turned cold. The greenness of Japan had vanished. A cold wind blew, scattering dead leaves across the pavement of Yasukuni Shrine. On either side of the concrete esplanade, some trees stood tangled and severe; they looked like rusted barbed wire.

Bob stood under the steel gate. It towered above him, two steel shafts rising fifty feet to two steel crossbars, one mundane for stability, the other the great soaring wing that was the universal symbol of Japan, the torii gate with its architectural communication of the glory, the breadth, the scope, the power, the beauty, the immensity of Asia. Bob looked up into a blue sky at the top bar and saw immensity.

He shuddered. He was wearing a black suit and a raincoat, slightly underdressed for the weather. Outside the shrine parklands, Tokyo's business hustled along its avenues, the honking and screeching of cars, the bustle of the endless parade of pedestrians. Here a few salarymen, a few tourists, a few visitors traversed the grounds in small knots, headed either to the shrine at the end of the walk or the samurai museum to the right of the grounds.

Bob checked his watch: 10:15 a.m. Of course, somewhere they were checking him out with binoculars, making certain he really was alone.

But then, from a knot of nondescript businessmen, one separated and ambled over to Bob.

Bob watched him approach. Was he expecting something special, someone whose demonic charisma seemed to carry its own internal light? He just saw a guy in a suit and a topcoat, with sunglasses, a broad but unimpressive face, dark hair cut into a bristly crew cut. As the figure approached, possibly he picked up vibrations of physical vitality, as if the man, under his dreary outerwear, possessed surprising strengths and agility. Or possibly it was his imagination.

'Greetings, I am the assassin Kondo Isami,' said the man in clear, accentless English, well polished, well schooled. 'Who are you working for?'

Now that he faced him, Swagger felt a weird sense of familiarity. It was peculiar. What was so familiar? He spoke. 'Philip Yano.'

'You're not representing certain American adult-entertainment industry groups? You're not a professional?'

'I would have nothing to do with that business.

362

I don't care for teacher-blowing-Johnny. But I'm professional enough to handle you.'

'You don't represent government or any such official entity?'

'Nope. Did some work for 'em once, didn't like it.'

'Who taught you the sword?'

'Toshiro Mifune.'

'Who's the woman?'

'Pal, I ain't here to play twenty questions.'

'What was Philip Yano to you?'

'A good man with a good family who never deserved what he got.'

'He was nothing. There are more important things than one obscure family living on a government pension and investments.'

'I would say, He was *everything*. I would say. Cut the shit, let's get cracking. The longer I stand here, the more I feel like breaking your neck.'

'I spent some time in America. You remind me of a football team captain who ended up a fireman. Stupid, loud, aggressive, but brave. He died on nine/eleven when the tower went down on him.'

'It makes me sick that a creep like you even knew him.'

'Yes, he was a hero, as you are. But in a different way. His was samurai's courage, rash and emotional and caught up in the moment. That I understand. You've had weeks to think this over, to consider, to find reasons not to act. Yet you persevere. What drives you on this bizarre personal mission that can end in nothing

but disaster for you? I suppose you've rational-
ized it elaborately. Really. I'm curious. Why?
Why?'

'*On*,' said Bob.

'*On*,' scoffed the man. 'You can know nothing
of *on*. Obligation. It's a Japanese concept,
endlessly convoluted and twisted. It's meaningless to any American.'

'I think I get it pretty well.'

'Impossible,' he said. 'I went to an American
high school. I had a year at an American
university. I know America. No American could
feel *on*.'

'Ask your pals at the polisher's how serious I
am. They'd know.'

'You had the advantage of complete surprise.
So possibly the feat is less impressive than you
imagine.'

'Sir, I really don't give a fuck whether you're
impressed or not. I want the child.'

'I want the sword.'

'You can see that I don't have it.'

'Where is it?'

'When I get the child in one hand, I'll cut your
head off with it with the other, and that's when
you'll know where it is.'

Kondo reached in his pocket and pulled out a
cellular phone.

'Two days from now, at five thirty a.m., you
will receive a phone call on that phone. You will
be given a route. You will proceed. I believe you
have a motorcycle? I'd wait for the call near the
Imperial Palace. That's centrally located. At five
forty a.m. you will get another call. It will direct

364

you to turn. This will continue for a bit until you arrive at a certain destination at around six a.m., though you will have to run some stoplights. But you'd better run those stoplights. If you are late I will cut one of the child's fingers off. Each minute, one finger. When I run out of fingers, toes. Then there'll be nothing trivial to cut, so I'll cut limbs. She'll probably bleed to death before I get all four off, but if not, I'll take out each eye, her nose, and her tongue. It means nothing to me. So you had better be on time.'

'I am really going to enjoy taking your head.'

'You bring the sword. I will release the child when I have the sword. The initiative is mine, I control the transaction. You may leave with the child. Later I'll call you on the cellular and set up another appointment. We will settle our business.'

'It sucks, of course. You could have sixty men there with AKs.'

'I could. But if you don't agree, I'll start cutting the child right now. You doubt it? Look over there.' He indicated and Bob saw, fifty yards away, a large man with a bruised, bandaged face — Bob remembered clocking him hard, twice, at the polisher's — and Bob saw Miko. The big man had his hands on her shoulders. She looked scared and wan. Her controller turned his hand, and the light caught the blade of a *tanto* held intimately against her delicate throat. There was also something about his hand, some sexual electricity. You could see he enjoyed the closeness, her smell, her helplessness.

'That boy will cut her in a second. He is true

365

yakuza, living for obedience to his *oyabun*.'

The obscenity of the large, strong young man holding the bright blade against the terrified little girl and enjoying it so much filled Swagger with rage. But rage was not helpful.

'I'm impressed with how strong you are against little girls,' he said. 'That's quite a trick, but we'll see how you do with someone with a sharper sword and faster reflexes. My guess is I'll see fear in your eyes before I cut you down.'

'We'll see you in a while, *gaijin*. Bring Beheader of Kira.'

'I'll be there. And when I'm done with you, I'll donate Beheader of Kondo to a museum.'

36

THE WHITE ROOM

They drove back across Tokyo in a giant black car. Miko sat in the back — on the floor, actually — between the two giant monsters. The two men said nothing to each other or to her. She just sat there, feeling the start and stop of the car in traffic.

She had recognized the Tin Man, the man from the good memories even if she wasn't sure what they were, what they meant. This time, he looked at her with such sadness in his eyes, and as she watched, the sadness flashed to rage, then went calm again. But she had caught it, that moment of rage, and somehow from that she took some hope. He knew, somehow. He was on her side. He would save her. But then the two giant monsters roughly returned her to the car, calling her only 'Little Girl,' never her name, as if she was the unwanted stepchild. And she drove back to the house, the room.

The giant monster dragged her out of the vehicle. In a kind of courtyard, she caught a brief flash of fresh air. The courtyard was walled, somewhere in the city, and she could hear the sounds of traffic, see apartment buildings off in one direction. She had the impression of many men. They seemed to lounge everywhere, young men without women, all in black suits, all somehow tough or ready to fight. They scared her, as they gambled or joked or looked at magazines, or boisterously shoved each other around. She knew they were some kind of army.

The giant monster took her upstairs to a white room. She knew it well. It contained a bed and a television set. There were no toys or books or dolls. The windows were painted white. There was a bathroom attached. Three times a day, she was brought food, usually by one of the angry young men or by the giant monster with the swollen face who was her primary keeper. It was always takeout food, hamburger from McDonald's or fish cakes, or pork cutlets wrapped in paper bags, or some such, a Coke in a cardboard cup. An hour later, wordlessly, someone would return, unlock the door, and take the garbage out. Meanwhile, she just sat and watched the television, or sat in the whiteness thinking and remembering, or sat in the whiteness crying.

'Little Girl,' said the Monster, 'you know the rules. You stay here. You obey. If you do not obey, I will punish you. I believe in punishment. Your parents did not punish you hard enough. I will punish you severely. Do you understand?'

'How long — '

'Be quiet! Little Girl, ask no questions. You need to know nothing. Be a good little girl or we will have to punish you.'

Then he locked her in her room.

★ ★ ★

'Nii, come here,' said Kondo.

'Yes, *Oyabun.*'

'How's the eye?'

'It's fine.'

'What did you think of him this time?'

'Without a sword, he's just another man, *Oyabun.*'

'He seemed calm. That impressed me. He had a moment when he saw the child and his eyes flared. He felt rage. But then he controlled it. He knew that if he tried anything, you would have cut the child's throat.'

'Yes, *Oyabun.*'

'Nii, you would have cut the child's throat, right?'

'Yes, *Oyabun.*'

'Sometimes I worry, Nii. Of them all, I trust you the most. These fellows are hard and tough and will obey and fight, even the new ones. But your job, Nii, that is the hardest. I cannot believe the *gaijin* won't try something. And it may be that you will have to kill the child. You must be *samurai.* You must be Shinsengumi. You must be Eight-Nine-Three. You must be all will and no heart.'

'Yes, *Oyabun.*'

'You can't go sentimental on me in some appalling way. Is that clear?'

'Yes.'

'You are *kobun.* I am *oyabun.* You understand that. All things flow from that.'

'I stand ready.'

'I can't imagine that it could happen, but if there's an attack, you will proceed directly to the child and cut her throat.'

'Yes, sir.'

'Are you sure?'

'Yes, *Oyabun*. Why — why do you ask?'

'Because I am aware that you have some feelings for this child.'

'*Oyabun*, I — '

'No, I've seen you in her presence. You cannot tear your eyes away. You look back. On the drive over, you kept looking down at her. When you hold her, I see a certain passion in your limbs. You enjoy holding her.'

'*Oyabun*. It's nothing. I swear to you, she is nothing, it — '

'I understand how comely the child is. I understand how her form can seduce you.'

'She is but an object.'

'Nii, don't lie to me. I am your *oyabun*.'

Nii swallowed harshly, caught in his lie.

'Nii, listen to me. I must know that you can kill her. Because if I don't know it, then *they* will also sense it. It will embolden them. Do you understand?'

'Yes, *Oyabun*.'

'So listen to me. Before you kill her, fuck her. Once you are done with her, she is no longer a little princess. She is a whore, used by you for momentary pleasure and now defiled, tarnished, made dirty. She is nothing more than that Korean cow we slaughtered in Kabukicho. At that point, you can cut her and walk away.'

Nii saw the logic. He liked the logic.

'Do you hear me, Nii? Before you kill her, fuck her.'

'I hear, *Oyabun*.'

'Good *kobun*. Good student. I know I can count on you.'

37

STRATEGY

'Here is our best option,' said Susan Okada glumly. They sat at a table at the Roppongi Starbucks, among software designers, clothing salesmen, mothers, teenage girls and boys with pins in their noses and lips. 'I have thought this over and it could work. I go to the ambassador. I explain the situation, its urgency, the timing. He goes to the prime minister. They go to the minister of the Interior. We get some sort of dispensation, and we make guarantees. Of no, or at best minimal, collateral damage. If we get their okay — notice I'm bypassing the Tokyo police and the whole infrastructure in which Miwa and Kondo may have influence — we can move a SEAL team in from Okinawa. Most of the teams are in the Middle East, but Seven is in Okinawa and they're very good. They've done stuff you wouldn't believe in North Korea and on the Chinese coastline. So when you get that call at five thirty a.m., Seven is above you in a helo, they follow you to the location, and we air-insert fast. We have Japanese police cooperation to the point that we've got the park or whatever it is cordoned off, so no civilians will get shot. So SEAL Team Seven takes out Kondo and Miwa, if he's there. Seven prevails. We get the little girl, you are not dead, Kondo and Miwa are dead or behind bars. Seven flies back to Okinawa, and we have our happy ending.'

'All due respects, ma'am, you can't fight them on their ground when they've had time to set up their ground. Lesson number one from Vietnam. When they hear them choppers, they kill the little girl. The SEALs are still at five thousand feet, drinking their coffee. When they land, the only thing there is a dead child. Maybe I'm dead too. Meanwhile, everybody in Tokyo hears the choppers and in two minutes there are fifty TV news crews on the spot. When the Japanese hear Miwa is involved, they go nuts. It ain't going to work.'

'Swagger, I never said it was perfect. But we have been dealt a crap hand and it's the best I can do with a crap hand. It controls collateral, it gets the best hostage rescue team on earth in play to save Miko, it takes out the bad guys hard, and it's over in seconds.'

'It's full of things that can't be controlled.'

'There are no other options. Oh, except the one where you go, you give them the sword, they kill you, they kill Miko because she's a witness, they disappear, and then the whole thing happens as planned and Yuichi Miwa is reelected head of that Japanese porno association, drives out the Americans, and convinces himself he's a great patriot because he's kept Japanese blow jobs Japanese.'

'No, there's another option. Night raid. *Before* they move to the site. We go in under cover of darkness and we get the child out. Then, when she's gone and safe, we settle up. We do it with swords, so there's no gunfight in downtown Tokyo to make the noon news and the cover of *Time*.'

She laughed.

'Are you joking? It's fine, except A, we have no idea where they are, where they're keeping her, and we have no fast way to find it. If I had a thousand men and a week I could probably find out. I have less than forty-eight hours and we are talking the biggest city in the world. And B, we have no people. I couldn't get a SEAL team on a mission like that, because nobody above me would approve it. So who goes? You alone? You're a good operator, I know that. You're not that good, nobody's *that* good. You can't go alone.'

'No, I'm not that good.'

'I return to point A: even if you find the people to go along, you don't know where Miko is. You have no idea where they have her.'

'They can be found in ten minutes.'

'Come on.'

'Maybe five.'

'Swagger, are you off the wagon again? How on earth would you — '

'I didn't say *I* could find them. I couldn't find them. But I know somebody who could.'

'Who would that be?'

'You, Okada-san.'

She just looked at him.

'I'm guessing assistant head of station, chief of operations. Central Intelligence Agency, Tokyo Embassy. Code Name: SCREAMING BITCH.'

'Christ,' she said.

'You are so Agency, it's written all over you.

You must think I'm as dumb as I look and sound. I've been around you guys all my life. I worked with the Agency to recover a Sov sniper rifle in 'Nam back in 'seventy-three. I helped the Agency with its housekeeping in the matter of a deputy director named Ward Bonson who wasn't exactly who he said he was six years ago. So I know Agency.'

'My code name isn't SCREAMING BITCH,' she said.

'I know. I was trying to be funny.'

'It's MARTHA STEWART. I hate it, but there you have it.'

'Some jerk at headquarters hung that on you?'

'He did. I've made some enemies.'

'You must be good, then. Anyhow, here's how I figure it. You tell me how close I am. This whole thing has been Agency from the start. The object was to find out who killed Philip Yano and his family. Because Philip Yano was your man and always had been. He was getting you the Japanese stuff on a target like North Korea or China.'

'Something like that.'

'That's why he had such a good career. That's why he got all the choice American schools, and he got the big job in Iraq, and got to go into battle finally. They even postponed his retirement for him to lead his men. And he did well, except he lost an eye.'

'He was a very fine man. I had the privilege of running him during his last three operational years. He never betrayed his country, and he served ours brilliantly. We were very lucky to have him on the team.'

'Then, two years into his retirement, he gets whacked, and so does his family. Now, you have a problem, a big problem. Who killed Philip Yano? Has your outfit been penetrated? Did someone outside the need-to-know list figure it out? Did the Chinese kill him? Did the North Koreans? Did a disaffected Japanese group kill him? Or, always a possibility, could it have nothing to do with his career in your business? Could it just be random shit going down, the way it always does in the wicked, wicked world? Things are made more urgent by the fact the Japanese themselves don't seem too eager to solve the mystery. Why? Who's pulling strings? What's going on? What does it mean?'

She nodded. 'I knew you have an instinct for this kind of work.'

'Maybe so. Anyway, someone comes up with the idea of hiring the eight ball, the wild guy from way outside — '

'Me, actually.'

'I thought so. What an answer to all your prayers I was: I know nothing, ain't a part of no system, but I got the advantage that I don't take no for an answer, I don't mind busting heads, I ain't afraid of the red stuff, and I knew and loved Philip Yano. That's how come Al Ino was able to get me such a good phony passport, that's why someone knew where I was to ship me the Yano autopsy file, that's why you've been so interested in me, and here I thought it was my redneck good looks and my real tight blue jeans.'

'Your jeans *are* too tight, Swagger,' she said

376

morosely. Then she added, 'I don't see how you breathe. Anyhow. North Korea. Not China, but North Korea. Phil had access to the Japanese networks there, he knew everything about it. He was months ahead of everybody.'

'Yes, and that's why, two days ago, you pulled the plug. When you found out Phil Yano died because Bob Lee Swagger gave him a sword that, one in a million, turned out to be the one that some old guy used to cut some other old guy's head off three centuries ago, and that it had nothing to do with the North Koreans. No American national interest. None of our business. It was like a traffic accident, that's all. Tough, sad, too bad, but not a part of your operation, so it was time to pull the plug. Game over, investigation over. Swagger go home.'

'Swagger, that decision was made at the very top. If it matters, I fought against it. You have no idea how I fought against it, how everybody here fought against it. But we all serve the daimyo.'

'I hear you. I done my time serving the daimyo too. The pay is lousy, the food sucks, but you get shot at a lot. Anyhow, now it's time for the daimyo to serve us.'

'Where are you going with this, Swagger?'

'I ain't going nowhere. I'm sitting here and I'm gonna get another one of those mocha frappe things. I think the Japanese add fish oil to 'em; that's a drink with some kick.'

'Swagger, I can't — '

'You're the one that's going someplace. You're going to the fourth-floor commo room and getting out your little magical encryptor, the one you got in that cereal box. Here's what you tell 'em in Virginia: you got a tip that someone is receiving explosives from North Korea for a terror strike on Tokyo. He's mounting a mission here to bring down the Hyatt or the Tokyo Tower or the Tokyo Dome. They'll buy that in Langley. You request a tasked satellite intel mission, flash. You have a bird in the sky zero in on every known Miwa property in Tokyo, and your research people can dig them up for you. I'm guessing that's the seven mansions, five or six distribution centers, ten warehouses, two or three TV stations, four or five printing plants. Twenty, tops. You put the big sky eye smack cold zero on them and inside of five minutes the bird will uncover unusual, abnormal activity at one of them. Lots of men on the grounds, lots of seemingly aimless milling about, maybe a lot of kendo practice, some judo, that sort of thing. Oh, and an unusual collection of vehicles, perimeter security, maybe even patrols. It'll look very military op. And I'm guessing it's near a park, or some wide-open facility with a single entrance they can control without a lot of travel. That's where they'll run the exchange, that's where Kondo will kill Miko before my eyes just to see the hurt on my face. and that's where he'll cut me down.'

She just looked at him.

'All right,' she finally said, 'so we've found them.'

'You want to know who's on the team we put over the wall?'

'Do you have forty-seven samurai waiting outside?'

'No, outside is where you have your four Korean ex-Special Forces guys, who aren't Agency contract boys but Okada-san's bodyguards. Every time I get near you, I gotta play bumper car with them. The kid in the second car is too aggressive. He almost creamed us on the trip back from Kyoto. I hope you reamed his ass for that. He was way too close. But I know the type. They're all probably in love with you and they like to fight. They'll go.'

'You're right, they'll go. That's four.'

'Now for the fun part. We call one-eight-hundred-SAMURAI.'

'What's that?'

'Here's another surprise. I have regularly been reporting to a Major Albert Fujikawa of the Japanese Self-Defense Forces. He's in the loop and right now he's in Tokyo with forty of his boys. He was Phil Yano's exec in Samawah. It was his life Phil saved when the IED went off. The unit is a recon company from the First Airborne Brigade of the Eastern Army. HQ'd at Narashino. They're paratroopers, but all they do is play sixteenth century all day long and smack each other with wooden swords. I'm betting they're the best swordsmen in Japan.'

'If we get them involved, we break every law on the books regarding JDF.'

'They've figured out the patterns of *on*. Some things trump others in this country, and loyalty to murdered lords means more than obedience to the shogun's law. They're here, all set up and ready to go. You get us the satellite dope and we go in twenty-four hours.'

She just looked at him.

'You *are* dangerous,' she finally said. 'This was your game from the start, right?'

'We hit 'em dead solid cold. They have no idea it's coming. It's over in a few minutes because swords leave a mess, but they don't make no noise. Then we go home. Sometime the day after, someone notices the flies buzzing around the joint. That's when they make the discovery. Everybody's home and in bed by that time, and Miko's fine. Kondo Isami's head is on a pole. The sword is in Dr Otowa's vault, where it belongs. You just made head of station.'

'So, forty JDF paratroopers, plus Major Fujikawa, four ROK Spec Ops guys. I count forty-five.'

'It's enough,' he said.

'Not quite. You forgot the forty-sixth.'

'Who's that?'

'Me.'

'Okada — '

'Don't even start, Redneck. Don't you *dare* even start. I'm not sitting home baking cookies while you are destroying my career.'

'You're too stubborn to argue with.'

'Forty-six,' she said. 'Just for the luck factor alone, we should have one more. Who did I forget? Oh, yeah. *You.* You're the forty-seventh samurai.'

38

NII'S DREAMS

It was well after dark.

Nii was alone with the little girl in the white room. He could hear, vaguely, the sound of other men moving in the large house, loafing outside, yelling and shoving and gambling, playing around. He knew that Kondo was back from whatever errands and that the thing would happen very soon, the day after tomorrow almost certainly.

He could hear traffic, though this house was on a quiet street in a quiet part of Tokyo, far from the major arteries that hummed with life and action.

He could hear the quiet whistle of wind in the trees, and he remembered how surprisingly cold it was, and he realized that the seasons had changed and he'd been so caught up in the drama of his life, he hadn't noticed it.

He didn't think of the future or even the past; he didn't think of his beloved *oyabun* or of his *oyabun's* daimyo, in whose favor they all labored so hard. He didn't think that it was almost over, that he would be a complete and full-fledged member of the dominant *yakuza* gang in Tokyo, that his name would be known and that he would be mighty and feared.

That wasn't what preoccupied him.

He stared at her.

She slept uneasily, her body spilled out. In the low, somber light, his imagination played tricks on him. He imagined she was naked, when he knew she wasn't. He imagined she wanted him as much as he wanted her, when he knew she didn't. He imagined, somehow, they could be together forever, when he knew it was impossible because she had to die.

Nii had never felt this before. She was everywhere in his mind. That she was four and he twenty-five had no meaning; it was supposed to be. He knew it had to be.

He could make out the soft up and down of her frail chest under the blanket, hear the melody of her breathing. He could see her small, perfect foot, her adorable toes with their flaky coat of the summer's last toenail polish. He could see the button of her nose, the repose of her face, the quietude of her pale eyelids. He could see her cupid lips, buttercups, rose petals, candy kisses. He could see a flare of tension and relaxation in the perfect oval precision of her baby nostrils.

Nii watched until he could watch no more, then rushed out to masturbate.

The day after tomorrow, he told himself.

39

THE KENDO CHAMPION

Bob pulled his bike into the museum parking lot. It was cold, getting on to nightfall. His chilled steel hip throbbed dully, broadcasting its message of deadness. He shook off the unpleasant feeling and its tendrils of memory. Tonight it all happened, he knew. He tried to wipe his mind blank. But he could not. No man could.

He checked his watch. It was 5:45 p.m. Tokyo time. Driving had been hellish, sliding in and out of the busy, mirror-image shunt of the cars, with things coming at him from odd angles. He didn't enjoy it a bit. It took too much out of him.

Of course all these ill feelings had their source in the immediate few minutes, where he'd have to deliver some very bad news to a man who'd been nothing but good to him. Not a happy prospect. Was it necessary? Yeah, it was. He couldn't proceed without what lay ahead in an office full of swords.

He thought of the parts assembling. Susan and her four Koreans, Major Fujikawa, the paratroopers, all of them quietly converging on a neighborhood in northwest Tokyo, far off the tourist way, miles from the famous spots like the Ginza and Shinjuku and Ueno and Asakusa, a place without major shrines or nightclubs or department stores. It was near there that the Agency satellites had uncovered intense activity on a Miwa property, a walled mansion in a secluded street next to a parkland called Kiyosumi Garden, once the playground of the Mitsubishi family and now a kind of wonderland of Asian garden themes. The mansion hit all the criteria perfectly: quiet, obscure, close to a park with one gated entrance, easy to command, walled off from society.

They would meet to stage at the close-by hotel banquet room, where, under a guise, Susan had made an emergency rental of the large room, claiming to represent a kendo club headed to an out-of-town meet and needing a rallying point.

Bob shivered. The weather had changed abruptly, the temperature had dropped, and he really didn't have the clothes for the midthirties, which it threatened to reach tonight. He drew his raincoat tightly about him, for warmth, but it was a thin coat and his black suit was thin cotton, summer weight, unable to stand up to the bite of the sudden gusts of breeze or the generalized bite of the falling temperature.

He approached the museum, feeling its cathedral-like grandeur tower over him. It was a modern building, constructed after the war, of course, but its lines carefully duplicated the harmonies of classical Edo architecture. So in a sense entering it was like being swallowed by Japan, as Jonah was swallowed by a whale. Inside, it was all Japan, only Japan, and no other place was permitted to exist. The somber, gray light lent everything a stoic dignity; in glass cases, kimonoed princesses and armored knights stood nobly, reflecting the grandeur of a past so glorious and bloody and complicated, so full of opera and murder, it almost defied belief. You could see the whole thing play out before your eyes in these vast rooms, from the little men the Chinese had found living in thatched huts to the brilliant men who had invaded China, raped its cities, cut it in half. You could see the Zen priest and the samurai warrior. You could feel the presence of men so mentally tough and sublimely confident, they could fight twenty at a time and win and not think much of it, with their long, curved swords of the most sophisticated metallurgy in the world. But it was all one thing: if you had those brave men, you also had sword testers who went out in the night and cut random strangers down to see how well the blades cut, you had secret diagrams of how to arrange a corpse to perform a cutting test on it, how many times a skull could be cleaved and from what angle. You had the brilliant men who destroyed the Russian fleet in seven minutes in 1905, and their grandsons, who fell from the sky in planes that were bombs, skipping between the blasts of American flak, hunting for a nice large gray superstructure against which to obliterate themselves. It was that same utter commitment that sank the Russian ships, blew up the American fleet off Okinawa, and built the skyscrapers of Shinjuku.

By this time, the security people knew Bob and nodded him through. He took the elevator to the fourth floor.

'Is the doctor in?'

'Yes, yes,' said his secretary. 'Dr Otowa, Swagger-san is here.'

'Oh, do come in. I was just getting ready to leave. Do you think it will freeze?'

'Feels like it in the air.'

'Yes, nippy out. Bracing, I must say. You have some news? Please sit, my friend.'

Bob sat in the familiar chair and faced the old man in his room of swords.

'The good news is, I think this will be concluded very shortly, and if all goes well, I will be free to dispose of the sword as I want. What I want is for the museum to have the blade. You-all would know what to do with it. It shouldn't be the possession of any one man but of your nation.'

'That is very thoughtful of you. I had hoped for as much.'

'It is my pleasure. But I actually came on another bit of business. I'm sorry to say, this news ain't good.'

'I am prepared.'

'Are you sure?'

'Speak, please.'

'There's a man calling himself Kondo Isami. Do you know the name?'

'Of course. Every Japanese does. Kondo Isami was the leader of Shinsengumi in Kyoto in eighteen sixty-seven. He led many raids, was in many fights. A hero or a villain, depending, but surely an extraordinary swordsman in the shogun's cause. He was executed in eighteen sixty-eight by the emperor's forces. He died well

386

but dishonorably, by beheading. He was not permitted *seppuku*.'

'This new Kondo Isami is also an extraordinary swordsman. In his fashion, he works for the shogun, fighting against outside domination. He's a *yakuza* contract killer, the very best. You can see by his name he has some kind of vanity for samurai history. He likes to think of himself as one of them old boys. But nothing stops him. He killed Philip Yano and family. The whole business with the sword has been his invention. Now we have the sword. I'm afraid to say he has kidnapped Miko Yano, and tonight, all that gets sorted out.'

'There will be blood?'

'A lot of it, I think.'

'Yours?'

'Possibly.'

'You will fight this Kondo Isami.'

'If I can find him.'

'You are very brave, Swagger-san.'

'No. I just don't see no other way. He's too good to fight the others; he'll kill them quick. So I have to run him down and face him off. That's what he wants. It's what I want too. It's why I came here.'

'I see. And from me you want?'

'I have gotten so much from you, but I must ask for one more thing. It's the hardest thing and you can be forgiven for not wanting to give it. But I felt I must ask.'

'What?'

'Your blessing.'

'Why would that be such a hard thing?'

387

'Because this 'Kondo Isami' is your son.'

There was a pause.

'I am beseeching the father of a man I must kill for his permission,' Bob said. 'I won't have a chance unless you free me. I can't see a son. I can only see an enemy.'

Dr Otowa looked at him dully.

Then he said. 'I have no son.'

'Then he is your brother's son or your sister's son.'

'I have no brother or sister.'

He met Swagger's gaze steadily.

'It is said of the new Kondo,' Swagger said, 'that some people he meets normally, that he goes clubbing, that he has a regular life. But sometimes he retreats into some kind of artifice. If he has to meet certain people he wears a mask. Or he designs some theatrical lighting setup so his face can't be seen. What's behind that? When I saw him, I knew. He can't meet people who know you. He met me because he doesn't know I've been in contact with you. But anyone who's seen him and you would see in a second the extreme facial similarity. It's all there: the eyes, the shape of the nose, the shape of the mouth, the texture and color of the skin, the width of the face, the hairline. It's a face I had seen before, sir. I saw it in a photo at Doshu's dojo in Kyoto. You, Doshu, and the boy, then possibly fourteen, and some big trophy.'

'My son died,' said Otowa.

Bob saw no point in adding a thing. In any case, he had nothing to add.

Finally, Dr Otowa spoke.

'I suppose I always feared such a thing. No one can hurt a father like a son, and no revenge is sweeter than the son's upon the father.'

'You should not blame yourself.'

'There is no one else to blame. That picture was taken in nineteen seventy-seven when the boy was sixteen. He had just won the eighteen-under all-Japan kendo championship open division, under Doshu's coaching. His life was set. He would win it at seventeen, and at eighteen: then he would enter the men's division and win that for five years running. Then he would be a national hero, a celebrity. He could go anywhere and do anything. Japan would be before him. He could be a politician, a CEO, an admiral.'

'What happened?'

'An appointment came up. It was an extraordinary opportunity. I supposed it would turn me into a national hero, a celebrity. I chose myself over him. I took him to America with me for three years. He had two years of American education at Scarsdale High and a year at Columbia. I don't think he ever really forgave me for taking him out of his competitive kendo for the three most important years of his life. But to this day I don't know how I could have turned it down. In any event, America changed him in some basic ways. It confused him.'

'It'll do that.'

'He came back in 'eighty at nineteen and we knew he was too far behind to score well in the eighteen-overs, that is, the national champion-ship. But he competed valiantly. It was astonishing. He made it to the finals. He was so heroic. But he lost, a close match. So it goes. But then in a split second, he threw it all away. Samurai pride, samurai rage. The helmets were off, the two opponents bowed, and my son went berserk for one second. He struck the man in the neck with his *shinai*, hurt him quite badly. Broke his collarbone. I had not been father enough to save him from his greediest hungers. The scandal was shattering. There was no hope. His *gi* and slippers were found on the beach at Enoshima. He had walked into the sea. No body was ever found.'

'I'm very sorry,' Bob said.

'You have no need to apologize. The shame is mine to bear, and mine alone. I love what my son was, I hate myself for my agency in his corruption, and I loathe what he has become. I can see the psychology, though. He did become the best swordsman in Japan, though not in a surrogate format with bamboo weapons. As a calculated affront to me and to the elders of the kendo world, he became a champion in the real world of the gutter, where the blades are sharp and the blood is real.'

Bob said nothing.

'Come with me,' said the old man.

He led Bob to the blank dark wall of the vault, cranked the handle, and slid the massive door open. He ducked in, gesturing Bob to follow, and Bob found himself amid yet more swords, even more beautiful, more valuable.

'There are many great collections,' Otowa said, 'but none so great as this.'

'I am privileged,' said Bob.

The doctor leaned and plucked one off the wall.

'Here,' he said, handing it to Bob.

Bob felt the electricity of the thing, the perfection of its balance, the hunger of its blade, the stunning artistry of its fabrication.

'May I?'

'Of course.'

Bob turned the blade upward and cleanly drew it from the *saya*. The *koshirae* — blood red *sago* of black sharkskin, a gold-tinted *tsuba* — were magnificent, but even that magnificence was diminished by the blade.

'That may be the most perfect blade in all Japan. It is certainly the sharpest, the strongest, the most deadly.'

'Sir, it's priceless.'

'Take it. Use it. Fight with it. Possibly it gives you a slight edge. My son will recognize it. He will know its power. It is one thing that may give him pause. It is your only chance. He had a superb natural skill set, and if he's worked hard for the past twenty years, he is indeed transcendent.'

'I couldn't risk losing it.'

'Swagger-san, it was built for this purpose and no other. It is fulfilling its destiny. Were it sentient, it would petition for permission to defend you. Think nothing of its value. Think nothing of its rarity. Think only of it as your weapon.'

'Yes, sir. A Muramasa, I take it?'

'It is indeed. The 'evil' swordsmith. His was

the blade — maybe even that one — in the stream in the famous story about Masamune. The leaves and twigs avoided the great Masamune's. Muramasa's attracted them, and it cut them flawlessly. Muramasa took pride in this when he should have felt shame. Thus his blades had a reputation for blood. They yearned to cut. They also had a penchant for seeking out members of the shogun's family, and killing or maiming them. They were banned, rounded up, and destroyed by the shogunate, which is why they are so rare today, and that is one of the survivors. My son will know this, and know that he works for a kind of shogun. That will cloud his mind. Again, a small thing, but victory is won on small things.'

'I thank you. I will return — '

'No. If you kill him, then the sword will have served its purpose. Maybe that is why it came to me so many years ago. Destroy it, that's all. Get it off the earth. Send it to hell. It came from hell, it represents hell. Use it and destroy it without a second thought.'

'I will, Dr Otowa.'

'That sword is my blessing. Now please go. I wish to be alone.'

40

THE BIG SHOTS

'You're sure,' said the Shogun.

'As sure as I can be. I told you, Lord, this is a determined and creative adversary. But now we have him.'

'I worry that at the park, it will be difficult to control. It will spill into a mess, and the news stations and the — '

'I will have ten men concealed. They are experts at camouflage. Ninja, almost. Not really, but close. I myself will be there. It's early, we control access to the park. No one will interfere. Certain suggestions have been made to the police to stay away. It's very, very early, barely dawn. We control the terrain. He has no choice but to come, if he loves the child, and he loves the child. I saw it in his eyes. At a signal I can get forty more men in the park almost instantly. He has some skill, I admit. But not enough to overcome me and certainly not enough to overcome fifty men. That only happens in movies.'

'Suppose he brings — '

'He can't. He won't have time. He cannot locate us until we call him. He will have to travel at extreme speed across Tokyo. We will be watching all the roads as he approaches and will know if he has allies. But he can't get allies close enough in time. It's a very solid plan.'

'The child — '

'The child must die. She's seen too much. It is a small matter. It means nothing.'

'It's just that I — '

'Lord, it means nothing.'

'Yes, Kondo-san.'

They sat in the living room of the mansion next to Kiyosumi Gardens. It was nearly midnight. Kondo had spent the day going over his preparations. He had his own trained men; he had his *kobun* Nii, his most trusted fellow, virtually connected by tether to the child; he had forty toughened soldiers from Boss Otani, ready to die for him. No, they weren't the best and they preferred to fight with Kalashnikov and Makarov than *katana* and *wakizashi*, but they would still rather die than yield, and would kill at the drop of a hand. And, if necessary, he had plenty of Kalashnikovs and Makarovs.

Still, the Shogun was nervous, Kondo could tell. He sat there, licking his lips, his face glowing in the light of the fire, swallowing, twitching occasionally, trying to control his nerves. He wasn't so brilliant at this kind of thing. The Shogun didn't even need to be there, but he had insisted. Still, regret seemed to cloud his thought.

'I just wish all this hadn't happened,' he said petulantly. 'We are running out of time.'

Pornographer! thought Kondo. There was no point in explaining to him that what happens is what happens. Feelings about what is past are silly; they contribute nothing; one must only look at the now.

'Lord, I have made all the arrangements. The *koshirae* will be completed in record time. The hard part was the polishing. Getting that done — and I understand the old man did a superb job, maybe his best — was the key. You will have the sword in plenty of time to announce it, to enjoy the prestige and attention, to empower your plans. All the things you desire will be delivered to you, exactly as planned. This unforeseen business — a trouble, I admit — is unfortunate, but we have it under control.'

'The stroke of the child. It was brilliant. We went from losers to winners in that single instant.'

'Strategy is very important.'

'You are a genius, Kondo-san. You will be well rewarded.'

'My service is my reward. But I'll still take that four million dollars. Tomorrow at this time I will have both my fortune and my opponent's head. I think I'll take a nice vacation.'

'Try Los Angeles. I'll give you some numbers. Fuck some blond white women. Very enjoyable. Once you do, you'll see why only certain Japanese should be allowed that pleasure. It would corrupt the general public and soon the concept of 'Japanese' would be gone! We must protect the sexual powers of our men, the submission of our women, and the purity of our — '

You had to stop him or he'd go on for hours and Kondo wanted a little sleep. 'I look forward to it,' he said.

Miwa went to pour himself another Scotch.

He watched the amber fluid splash across the ice cubes. Then he raised his eyes and peered out the window, where the many spotlights created an intense and impenetrable zone of illumination.

'Kondo-san,' he said, 'look! It's snowing.'

41

STAGING

An observer could be forgiven for thinking that indeed a kendo club had commandeered the banquet hall of the Kasaibashi Hotel on Kasaibashi Road a block from Kiyosumi Gardens in East Tokyo. The young men were husky, handsome, quiet, athletic, graceful, and all carried kendo bags, long enough to accommodate *shinai*, the bamboo sword of the sport. Other bagged gear surely contained the armor kendoists wore, and the appearance of medical technicians merely confirmed the impression, as kendo can be a rough encounter, leaving abrasions, bruises, sometimes even cuts. Their coaches, a few years older, were also husky, handsome, quiet, athletic, and graceful. All wore black jumpsuits under sweatshirts, all carried black watch caps wedged into their belts, all spoke only to friends if at all. So many young men — but they had to be a team because there was no joshing, no horsing around, no shoving or needling. Certainly, a big match loomed ahead.

The observer would have wondered about the *gaijin* who seemed to be some kind of consultant to them, for he enjoyed the confidence of the older fellows and soon took over the pep talk from the head coach. But what to make of the slim, beautiful woman in glasses, who also seemed to enjoy everyone's confidence? Was she a kendoist? She was wearing blue jeans, New Balance sport shoes, and a black turtleneck, almost a kendoist's outfit. And yet again, what of the final touch, the four Korean men, much squarer in face and blockier in build than their Japanese counterparts, who spoke to no one and hovered close to the woman? All in all, it was a very strange gathering.

But of course there was no observer. The Kasaibashi was a two-star business joint well away from tourist areas. At midnight, when this strange confab began arriving in ones or twos, checking in with a fellow who looked as much like a sergeant as a coach, only a single employee was on duty at the hotel, a night clerk who doubled as a telephone operator. He was earnestly advised to mind his own business by someone whose seriousness of purpose impressed him. And his switchboard was quietly disconnected from the outside. All this was done with utmost politeness but, at the same time, utmost sincerity.

In the big room, the men eventually assembled before a blackboard, each silent, each ready, until at 3 a.m., the meeting commenced, the head coach welcoming them, promising them that this would be their night, the night they had so long awaited, the night when their team would triumph. The men seemed, like all men in preathletic stress, tight and nervous and hungry at once.

Finally the *gaijin* stood in front of the men. Hmmm, what would a *gaijin* know about kendo?

398

But this one held their attention, even if he didn't seem to be talking about kendo.

'Last-minute check,' he said, speaking in an English that more than half understood, but which was translated by the woman with great technical fluency in near real time. 'Medics, there are medics here, Major Fujikawa?'

The major nodded, as three men raised their hands.

'You've all got O-neg, plenty of needle and thread, plenty of QuiKlot, plenty of clamps and transfusion equipment? Wounds tonight will be cuts. You medics, I hope you've been practicing clamping and sewing, that's what it'll be all about.'

The appropriate men nodded.

'Okada-san,' he said.

The woman handed out Xerox sheets.

She said in Japanese. 'That's the latest satellite photo of the target, taken approximately six hours ago. Don't ask who took it or how I got it. You can see the layout of the building, the layout of the walls. We have ID'd approximately fifty men on site. They seem to be quartered in the basement, because they go in and out of one lower-story side door. They were all inside as of nineteen hundred hours. The front gate is locked. You can also see that we've indicated by marker your approach to the target. It's no more than half a mile from here.'

'Let me run through this one more time,' said the *gaijin*. 'You've been briefed, but let's take it by the steps.'

He ran through it again: how in small groups the men would infiltrate Kiyosumi Gardens, come out at the far end, and gather in two groups on the north and south sides of the wall around the Miwa mansion. The four snipers would take up positions on the walls. At that point Susan and Bob would approach in her RX-8, park next to the west wall midway between the two teams. The signal was a loud blast from the horn, and then the men would proceed over the walls.

'Captain Tanada takes the rear team over the south wall. Major Fujikawa will go over from the left of the gate, the north wall. I don't want to breach the gate because I don't want to use explosives, and if there are sentries inside with firearms, their first instinct will be to zero in on the gate. As they look at the gate, the snipers should find them in the windows and take them out. Okada-san and I will go over from our position on the east wall.

'You get to the house, then you toss your flash-bangs: each window, each door. I don't want you entering the house because you don't know the layout and the arrangement of the furniture or the closets, and Okada-san and I will be inside, and I don't want us getting all mixed up. With the flash-bangs, those guys will come pouring out.

'I should tell you: the one feature of a sword fight is a lot of blood. It ain't like no movie. There will be blood everywhere. You cannot cut with *katana* hard into the torso without severing major arteries. It will be slippery and sloppy. You cannot allow yourself to be shocked by it. When you cut him, he'll bleed bad. If he don't go down, cut him again, hard, and he will. Then move on. If you are cut, disengage, get your bandage tight on it, and fall back to the medics, who will be the last over the wall. They will get you clamped and get an O-neg line into you. You have a lot of blood. You can lose half of it before you pass out. If you see a lot of your own blood, do not panic. Move swiftly to the medics and you will be all right.

'There is one man you should avoid. This man is called Kondo Isami. He will be older, about forty-five. His skills are beyond yours, believe me. If you see him, do not fight him: if he means to escape, let him escape. If he is guarding someone — I'm imagining he will be guarding Miwa, the big boss — then you surround them but do not attempt to take him down. He will kill six or seven of you before you can finish him and those are unacceptable casualties. Simply hold him at bay; we'll get the snipers in quickly, and if they won't surrender we'll shoot them. Or tell me where he is. If it comes to it, I will handle him. I've done a lot of fighting in my life and I am not afraid to fight.

'Finally, remember our priorities: saving Miko Yano is first, justice for the man who murdered her father and family is second, and this fellow Kondo is third. Okada-san and I will find the little girl. Okada-san has night vision and we will penetrate the house first; we think the kid's probably in a cluster of bedrooms on the second floor. After we get the girl out safely, I will be looking for Kondo; Major Fujikawa, who is in charge of the ground forces, will be looking for

401

Miwa. Captain Tanada, I think, will just be looking for heads to take.'

There was laughter.

'Now, I just want to thank you. I am a stranger to this country and the men of this platoon have made me feel at home. I know I am among professionals. Our interests are the same: justice for Philip Yano and his family, and life for his surviving daughter. The people who took the first and threaten the last are a half-mile away, sleeping the sleep of the wicked, confident that they own the world. This is the night they find out different.'

After that, it just seemed to happen without much drama. The men, clutching their kendo bags, pulling on their black watch caps, began to form up into the two- or three-man teams. The medics with the larger bags of gear fell in to the rear. The staff people — Fujikawa, Sergeant Major Kanda, Captain Tanada, and Bob and Susan — were at the front, looking at the map one last time.

★ ★ ★

Bob and Susan sat in her car outside the hotel, watching as the last of the teams moseyed out and disappeared into the night. It was about ten minutes from go-time. Bob looked at his watch.

Suddenly a buzz filled the empty space.

'Shit,' Susan said. She pulled out her cell phone, switched it off.

'Your date is annoyed because you stiffed him?' Bob said.

402

'My boss is pissed because I stiffed *him*. That's the fifteenth time he's called in the last two hours. He's also sent me ten text messages. He wants to see me right now.'

'Christ.'

'He can't reach me. That doesn't please him. He's mad, he's desperate, and tomorrow I get fired.'

'You could go now.'

'No way. If my career's going south, I want to be there for the fifth act. I want to see it all turn sour. Now, Swagger?'

'Yes?'

'Some questions, all right? No bullshit. I have never bullshitted you. We may both be dead in twenty minutes, so no bullshit.'

'Yes, ma'am.'

'Swagger, your little drama is about to come off. You made it happen. Subtly, carefully, skillfully, with a great deal of sound planning, you've got a career CIA officer and fifty Japanese Self-Defense Force paratroopers about to raid a *yakuza* strong point, in contravention to the basic laws of both groups. It shouldn't be possible, but you made it happen. The question is simple: why?'

'Why? Well, I cared a great deal about Philip Yano. I felt involved because I gave him the sword.'

'Bullshit. That's what you've been saying, but I see now you're too smart for that. You think things through too carefully. That's just a cover story. You know that giving him that sword was pure chance. You could not have known what the consequences were, and you were not responsible for them. You know that. And another odd thing: why did you work so hard to give him that sword? You told me you went all over America looking for the sword. So even before you'd stayed with his family, the Yanos meant something special to you. What, Swagger? Tell me.'

Swagger considered.

'All right,' he finally said. 'I was raised not to talk of such things and I never have. But you deserve an answer, Okada-san.'

He looked off. The snow was falling more heavily, sifting down through the trees, muffling the earth, driving most of the traffic away. Swagger thought of the men moving through the dark, creeping toward their destination, violence in the air, another night of war. So much war in the Swagger family.

'My father,' he finally said, 'never talked about the war. He was a great man, one of very few surviving five-invasion marines. He hit five beaches, was shot up seven times, once close to death, but he kept going back. Finally, two days after the fifth beach, Iwo Jima, he won the Medal of Honor. I suppose he liked having won that medal and the respect it earned him. But he never, ever bragged on it or mentioned it, and he told me once. 'You are *never* to tell anyone about that medal.' That was very important to him.

'But one night in nineteen fifty-five, a few weeks before he died, he was out on the porch talking with a friend of his, the county prosecutor, a wonderful old goat named Sam

404

Vincent. The two of them were talking about the war. Sam was running himself down and Dad said, 'Mr Sam, you think I am such a goddamned hero and you are a failure because of Thebes. Let me tell you a thing or two and maybe you don't know so much and things ain't so clear. You know that big medal I won in the war?'

'And Sam said, 'Earl, everyone knows you single-handedly took on a Jap pillbox and killed forty men that day.''

'Well, sir,' said Dad, 'it wasn't quite like that. And he told him what really happened.'

42

MOON OF HELL

SHOWA YEAR 20, SECOND MONTH. 21ST DAY 21
FEBRUARY 1945

The third chamber had caught most of the blast. As he squirmed into the entranceway, Earl saw that the big automatic weapon was atilt and two men, standing over the body of a third, struggled to restore it to a firing position. Goddamn, they were good, the little bastards. Fighting so hard, no matter that death was here for them, to kill a few more marines. You had to respect them, even as you killed them, and kill them he did, one spray that caught them in tracer and clouds of debris from the bullet-strikes against concrete behind them. He stepped forward in aggression. Then he caught a flash of movement in his peripheral, turned, and saw that it was too late, as a man with a sword drove forward, had him cold and uncoiled, the sword diving toward his neck.

But then it stopped. There was a frozen moment when the sword caught on the ceiling for some reason, and the arc was interrupted.

Earl pulled back in panic, swept left and fired. The gun fired three times, went empty, but the three had all hit. The Japanese officer went down. He squirmed into the fetal position, blood pooling beneath him hard and black and glossy in the low, smoky light of the gun pit. He moaned, convulsed, thrashed.

Kill him! Earl thought.

He dumped the light machine gun, and his hand flew to his .45; he got it up, jacked back the hammer, and put the sight on the man's head.

Kill him!

But he couldn't. The man was twisting in great pain, his jaws clamped shut. Earl quickly stuffed the pistol back in its holster, reached around for his first-aid kit, and pulled out a Squibb morphine syrette. Quickly, he broke the glass casing that shielded the needle, removed the needle, and reversed it to puncture the tube seal, then screwed the needle onto the neck. All he had to do was inject the needle point and squeeze the tube.

He bent to the man, pulled back his tunic collar to expose some neck, and placed the pinprick against the flesh, and —

★ ★ ★

The American fired from just outside the entrance. His gun threw light into the room, like the sparkly contents of a pail of water. Then the man stepped into the room to make sure and Captain Yano uncoiled.

He had done it a thousand, a hundred thousand times, felt the muscles charge with power as the sword acquired speed and certainty, flashed through its arc and hungered for flesh.

407

He had him cold, for he was so ahead of the reaction time that the hairy beast could do nothing but die. The blade would shatter the clavicle bone, cut through spine and lungs and heart, continue to the intestines; he would drive on, cutting, then withdraw on the same plane and —

Then he felt his foot, thrust forward in the stroke, alight atop something hard, so he was two inches higher and the sword caught on the ceiling and its vibration of disaster flowed from point down shaft to grip — from *kissaki* down to *nakago* — and in the second he lost, the hairy one squirmed right, spun the gun, and it erupted.

He did not feel himself fall. He did not feel his legs. What he felt was that he'd been drenched in hot, steaming water. The pain soon localized into three bad sites, and his fingers clawed at them, to hold the blood in, but he could not. He lay on his side, his knees up, feeling his life drain away.

He felt the American on him. He felt the pressure of the other body, he felt the hands go to his neck.

He cuts my throat!

His hands bunched at his stomach, his elbows drawn in, he suddenly realized he had a whisper of advantage, for his enemy considered him dead already and in that second his elbow achieved force and speed and it slammed hard into the man's face just under the eye driving him back, and again the captain elbowed him in the face, driving him back still more in a moment of stunned weakness. The captain, liberated from the weight of the man, drove himself at him.

They rolled in the dirt. The captain seemed to get his hands around the American's throat, but a punch arrived from nowhere, breaking his grip, knocking out two teeth. He slammed the American under the eye with the palm of his hand, feeling the blow strike hard, hearing the other man grunt. They pounded into each other's torsos with fists and open hands, their sweat fell on each other's faces, they tried to find leverage bracing against the floor.

He knew he would die; his strength was ebbing and the pain in his guts rose.

Gradually the stronger American seemed to prevail, but the captain thought of kendo, of perfect emptiness, and found a blow to the throat, and the man jacked upright, lost his grip, and somehow the captain put strength in it, then took it away, and the American's own strength toppled him, so the captain slithered over him, and was atop him in terrible intimacy. His right hand flew to the leather haft of a knife the American wore on his belt; he snatched it, again feeling the friction as the blade freed itself from a metal scabbard. He rammed his wrist into the man's throat, driving him back, and continued on the roll, thrusting the knife upward, nesting it between two ribs so that it would slide easily into the central chest cavity. The grip was wood or leather, grooved heavily, a little thick for him, but he controlled it quickly enough, securing it in his strong fingers. He felt the knife point pressuring the skin, the skin fighting, then yielding, as the blade penetrated a quarter of an inch. Two ounces more of pressure and he could thrust through to the man's heart and take one more with him.

★　★　★

Earl was dead. Where did the scrawny man find the strength? He looked into the Japanese's eyes, felt the pinprick of the blade of his KA-BAR between his ribs, and fought to get his hands around the man's throat but was too late.

I am dead, he thought.

He got me.

He beat me.

He closed his eyes. He felt the wrist heavy against his throat, smelled sweat and oil and fish, felt their two hearts beating almost against each other, locked in the murder embrace.

The deadly point of the KA-BAR probed his skin, bent it down, maybe drew a drop of blood. It would slide in easily, climb through lung tissue, and find the clump of muscle called his heart.

Oh, Christ, Junie, I tried so hard.

★　★　★

The captain leaned into the knife hilt and — stopped.

He saw on the ground next to the American's head a flexible metal tube with a syrette screwed to its mouth. He realized instantly it was morphine. The American hadn't been trying to cut his throat; he'd been trying to ease his pain.

He drew back. It seemed suddenly wrong to kill a man who meant to save him.

But it seemed wrong to surrender to him too.

★ ★ ★

I wish I done gave you a child, I am so sorry to leave you alone. There wasn't no time. I had so much to tell you.

But he felt an immense liberation as the pinprick went away and the man somehow heaved himself off Earl's body, and lay a foot away, breathing hard.

A smile came to the man's grimy face.

'*Samurai*,' he said.

Then he reversed the heavy war knife, plunged it into his own neck, where a major artery carried a river of blood to his brain. The jab was expert, and the blood spurted out in a bright and gaudy fountain. In eight seconds his brain had devoured the oxygen and glucose that remained, and his eyes closed.

★ ★ ★

'He killed himself,' Susan said.

'Yeah. Dad told Sam he thought the guy may have seen the morphine single he was trying to inject. It was right there on the floor next to them. Or maybe Hideki Yano had had enough killing. Or maybe he was saying, I'm the better man, I can kill you or not, and then I can embrace death. Whatever, my father always felt he'd lost that battle. The Japanese officer won it.

411

And for whatever reason in the middle of a battlefield, the worst battle on earth, the most dangerous — on a 'moon of hell,' as someone called it — the officer let Earl Swagger live. That's why my dad gave up that sword. Maybe that's why he never talked about the medal. And also because of that, Earl got to go home, where he got his wife pregnant and they had a little boy called Bob Lee. And how Mr Earl loved that boy, and helped him and taught him. So Bob Lee not only got his own life in the deal, he got nine more years with his daddy, who was a great man. And thirty-odd years down the worthless road, Bob Lee himself got a daughter out of it, and she's a great one too. It all goes back to the decision that Japanese officer made in that pillbox. So you could say Bob Lee, he owes the Yanos something big. Call it on, call it whatever you want. But what he owes them is everything.'

'He does,' said Susan.

Bob looked at his watch. It was 4:59:57 a.m.

:58.

:59.

'Okay,' she said. 'Samurai up.'

43

CHUSHINGURA

The last thing Swagger said was, 'When you hit the ground, wait a second, then pull down your goggles and go to night vision.'

But in the one-tenth of a second of fall, she forgot, and she landed with more thud than she expected: it was seven feet, she felt her body elongate to full extension then accordion shut with a bang when she landed, snapping her head hard enough to drive bangles and spangles before her eyes.

She could see — nothing. It made no sense. Light and dark, nothing focused, nothing where it should be, all confusion, her will scattered and gone.

'Goggles,' whispered Swagger, who had come down beside her.

She got the goggles down — PVS7s, she'd had a day on them at a Delta Force counterterror workshop at Fort Bragg a few years ago — and hit the toggle, which was no longer where it should be but an inch to the right, evidently resettled on her head in the landing. This led to another moment of confusion, but then she got them aligned right and it all popped to. Things were beginning to happen.

It was a green, fuzzy world. Still, she made out the house. To the left, a glowing amoeba seemed to be disintegrating before her eyes. It was Tanada's rear team, coming hard over the back wall, in fact most were down, pausing only to withdraw their *katana*, then peeling off individually to the left rear. Meanwhile to the right, the same optical phenomenon reiterated itself, this being Fujikawa's front team, maybe a tad behind the curve, but peeling right. She swept the house, saw nothing, but then the front door opened and she saw a man with a rifle — AK-47, she ID'd it, again from her Bragg tutorial — and behind her she heard the sound of — well, of what? It was light, a wet piston floating through the grease of a hydraulic tube, nothing sharp, but surprisingly vibratory. It was a silenced rifle, wielded by Sniper 3 Kim, and before the sound had even dissipated, the rifleman went down as if someone had cut his knees and they no longer held, and he just flopped down hard and fast.

She realized, I just saw a man die.

'House clear,' came the voice of 3 Kim from above.

At that moment a series of bright flashes syncopated to hard pops lit off in the basement of the house, as the first team of intruders had gotten their flash-bangs into the area where the yaks were.

'Go, go,' said Bob, but she was already on the way, low, hard, cutting directly across the courtyard to the house, reaching it and sliding along it. She felt Swagger beside her. She reached the open door, stepped over the body of the guy with the rifle, and, clutching her *wakizashi* in her right hand, ducked inside.

Captain Tanada was not the sort to direct; he was the sort to lead. So he hit the ground and took off, and fuck anybody who couldn't keep up with him. But that got him close to the rear of the house first, and he pulled his flash-bang, got the pin out, and almost — but not quite — launched it through the window.

He got himself under control.

Four other men reached him and to each he gestured with the small munition, and each duplicated his move. Flash-bang out, pin out, lever secured, each man placed himself next to a window and in the next second, on Tanada's nod, each shattered the window with a pad-protected elbow, tossed in the illumination device, and peeled back, withdrawing *katana* from scabbard, waiting for a target.

The things went off almost simultaneously, not in concussive explosion — they weren't bombs, after all — but with a harsh bang and a white phosphorous flash that blasted anyone's night vision to pieces. You could be forgiven for thinking that the devil himself had chucked a nuclear device through the window. They caused one of two responses: utter paralysis or complete panic. Four of them quadrupled the effect.

In a second the first man came out, unarmed, and Tanada hit him with the hilt hard in the head. Two more came out, one to be conked, the other took a roundhouse slash at Tanada, who neatly evaded and watched one of his men hit the yak with a hard diagonal cut, left to right, so that he jacked, pirouetted, dropping his weapon, and went down, spurting blood.

And then suddenly it was happening, exactly as the men had dreamed about and believed they wanted, exactly as had not happened in Japan, except on movie sets, for more than a century: the yaks poured from the house and began to spread out, each unleashing a sword, and the soldiers moved forward to engage them, a kendo-to-the-death in dull light as the snow swooped downward, the cuts hard and serious and meant to kill, the evasions equally hard and serious and meant to avoid, the whole thing happening in slow motion and fast motion at the same time.

Tanada killed two men in a single second as they came at him, his technique superb: *kesagiri* on the first, diagonal, a flowing block from the second assailant's *kesagiri*, which led quite naturally into a horizontal *yokogiri*, with four inches of blade opening eight inches of body. The destroyed man made a gasping sound, tried to step back, and fell.

Tanada looked about and saw war everywhere and was happy. Then he got back to work.

★   ★   ★

Nii was dreaming, filthily, completely, in anatomical detail, dreams that would shame most but only gave him a boner the size of a V-2. But then the V-2 exploded, and he came hard awake in time for another V-2 explosion, then a third and a fourth. Around him, he heard screams, starts, lurches; men jumped, some wailed, some grabbed weapons. The door was open, and someone rushed out, and Nii caught a glimpse of him brought down with a wicked blow.

Attack, he thought.

His mind dumped clear and empty. He had a moment of stupendous confusion as all his reflexes broke down. Two more, then two more explosions went off, but after the first, he got his eyes shut and buried in his fists.

When he opened them, the big room was half empty. He saw a man jump in, blade whistling, and take one of his friends down with a single blow, and in the ferocity of the blow, he knew there was no mercy this night, it was to the death. More men flooded the room, blades slicing the air, cutting through meat, killing. Someone threw a charcoal hibachi at an invader, who ducked and killed him with a cut across the belly.

Nii rose to fight, then remembered his mission.

Kill the little girl.

It wasn't a judgment call. It was what he owed *Oyabun*. It became the only thing in his life, that plus the fact he would fuck her first, then kill her, then commit his beloved *seppuku* and go happily to his ancestors, his honor restored.

He rose, grabbed his sword, and as men surged forward and death and chaos were everywhere, he cut against the tide, found the steps, and rushed up, one flight, then another, and, entering the upper hallway, saw that so far it

417

was empty. He counted the doors, which were popping open, and men were pouring out, until he reached the door to the white room that contained the little girl. He got out his key and fumbled to insert it.

★　★　★

Major Fujikawa saw that the plan was not quite working. That is to say, the congestion point seemed to be the doorways, where the violence was sharp and ugly and the whole thing coagulated into a subway platform at rush hour with swords. Not pretty.

He pulled out a whistle. There was no plan; in the hurried assembly of assault details this one had not been considered. But he understood that his people couldn't kill efficiently enough at this rate. He blew the whistle, hard, and watched as dozens of eyes popped to him.

'Let them out, goddammit,' he screamed, '*then* kill them.'

What a good idea, everyone understood, and the crowding at the doorways immediately broke out as the raiders made way and the *yakuza* spilled out into the falling snow. There was a moment of near poetry, if the death even of evil men can be considered poetic.

Someone's flash-bang went off in the crowd of fighters. It was a moment with the snow falling in the gentle Japanese fashion, and behind the screen of lulling white, men were briefly isolated by the flare of white chemical light in postures of attack and defense, the cuts stopped in midflight

418

so that the whole had the clarity of one of Kuniyoshi's woodcuts, an orchestration of muted color and delicate grace though applied to the subject of maximum violence. Fujikawa wished he had seventeen syllables at his command to press into a poem, but then he remembered he was a soldier, and he rushed forward, sword in hand, looking eagerly for someone to kill, aware that the chance to fight with a sword would never arrive at his doorstep again and he'd better take advantage of it.

★　★　★

The raid caught the great Kondo in an unfortunate position. He was in the shower, performing ablutions, readying for the next day's events, when the first bomb went off, followed by three more.

His first thought: *Fuck!*

He knew immediately that by some magic, the *gaijin* had located them. He had a moment's rage for the fellow's guile and wondered who had helped him, and imagined their heads on the table next to the *gaijin's*.

He got out, threw on his robe — naked, they caught me naked! — and edged quickly to the door. His bathroom was on the second floor, above the living room. He edged down the hall, looking for a view of the events, to decide upon an action. Though he couldn't see much, he noted shadows on the wall from a stairway leading downstairs. The violence of the shadow-work dancing hard on the wall conveyed the

419

violence of actuality. Then another flash-bang went off.

By chance he'd been looking directly at it and the brightness stunned him. He could not think, he could not see, he was defenseless.

Fuck!

He knew he could not retreat into the bathroom, for to do so would equal his death or his capture, actually the same thing. Yet he could not go back to his room where his swords were, because he could not see.

He heard the rising screams and smashing of fists, flesh, and swords as the fighting rose and knew that his men had been engaged by a force as large as they. He yearned to rush to his swords, claim them, and turn, whirling with violent purpose into the melee, cutting and cutting and cutting, knowing that he could turn the tide.

But he was blind.

He thought, The bathroom window.

It was a low drop — say ten feet to earth.

Blindly, he groped his way back to the bathroom window, slid it open, tried to remember exactly where the bathroom was with regard to the floor plan of the estate, realized that thinking cost him time and he had no time, so he launched himself forward, fell through cold space, and hit the ground with a thud.

'There's one,' someone said, 'grab him.'

In seconds four men had him.

'Give it up, brother. We won't kill you if you surrender.'

'Don't hurt me,' he said, going limp and sad.

420

'I am a cook. Please, I only work here, don't hurt me.'

* * *

Miwa tried to be calm. He listened to the general roar outside and understood what was happening. His only thought was to escape, but of course he was too frightened to attempt such a thing on his own. Therefore he assumed that Kondo, the ever-loyal retainer, would come for him.

After a few minutes, he realized that Kondo would not come for him.

Cursing his luck, he crawled to the doorway, slipped it open half an inch, and saw the same shadows on the wall that Kondo had seen.

They really frightened him.

He fought panic.

He thought. If I can hide, I will survive. They cannot stay long. They must attack, kill, then flee. I will never escape, but I can hide.

On all fours, he scrambled down the hallway, found steps downstairs, and like a snake, slithered down, into darkness.

* * *

'Please don't hurt me, I am a cook,' Kondo said, as the arms locked him down, and someone pinned his arms.

'He's nothing,' said a raider. 'Akira, take him to the courtyard; we'll continue.'

Three of his captors dashed away to join the

general melee, still intense behind them.

'Come on, asshole,' said the remaining raider, 'get going. Christ, you're not even dressed, you poor son of a bitch.'

True, he wasn't dressed, but Kondo blinked and watched as the strobes flashing in his brain shut down. He blinked again, watched vision assemble itself out of sparkly chaos, and he found himself alone in the backyard with his assailant, his arm pinned behind him as he was being roughly driven ahead.

'Sir, my arm?' he said.

'Shut up,' said the raider, or perhaps meant to say, but somewhere between the *Sh* and the *ut*, Kondo got leverage, hit the man with a left-handed dragon punch out of the most basic aikido text, knocked the man to the snow, then drove a palm into his temple with a thud, not knowing whether he'd killed him or not.

He felt the man collapse with a groan.

He snatched up the man's sword, a good utilitarian cutter, and went to the wall. He was over it in a single bound, lay on the other side, breathing hard, waiting to see if anybody had followed him.

No.

He stood, naked but for the robe, and ran barefoot through the snow. He found a nearby house, broke a window, and entered. He raced upstairs to face a scared man and his wife in bed.

'You stay there or I'll kill you. Now I need some clothes. And a cell phone.'

★ ★ ★

Nii got the door open and stepped into the white room. All was dark. To the left he recalled a light switch and, not thinking clearly, popped it. The room leapt to view, all its detail brilliantly exposed — the knotted bed, the television, the painted white window, all of it, white, white, white. But where was the child? A bolt of panic knocked through him, then fear: he could not fail. He ran to the bed, pulling it apart to find nothing, dropped low and looked under it, saw nothing. Then he thought to touch the sheets, found them warm.

She's hiding, you fool! he thought.

He raced to the closet, pulled it open, finding nothing. That left only the bathroom. He ran to it, pulled the door. It was locked from within. That's where she was!

'Little Girl, open the door! You will be in big trouble if you don't open the door! Little Girl, do what I say, damn you.'

The door was silent and still.

Outside, the din of fighting rose to a still higher pitch, the grunts, the shouts, the cries of being struck, the thud of strikes. A part of Nii yearned to join the battle. But he had duty.

'Little Girl! Little Girl, I am getting mad!'

But the child said nothing.

'All right,' he said, 'you'll be sorry.'

With that, he drew back and with his *katana* began to cut at the door, which, being a cheap and typical modern product, quickly splintered under the assault. He watched it dissolve with three or four great whacks, and when a ragged gap had been cut through it large enough for his shoulder and arm, he reached in, found the lock, and popped it.

Then he heard someone shout, 'Back off, fatso.'

He turned, furious, and found himself confronted by what appeared to be an actual Mutant Ninja Turtle. Donatello? Or maybe one of the others. Leo? Raph? That is to say, his antagonist was unusually tiny and thin, dressed all in black, and had a single eye protruding from a mask.

Suddenly the turtle reached up and flicked off its heavy eyepiece and as the thing flew away, it pulled the hair loose and the hair cascaded free, a dark torrent, long and beautiful, and Nii realized he was facing a woman.

'Bitch!' he screamed at her.

★　★　★

Susan leapt through the door; her night vision goggles captured exactly what lay before her. To the left were big rooms, and from them rose the racket of battle, a humming, throbbing fusion of grunts that men made involuntarily as they came together and tried to dominate each other. Before her on the right, a short stairway led up to a hallway, while below it, at this level, another stairway led to bedrooms and the like.

Down which hall? Certainly the top one; they wouldn't put a prisoner, even a small child, at ground level. Up she went in one bound, Swagger just behind her. They were met at the top by three men, but they weren't combatants. They were fleeing in panic, so Susan and her companion stepped aside as the three — cooks possibly, or accountants, hard to tell as they were in pajamas — raced outside to be secured by raiders.

But suddenly two men came at them from the left, and they were *yakuza*. Beside her, Swagger leapt forward, evading a cut, and clocked one with his elbow hard, sending that boy to the floor in a heap, and was then so close he had no room for swordplay and instead grappled, rolling against a wall, kneeing his opponent, slamming him several times hard against the wall.

'Go, go,' he shouted.

Susan peeled off from the struggle, kicked in the first door, found the room behind it empty, sped down the hall to another, kicked it, another empty one, then heard screams and shouts from ahead.

She raced to a room whose door was already open and from which bright light flowed like water. She ducked in and beheld a strange sight, amplified by the night vision goggles, though it was completely illuminated already. A large man was brutally cutting a closet or a bathroom door to ribbons in a frenzy, his blade splintering the thin wood. He was screaming, 'Little Girl, come out. Little Girl, you must obey me or I will hurt you. Little Girl, you must cooperate or I will be very, very angry.'

Susan stepped in.

'Back off, fatso,' she commanded.

He turned to her, his face bunched into a sweaty rage.

He was large and green.

Then she realized she was still wearing her night vision goggles, and she tore them off, feeling a slight snare of pain as one of the straps caught in her hair.

Her womanhood seemed to enrage him even more.

'Bitch,' he screamed.

'Cow,' she replied.

★ ★ ★

Swagger found himself in a room with six men, evidently some kind of security guard for the upper floors. He flailed about, driving them back. Now they faced each other, one on six, in the relatively close confines of the small room.

Oh, shit, he thought, wondering if he had a chance against six.

Without willing it, he went into full aggression mode, going quickly to *jodan-kamae*, right side, and stepped forward, ready to issue from on high, feeling that pure force was the only solution to this tactical problem.

It was, but not in the way he imagined.

His war posture, the ferocity of his fighting spirit — 'The moon in the cold stream like a mirror' — and his eagerness to cut people down immediately melted the will of his opponents. Six *katana* dropped quickly to the floor, and the men fell to their knees, wishing to offend him with their lives no more.

This was fine, it was even an ideal outcome, for at this point killing seemed pointless, but it left him with the problem of administering to six prisoners. He ran to them, reaching in his pocket for the yellow plastic zipcuffs and discovered — shit! — only four.

He worked around behind them until he ran out of zips. It was two-handed work and he had to wedge the Muramasa *katana* between his arm and body.

With each man, he shouted, 'Kondo Isami?'

Each man looked at him with fear redoubled in his eyes and his face yet paler by degrees. If they knew Kondo, it was only by reputation.

Ach! The assault clock continued to grind on, the seconds falling away, as Bob struggled with these boys, of no consequence but still men who couldn't simply be released. At any moment they could have turned on him, the six on one, and knocked him down and killed him. But there was no fight at all left in them, and after still more time, he had them all neutralized, four in the restraints, two tied in their own obis, not that such binding would hold but it was symbolic of surrender.

He pushed the first one out, pointed down the hall, and marched the small parade to the stairway, from which the front door was visible. Possibly, outside, the fighting had died down, as the din wasn't so loud. He pointed again, watched them file out to their fates.

Suddenly he heard screams, male and female, signifying the coming together of two warriors at death-speed.

One voice was Susan's.

★ ★ ★

427

Outside, suddenly, it was over.

The blades stilled, the grunts died, the spurts of harsh breath rising like steam, all finished. Only the snow continued its drift downward, settling in increasingly delicate piles on the brick courtyard.

Everywhere Fujikawa looked, the men had ceased to be opposed by the enemy. Some of the enemy were down with red smears across them or lay still in large puddles, where blood and snow had fused to slush. More, however, were on the ground, either tied or obligingly raising hands to be tied.

'Secure them,' he yelled pointlessly, for that process was already happening.

'Snipers?'

The snipers were still perched on the walls, hunting for armed targets in the house.

The calls came quickly.

'Sniper one, clear.'

'Sniper two, I have nothing.'

'Sniper three, all quiet.'

'Sniper four, no targets.'

'Secure the compound,' the major yelled, again more ceremoniously than to real effect, for his well-schooled men had already begun to spread out and hunt for the hidden, the missing, the escaped.

He watched as Tanada came around toward him.

'Secure, Major,' said Tanada.

'Yeah, here too. Sergeant Major Kanda?'

The sergeant major, who'd had a fine old time laying about with a *bo* — a four-foot-long stout fighting stick — stood up from securing the yaks he'd clobbered solidly.

'Yes sir?'

'Get a head count.'

'Yes sir.'

The sergeant major ran off to consult with various squad leaders.

'I can't believe it went so fast,' said Tanada.

Major Fujikawa looked at his watch. It had taken seven minutes.

'Any sign of Miwa or the child?'

'Swagger-san and the American woman are inside.'

'Get them some help, fast.'

'Yes sir.'

★　★　★

His rage flared: kill, smash, crush. All his anger turned chemical, the chemicals went to his muscles, which inflated with strength and resolve.

He would cut her in two. He would destroy her.

He ran at her and she at him. His sword was high, and he meant to unleash *hidari kesagiri*, diagonal cut, left to right, exactly as all those nights ago he'd seen his *oyabun* perform it on the Korean whore and he visualized it more clearly now: the progress of blade through body, the stunned look upon the face, the slow slide as the parts separated.

Agh! He let fly and felt the blow form itself perfectly and issue from above with superb speed and violence as driven forward by the grunt, which propelled oceans of air from his lungs.

She was quick, the little bitch, and he missed her by a hair as she slid by.

But he recovered in a split second. Improvising brilliantly, he snapped his left hip outward and felt it smash into the running woman, who was so light that its momentum flung her through the air. She struck the wall with a satisfying crash. She must have hit it midspine, for her arms flew out spasmodically, the sword in her hand flipped away, her face went dull with momentary shock, as she began to slide down the wall toward unconsciousness.

Now, the end.

Tsuki, thrust. He —

'*No!*'

It was English. He halted.

'Daddy's home.'

He turned.

It was the *gaijin*.

It was the source of his humiliation; he had a rare chance to erase a failure. His warrior heart swelled with pleasure.

'Death to the *gaijin*,' he said, 'then the child, then this whore.'

'The reason you are fat,' the *gaijin* said, 'is that you are full of shit.'

Nii rushed the man, sword high, issuing from on high, and cut a large slice in the universe, though alas the *gaijin* wasn't in it.

He spun, went to a cocked position, and thrust forward at the man.

With both hands, he drove the sword forward

to impale his opponent's opened body and nothing halted him as he plunged onward and onward, waiting for the resistance, when at last the sword's point passed through the flesh. The point and the blade it led must have been very sharp for the flesh didn't fight it a bit, he just kept on going.

Then he noticed he had no sword.

The second thing he noticed was that the reason he had no sword was that he had no hands. The *gaijin* had cut them at the wrist, both, neatly and nearly painlessly, going into what Yagyu called 'crosswind,' specifically designed against *kesagiri*, and culminating in the direction 'cut through his two hands.' The *gaijin* had been the faster.

The blood did not fizz and spray. Instead, far still from coagulation, it squirted out in pitiful little spurts, each driven by a beat of his heart. He looked at them and wished he had a death poem.

He turned to smile bravely, and then the world cranked radically to the right and went to blur and he had a sense of falling but no sense of body. Then his eight seconds ran out.

★ ★ ★

Bob stepped back from the carnage he had wreaked.

The fat one's body lay in the bed, where it had emptied a great red tidal wave across sheets and blanket. The head had bounced and rolled somewhere else.

Then he picked up Susan, who moaned as she came to.

'Oh, Christ,' she said.

'It's okay,' he said. 'Where's the child?'

'The bathroom.'

Bob turned, went to the bathroom, reached in the gap, found the lock, unlocked it, and entered.

'Honey? Honey, are you here? Sweetie, where are you?'

'Tin Man, Tin Man,' cried the girl in broken English.

'Here I am, sweetie.'

He ran to Miko, who crouched in the bathtub, and picked her up and squeezed her hard, feeling the tiny heart beat against him.

'Will the Giant Monster hurt me?'

Swagger spoke no Japanese. He just said, 'It's all right. They're all gone.'

'Oh, Tin Man.'

'Now listen, sweetie. I'm going to take you out of here, all right? Everything is going to be just fine.'

The child spoke in Japanese, but then Susan was there.

'Don't let her see anything,' Susan said.

'I won't.'

Susan spoke in Japanese. 'You have to make us a promise.'

'Yes, ma'am.'

'I will carry you. But I want you to close your eyes very tight and press your face against my chest until I tell you it's okay. It'll just be a minute or so. Can you do that for me? Then we'll get some ice cream. I don't know where, but we'll get some ice cream.'

'Yes, Auntie. Will the Tin Man come?'

'Yes, he will,' she said in Japanese, and to Bob said, 'She thinks you're the Tin Man.'

She picked the child up and turned.

'All closed now?'

'Yes, Auntie.'

Okada-san stepped from the bathroom and immediately saw two of her snipers, carrying their M-4s at the ready, standing there to escort her to the car, and then to wherever.

'You did good, Cheerleader,' said Swagger.

'So did you, Redneck,' she said, and carried the child out. Miko obediently kept her eyes shut and never realized that the room was no longer white.

44

EDO JUSTICE

He reached the compound just as the buses that would take the raiders out of the area pulled in. He walked to Fujikawa.

'What are your losses, Major?'

'We got out clean. A few bad cuts, now stitched. A few concussions, sprains, a lot of bruises, that sort of thing. The worst was a trooper knocked unconscious by a cook, who escaped.'

Swagger knew who that would be.

'How many kills?'

'Fifteen. Lots of wounded, though. Our people are stitching up the badly hurt yaks and getting plasma into them. They're pretty goddamned lucky. Another yak crew would have let 'em die.'

'Sixteen. I had to take a fat one down. Anyhow, it looks like you'll be out of here before light.'

'We have a last job.'

He turned and gestured. Bob saw Yuichi Miwa, shivering in a kimono-bathrobe that exposed his scrawny old man's chest, kneeling in the snow. Nobody was touching him or abusing him, but his face was down and grave.

'Possibly you don't want to see this,' said the major.

'I've already seen it.'

'This is the old way.'

'It's the right way.'

'The men think so. We voted. It was unanimous.'

He nodded to Sergeant Major Kanda, who approached with what Bob recognized immediately: a red silk sword bag, neatly tied. Quickly, Major Fujikawa untied it, removed a blade in *shirasawa* that Bob knew intimately, as it was the blade his father recovered on Iwo Jima.

Major Fujikawa approached the kneeling man.

He spoke in Japanese, but Captain Tanada whispered the translation in Bob's ear.

'Miwa Yuichi, this is the sword Asano retainer Oishi used in the fifteenth year of Genroku to behead Kira, who had betrayed his lord. It's the blade that was presented to Philip Yano by this American, and had become ancestral to the Yanos by reason of Major Hideki Yano's last battle with it on Iwo Jima. It is the blade you murdered Philip Yano and his family to obtain, for reasons of career and ambition, you who have so much, who wanted so much more. I, Fujikawa Albert, of the First Airborne Brigade of the Japanese Self-Defense Force and former executive officer of Philip Yano, claim a retainer's right by ancient tradition to avenge the death of my lord. I do offer you a choice. If you wish, you may use the sword to end your own life, and thereby, in samurai eyes, regain your good name and honor. If not, I shall execute you like a common criminal.'

Miwa's chest puffed importantly.

'Do what you will. Just know you are killing a

435

man of vision. I will say that the deaths of Yano-san and family were necessary. I fight to keep Japan whole and pure. I stand for the old Japan. I fight the foreigners, and Yano-san, as is well known, had sided with the foreigners. Now, you kill me. That is your way; I would not talk you out of petty vengeance that only attests to your smallness as men. But when I die, a part of Japan dies. Let it be said, I gave you my neck, and in nights far distant, many will regret what you have done and who you have killed.'

The snow fell, drifting this way and that, covering all, cloaking all sound. The moment was silent. Even the prisoners, secured on the ground, watched with respect, acknowledging the ultimate meaning of the moment. The old man leaned forward, stretching his thin neck for not merely the ease of the executioner but also for his own ease, and the major set himself. He offered his blade for cleansing; a bottle of Fuji was emptied upon it, consecrating it. Then the major stepped into a fluid *shinchokugiri*, the straight vertical, and the polished blade sang in the cold air. The separation was almost bloodless. The head fell with the thud of a book hitting the floor. Then the body pitched forward, twitched, and went still. A red flow began to print odd patterns onto the snow.

The major performed a quick *chiburi*, flinging the blood off the blade to form a spray of red abstraction in a snowpile, then someone began to play 'The Star-Spangled Banner.'

It wasn't until 'proof through the night that our flag was still there,' that Swagger realized he

436

was the source of the music; it was the ringing of the forgotten cellular phone that Kondo had given him to manage his transit to the point of exchange.

He flicked it open.

'It's five thirty a.m. As I said I would, I call you. We have some business,' said Kondo Isami.

'We do,' said Bob. 'Time and place, please.'

'It's not so far, *gaijin*. It's next door, over the wall, quite a lovely place. Kiyosumi Gardens. Turn left at the pond. Look to the left. I await you on an island. I'll be easy to find. I'm the one with the sword.'

45

STEEL TO STEEL

Swagger turned and strode out the gate, the Muramasa blade over his shoulder, the folds of his *hakama* jacket tied back by a figure eight of rope around his shoulder, his obi tight, his creases still sharp. He turned right on the little street, walked fifty yards, then diverted to the left through the open gate of Kiyosumi Gardens in the somber rise of light.

He entered a kind of wonderland. Light snow lay upon everything, as did the utter tranquillity of dawn. Before him he saw the pond, a flat sheet of reflection, its surface broken now and then by the ripple of one of the ceremonial carp the size of trout breaking the surface in a flash of golden torso. In one corner, reeds, still green because their verticality gave snow no purchase, waved ever gently, more on their own internal vibration than by any force of atmosphere. Across the way, a pavilion, ivory with a sequence of tile roofs and the elfin upturn of Asian style over stout mahogany pillars and a sea of paned, opaque windows, supported its own mantle of snow. The trees were variously dressed in white as well, the pines supporting it, the willows less cooperative and, like the reeds, still mostly green. Ducks cruised, the big fish fed, the snow lay crisp as sugar, everything was etched to a woodcut genius's perfection. No modern buildings could be seen. It was a haiku called 'Garden, 5:32 a.m., Break of Dawn.' He might have added, '1702.'

He saw the man standing on an island to the left, still a hundred quiet yards away. Swagger followed the path, skipping over rocks where they transected a cove for a shortcut, ducked under willows, turned again to find a wooden bridge, and crossed to the island.

The circle of earth lay possibly thirty feet across, with a shore of rocks artfully arranged, some glazed white in snow. Its trees were willows, bent with their own load of snow, the white on the green, the whole painted magenta by ribbons of sunlight broken through and captured on the surface of the low, dense clouds. Now and then a bubble popped, as a fat carp came up in search of food or merely to belch.

Kondo stood, one hip cocked, with a warrior's utter narcissism. Like Swagger, he held the *saya* over a shoulder, almost like a rifle. A smirk marked the handsome face on the square, symmetrical head. He looked like a jazz musician ready for a riff or a ballplayer in the on-deck circle, his muscularity held taut under a black, formal kimono, his radiant vitality almost a heat vapor off his posture.

'So,' he said as Swagger approached, 'did Miwa die well?'

'Not particularly,' said Swagger. 'He gave some bullshit speech.'

'Alas, I heard it many times. You, Swagger-san, I know you will die well.'

'I doubt it,' said Swagger. 'I plan on screaming

like a baby. But since it ain't happening for thirty more years, it ain't worth worrying about now.'

The jibe brought a sharper smile to Kondo's confident face. Then he noticed something.

'Oh, I see my father gave you Muramasa's blade. He actually still believes in all that crap. It'll be a pleasure to give it back to him without comment this afternoon. He'll know what it means. That will be my revenge on him. Oh, what a warm family moment.'

'What he'll get is a bag with your head in it.'

'If Dad's been helping, that means he sent you to Doshu. I studied with Doshu too. It's too bad, you know; you can only get so far with Doshu. You're limited by Doshu's imagination. You better have more than eight cuts if you're going to last a minute against me. And when I take your head, Doshu will hear too. I wish I could see *that*.'

'You must be nervous. You talk too much. I come to fight, not talk.'

'No, I am not nervous, I am eager. This is a red-letter day for me. I didn't help Miwa win his dirty movie election, but so what? As I say, he was only a pornographer. But I am about to fight and defeat a really great samurai, as I have dreamed of for years. Then I will have defeated in proxy my father, and as he is the living memory of samurai in Japan, I will have entered legend.'

'You're talking so much you must think you have all the time in the world.'

'I do. And let me tell you why. I have genius, and genius always triumphs. It's the law of

440

genetics. I have a thousand years of swordsmen's blood in my veins. Then I have experience. I've fought man on man to the death thirty-two times and won all. I know what happens in a duel. I have strength and stamina. I have foreknowledge: I know Doshu's style and the eight cuts he taught you, and I can easily counter every one with either hand. I also know *your* particular style: the cuts are shaky, except for your best, *migi kiriage*, and your footwork is always suspect,' said Kondo.

Swagger said. 'You forgot one thing: I cheat.'

The swords came out fast, like the flickering of a snake's searching tongue, with doubled rasps of polished steel against wood loud against the silence of the dawn. Kondo was much faster. He was so swift in the unleashing, Swagger knew he'd been smart to keep his distance, so that he couldn't be chopped down in *nukitsuke*, the draw, and fall ruptured before the fight had even begun.

The island afforded little enough room: Swagger thought that was to his advantage, because the less he ran, the more strength he'd have. The closer he got, the better chance he'd have. If it became a running, cutting thing, like all the movie fights, he was done when his gas ran low, so why bother with the technicalities just to die tired.

Trusting aggression, his old friend, he moved in, quickly cutting the island in half, bringing his blade on high right to an enemy that awaited on the balls of his feet, bent utterly in concentration, his blade thrust before him.

441

Bob closed, forgetting the swordsman's shuffle over the bare wood of a dojo. This was in the real world, over clumps of grass, drifts of feathery snow, the odd stone. He launched forward — '*Ai!*' — with his right-handed *kesagiri*, but the mercury-slippery Kondo rotated out of sword's fall, repaying with a fast sideways cut, very strong, classic *yokogiri*, but Swagger with a speed he never guessed he had (but knew he wouldn't have for long) got his blade up in time to turn it away, as the steel on steel hit an almost musical tone. Swagger felt the muscle and precision in the blow, even as he turned it and got himself out of range for a second.

'Yes, that's good, close in, finish it fast. We both know you can't stay with me. Each second is a point for me. I don't need to cut you down quickly to win, merely to last until your arms fade,' the *yakuza* said, that fucking smirk still on his face.

In that second he made as if to relax and exactly as Bob's subconscious read the relaxation in his body, he knew it to be a fake, and in the next moment, from the pose of muscular softness, Kondo exploded. His move had no coefficient in nature, it was beyond metaphor. What Swagger was doing still alive after that, he never knew, because something catfast in himself took over, as his blade didn't fight Kondo's for the space, but vacated pronto, turning with a way-less-than-good cut, which Kondo easily thwarted. But Kondo didn't press the advantage, instead eased backward.

'Not bad. Slow, imperfect, but you still

breathe. Let us try you again.'

Tsuki, a straight thrust driven by lunge and locked elbows, flew at his face, a fast-closing raptor, seeking his eyes or his mouth or his throat, and it was only an ancient dinosaur brain somewhere in Swagger's pelvis that saved him this time, jacking his upper body back an inch beyond the gleamy tip of the *katana*. Then, stepping to the right, he tried the sideways cut, *yokogiri*. He cut something, but it was only cloth.

'Agh!' groaned Kondo, deeply affronted, and his rage transferred itself instantaneously to the wicked diagonal *kesagiri*, which Bob redirected just enough to miss him. Then came a thud as something hard plunged into Bob's face. It was the hilt, as the enemy swordsman, with not enough room to reverse and get his blade into play, simply reversed and drove, clubbing him hard in the face with his hilt, knocking spiderwebs and fly wings and gunflashes into his mind, setting him up for the kill.

But Swagger wasn't ready for death yet and grappled the man. Bob chose the moment to repay favor with favor, unleashing a head butt that caught Kondo flush and would have knocked a lesser man to the ground, but Kondo used the energy to break away and reset.

The two stared at each other, each gulping for air, each taut face leaking blood, each set of eyes bulging in the need for information.

Kondo took a small breath.

'You fight like a peasant,' he said.

'I am a peasant,' Bob replied.

Now it was his turn for the *tsuki*, the fast

thrust, though he aimed lower, meaning merely to puncture heart and center chest and bleed his enemy dry. The thrust seemed to take an hour. He stabbed air, withdrew, took a feint cut to his left, and knew that Kondo wouldn't feint left then cut right the first time and so was stable and locked when a nanosecond later the withdrawal abruptly ceased and became another launch from the left. He rode the strike, tried to turn it to his advantage by stepping inside, but, although the sword was past him, he had momentarily forgotten that his enemy had two arms and with his other one, the guy roped him around the neck. Swagger drove backward, then yielded with a trickster's cunning, dropped to one knee, and heaved the man over his shoulder, bracing himself on his own blade to stay upright.

That saved his balance but it meant he was behind the curve in getting the blade back in play, and by the time he was ready to cut, so was the other man, having rolled adroitly through the throw to arrive standing in a cloud of snow sprinkles his fall had raised, his hair a mess. Bob shivered, ordering some small pain to abate for the moment.

'Again, you surprise me. Two minutes of fighting, you have even drawn blood, and you're still standing and spitting.'

Bob had no words for the man. He yearned to nurse the terrific clout he'd taken under the eye and now battled a new enemy beside the real one, his age, his lack of experience, and his fear: his left eye was swelling. One-eyed, he might as well be blind.

He gathered in some breath, trying not to make it obvious, and ran through homilies that might help him.

The moon in the cold stream like a mirror.

Nah. Nada.

Think of sex.

Bad idea.

Think of the scythe, the smooth sweep of the blade through the clear Idaho air.

But as he was reminding himself to think of the scythe, a scythe came at him, that hard-powered *kesagiri*, what a magnificent thing it was, maybe the best ever, all power concentrated in four inches of flying *yakiba*, and if he weren't again lucky as hell, it would have cleaved him, clavicle to belly button, and left all his secrets to spill out on the nice white snow.

Inside the thrust, he head-butted again, at the same time trying to find enough play to get his own point into flesh, but the butt was a glancing thing, more of an ear slap, and by the time his blade was where Kondo was, Kondo was no longer there.

Bob gulped.

Christ, he felt old and used.

'Feel fear? I see it in your eyes. You have accepted your defeat. Wonderful. I can do it quick. You won't feel a thing. They just fall, wordlessly, without a sound. I've never heard a cry. The eight seconds of oxygen in your brain goes fast. The pain never catches up with it.'

Bob's answer was *yokogiri*, left to right, driven by the proper '*Ai!*' because expelling the air in perfect timing hastened the blade. He sliced the

445

air cleanly in two. A lesser man would have fallen in both directions at once. Kondo pirouetted into a new defensive position, then stepped forward with a high kick and a '*Hai!*' and drove a superspeed diagonal at Swagger who fortunately had a nervous system still enough in the fight to react and leap ahead. In a blinding flash Kondo unleashed another giant power cut, this time his own version of *yokogiri*, left to right, much more perfectly formed than Bob's, much more elegant and worthy of a movie. The wicked point of the blade cut Bob's *hakama* sleeve and maybe an inch or so of skin. Swagger smelled blood, his own. That was a serious cut, deep, almost to the bone. It needed stitches or it would bleed him out in an hour or so. But it wasn't to guts or heart or lungs, it took down no bone structures, it didn't interrupt the flow of neurons, it just fucking hurt.

He rotated leftward, bumped into something hard, the thin trunk of one of the ceremonial willows, and maybe lost a step. At that moment, from utter repose, Kondo fired another *yokogiri* at him and he winced, not fast enough to block, too tired to duck.

But instead of opening his throat like a broken gutter, the blade lost possibly a tenth of its speed as it hit the willow trunk, glided through without breaking a sweat, and then halted and withdrew a few inches from his face.

'Pretty cool,' said Kondo. 'You haven't seen that in a movie, have you?'

Indeed, he hadn't. Suddenly snow on the willow leaves shook itself loose as the top half of the tree tumbled, trailing spirals of snow.

Swagger took a shot at *kiriage*, the rising cut, left to right, his best option, but it was too slow.

'I've seen better,' said Kondo. 'Really, I think Doshu would admonish you for that one.'

Bob gulped air.

'No snappy patter? You're spent. That was your last cut. You have no offense.'

With that Swagger lunged again, *tsuki* hard, but spent most of his energy in the thrust, which connected with nothing except the void that Kondo had so recently occupied.

Swagger sucked hard for oxygen. God, where was his second wind?

'Swagger, let me finish it. No need to go out on a bad cut, screaming, your guts hanging out. I can put an instant end to your suffering.'

Swagger responded to the offer with a diagonal issued from on high that was so awkward and poorly timed it was almost an insult to Kondo. It missed by what felt like seven yards. He had almost nothing left.

'Just let me end it now, fast and clean, old lion.'

Bob didn't take the advice, as expressed in *shinchokugiri*, a vertical downward, but badly out of timing and harmless.

'If you didn't kill me early, you aren't killing me at all,' Kondo said. 'Okay. I offered. I pay my respects. This has been great. You're a valiant guy. But the party's over. Five hard cuts and you'll only be able to stay with me through four. I know you will die strong, great samurai.'

'Fuck you' was all the blown man's wretched

mind could come up with.

'*Hai!*' screamed Kondo.

The blows came so fast Swagger's eyes could not stay with them, only the dying warrior reptile far inside took over his instincts and got soft parries on the first left-hand diagonal, the second left-hand diagonal, somehow got horizontal for a harder, low-blade block on a vertical, lurched to the right to dissuade the fourth, now right-handed diagonal, and dropped to come against the final side cut, the *yokogiri*.

No time.

No gas.

No speed.

His blade couldn't catch up with the blur of steel that seemed to pick up acceleration as it vectored hard to his body.

It was perfect *yokogiri*, with Kondo's full might and genius behind it, and as he knew it would, it flew true into the shred of opening under Bob's lagging defense. Kondo had an image, almost of woodcut clarity, of what must happen next.

Yakiba — tempered edge — sheers through hip bone, shattering it, continues downward, shattering the femur ball by the inevitable physics of its own impact reverberation, then shatters the femur itself and with it nips the femoral artery, that torrent of blood. Sundered, the femoral deposits its fluid in midair in a fine and driving rush to turn the snow below to purple slush. The blade itself, far from spent, cleaves through what remains of flesh, breaks free, its amputation complete, and Bob falls as

448

he exsanguinates. Clinical death is possibly not instantaneous but certainly occurs within eight seconds.

Yet even as his brain told Kondo that must happen, it did not happen. Instead odd vibrations of uncertainty came his way, as he felt the cut stop hard and shallow and his own hilt torque wildly, almost out of his hands, though he was fast enough to recover even as an old adage somehow came to mind. Who said it? Where? When? Why was it so familiar?

Steel cuts flesh, steel cuts bone, steel does not cut steel.

He struggled to regain timing but was not quite fast enough.

It was the *migi kiriage*, the rising cut, left to right, the scythe cut, Swagger's best, honed on desert slopes under a hard and ceaseless sun. For his part, bad old Muramasa was with it all the way. His blade hungered for blood, driving up from just above the hip, through hoses and ducts and wet linkages and mechanics, through a whole anatomy lesson of viscera, splitting them wide so they could jet-empty their contents upon the snow. It wasn't Swagger's best cut, for it wore out at the halfway point before cutting the spine, much less the lungs. But even Doshu would have counted it adequate.

He withdrew, and seeing that which was far as if close and that which was close as if far, segued rather gracefully from recovery into the next most accessible position, which was *kasumi* ('mist'), a horizontal, over-the-shoulders construction supported on reversed wrists.

449

'Feel the fear at last?' Bob asked, and maybe saw a glint of it in the man's stricken face: I am mortal, I will die, my time is up, why why why?

Bob's *kasumi* then transcended miraculously and of its own volition into *tsuki*, not well aimed but well enough as it punctured and passed through Kondo's throat, splitting his larynx and jugular, half-severing his spine, and weirdly sustaining him in midfall for a half-second before withdrawal.

Kondo toppled, issuing fiery liquids from his ruptures. His face was blank, his eyes distant, his mouth slack. When he hit, a reddened puff of snow flew up.

Swagger stood back from the carnage and his hand flew to his hip, where the steel inserted courtesy of a Russian sniper in Vietnam decades ago had stopped Kondo's brilliant cut. It was Swagger's only card, and he'd been wise enough to play it last. The cut was precise butchery, smooth but shallow, and some black gruel pulsed from it, but it wasn't geysering spectacularly, meaning no artery had been cut. Bob got a pouch of QuiKlot out, tore the top off with his teeth, and poured the clotting agent into the wound, knowing again that stitches were mandatory within an hour, if he had the strength. Then he poured more on the bloodier cut on his left shoulder.

Christ, it hurt.

He retreated, found his *saya*, and stood for a second.

Do it right, he thought. Thank the fucking sword.

Feeling foolish and white, he held the weapon horizontally before him and bowed to the little Japanese god inside the steel, and said *arigato* as best he could. Then since the thing wore a dapple of disfiguration, he snapped it hard to the right, flinging its contents off to splatter an abstraction on the snow — *chiburi*, in the vernacular, big in all the movies.

Now *noto*: he sheathed the sword, as ceremony demanded, drawing the dull spine of the blade through his left hand and fingers while clutching the *saya*'s opening until he reached the tip, then smoothly snared the tip in the opening, then ran the wood casing up to absorb and protect the blade, the whole move ending with a gentle snap as *tsuba* met wood.

His watch read 5:39 a.m., Tokyo time. He turned and looked at the body of the man he had killed. Kondo lay in a sherbet field of blood and snow, and the spurting had stopped. It was only drainage now. Somewhere a big fat golden carp came to a placid surface and seemed to burp, leaving a widening burst of rings in its passing.

Swagger looked back at the body. He could have taken the head as he'd promised. But really — what was the point?

46

OFFICE POLITICS

She arrived at the American embassy promptly at 8:45 because nowadays it took a good fifteen minutes to get through security. She wore a new Burberry pantsuit she'd bought recently at Takashimaya, a smartly tailored pinstripe on gray wool, a white silk blouse and pearls, a pair of Christian Louboutin round-toed platform pumps, her Armani horn-rims. Her hair was pulled back into a severe ponytail, her foundation Lanvin, her blush Revlon, her mascara Shiseido.

She got to his office exactly at nine and, of course, he let her wait ten minutes, a kind of humiliation ordeal — more of which would be coming her way, assuming she survived the next few minutes in any case — then he ushered her in.

'So nice of you to join us, Susan.'

'Doug, I'm very sorry, I — '

Doug had graduated from Annapolis, and though he had never had a command at sea, his office was filled with nautical gewgaws, like brass sextants, charts, gaffs. In office lore it was called 'the Bridge,' though never when he was around. He was the sort of man who demanded results yesterday but then forgot to ask for them tomorrow.

'Sit down, sit down.'

She sat opposite: he was a large-headed, red-faced beefy man, ten years older, from an old family that was by reputation third-generation Agency. His hair was a brusque graying crew cut and he wore his suit jacket at his desk. He was a well-studied imitation of the man Swagger represented naturally, without self-consciousness or reflection.

'Look, I shouldn't have to give a pro like you pointers, but goddammit, I have to be able to reach you twenty-four hours a day. That's why we have cell phones, pagers, the like. It doesn't work if you *turn the goddamn things off.*'

'I didn't turn anything off. I just didn't answer because I was in an awkward situation.'

'Anything you care to discuss with your chief of station?'

'It's all right, Doug. It was a Swagger issue.'

'I told you the Swagger thing wouldn't work. He's too old, he's too slow, he's too stubborn, he's nothing but trouble.'

Like to hear you say that to *Swagger*, asshole.

But she played his game: 'I know it was my idea to bring the guy back. He proved harder to manage than I thought. However, now it's fine, it's great. I'll have him out of country as soon as I can make arrangements. He made some progress. He — '

'I want a report. First thing tomorrow.'

'Sure. Is that all? I — '

'Oh, no. Oh, no, it's not over. Susan. This isn't just more Swagger bullshit. That was just the start. The issue is much more serious. As in, Why the fuck did you send an unauthorized request to

453

SAT-D to orbital on seven houses and thirteen business locations in the greater Tokyo area?'

'Oh, that?'

'Yes, that.'

'It was mission-related.'

'There is a big flap at Langley.'

'I made a judgment, possibly it was wrong. I had to confirm something fast.'

With an egomaniac like Doug it was important to show contrition. Defiance simply enraged him, and enraged, he was even more erratic than when calm.

'Tell me why it was so goddamned important for the birds to eyeball Japanese mansions and warehouses when they could have been looking at North Korean launch sites, Chinese naval bases, Taliban outposts, or god knows what?'

'I have a guy who has a network, mostly low-grade stuff, but you never can tell. Somehow he picked up a whiff that a certain ultra-wealthy Japanese national had sympathies in a certain direction and was unstable. It wasn't enough for any hard action. I didn't put surveillance on him, I didn't discuss him with Japanese intelligence, because we knew he'd hear. I didn't try to penetrate or eavesdrop. I didn't recruit within his organization. But I decided on a look-see.'

'Come on, Susan. You're stalling. Why, please?'

'Doug, there are a lot of tall buildings in Tokyo. If someone flew an airliner into one of them, we'd look foolish. Plus, it would kill a lot of people. I was trying to split the hair between being overreactive and being responsible. I was trying to do my job. I flash-prioritized it over

454

your signature because if you don't, it takes weeks. You weren't around to sign off, as I recall.'

'You can use that one to justify anything, Susan.'

'Yes, Doug. I know. However — '

'What did you find out about Mr Miwa?'

'Oh, at Langley they made the connect?'

'And how. They are not pleased. What did you learn?'

'Well, frankly, nothing. At one mansion there was what might be termed unusual activity. That is, a great many people, vehicles, a lot of movement outside in the courtyard. Possibly it was a business conference, possibly a company retreat of some sort, even some kind of reunion. Then it occurred to me, since I'd looked into him, that it might have been *yakuza*-related. I believe he has *yakuza* ties. But the infrared picked up no concentration of explosives, the spectroscope didn't indicate nuclear, and we don't have bio-chem sensors yet.'

'Susan, assure me you didn't muss, even slightly, Yuichi Miwa's hair.'

Hmmm, Susan wondered, does *cutting his fucking head off* count as mussing his hair?

'Doug, no entity under any possibility of my influence or under my direction has had anything to do with Yuichi Miwa. We looked at him from three miles up, that's all. It couldn't have been softer or more discreet. If anybody finds out, it's because of a leak somewhere, nothing that I have done or caused to have done.'

'You're sure?'

'I was going to eyeball him from upstairs another few times, just to make certain. Maybe I'd put some discreet feelers out. That's it. I was just checking.'

Doug sat back. He looked immensely relieved.

'Okay, fine. Good. The man is not to be touched, even watched. He is to be utterly ignored.'

'Of course.'

'Strictly hands off. Do you understand?'

'Of course.'

'Until you figure out how to destroy him.'

'Ahhh — '

'*That's* why they're in such a frenzy at Langley. *That's* what this is all about.'

He reached into his desk, pulled out a large folder wearing the usual TOP SECRET stamps across its top.

'The file on Miwa-san. It's come to our attention that some years back, Miwa-san almost went under. He owed *yakuza*, he owed banks, the whole thing was going away. He convinced himself it was an American plot against him, that the mafia wanted to crack Japanese porn and to do so they had to destroy him. He *was* Japanese porn; he was *Japan*, for god's sake. So he turned for help to the enemy of his enemies, the North Koreans; he told them if they helped him, his newspapers would always sing their song. They funded him. They can't feed their own people, but they're giving millions to a Japanese pornographer to produce DVDs the likes of which I can't even begin to describe.'

'Teacher-blows-Johnny.'

'Thank you, Susan. I knew I could count on

you. Anyhow, he turned it around, got in on the Internet early, found some disgusting niches, pushed the technological edge, made sharp investments, and became a major, major billionaire. So your boy's sense of him may be right. We just have to coordinate all this and stay organized.'

'I have it.'

'Now he's involved in some election for the king of pornography or something. It's all in here. He's got to win that election, he's got to find some way to make himself an institution. He's got to do something big, to get all the mucky-mucks and all the little people behind him.'

She just smiled a bit. Nick had it a week ago. He beat Langley's bright boys by seven full days.

'If he wins, the next step will be the bestowal of something called the Supreme Order of the Chrysanthemum on him, Japan's highest civilian honor. He's had lobbyists pushing that in the Diet for months now.'

Now *there* was something new.

'That will have the impact of instantly legitimizing him, and it'll gain him access, influence, and so forth. He's a North Korean agent. He'll be set to get them stuff on the Japanese and on us they've never gotten before.'

'Do the Japanese know this?'

'No. One of our listeners is in North Korea, and if we tell the Japanese, they will understand we have a good North Korean earhole. Then maybe someone finds that out from them. Do you see?'

'Of course.'

'Susan, make up for your bad judgment on Swagger and put it all behind you. This will take all your creativity and imagination. It's your number one priority now: you must figure out a way to derail the Miwa express, but you must do it in a fashion that leaves no footprints to us. We must appear entirely innocent and uninvolved. But he has to go down before his big PR push makes him legit and the emperor gives him that award. You've got to somehow move through Japanese entities, perhaps in ways that they themselves won't even recognize. It won't be easy; you have somehow got to do it, Susan. Your job and my job depend on it.'

'What's the time frame?' Susan asked.

'Well, you'll need a week or so to recon and develop some sources, another to come up with an operating plan, we'll have to get it approved, then you'll have to staff it. You've got at least three months. No more. I know it's hard, but sometimes we have to do the hard thing.'

'Okay,' said Susan. 'suppose I can bring it off by . . . four thirty this afternoon?'

'What? Susan, this isn't a joke. This isn't — '

'Doug, do I look like I'm joking?'

'I — well, aren't you overconfident?'

'Doug, you're scheduled to rotate back to Langley in the spring. Are they going to bring in another stateside tool to be head of station?'

'Susan, that's not fair.'

'Focus, Doug. Nothing personal, but I'm so tired of answering to tools. By four thirty today, Doug. All right? And then by five thirty you've

458

sent the first of many, many wires in which you single me out for extraordinary praise and recommend to all your old-fart buddies I get head of station here. Do we have an understanding?'

'What do you know that — '

'Do we have an understanding?'

Actually, the announcement of Miwa Yuichi's death of 'natural causes' came at 3:25; she beat the deadline by an hour and five minutes.

47

NOTO

He came out of unconsciousness on the second day and floated through a semiconscious state, aware of bindings on many parts of his body, aware of the ceiling, of the occasional Japanese medical staffer, and the slow passage of time.

On the third day, he could sit upright, and some clarity and memory returned; on the fourth, more clarity, more memory. It was around then that his Japanese caretakers were subtly replaced by two clean-cut American boys, whom he took to be, on no evidence except that they called him Gunny, navy corpsmen working in mufti. They were good kids, though, and who knew from what secret installation they had been assigned.

On the fifth, his brain had settled enough so that he could watch the television. He quickly discovered a nation in — well, not exactly mourning but something like morbid fascination, perhaps, a sense of mass irony, perhaps, a secret pleasure in the tragedy of the other. This was occasioned by the sudden death of Yuichi Miwa, aka 'the Shogun,' one of Japan's leading geniuses of the silver screen, the porn billionaire, the founder of the aggressive Shogunate AV company, and later publisher, radio station owner, media mogul, playboy, and nationalist crusader.

Swagger watched without comment the coverage on bilingual TV news. The man, by rumors all but awarded the Supreme Order of the Chrysanthemum, had died suddenly of a stroke. Swagger was one of the few who knew whose stroke it was, and with which weapon it had been delivered. But watching, Swagger could tell; the Japanese weren't that broken up about it, not really. Miwa was, after all, a pornographer. In any event, soon enough the news passed from attention.

He managed to gain access to a laptop, pulled up the *Japan Times* site, and got the articles from two days after his fight on the island. On the national page, he found the brief item he was looking for: an unknown body had been located in Kiyosumi Gardens, presumably a *yakuza* or someone who had run afoul of the *yakuza*, given the gravity of the cuts that had killed him. A police captain was quoted expressing concern that while the Brotherhood of the 8–9–3 was frequently violent, these crimes almost always took place in tenderloin areas such as Kabuki-cho; the captain worried that a corpse in the elegant, historical glades of Kiyosumi Gardens indicated some new phase in criminal culture.

There was no other coverage; no one visited him, no one asked for a debriefing, a statement, a comment, an account. He simply lay there, regathering his strength, reading newspapers, watching the tube, eating cold eggs, cucumber sandwiches, and many kinds of fish and cutlets.

A week into it, his wounds were checked, rebandaged, painkillers and more antibiotics

461

provided, and then he was declared well enough to travel. The young men brought him a new suit, as well as his fraudulent passport under the name Thomas Lee.

'Gunny, I'm told that when you get to LAX, someone from State will meet you. He'll ask you to surrender this passport. It'll then disappear. I don't know a thing about this, but they told me to tell you that Thomas Lee will also disappear.'

'Who's 'they'?'

'Oh, you know. The guys in the suits. That's all I can say.'

'Got you, son.'

He got into his clothes and assembled his meager possessions — the passport, the United ticket for the flight scheduled for 7 p.m. that night. The keys to his bike were missing. It didn't matter.

The hospital insisted on a wheelchair, and one of the corpsmen wheeled him, ridiculously, to the van, a tan, unmarked Ford. The cold air was like Boise in January. He climbed in slowly, using his uncut arm and his uncut leg for leverage.

'Got everything, Gunny?'

'Enough to get me back.'

'We're off. We'll get you there in plenty of time.'

Nobody talked on the long drive to Narita. It was essentially the second time he'd been ejected from Japan, and he knew he was lucky he wasn't in prison. The traffic, the small, crowded neighborhoods, the driving ranges, all fled by unremarkably, and two hours later, the low, sleek hull of Narita's No. 2 terminal came into view.

At the curbside, he got out, as did one of the corpsmen.

'Ben's going to park the van. I hope you don't mind, but we're supposed to stay with you till you get beyond security.'

'Sure, you have a job to do, like everybody.'

That ordeal went smoothly. He checked in, displayed his passport, got his boarding pass — well, well, the flight was first class, so much easier — and the two young guys took him to security.

'This is always a pain,' he said. 'I have a steel hip, so bells go off.'

'No problem,' said one of the kids. 'We'll help.'

'Look,' he said, 'is this it?'

'What do you mean?'

'Well, nobody's debriefed me, nobody's taken a statement, nobody's even asked any questions. I don't know what happened to some people who were involved with me. There was a little girl who — '

'Gunny, we're just pharmacist's mates. We don't make policy. This is the way they want it.'

'Them again.'

'Sorry, Gunny.'

'I just have to make sure this little girl is all right. I mean, she was just a kid.'

'I don't have any information for you, Gunny. They didn't say anything.'

'Oh . . . okay, okay.'

So he turned to security and this time, at least, the bell didn't go off. Without ceremony he was through. He nodded at the boys across the rope line, and they nodded back but made no move to leave. As this was the only exit, clearly they were to stay until eight-ball Swagger had safely departed.

He walked toward the gate, skipping the mall area where, a few months ago, he'd so memorably fallen off the wagon. He felt — well, what? Not satisfied, not really. Old. His wounds hurt, his gait was stiff, he needed another painkiller, but at least he wasn't on crutches or in some kind of a chair. He also felt oddly empty. The light was gray and somber, perfect for his mood: used up, useless, spent, irrelevant. Maybe even disappointed. Couldn't put a finger on it. It was over, was all, back to the world, DEROS, all that good shit.

Till the end, he kept his hope up. Perhaps Okada-san would show up, perhaps she'd have Miko along and they could have a nice farewell chat. That way there'd be some finality to it, some sense of ending. But it didn't happen and then the flight was called.

★   ★   ★

The blade flew against the scrub, bit hard and clean, and sent a sheaf of cuttings flying through the air, where a harsh wind sprayed them across the slope. Back and forth, back and forth, the scythe ate the brambles as Bob found his rhythm, leaning in, uncoiling lightly, and cutting.

He had to start over, of course. During the months in California and Japan, the slope had grown out. Now, under a lowering winter sky, you could hardly tell where he'd cut and where he hadn't. This was his fourth day here, the air was raw and the wind sharp, but on some principle that he could not name, he had come back, taken up the scythe, and again laid into the long job.

'That is not what is eating you,' Julie said. 'You don't give a damn about that slope. Something is eating you alive. I can tell. You'd better get some help.'

'Sweetie, I am fine. I started a job, now I will finish it.'

'You should talk to someone about Japan. Maybe not me, maybe not anyone here in town, but a specialist. I have never seen you so low since the day you showed up in my front yard shot full of holes all those years ago. Bob, if you don't deal with it, this'll be the one that kills you.'

'Nothing bad happened in Japan,' he said. 'Everyone says it was a big success, and that we got a job done. Now I am back, everything is fine, and I have this thing to do.'

'Yes, and you came home like you always do, tired and sad with a whole new set of scars. You only get scars like that in fights to the death. But it's even worse than that. I can tell. Someone died, someone you cared about, and you don't have any way to scream about it. Honey, you've got to find a place to scream.'

'There were some rough times. Yes, some people died. Nothing I could do about it, unfortunately. But that's not it, I have to tell you, there's a child I wanted so much to help. And I couldn't, not really. So she's lost. Not dead, just

465

lost. That's all. I'll tell you more sometime, not now.'

'Well, I'm sorry. A child would be nice,' said Julie. 'Liven this place up. I might even love a child. Tired of living with a grouchy bear, how much worse could a child be?'

Not even Nikki, who'd come home for a spell, could really get through to him.

'Something about a child that he didn't want to talk about has him all hurting,' her mother said, 'and he's too goddamned stubborn to take a rest and get some help.'

'He'll be all right. You know him. He comes back from everything.'

'But someday he won't, and maybe that day has come.'

'No, he's fine.' But even as she said it, she didn't believe it: her father was somehow there/not there at once, as if a hole had been opened, then lightly covered over.

A child? What child could that be?

So the three lived in the nice house on the outskirts of Boise, and from a distance, everything seemed fine. The doting father, the handsome wife, the beautiful daughter, now and then in town at a fine restaurant or off to the movies. Why, it looked so fine; there was plenty of money and the three of them so bright and attractive you'd have thought, Those are America's aristocrats, not of birth but of skill and strength. They are so blessed with health and courage and even some wealth and so proud of each other. They are the best we make.

He cut, he cut, he cut. First day was the worst.

466

Each cut brought an increment of pain. His stamina was way down too, and he wasn't as hard as he thought he'd be. He'd lost a lot. By the end of the first hour, he breathed hot and hard through dry lips. Over the next few days, it got a little better, and by the third day he stayed out even as a squall blew through, pelting him with ice particles.

It looked like today might bring more of the same, though the heat he'd raised was insulation against the rain and the cold. In the distance, of course, stood the mountains, dark to the point of purple, their peaks lost in the low strata. The prairies between them and him had turned yellow in the winter, dried out and cleansed of wheat or let simply go if they were only grass, so the whole earth had a yellowed, used, even dead feel to it. Yet it was so western: nothing at all looked like it could be of Japan or the East, just rolling hills and plains and the scars of the mountains lost in the dark clouds thirty miles to the east.

It was about four when he saw Nikki's truck. What was that damned girl doing all the way out here? He'd driven her out to look at his land once late last summer, before all this, but she'd not returned since and there'd been no talk of a visit that morning or any other morning. He was surprised she even knew the place, for it involved a cutoff and a couple of unnamed back roads before it yielded the Swagger retirement property. Maybe she'd had a bitter fight with her mother and was pulling out early and stopped off for a good-bye. It had happened before.

467

Nikki's truck pulled up at the foot of the slope, and Bob came down to greet her.

He could see his daughter in the driver's seat, laughing. Then he saw she had a passenger, and the door opened and out climbed Susan Okada.

Something went off inside him; it might have been a sense of hope. He took a deep breath.

'Well, lookie here, the lady from the embassy.'

'Hello, Swagger. I had to come.'

'My god, it's so great to see you!'

'You saved my life. I never thanked you.'

'You saved the child's life. I never thanked you.'

'The child's life is thanks enough.'

'Fair enough.'

'You deserve a report on how it all shook out.'

'I been wondering.'

'Well, to start with, the Japanese government clamped down on it right away. The fight, the deaths, never reported. No scandal. They got there and closed it all down. They don't want it public.'

'It would take a lot of explaining.'

'And they don't like to explain. But two days later, Major Fujikawa and Captain Tanada surrendered to the authorities.'

'Good lord!'

'Yeah. They felt they had to do it. Japanese thing, don't ask.'

'What's going to happen to them?'

'Not known yet. Depositions have been taken and all have been released on administrative leave while the government figures out what to do. You might think, eighteen men are dead, including a multibillionaire, huge deal. But seventeen of the eighteen are low-ranking *yakuza* who could have died in any of a hundred squalid ways and the eighteenth is Miwa. But dead, Miwa has no power, no heirs, no legacy. And it turned out he had some unsavory foreign connections that made him very problematic. Finally, the *yakuza* people don't want to upset the working relationship for vengeance, since he wasn't really one of them. I'm hoping that the whole thing will be brushed under the carpet. The Japanese are very good at brushing things under carpets.'

'Can you help the officers?'

'There's not much I can do. Maybe it'll work out. At least they won't be ordered to commit *seppuku*.'

'That's something. And how about you?'

'Well, it worked out to my advantage. Long story, still classified, but as I said, Miwa had some contacts that had lots of Agency people worried, and getting him out of the picture — well, *you* got him out of the picture — worked out to my benefit. I'm going to get a promotion. I'm the new queen.'

'You were born to be a queen, Okada-san. Glad I helped. Still, I have to ask about the child. Is she — Is she all right?'

'She's better. She's sleeping through the night.'

'I guess that's the important thing. Still, I wish I had seen her one last time. There at the end, it was so crazy, I just lost sight of you and her. You just disappeared. It was so sudden.'

'I got her back to my place and then we got her back into the system. She's safe now.'

'I just hate the thought of her in that hospital.'

'She's not there anymore.'

'Oh, they found someone to take her? Well, ain't that nice. I suppose that's all for the best.'

'She went on a long trip.'

'She went to *gaijin?*'

'There was no one left in Japan. We had to look hard to find someone to love her.'

'I hope it's a good family.'

'I know it's a good family, Swagger-san. Nikki!'

She called, and Nikki climbed out of the truck, delighted, holding a wrapped but lively bundle that twisted in her arms mischievously, and he recognized Miko.

She looked over at Swagger and her eyes filled with something.

'Miko, it's the Tin Man. He came and rescued you. He helped you so much.'

The child looked at him, then buried her shy eyes in Nikki's chest, then found the courage to look again, decided it was okay, and smiled.

'Hi. there, sweetie,' he said. 'Don't you look swell today? Oh, you're a peach, I'll say.'

'Here, give her a hug,' Nikki said, handing the child over.

She squeezed him, he squeezed her.

'It's so nice to see you,' he said to her, now worried that his daughter and Okada-san might see him cry. Big guys don't cry, it was a rule.

'It's so nice that she's here.'

He was trying to put it together. Somehow

Okada-san had taken charge of the child and was bringing her — well, where?

'You say that now, but maybe you'll change tunes in fifteen years when she brings home a boyfriend with fishhooks in his eyebrows,' Okada-san said.

'What?'

'It's very tough for a foreigner to adopt a kid in Japan, but it turned out that Miko tragically fit all the criteria. When I found that out, I couldn't just leave it alone. So I went to the ambassador, who went to the prime minister, and maybe someone whispered something in someone's ear about certain behind-the-scene occurrences. Anyway, there's still paperwork to catch up on and some pro forma interviews, but everybody concerned thought it was better to get her over here sooner rather than later and play catch-up on the other stuff. Swagger-san, say hello to your new daughter.'

'Oh, god,' said Bob. 'I don't believe this.'

'Mom is so excited!' said Nikki. 'She's out buying a child's bed and toys and the whole shebang.'

'Okay, sweetie,' said Bob, holding his child closer, 'it's time to go home.'

ACKNOWLEDGMENTS

Readers of the entire Swagger saga will see that the account of Earl's heroics on Iwo Jima, even as to date and unit, have evolved slightly from previous accounts. As I have progressed through what has become a life's work, I keep encountering small areas where the joinery between volumes is untidy, and I can only plunge ahead, correcting or reinterpreting as I go. I count on your goodwill to understand that such awkwardnesses are unavoidable and make a promise that if I can ever convince a publisher to negotiate the complicated rights (among the issues: a trilogy in which each volume was issued by a different publisher!) and put the whole thing together in a uniform set, I'll try and reconcile all such annoyances.

I must also say that the great Musashi, oft-quoted here, said many provocative things about the art of the sword, but 'Steel cuts flesh / steel cuts bone / steel does not cut steel' was not one of them. It was Hunter who said that, sitting in his third-floor office in Baltimore. Maryland.

This is another way of pointing out that no reader should impute to me any deep knowledge of the way of the sword. I'm a writer, not a samurai; I tell stories, I don't cut enemies down. My weapon of choice is the adjective, not the *katana*. I based my accounts of sword encounters mainly on secondary sources, a slew of texts, and

472

dozens of DVDs of samurai films, high and low. I took sword-cut terminology from *Shinkeudo: Japanese Swordsmanship* by Toshishiro Obata. Devotees will possibly be upset that I've mixed kendo and combat terms in my quest to give the encounters a different feel; send angry e-mails to Hunter-doesn'tcare@aol.com.

I relied on friends for support and encouragement. My old pal Lenne Miller gave me the advantage of his insightful enthusiasm; Gary Goldberg did as much, plus Gary — the world's most advanced net-worker! — set me up with Dr David Fowler, the medical examiner of the state of Maryland, who gave me an hour of his time to discuss the biomechanics of sword cuts, very helpful in a book as bloody as this one. My pal and hunting pard and former collaborator John Bainbridge gave me the gift of his great eye for proofreading. Jeff Weber, way out in California, was uniformly enthusiastic and had a number of extremely useful insights I was happy to incorporate into the text. James Grady, great navigator of the Condor and a Washington fixture, also was a shrewd and helpful early reader, as was Jay Carr, the former film critic of the *Boston Globe*, who in retirement has become a Washington screening-room regular and a good and valuable friend.

Bob Beers continues to maintain the unofficial Stephen Hunter website, there being no official one. What he gets out of it, I'll never know, certainly nothing from me, but he's made it into something solid. Check it out at Stephenhunter-.net. Thanks again, Bob. Alan Doelp, as always, was an invaluable advisor on computer issues.

In the world of the *Washington Post* four colleagues gave of themselves to my advantage. The great Kunio Francis Tanabe, retired after forty years on *Book World*, advised me on Japanese names and gave the manuscript a close reading. He also wrote Hideki Yano's death poem, after pointing out that my version wouldn't pass muster in Japan. Anthony Faiola, the *Post*'s brilliant Tokyo correspondent, looked into and then briefed me on the structure of the porno business and its various governing bodies in today's Japan. Finally, Tomoeh Murikami Tse took the trouble to render an early version of the death poem into kanji. Paul Richard plied me with Japanese art books. I'm greatly indebted to all of them.

Finally, late in the process when news of the book's publication had somehow reached the Internet, I received an e-mail from Mark Schreiber, a freelance writer, translator, and all-around man-about-town who has lived in Tokyo since 1965. Among his many accomplishments, he is the organizing genius behind the *Tabloid Tokyo* books, which compile some of the zanier tales of the Tokyo weeklies for American readers. Mark volunteered to read the manuscript for accuracy in all those little areas through which Hunter sometimes dozes, and there were times when it seemed to me he was working harder than I was. One weekend he went to Kabukicho on a scouting trip, found the ideal spot for Kondo Isami to test his blade, measured it, photographed it, mapped it, then e-mailed it to me. That same weekend, I drank, watched football on TV, slept, and of course drank. Moreover, he caught dozens of mistakes of the sort that would have deeply annoyed readers who were more familiar with Tokyo than I was after a two-week trip. I should also point out that mistakes that remain are not Mark's fault or any of my other contributors', but my own entirely. As I said before, angry e-mails may be sent to Hunter-won'trespond@aol.com.

I should mention my professional colleagues as well, all of whom were enthusiastic and supportive throughout: Michael Korda and David Rosenthal of Simon & Schuster, and my agent, Esther Newberg, of ICM.

Let me broadly thank the Japanese themselves for being so damned interesting. I must make special mention of my three muses, Sakura Sakarada, Yui Seto, and Shiho. The dedication page expresses my profound gratitude to the artists of the theory and practice of samurai on the screen. I should say, also, that in a certain way those movies saved my mind. The origin of this book, for anyone interested, was a personal depression in my life as a professional film critic, when American movies seemed to have reached a new low. In this morass of mediocrity, I saw Yoji Yamada's great *Twilight Samurai* and was instantly reborn. That set me off on a two-year samurai movie rampage (interrupted by *American Gunfight*) and the obsession took its final form in the idea of writing a samurai novel set in the era of warring clans. Being smart enough to realize that a novel set then by a *gaijin* who'd seen too many movies wasn't the soundest of ideas — what would you call it, *Memoirs of a Samurai?* — so I tried to figure out a way to fuse samurai issues and fighting styles with a traditional American thriller. The result you hold in your hand.

Finally, I must thank my wife, Jean Marbella, the world's greatest trouper. She's lived patiently for a year among swords, samurai movies, books on sword fighting, sword making, sword polishing, and sword collecting, all in piles spread randomly throughout the house and seldom policed. Never complained, never whined, and even pretended to be interested in sword fighting and *yakuza.* What a gal.

We do hope that you have enjoyed reading this large print book.

Did you know that all of our titles are available for purchase?

We publish a wide range of high quality large print books including:
Romances, Mysteries, Classics
General Fiction
Non Fiction and Westerns

Special interest titles available in large print are:
The Little Oxford Dictionary
Music Book
Song Book
Hymn Book
Service Book

Also available from us courtesy of Oxford University Press:
Young Readers' Dictionary
(large print edition)
Young Readers' Thesaurus
(large print edition)

For further information or a free brochure, please contact us at:
Ulverscroft Large Print Books Ltd.,
The Green, Bradgate Road, Anstey,
Leicester, LE7 7FU, England.
Tel: (00 44) 0116 236 4325
Fax: (00 44) 0116 234 0205

Other titles published by
The House of Ulverscroft:

HAVANA

Stephen Hunter

Havana, Cuba, in 1953 is flush with booming casinos, sex and drugs. The city is a lucrative paradise for everyone from the Mafia to pimps, porn-makers and anyone looking to grab a piece of the action — including the Cuban government, which naturally honours the interests of its old ally, the United States of America. Of course, where there's paradise, trouble can't be far behind. Trouble, in this case, is in the charismatic form of a young revolutionary named Fidel Castro. The Caribbean is fast becoming a strategic Cold War hub, and Soviet intelligence has taken Castro under its wing. The CIA's response is to send the one man capable of eliminating Castro: the legendary gunfighter and ex-Marine hero Earl Swagger . . .